# DIARIES OF THE DAMNED

## ALEX LAYBOURNE

SEVERED PRESS
HOBART TASMANIA

# DIARIES OF THE DAMNED

Copyright © 2015 Alex Laybourne
Copyright © 2015 by Severed Press

## WWW.SEVEREDPRESS.COM

## ISBN:  978-1-925342-37-6

## ACKNOWLEDGEMENTS

*There is so much more to creating a book than just writing the words. There are a lot of people who have helped me along my writing journey thus far. Thank you to Paul Flewitt and Patti Geesey, Cecilia Clark and Julieanne Lynch.*

*Of course, the most important person behind my success is my wife, who has put up with me for almost a decade now, while somehow resisting the undoubtedly strong urge to kill me in my sleep.*

## DEDICATION

*This is for my wife Patty, and our wonderful children; James, Logan, Ashleigh and Damon*

# CHAPTER 1 – BOARDING

Paul Larkin sat in his seat and fastened his seatbelt. His body was caked with sweat and dried blood. His ears rang from the gunshots, and his ankle was swollen again, remnants of an injury he acquired jumping from the first floor window of his suburban home. At least, it used to be suburbia before everything went to shit.

He sat back and let out a long, deep breath. Shock threatened to take hold of him, so he closed his eyes and waited. The plane filled up, and the cries of those refused admittance echoed down the walkway, swiftly followed by the sound of their execution.

Paul spared but the most fleeting of moments thinking about it. He found it strange how killing and death had become such a large part of his life.

"Excuse me." A fragile sounding voice stirred Paul from the calm place he had just started to settle into. "I believe this is my seat." An elderly woman, late seventies at best, stood before him, her face was smeared with blood while one eye had been covered by a filthy rag that had been hastily secured to her face with what looked like duct tape.

"I'm sorry…" Paul asked, confused.

"Seat 17b. This is my seat." The woman waved the ticket in Paul's face.

Paul said nothing, but gave the woman a look which screamed, *'the world as we knew it has ended, are you seriously going to complain that I'm in your seat'?* If she could read his expression, she showed no signs of it. So with another heavy sigh, this one of frustration, Paul undid his belt and scooted one seat over.

"Thank you. I don't mean to be rude, but after all that has happened I feel the need to remain proper about some things," she said as she sat down. There was an odor to her person that Paul found distinctly repelling, yet she had clearly gotten through the scanners at the gate.

"It's fine," he answered her, closing his eyes once more.

The seat he had taken was a window seat, just before the wings of the Boeing 737 which the military had been using as an emergency evacuation vehicle for the past two weeks. Looking out across the tarmac, Paul saw the troops standing guard at the perimeter of the small airfield. The sun had begun to disappear beneath the horizon, and in the dull afterglow of yet another survived day, Paul found himself staring at the firework like bursts of gunfire and wondering how it could have all gone so wrong so quickly.

He tried to stop himself, but before he knew it, his mind was cast back. He saw his wife, Julia, and their two children, Doug and Maddie. They were outside, Paul standing behind the barbeque as Julia busied herself by setting the table while their kids played in the garden, enjoying the summer weather. He blinked, trying to force the image away. It worked, but was replaced by the memory of his wife's battered, bloody corpse lying on the floor in their living room; her face blackened and swollen by the sickness, her body broken from the repeated strikes he had delivered with his son's baseball bat. Her blood was splattered over his clothes, his face, everything.

"Daddy, I don't feel well," his daughter had called. Paul had turned around just in time to see the blood flow from her mouth like vomit. She collapsed to the floor, the convulsions already upon her. His son followed suit within the hour. Their small bodies were an easy target for the virus.

"I love you," Paul had whispered as he hugged them both tightly and then pushed their heads beneath the surface of the water. They struggled, of course, but their bodies were too weak from the disease to provide much resistance. His daughter fought the longest. "You're with the angels now," Paul whispered to them as he dried their faces, dressed them in clean clothes, and laid them in their beds.

The sound of an explosion within the terminal rocked the plane and pulled Paul from the nightmare. The sun had fallen behind the trees, yet the plane did not seem anywhere near full.

"Close those doors!" the lone flight attendant called out, running down the aisle, pushing passengers out of the way without a second thought. "Close them now!" she screamed again just as the roar of machine gun fire reached them.

The screams of those still in the walkway were cut off as the doors were closed, and the engines roared into life.

"Ladies and Gentlemen, please take your seats. We are making an immediate departure," the now out of breath young women spoke into the intercom. "God help us all," she added.

The plane shuddered into life and rolled away from the gate. The coupling that connected it to the terminal was still filled with bodies. Paul watched them cascade to the floor like lemmings; a human waterfall. "Lucky bastards," he whispered as he stared at their still, lifeless forms.

The plane rolled onto the runway and stopped. They sat there for ten minutes, and then just as people started to get nervous, three armored

Jeeps came to a screeching halt either side of the aircraft, the machine guns mounted on the top of each firing into the unseen enemy.

"Oh God, they got past the perimeter fences!" a voice cried out. This was accompanied by a wave of panic that saw people leap from their seats. Paul however, sat still; shock and weariness had overcome him. As a result, he saw the guns cease firing, and the gunner of the car nearest his window waved his hands in a signal which even Paul understood meant, *'Get going, NOW!'*

Paul opened his mouth to warn the panicked mob, but he was too late. The engines roared, and the plane sped down the runway. People were thrown to the floor and into their seats as the plane gathered momentum. Through his window, Paul watched as the bodies of those that had caused the delay were mown down by the speeding jet. Even that wouldn't be enough to kill them all, but what did it matter now? They were airborne, and the legions of the undead were behind them.

Looking back, Paul was just in time to see the main concourse explode in a ball of flame. The mushrooming ball of fire looked, for a few seconds at least, as though it would engulf the plane, too, but their ascent was steep; too steep to be safe. They avoided the blast, but the resultant concussive wave shook the aircraft enough to dislodge an extra round of screams from his fellow passengers.

Once they leveled out, and everybody had pulled themselves to their feet, an eerie hush fell over the cabin. Nobody moved; nobody spoke. They had all lost people to the disease. They had all killed as a result of it, and while they were alive, the world beneath them was locked in a bitter fight for survival. The city burned below them; the air dark with ash and soot. The military presence was immense: tanks, aircraft, and platoons of men armed to the nines with every weapon that could be issued. They had a lot to mourn and a lot to be thankful for.

Of course, Paul had seen firsthand how the creatures...infected - it was all too easy to forget that they had been human beings just two weeks ago - had eaten bullets and kept on walking, so what use the military presence would serve in the long run was beyond him.

Beside him, the old woman began to weep. Within a few seconds, the whole plane echoed with the sound of tears being shed; the conflict of emotions too overwhelming. As a collective they had stayed strong, but now, like a house of cards, when one fell, the rest would never be far behind. Apart from Paul that was. He didn't cry, he felt nothing; his entire body was numb. He was not an emotional man. That is to say, he was a man that had learned to deal with the dark tide of his emotions internally. He didn't keep it bottled up in an attempt to look tough. At five feet eight and seventy kilos, a tough guy he was not—not under the traditional definition. He did it because he didn't know how to let it out. Instead, he watched and listened as those around him gave voice to their pain.

The sobs died down, and the gentle thrum of the engines seemed to ease the entire group into a semi doze. Even Paul found himself struggling to hold his eyes open. Climbing over the snoring elderly woman beside him, Paul made his way to the back of the plane. The bathroom stall was unlocked, but when he opened the door, he let out a cry of alarm when he saw the young air hostess who had run down the plane and closed the door when things got too heavy, sitting slumped over the toilet seat. She was covered in blood which spilled from the two slashes she had made in her wrists. The mirror above the sink had been smashed, and in her left hand she held a bloodied shard. She clutched it like a knife. Even as Paul reached over the spreading pool of blood on the floor to check her pulse, she managed to lash out feebly.

"Get away from me," she whispered her words, sluggish from the loss of blood.

Paul froze for a moment; even considered just closing the bathroom door and leaving her to die, but at the last moment he raised his voice, and called out, "I need some help here." As he stepped into the small cubicle, his foot slipped on the slick floor, and he almost fell, catching his balance at the last second.

"No," the young woman protested, but Paul took hold of her and pulled her into his arms. She was unable to hold herself upright, her legs dragging uselessly behind her, drawing a white line on the scarlet floor.

"Oh my God!" a few voices screamed, and a general clamor of interest sprang up as Paul laid her down on the row of chairs he had singled out as a good place to have a nap. He held her arms in the air, elevating them to stem the blood flow. Paul looked around and noticed how unfazed people were by the scene; how little they reacted to the shedding of blood or the taking of one's own life. After all, they had all witnessed much worse, and the act of suicide, of opting out, was an option they had all considered at various points in time.

"Is anybody a doctor?" he called to the small group of passengers. There were only a handful, maybe thirty at most, but it was a legitimate question to ask.

"I'm a paramedic," a voice spoke up, and a tall black man with a shaved head strode toward them. Behind him, his daughter sat crying, afraid that he had strayed too far from her side. "It's okay, I'm only going over there to help the young lady who gave you that blanket." He soothed her, pointing to the airline blanket the stewardess had taken the time to retrieve for the young girl.

"We need to stop the bleeding," Paul called as he held his hand over the two gashes. Blood seeped through his fingers making his grip precarious on her slick wrists. He could feel the stewardess losing consciousness; her body grew weaker and weaker.

"You, grab the first aid kit from the galley," the paramedic instructed the nearest bystander the moment he saw the scene. "Here, let me take a look," he spoke, reaching out toward Paul who carefully slid the young girl's arms into more capable hands.

The man inspected the wound, tilting his head to the side as he examined it as though it were some rare find. "If we can stop the bleeding and get these things covered up, she should be just fine. The cuts aren't too deep, and this one, I guess it was the second, doesn't even span the whole wrist," he spoke in a serious tone as he took the offered first aid kit. "Hand me the gauze, will you?" He passed the kit on to Paul, the appointed nurse for the flight.

It took a little while, but the paramedic who, when it was all said and done, had introduced himself as Leon Melcher, stopped the bleeding long enough to crudely stitch the wounds and bandage them both. "It won't heal all too pretty, but she'll live." He wiped the sweat from his brow and replaced it with a bloody smear. "Somebody will have to watch her. We need to get her talking as soon as possible, keep her awake." His look at Paul made it clear he had been elected to watch over the girl.

"Ok," he agreed. His head was pounding, but at least it would give him something to do to keep his mind occupied and hold the nightmares at bay.

The sun set, and the cabin fell into darkness. With the stewardess out of action, the passengers had taken to helping themselves to drinks from galley, and thanks to the decently stocked supply of beer, wine, and spirits, soon began to relax. Paul refused the drinks when they were offered. It wasn't that he didn't drink, but he had consumed enough after the outbreak to keep him turned away from booze for a good time yet.

Sitting beside the woman he had rescued, Paul found himself drifting off into sleep. She stirred intermittently but had yet to regain full consciousness. Paul knew the only thing he could do was wait. He tried to fight it, but there comes a point when exhaustion cannot be held off any longer. To his relief, it was not so much sleep that consumed him, but more an inability to stay awake. He fell into the darkness, a period of seemingly endless silence, and welcomed it.

A shooting cramp in his left leg jolted Paul from sleep. He jumped to his feet and tried to stretch it out, gritting his teeth to stop from causing a scene. The cramp passed, and Paul looked around. It was dark in the plane, the sun not even beginning to tease the horizon. He couldn't have been asleep for more than half an hour, but he felt better than he had in weeks.

A groan to his right caught his attention. The air hostess began to stir, the throb in her wrists finally coaxing her from slumber.

"Miss? Miss, can you hear me?" Paul whispered to her, conscious of the exhausted passengers that surrounded them. "I need you to open your eyes for me," he coaxed gently.

At first Paul got no reaction, and the moans fell silent. He went to stand again, feeling the cramp threatening to return with a vengeance, when a brittle whisper stopped him.

"Why?" she asked, her voice barely audible. "Why?" she asked again, and slowly her eyes opened. At first they had this distant, unfocused stare of a person woken suddenly from a deep slumber, but that soon changed, and they stared straight at Paul. Although her words were questioning, the look in her green eyes was one of thanks.

"Don't mention it." Paul sat down, and his hands had started to shake. He couldn't remember the last time he'd had a cigarette.

"How do you feel?" he asked, mildly embarrassed at the seeming stupidity of the question, but remembered Leon's advice to keep her talking. Paul kept his voice to a whisper, mindful of the sleeping passengers around him.

For a long time the woman remained silent. She looked at Paul, closed her eyes and when she opened them again, her tears fell freely. "Dirty, I feel dirty," she answered, her voice breaking. "What we did back there…I just…all those people…" she began to sob.

Paul hated it when women cried; he never knew what to do. He reached out and clumsily placed a hand on her shoulder. She couldn't be more than twenty-four; he was almost old enough to be her father, but what they had all been through could not be explained or prepared for in any walk of life. "I know, but we did what we had to…" he lied. "We needed to get away. Besides, we are out now, and we're safe." He paused. Were they really safe? Did anybody know if the virus had spread from the island or not? It wasn't as though they were in the middle of nowhere. They were in England. The jump to France wasn't a big one, and with the tunnel, maybe it could have gotten through before they blew it up! Paul felt his mind begin to unravel, all of the questions nobody dared ask had started to bubble to the surface. He concentrated his mind and forced them back down.

"We don't know that," she said, seeming to read his mind. "What if it spread? What if someone got through the checks and infected one of the other planes?" she asked, her own mind whirling at a thousand miles an hour. The only difference being that she was in no condition to control it.

The plane bounced around slightly, and Paul noticed, much to his own amusement, that the fasten seatbelt light came on.

"Best not to think like that." He spoke calmly. "Do you want anything to drink? Something to eat maybe? You lost a lot of blood." Paul wasn't sure if he should be giving her anything, but it seemed like the right thing to offer.

"I could go for a smoke." She sighed.

"You and me both." Paul flashed a smile and felt his spirits rise as the woman returned his smile with genuine good humor. "I'm Paul, by the way." He introduced himself, offering his hand before remembering her condition and withdrawing it sheepishly.

"Jessica," she answered, "and thank you for saving my life." Her eyes still welled with tears, but she managed not to let them fall.

"It was my pleasure. It feels good to save a life for once." Paul spoke without thinking, and suddenly the jovial mood that he had built was deflated.

The pair sat in silence for a few minutes, both mulling over the situation; both remembering those that had been lost. Twice Paul raised his gaze, only to lower it again as another horrific image invaded his mind: His sister stumbling down the street chasing him, her body blistered and covered with weeping sores. He remembered her calling his name and the pain in her voice when he turned his back on her. Yet he couldn't shed a tear. Every time he came close to that emotional release, his mind focused and he found himself pulled away by some menial task or chore that needed to be done. It didn't matter how small the job, the distraction was all he needed rather than any specific notion of accomplishment. Paul stared at his hands—the blood under his fingernails, the grazes and bruises that covered his forearms. Callouses had formed at the base of each finger from the near constant wielding of the machete he had collected the first night. The night he had…Paul closed his eyes and slammed the door on the memories. His hand clenched tightly, nails digging into the palms. Slowly he opened it again. It was a subconscious action that he repeated for as long as it took for memories to cease their pounding on that door.

"It's alright you know. To feel the pain," Jessica whispered as she dragged herself into a semi-seated position.

"I…I'm not ready," Paul stammered after a moment's pause.

"Neither was I, and take a look at what I did." She held out her arms.

Paul had no reply. He simply curled his lips inwards and gave a slight nod of his head. The necessary words escaped him.

"You remind me of my father," Jessica said.

"How so?" Paul replied.

"He was a writer, too." The accuracy of the woman's guess had Paul floored. "You both have this…look; it starts in your eyes, and then consumes you. I've seen that stare a thousand times over," Jessica continued, having caught a glimpse of Paul's face and the look of surprise etched upon it.

"That's very astute of you," Paul confirmed.

"Yeah well, once you live with somebody like that, you begin to learn the signs. What was your genre of poison?" she asked, her interest peaked. Whether it was because she too liked writing or simply because of the close relationship she had had with her father, Paul didn't know, but it offered him a chance of distraction, and so he ran with it.

"I was more of a journalist. I worked for one of the tabloid newspapers. I took the real news and dumbed it down." He paused for a second. Jessica fit into their target demographic.

"Yeah, I never liked the tabloids much, nothing but gossip for the most part." She grinned. "No offense," she added, and this drew a small chuckle from Paul. "What's wrong?" she asked him.

"Nothing. I despised working there. It certainly wasn't the big, main breakfast table newspaper I had always dreamed of, but it paid the bills. Fiction, now that is my true passion. I always wanted to write a book, one that would change the world. Now look, the world has changed, and I'm…well, nothing," he answered. Unable to take it anymore, he rose from the seat without saying a word and grabbed his jacket. As he sat back down, Paul pulled a crumpled packet of cigarettes out of the pocket, and after some digging, a lighter.

Jessica watched him. "Can I have one?" she asked, "Don't worry about the alarm," she said as she took the cigarette she was offered and placed it between her lips. "The sensors just make a few lights blink up front. I don't think the pilot will care very much." Jessica dipped the smoke into the center of Paul's offered flame and took a deep drag. Paul did the same, and the change in his mood was almost instantaneous. "It's not too late, you know." Jessica spoke between puffs. A few seats before them, one of the passengers gave a slight cough in response to the smoke that filtered down the cabin.

"What do you mean?" Paul asked as he blew smoke through his nostrils like a dragon

"Your book. It's not too late to write it; to change the world," she whispered, keeping her gaze low.

"I guess you're right, but I don't think a publishing house will be the first thing they set up when we get to…wherever the hell it is that we are headed." He stared at Jessica, waiting to see if she got his message.

"I don't know, they only tell the pilots. But I'm serious. I mean, why not tell our stories? We survived the fall of civilization." Her voice grew in strength as she spoke. "Some with more grace than others, but still, we are the survivors. If you can tell our stories then I am sure someone important will want to read them. Maybe we have missed something, overlooked it. Getting peoples stories on record might just answer a few questions." She pushed. "Besides, self-publishing is the way to go, haven't you heard?"

Paul considered it for a few moments, raising his head to check the cabin. "Could I?" He spoke aloud but addressed himself. He always carried a pen and paper with him, and there weren't too many people on board. Even if the flight was only a few hours long, he could get a few of them talking.

*Why not? Maybe you're the only writer who made it out alive.* Paul shivered at the thought, which made the hairs on the back their necks stand on end.

Rising from the chair once more, Paul carefully opened the baggage compartment above where he had been sitting, and pulled out a beaten up, old backpack. He brought it back to the last row of chairs, sat down, and pulled out a bloodied and crumbled pad of paper and a cheap pen which, after everything he had been through, still worked perfectly. With his bag on the floor and his paper in hand, he turned to look at Jessica.

"So tell me, Jessica, what is your story...?"

# CHAPTER 2 - JESSICA BOUGH

Jessica Bough stood in line at the supermarket. It was busy and filled with people panic buying ahead of the supposed snowstorm that was heading their way. It was the same story every year. A horror winter that would mark the start of a new ice age, when in reality it would end up being an icy wind, a few flakes of snow, and then rain. Besides, it was almost February; how long could it last?

Much to the annoyance of the other shoppers, there were only three checkouts open despite the shop being packed. In their defense, the store had hung a sign apologizing for the delays, but there was a severe staff shortage. Everybody was at home with the flu that had been going around. Jessica was lucky in that she very rarely got sick; a good thing, too, because from what she had heard, this season's flu strain was a bitch.

She stood there, slowly tapping her toes to the rhythm of an imaginary song. A rather large man standing a few places behind her in the line began to cough, once at first, then several times. The third fit made it sound as though his lungs were about to be ejected from his body. Jessica felt drops of his spittle land on her neck. She turned around to confront the man, but held her tongue when she caught a glimpse of his face. His skin was pasty and coated with a layer of sweat. His eyes were red and watery while his nose ran - the mucus had a slightly pink tint to it. Oh, how Jessica hated her apparent ability to notice the small things about a person! His lips were dry and cracked, and each breath sounded as though his lungs were filled with water.

"Sorry," he offered before falling into another coughing fit. This time, when he pulled his hands away, his lips were speckled with blood.

"It's fine, sir," Jessica answered. That week alone, on a flight back from Ireland – not the normal run she did, but short staffing levels had caused for some shift changes within the airline she worked for – she had been coughed over, spat and vomited on. The passenger in question had not been sick but drunk. He had even made a grab for Jessica's behind, but she had dodged it. Jessica had never hit anybody before, and had she not loved her job, she was certain her non-violent record would have been gone.

The queue moved forward slightly, and with the song in her head over, its composition complete and never to be used again, she began to look around the store, and to pay attention to those she shopped with.

Everybody seemed sick - at least two thirds of them. The red eyes seemed to be the most common symptom, although the cough, which had begun to echo around the store, was also a somewhat less subtle indication. Jessica felt a chill run up her spine as it dawned on her that the store had been cough free when she had arrived.

Agitated and eager to be out in the fresh air, Jessica began to bounce around, moving from one foot to the other. Behind her a commotion rang out. Whatever it was, caused the store manager who, to his credit, stood behind the checkouts offering his apologies and some sort of voucher / coupon thing to everybody that went past, to drop his tickets and run into the store. A few cries rang out, but a rising wave of coughing and wheezing drowned them out.

An uneasy feeling settled over the store, and Jessica was glad when she could pay for her things. The man behind her had deteriorated in a matter of minutes, and when she cast a glance over her shoulder at him - in genuine concern, she jumped at the sight. His face had turned a pale green color, the first time she had ever seen the expression in real life. His chest quivered as he took rapid, shallow breaths. His eyes had a glazed expression, and he had a problem standing still and steady. He steadied himself on the counter and hung his head. The whole atmosphere made Jessica feel uneasy, so she ran from the store, throwing a ten-pound note at the cashier, not waiting for her change.

It was a cool day outside, but certainly nowhere near horror winter standards. A few snowflakes fell, and an icy wind swirled around the car park. *Wow, that's two thirds of the winter already done,* Jessica thought to herself as she placed her groceries in the well beneath the seat of her scooter. She only lived a few miles away from the store, and a ten-minute bike trip even in bad conditions, but before she got home, the man who had been standing behind her was dead. So, too, were the couple that had collapsed in the rear of the store. The store manager and cashier were also infected and would be dead by morning.

Once inside her small one bedroom apartment Jessica turned on the TV and made a bowl of instant noodles. It was late in the afternoon, and she had a date that night, but Jessica was the sort of girl that liked to eat. She hated seeing people take a few bites of something and then leave the rest, claiming they were full. If a meal tasted good, she would eat it all…except in those restaurants that pile the plate so high it was impossible to clear the plate. Even then, she would take the leftovers home. However on dates, especially first ones, it was a different story. She had learned that most men didn't want to see her eat a whole plateful, so she ate at home to ensure she left at least half of her meal. Unless, of course, the date went well, and the man was one of the rare few that wanted a girl to enjoy her food. Then she would joke about her earlier meal and then eat to her heart's content. It didn't happen very often, but when it did it was almost a guarantee for a second date; normally breakfast. As she ate, she flicked through the channels and found that every news show being broadcast talked about the flu; how it had reached pandemic proportions, and how a vaccine would be distributed in the coming days. *It's the fucking bird flu, Mexican flu crap all over again*, Jessica sneered at the TV. There was no doubt that this strain was serious, and shots would be a good thing, but there was no doubt that the media would ham it up as much as they could. The thing that shook Jessica the most was that Norwich had been the first place in the UK to report a case.

The traffic was unusually light as Jessica made her way downtown, heading toward the Italian restaurant her date had picked out. She had never been there before and loved pizza, so she was in a happy mood as she weaved through the streets. It had already stopped snowing, and while the temperature had dropped, so, too, had the wind. The ride had been so simple that Jessica arrived fifteen minutes early. She headed to the bar a few doors further up to have a drink before her date arrived. It was of the blind sort, the friend of her best friend's brother to be precise. Jessica always liked to bring herself to the first date; the second date too. Given that her job meant she was away from home a lot, she didn't want her address to be known by everybody she dated. It also stopped her from rushing in too fast and inviting men straight into her bedroom at the end of the night. That was not to say it never happened, but with less frequency that it had during her college years.

The bar was as good as empty, and the first thing Jessica heard when she walked in was the hacking cough of the bartender. He sounded as though he had the lungs of a terminally ill emphysema patient. An odor hung in the bar like a scented fog, a stench unlike anything Jessica had ever smelled. It was the smell of sickness mixed with stale sweat and beer. It was a pungent aroma that made her recoil, her skin tightening over her frame. The bartender looked up at her, a young man, who would have been attractive had it not been the thick trail of pink tinted mucus and blood that descended from both nostrils.

Jessica turned, left as quickly as she could, and headed to the restaurant. She would just sit at the table and order a drink there. She would explain everything and offer to pay for the drinks herself if need be.

The restaurant was very quiet, but it was early on a Wednesday, so Jessica had not expected a big crowd. She was shown to her table and ordered a beer, another drink she could sneak in quickly before her date arrived and she had to switch to something more feminine. As it happened, she had time to drink three—not that she ordered them—as her date was late. When he did arrive, he was full of apologies. He had been caught up at work, the flu had wiped out the personnel, and he had ended up doing the work of an entire department. Jessica forgave him, mainly because of his intoxicatingly beautiful blue eyes. They were almost icy, their color was so clear.

The date went great. They laughed and joked. They shared stories and memories, even a few secrets; the kind that meant nothing, but created a feeling of trust nonetheless. Jessica ate the entire plate and drank beer the whole evening long. When the end came and the check had been paid, something that Jack insisted on paying in full, Jessica was adamant that they return to her house for coffee. She would return to pick up her bike in the morning. She'd had too many beers to drive anyway.

Jack was more than happy to escort her home, and had said that was his plan regardless, especially with the craziness of the previous few days.

They slept in each other's arms and found feeling the warmth of another person's flesh against their own to be both comforting and heartbreaking.

Jessica didn't have a flight scheduled until later in the afternoon, so groaned expletively when her phone rang at eight the next morning.

Rolling over, she grabbed the phone and looked at the caller id. It was Rachel, her best friend. She was an artist and never awake before noon. "Hey Rach…" Jessica began, her mind already gathering speed for the reason behind the early call. Rachel still lived in the same town they grew up in, and the first thought to flash in her mind was that there had been an accident; that her parents, or even worse, her younger brother, Eric had been hurt.

"Jess, where are you?" The panicked voice of her best friend cut her off mid-sentence.

"I'm home. I don't fly anywhere until this afternoon. What's wrong Rachel? You sound upset." Jessica wasn't used to hearing her normally laidback friend so worked up about anything other than her current project.

"Lock the doors, Jess. Lock everything in your house now, and turn on your goddamned TV!" Jessica sat on the bed, her overnight guest forgotten, and turned on the television. "Are you seeing this Jessica? Those things are everywhere," Rachel cried. "What are we going to do?"

"Rachel, Rachel, slow down a second. I don't get it, what things; what's going on? My TV won't pick up a signal." Jessica tried to calm her friend.

"They have said that it is all because of this flu that's going around. Everybody is dying, Jess. Everybody!" Rachel cried, "Mike didn't come home last night, either. We had a fight; he stormed off and never came home. He always comes home… they got him, I know they did. Oh God, I got him killed!" Her friend entered a new level of hysteria as she referred to her long term, on-again, off-again boyfriend, Mike. The pair was like Tom and Jerry. Their fights were known to be legendary, and their make-up sessions even more so.

"Rachel, wait a second, slow down. Breathe, Rach, breathe. What happened to Mike? Who killed him, and what does any of this have to do with the flu?" Jessica was used to her friend's breakdowns—the perils of an artistic mind—but early in the morning was not the time for it.

"The zombies, Jess, I'm talking about the motherfucking zombies!" Rachel screamed. "Everybody that has died from the fucking flu has come back as a zombie!"

Jess didn't really hear her friend's words; her attention was diverted by the sound of screams that came from across the street. Jessica lived in a cozy terraced house in a small suburb on the outskirts of Norwich. It was a nice enough area, so the screams were certainly out of place, unlike the area she lived in while at college. Rising from the bed she looked outside. Her neighbor, a woman she had never met but knew to be Barbara Johnson, staggered out of her house screaming. Her hands were clasped to her neck which hemorrhaged blood at an alarming rate. She didn't even make it down the steps that led to the raised front door of the house before she fell to the ground dead.

"Oh my God!" Jess cried as she saw Barbara's son (she thought he was about eleven) appear in the doorway, his face covered with blood. Even from across the street she could see that he was chewing.

"Jess, Jess what is it?" She heard Rachel calling her name.

"It's…my…my neighbor. She's dead, her son…he…bit her," Jessica stammered, her mind busy trying to process what she had seen. "Rachel, what's going on?"

"That's what I have been trying to tell you, Jess! It's zombies. The flu has created zombies. The news is telling everybody to stay indoors, to close all windows and doors, and to wear masks. It's fucking crazy. Half of the town is dead…" Rachel's voice trailed off, and the resultant thump told Jessica that she had dropped the phone.

"Rachel? Rachel? Are you there?" she called. She could hear something on the other end of the phone.

"Mike, Mike, thank God you're safe. I love you baby…Mike, stop, no…No oh God no," Jessica heard her friend start to scream. "Get off me! No, Mike, please, stop." The words were mixed with a series of deep growls and grunts.

"Rachel!" Jessica screamed. The sounds of a scuffle filtered down the phone. The noise that ended it all was one that Jessica would never forget. The sound of her best friend having her skin ripped open created a lasting impression in her mind. It was a cry filled with such agony that it transcended all means of description. What made it worse were the satisfied smacks of a greedy mouth as it was stuffed with fresh meat.

Jessica dropped the phone, her world a blank and noiseless place. She felt cold and hot in the same moment. Unable to focus her thoughts, the final moments of her best friend's life replayed in her mind like a broken record. When the hand fell onto her shoulder, Jessica jumped from the bed, the fright so great that she screamed and fell to the floor. She had forgotten all about the man she had shared her bed with. Even upon seeing him, her mind couldn't place him. Screaming, she backed away into the corner, losing control of her bladder in the process. As her cries quieted down and the world came back into focus, and she stared at the man. *Jack, his name was Jack*, embarrassed by the puddle that spread on the floor around her, and for the first time since waking, she was conscious of her own nudity.

"Jack…Jesus Christ, you scared me. You won't believe what's happening…" Jessica stopped talking and took a good look at her guest. His skin was pasty, his eyes sunken and lifeless. His breathing was shallow and raspy.

"I don't feel good at all," was all that he could say before a stream of bloody vomit erupted from his mouth and showered the bedroom with gore.

Jessica screamed and scrambled to her feet, forcing herself even further into the corner to avoid the blood.

"Jessica, I am so sorry," Jack gasped before a final spasm gripped his body and erased all traces of life from it. He fell back into the bed, still. Tentatively, Jessica moved from the corner, walking on tiptoes to avoid the rapidly spreading puddle of blood. She gathered her clothes from the floor and ran out of the room, hurrying downstairs so fast that she tripped down the final few. Jessica managed to keep from falling, but twisted her left ankle which started to swell almost instantly. Acting on instinct, she ran and locked the front and back doors and then turned on her living room television. The picture was fuzzy, but the sound worked well enough, and judging by what she had seen already, a live broadcast from a heavily populated area was the last thing she needed.

She pulled on the shirt and trousers that she had worn the previous evening, conscious above all other things that she wore no underwear, and that the cold weather made the fact somewhat obvious. However, the recorded message that repeated on all channels was enough to focus her mind.

*This is a public service announcement. Quarantine laws have been put into effect. People are requested to remain in their homes and ensure that all doors and windows are locked. The military has set up roadblocks in order to contain the virus, and any person attempting to leave the containment zone will be apprehended. Hospitals are currently at maximum capacity. Should anybody in your immediate family show flu like symptoms, they are to be isolated. Sufficient fluid ingestion is imperative. Face masks should be worn at all times. We urge you all to remain calm. Help is on the way.*

Jessica stood and stared at the TV until a sudden thump at the living room window made her jump. She snapped her head up but saw nothing. Rising from the sofa, Jessica slowly walked to the window. She peered out. The street was empty, and everybody was indoors...the body of Barbara Johnson was gone. Jessica heard another heavy thump - this time it came from above her head. She spun around, her body wrapped in an icy blanket of fear, her heart hammering in her chest. There was nobody. Jessica turned back to face the window, and felt her heart go from thundering to frozen in an instant. Her neighbor, Barbara, stood on the other side of the glass staring at her. Her face was covered with blood, and the gaping hole in the side of her neck continued to leak vital fluids.

Barbara hammered the glass with her fists. Three blows were enough to break the glass. Her arms pushed through and grabbed hold of Jessica's shirt. The power of her grip caught Jessica by surprise, but also gave her the mental kick in the ass that she needed. Pulling hard, Jessica wrenched herself free. She watched as her neighbor continued to reach, shredding her arm on the shards of glass lining the windowpane like teeth.

Barbara made no sound as she struggled, and when she twisted her head in response to a noise farther up the street, Jessica saw why: it had not been a single bite that her son had taken, but many. He had chewed through to the bone. Her head leaned to one side, opening the wound into a vicious grin as Barbara tried to groan before taking off down the street, ripping her arm free of the glass in a shower of flesh blood. It only took a few seconds for Jessica to hear the screams. The house three doors down was under attack by five zombies. One had adopted the same approach as Barbara, only he had succeeded in his quest. He pulled a young woman from the window, and within seconds they were upon her, their frenzy so heightened that they dug in with their hands, scooping steaming handfuls of raw flesh into their ravenous mouths. A retch rose from Jessica's stomach as the woman's screams fell silent to be replaced by a sickening, tearing sound as the mass dug deeper, ripping her apart in search of the juicy bits. Jessica showered the window with vomit, pushed over the edge by the appearance of the woman's liver, which was thrown into the street, discarded. Apparently, even zombies didn't like an excess of Vitamin A.

Where Barbara had failed to growl, Jessica didn't have to wait long to hear the sound of the zombies' signature call; a sound that would become very familiar to her ears. This one came from within the safety of her own home. Jessica spun around just in time to duck away from Jack's reaching hands. His face was caked with the still drying gore he had disgorged upstairs. His eyes were dark, and Jessica could see that there was no hope for him; now that he had become one of the zombies. She knew she had to get away, to get out, and get somewhere…anywhere. The problem was that she was inadvertently allowing herself to be backed into a corner. Jack's hunger for her now far greater than it had been during their love making the night before, his hands now desperate to get a grip for a different reason. His motive for eating her was now far more literal; his craving for her warm moist flesh had consumed him.

Jessica changed the course of her retreat and directed herself into the kitchen. There was only one course of action if she wanted to get out of the house alive. Getting past Jack, however, was not her only problem. Her scooter was still at the restaurant. That only left Jack's car. The keys were by the front door where he had dropped them as part of an automatic reaction to coming home at the end of the day. Opening the drawers in the kitchen, Jessica fumbled around, never once taking her eyes off the zombie that bore down on her. Her fingers wrapped around the heavy rolling pin that her grandmother had given her. She was an old-fashioned woman and had given it to her as a gift when Jessica moved out of the house with the message: know how to take care of yourself, and you will always be fine.

With her grip secured, Jessica waited for Jack to get close enough. The roller was heavy, but she had no idea how effective it would be as a weapon. Jack took another step, and Jessica's heart leapt into her throat. She swung the heavy rolling pin, her arm descending at a forty-five degree angle, more through indecision as to whether to follow the horizontal or the vertical than anything scientific.

Jack stumbled back from the blow, and a welt the size of a golf ball erupted on the side of his head just before his ear, but it didn't stop him or even make him fall. His approach began again, and again Jessica swung. She gave a scream of exertion as she put her whole body behind the strike. The sound of impact was a dull thud, and the spray of blood that it caused a sign of its effectiveness, but still Jack moved forward. There was a hole in his face, and rapidly thickening blood fell from the wound like cottage cheese, but it wasn't enough. In disbelief, Jessica took a few more paces backward, the last she could make, for it brought her to the row of cupboards that lined the inner wall of the kitchen. In frenzy, her survival instinct kicking in, Jessica began to swing. Not once or twice, but repeatedly. She hammered away on the skull, working the same spot like a man cutting down a tree. Each strike embedded the rolling pin further into the skull, and it wasn't until the walls were spattered with blood, brain, and shards of bone that Jessica stopped. At some point Jack had fallen to the floor, but his crawl had continued. It was then that Jessica abandoned the roller and began to stamp on the zombie's head. She gave a howl of triumph when she realized she had won.

She was sticky with gore when she stepped outside. Judging by the reaction of the rapidly expanding crowd of zombies in the street, the woman whose liver lay by Jessica's front door had risen and joined the fun. The gaping hole in her abdomen proving to be of no hindrance, and even the fact that her intestines dangled from the wound like a tail causing her to stumble seemed to be of no concern. Her husband or partner had also been added to the mix, and in the distance a large mass of the undead could be seen shambling down the road.

*They can smell me,* Jessica thought when she saw her bloodied reflection in the car's shiny paintwork. Jessica's hand shook as she slipped the key into the lock and wrenched the door open. She had never driven a manual car before, and had no real idea as to where she was headed, but the zombies were upon her, their fists clubbing the roof of the car. The rear passenger side window broke, and an arm appeared.

Turning the key and forcing the car into gear, Jessica slammed her foot to the floor and shot out into the street. The car was new and far more powerful than her scooter. She had not owned nor driven a car since she gained her license at the age of eighteen, and she almost lost control. The tires found their purchase at the last moment and made the sharp turn to narrowly avoid the trees which grew intermittently along the street; large brutes of nature which the houses had been built around.

The road was blocked by a wall of the undead, and in the passenger side mirror Jessica saw that the owner of the arm was still dangling from the car. She knew she couldn't slow down, they would rip her apart like they had her neighbor. The mere thought caused her to wince in pain, so she pressed her foot even harder against the floor, plowing into the mass. The car was a pseudo-sporty thing with a front end that was more wedged than rounded. Perfect for cutting through a crowd, she soon discovered. One after another the zombies fell. Their legs shattered upon impact, and they began falling left and right depending on which leg gave first, only to be crushed by the speeding wheels, or they fell forward into the car, whereupon they disappeared under it.

The crowd had only been a few lines deep, maybe a hundred zombies in all. When the car burst through and into the open space beyond, Jessica finally took a breath. She hadn't realized that she had been holding it until her lungs burst into flame to help get the message across. In the rearview mirror she saw to her horror that not only had the zombies turned to give chase to her, but that many of those she had hit were still alive, crawling along the road with their legs nothing but mangled lumps of useless flesh trailing behind them.

Jessica wasted no time in getting the car moving again. Every street she passed told a similar story. Bodies littered the roads, hung from windows, or ran screaming from one house to the next, desperate to find shelter. The road was slick with blood and dotted with scraps of flesh and organs. She noticed several livers lying on the ground near bodies that had been dismembered beyond the point of recognition, yet still they lived, flapping on the floor, immobile yet still gripped by the cannibalistic cravings.

The sound of the car attracted zombies to it like moths to a flame. It was early, and the area was quiet at the best of times, so Jessica was the only real target they had. Thanks to the missing rear window, the sound of their undead growls filled the car and chilled her to the bone. There were also more than a few genuine cries for help, but Jessica didn't stop. She didn't look, for she knew that she had abandoned those people, condemning them to death. Her subconscious had taken over and kept her focused on the task at hand, protecting her as best it could by shutting out all things that would slow her down or cause her problems once she resumed full control.

The motorway was not too far from where Jessica lived, the ring road that looped the city, and she could see the road that led to the airport around the midpoint. It was there that she was determined to reach. Her mind operated on the single hope that maybe, just maybe, there would be a plane ready to leave.

Despite the infancy of the outbreak, the zombies were everywhere, and it seemed to Jessica as if every street she passed grew worse. Her escape was aided by the many families who, listening to the news broadcasts, had barricaded themselves in their homes. Every house seemed to have a group of the undead pounding at the doors and windows. They may not be smart, but with the power they could produce, especially in a group, it was only a matter of time before the locks and chains caved, and the buffet opened.

Once Jessica was on the motorway the activity seemed to lessen, although there were several zombies wandering aimlessly along the lanes, moving through the abandoned cars in search of food. Cars, lorries, and more than a few buses littered all four lanes which caused Jessica to have to slow the car down to not much more than walking speed in some places in order for her to maneuver through the gaps.

As she navigated one of the gaps, Jessica came closest to losing her life. After having negotiated her way through a series of abandoned vehicles, Jessica happened to glance in her rearview mirror and saw movement coming from the inside of a severely dented station wagon. The occupants of the front seats were clearly dead; however, as she watched, she saw it again. A child struggling to climb over its dead parents and escape. Without thinking, Jessica stopped the car and got out. The child pounded against the window. Her fist and the glass were smeared with blood from the effort. The child could not have been more than three or four years old judging by her size.

"Wait. Wait a second, I'll get you out," Jessica called through the glass, aware of the three zombies that bore down upon her. Their bodies were burned, blackened to a crisp and still smoldering. They had clearly come from within the burned out group of cars she had passed a few miles earlier.

Trying the handle to no avail, Jessica looked around and grabbed a broken number plate from the car nearest her.

"Stand back," she called. Not waiting for the child to listen and with no time to ask again, Jessica smashed the window and unlocked the door from the inside. She cringed as her hand brushed the hardened, cold skin of the child's father. "It's ok, I've got you. Come on, your safe with me," she soothed, reaching inside the car to grab the child. The group of zombies were less than ten meters away, but their mangled limbs made any form of motion difficult and slow. Jessica knew she had time to save the kid. "Come on," she urged, and as the child leaned forward, she grabbed the girl by the arms and yanked her free.

Jessica hugged the girl close to her and turned to run for the car, when she felt the child's grip change. Her head was forced to the side by arms stronger than those of any living child. Jessica's neck was exposed, and had it not been for the hungry growl that the girl gave she would have been bitten. Once again her natural survival instincts took over, reacting just quickly enough. She dropped the girl, and without waiting for a second opinion on the diagnosis, kicked out and sent the small body tumbling through the air. Her head hit the grill of the car she had been trapped in, and the neck snapped from the whiplash effect of the impact.

Jessica ran and jumped back into the car, thankful that she hadn't turned it off, yet equally aware of how foolish she had been. She gave one last look in the mirror as she drove away. The child had gotten to her feet and had given a slow and lumbering chase after the car. Her head was lopsided and twisted on an angle that meant she would forever walk with a tilt.

With her foot on the floor once more, Jessica sped toward the airport, hoping that she would not run across any more survivors.

The airport was not a busy one, with flights scheduled in such a way that it never became over-crowded. However, as she drew closer, the number of zombie groups she ran across increased, as did the number of severed limbs that she saw scattered about. The zombies in this part of town it seemed more aggressive; either that, or had put up more of a fight before finally falling to the endless wave of the undead.

With the airport in sight, Jessica began to get nervous about her chances of making it. The crowds around the car were thick, and several times she had to mow down a few lines of the things. The car had at least two flat tires, and the engine was overheated in the extreme according to the gauge which tried to push past its maximum level. Suddenly there was a flash of light, and the zombies began to fall to the pavement.

Jessica slowed down, shocked by what had happened. It took a moment to realize that it was not that the zombies had succumbed to their inevitable demise, but rather as a result of heavy machine gun fire. The flash of light had been a handful of smoke grenades thrown into the crowd. As it began to clear, the army personnel came into focus. There was one tank and three jeeps with gun turrets mounted on the top, along with a small group of armed soldiers standing on either side. They all fired into the crowd, with the exception of the tank.

As she drove toward them, Jessica was motioned to slow down. She did as they ordered, following their pointed directions to the short stay car park where a host of medical tents had been erected, the kind you would see in disaster zones when a flood or hurricane had hit.

Jessica was ordered out of the car by two soldiers, one male and one female. Both waved automatic weapons at her and had their faces covered by masks which distorted their voices enough to cause them to give their orders repeatedly. It was something that seemed to annoy them, for ultimately, the female soldier grabbed Jessica by the arm and pushed her over to the tents. Here Jessica was met by a team of doctors who wore a similar collection of protective masks. They worked quickly and without too many commands. Jessica was stripped naked and inspected for wounds and other injuries. She was sprayed with a liquid that caused the cuts and grazes she had acquired during her struggles to catch fire. With the tests seemingly passed, she was given her old clothes which felt far too dirty to put back on, but there was no other option. She was swiftly ushered into the terminal building, passing several large groups of survivors who looked equally, if not more shell-shocked than she felt.

"Jessica…oh thank fuck, you're alive. I knew it was you, I just knew it!" a familiar voice sang out, breaking through the background noise.

Jessica turned, her mind and body still not under her full control, and saw a pair of arms waving at her. Her mind focused and she smiled; an automatic reaction. She only returned the wave once the full recognition process was complete. "Rita, oh God, Rita." Jessica felt the tears start to flow, and she ran into her friend's arms. The pair embraced and held each other tight. "I told them it was you. I told them." Jessica's colleague and travel partner sobbed into her friend's neck.

After a while, Jessica broke their grasp and stared at her friend. "Why is this happening?" Jessica half cried, half whispered. "Look at us… me." She stared at her blood-encrusted clothes and noticed for the first time since it all started that she was barefoot, and there was a large piece of grey, gelatinous brain stuck to the top of her foot. "I'm gonna be sick," she whispered.

"Don't Jessie, if they see you so much as look sick, they'll kick you out there…with them." Rita pointed to the horde of survivors that were huddled together in various states of shock. They seemed to be split into three definitive groups: injured, blood covered but otherwise fit, and those that seemed unscathed.

"What's going to happen to them?" Jessica asked as the steady drumbeat of machine gun fire started up again.

"They're being checked out and evacuated," Rita answered. She still wore her airline uniform and seemed to be anything but disheveled.

"How come you look so good, Rita? Where were you when this happened?" Jessica asked, embarrassed by her appearance.

"I was in the air. We landed, and as we walked into terminal they…they just attacked us. We never stood a chance." Rita began to tear up, and she looked at the floor. "They got James, ripped him apart in front of me. It's the only reason I got away. I hid in the baggage area." Rita pointed toward the key card operated security door. "It was still open, so I ducked inside with a couple of others and hid. The army came not too long after that and cleared them out. They rescued us and immediately started planning the evacuations. I guess it was all true, those newspaper reports." Rita changed the subject suddenly, eager to be done with talk of their attack.

"What do you mean?"

"What they said about the zombies... that the government always had a plan in place for something like this." Rita looked around. "It's all too organized for it to not to have been rehearsed," she whispered.

At that moment two army officers approach the women. Jessica knew they were officers from their clothes and the fact that they were nestled safely inside, away from the action. They stopped before the pair, and one of the men asked, "Are you Jessica Bough?" Military through and through.

"Yes..." Jessica stammered, as her mind spun out of control.

"Ma'am, I must request that you to come with me. You need to get changed right now. We need you to start showing passengers to the planes." The other man, the younger of the two spoke. "We have two planes fuelled and ready to leave. You arrived just in time," he continued, flashing a smile.

"OK, I um... I have some spare clothes in my locker," Jessica stammered. She was suddenly exhausted as the true consequences of everything filtered through. She thought of her parents and her baby brother. The zombies were in her hometown. Rachel had been eaten by one - her boyfriend. Jessica felt an officer place a hand on her shoulder and gently lead her in the direction she needed to go.

"Remember, Miss Bough..."The older man called after Jessica, who turned to look his way. "You're in the army now."

# CHAPTER 3 – SOMETHING, ANYTHING

"That is pretty much it, Paul. For the past two weeks I have been flying trips to and from the airport, dropping people off in safe zones, and evacuating them." Jessica finished her story and sat back down. During its telling, several people had stirred and sat listening intently to every word she uttered.

Paul said nothing. He wrote feverishly, scribbling as many of the details as he could remember. Even as he listened to Jessica's story, the verbal narration of her history, he began to pose questions—forever the journalist, it would seem—which he scribbled in the margins. Everything he wrote was in his own form of shorthand; utter nonsense to anybody but himself.

"There's nothing else?" he asked. "You've been flying these evacuation flights for the past two weeks. Have you not heard something, anything about what has happened since? What started it, why did it spread so quickly?" Paul flicked through his notes. He was certain that Jessica was hiding something from him. They had only scratched the surface of her tale, but clearly, she had finished speaking...for now.

When she looked up at him, Paul saw her in a different light. Sure, she hadn't been out there fighting the undead, putting them down where they belonged, but she had been doing something far worse, something far more damaging to the human psyche: She had been escaping, and then returning to the heart of the action, time after time. Paul knew that, unlike the others, Jessica had experienced the outbreak from a unique perspective, and that fact alone told him that she knew more.

Jessica shook her head. She was still pale from the loss of blood, and even though she was awake and talking, the danger was still present, and not just from side effects, but from a repeat performance. "No...I don't know. We never really leave the plane. We fly out, never to the same location twice in a row; we unload the passengers, refuel, and then come back. We load the plane, most of the time the people are already lined up in the concourse. I run a head count, report it to the pilot, and we take off again. The only time I get off the plane is to sleep, and even then it isn't always that simple."

Paul thought a moment longer. "So where are you taking us? It has to be an airfield, right? Is it still in England? Britain? You said that you fuel when you unload, so it can't be that far," Paul mused, the questions were meant more for himself than for Jessica.

"It is Europe. The virus spread all over the UK, but they shut everything down quickly. They have five bases that I have seen so far, all military operated now. Only the pilot knows where we are going, and even that is only after takeoff. I'm sorry, Paul, I wish I could tell you something else. I really do." She had started to cry once again.

"It's okay, you did great. I am sure people will be just as fascinated by it as I am." Paul smiled as he put his pen and paper to one side. He scooted closer, and put his arm around Jessica. "It's a noble thing you are doing," he whispered, giving her a friendly squeeze. "This will be the best damned survivor story anybody has ever read," he joked. It was odd, the effect writing but a few pages of notes had on him.

"Maybe someone else will know something," Jessica whispered as she wiped her eyes on the back of her bandages.

At that moment, the paramedic who had truly saved Jessica's life spoke up. He sat three rows before them. His daughter was asleep and was stretched out on the chairs before him. He had been listening to the entire conversation.

"You want to know more about what caused this thing?" he asked rhetorically. "I think I can help a little," he added as he slipped into the chair on the opposite side of the aisle to Paul.

"I'm all ears," Paul replied with a smile and a wink aimed at Jessica. He bent down, collected his things, and turned to a fresh page in his book.

# CHAPTER 4— I CAN HELP YOU THERE

Leon sat back in his chair and looked carefully at Paul and then to the suicidal flight attendant behind him. Both stared at him as if he held the secret to the Holy Grail in his head.

"I don't want you getting your hopes up now." Leon smiled at them. "I just heard a few things is all." He was a tall man, and he shuffled himself into a more comfortable seating position. He eyed the pack of cigarettes. "Mind if I bum one of those?" he asked.

"Sure, anything for a good scoop," Paul joked as he handed the pack across to the man.

The plane bounced around as the turbulent winter sky buffeted them this way and that.

Leon stalled, a tactic Paul knew well. His hand shook slightly as he lit the cigarette and took a shallow drag. The resulting cough said enough.

"You weren't a smoker before, were you?" Paul tried to get the conversation going. He had learned during his years of interviewing people that a conversation was like pulling a truck. Hard to start things rolling, but once momentum was there, keeping it going was simple.

"No, I used to be a complete health nut. Strange, it all feels like so long ago now. It's hard to believe it's only been a couple of weeks." The sadness in his words hung heavy in the air. Nobody said anything, for nothing needed to be said.

"If you're not ready for this, Leon, just say so, and we can stop. I'm sure someone else…" Paul tried a different tact, his failsafe technique.

"No, I want to…I need to," Leon interrupted. "Like I said, I couldn't help but overhear your story, young lady, and well, your questions there at the end. I think I can help you answer a few of them, or at least add a little bit of something," he answered.

"Ok, well, I'd love to hear it, Leon. Why don't we start with something simple? Where were you when it all started?"

# CHAPTER 5 – LEON DE GUZMAN

"Hand me some more bandages! Jesus Christ. I cannot stop the bleeding. Hurry up with those bandages!" Leon De Guzman called as he clamped his down on the woman's injured shoulder. They had received a call from the local Morrison's supermarket about a young woman who had been attacked in the middle of the store.

Leon and his partner Danny Knowles had been in the area and had gotten there within three minutes of the call coming through. Blood was everywhere. The patrons of the busy supermarket had formed a cloying ring around the area and watched with a mix of horror and fascination as the two paramedics got to work.

"Miss? Miss, can you open your eyes for me? Miss, I need you to stay awake for me now," Leon almost shouted. Adrenaline surged through his veins. Something hung in the air, and it had Leon on edge.

The girl on the floor gave no answer. She had lost too much blood, Leon knew, but with so many people around it would be unprofessional to lob her body onto the gurney and drive away. Sometimes real life was about the show or so Leon had learned over the years.

"She's gone man," his partner Danny whispered to him when he returned with a thick pile of bandages.

"I know that, and you know that, but they don't," Leon whispered, swapping the sodden bandages for the fresh stack. In doing so, he chanced a look at the wound. The bleeding had begun to stop, more as a result of the body being empty than any reasons pertaining to clotting. There was a strange shape to the wound, a series of small crescents that in turn formed a rather distinct larger crescent. While not a perfect outline—the edges jutted outward in two places—the tool used to inflict the wound was unmistakable.

"Danny, take a look at this shit," Leon whispered, nudging his partner with his elbow.

"What is that? It looks like a …"

"Teeth! That is a fucking bite mark." Leon stood up from the body, the setting suddenly forgotten. He could no longer stand the cold chill that caressed his spine like a lover. "Where did the guy that attacked her go?" Leon asked, looking around the crowd. Their faces had paled considerably. The blood had spread, almost filling the circle that had formed.

"Is she dead?" someone asked.

"Yes, but we really need to see the person that attacked her. He could be ill," Leon lied. He was not sure why he wanted to see the attacker. He just knew he needed to.

"He ran off into the store room," another faceless voice answered.

Leon turned to move away, when he was startled by a sharp cry. The body of the girl was moving; not the twitches of the recently deceased, but moving. The legs kicked out at the air while the arms flapped, but not in seizure. The fingers had hooked and scratched at the ground. She was trying to get up.

"What the hell...Danny, Danny, grab the Medikit," Leon called as he ran back to the young woman who strained and groaned on the floor. "Miss, Miss, calm down, I'm going to need you to keep calm." He reached out and placed his hand on the woman's shoulders in an attempt to get to her lie back. Leon recoiled from the touch; the woman's flesh was hot, hotter than any fever could cause.

Danny returned with the medical bag, and immediately began reaching for the morphine pen they all carried. He grabbed it and handed it to Leon. Working quickly, he pulled off the cap and pushed the needle through the skin of the woman's upper arm. Rather than calm her, the morphine seemed to agitate her further. She thrashed on the floor, splashing her spilt blood over everything. By this point, the shoppers had all turned to leave, only to find their path blocked by the very same man that had started it all.

Blood streaked his face and soaked the front of his shirt. He stood, not still, but stiff and took deep rasping inhalations. He stared at the shoppers, his head tilted slightly to one side, and smiled. He lunged for them. He was slow, but their panic allowed him the time needed to claim another victim. Blood lust descended, and the man buried his face into the face of a middle-aged shopper who had been out with his daughter buying the final decorations for the birthday cake they had planned to make that afternoon. The man fell to the floor in seconds, his aorta severed by hungry teeth.

The cries and commotion startled Leon who continued to try and restrain his patient. Danny was frozen, his eyes bulging as he watched the scenes unfold. He was a lot younger than Leon and still green, and despite repeated calls for help, Danny lent none.

"Hold still," Leon growled, his patience wearing thin. As if only hearing his voice for the first time, the women raised her head and looked at him. Leon gasped and jumped back, slipping in the thick layer of congealing blood that he knelt in the center of. He careened backward, arms flailing, falling into the fully stocked shelving unit, and knocking its contents to the floor. Jars of vegetables fell to the floor, shattering on impact. Crawling, unable to fully right herself, the woman dragged herself over to Leon, who quickly found his footing and beat a hasty retreat. He knew the woman was dead—the grey pallor to her skin, the blue tint to her lips—but most of all, it was her eyes; they were cold, dead. "Get back, stop right there!" Leon ordered, but the woman kept coming. She dragged her body over broken glass, slicing open her skin without so much as a hint of recognition. Turning, Leon ran, assuming his friend and partner was behind him. The commotion in the store had turned into the full-fledged panic by the time Leon reached the door. Several people had the same idea he did—to escape. Most simply ran blindly. Bodies littered the floor, and the heady aroma of blood filled the air like an abattoir drainage pipe.

Leon sprinted to the door, but before he made it something grabbed hold of his leg. The grip was strong, and Leon fell to the floor. His head slammed to the ground hard enough to make him see stars. He must have blacked out for a few seconds because when he opened his eyes the man who had tripped him was upon him, pinning him to the floor. The man was dead, and Leon knew it just as easily as he had seen it with the woman. When you dealt with death as often as Leon did, it was just a case of 'You know it when you see it'.

Leon pushed and struggled to slowly work his way free. He was a strong man, in great shape, but the strength of the freshly risen dead shocked him. The dead man fought back, changing tactic. It tried to take a bite out of Leon's leg. Its maw began to close, and just as Leon felt the teeth make contact with his skin he struck out. Leon threw a flurry of punches and knocked the dead man off balance and eventually, off him entirely. Leon sprang back to his feet. Running on adrenaline he looked around, unable to fully process what had happened. All around him people fell, their bodies ripped apart, only to stand back up and come after those still alive.

"It can't be," Leon spoke to nobody in particular.

At his feet, the man he had just escaped from attempted to claw his way back toward Leon. He reacted with aggression and kicked out at the man whose snarling lips and gnashing teeth were anything but positive signs. The man's nose shattered, and the skin surrounding his left eye split open like a piece of over ripened fruit. Yet still he came, hauling himself to his feet. Leon struck out again, this time with his fist. Though knocked to the floor, the zombie immediately began to struggle again, giving Leon the time he needed to escape.

He reached the door when a scream rang out that stopped Leon in his tracks. "Danny," he called as he spun back to face the store.

A second scream followed the first, and Leon set off without hesitation in search of his friend. He found him just one aisle over from where he had left him. The young woman they had tried so hard to save had straddled Danny's chest. She began to slam his head into the floor, creating a second, less substantial pool of blood. Leon was too late. Before he could reach his partner, the undead woman had opened up a hole in the back of Danny's head and had slipped her fingers inside it. With a powerful yank she ripped the skull open, the bone breaking with a strangely delicate snapping sound. She threw the top of the skull over her shoulder as if it were nothing, where it spun on its neatly trimmed, overly gelled top like an empty cereal bowl.

With a triumphant growl, the woman buried her face in the open cranium, greedily stuffing her face with the juicy brains that lay within. She ate with a noisy fervor which caused Leon to spew his breakfast and half-eaten lunch all over the floor. Not that anybody paid attention.

*Run Leon,* he ordered himself, but his legs would not respond. They were frozen.

"Daddy, no, stop it!" A young girl screamed and snapped Leon out of the shocked trance that enveloped him in a dark nightmare. He turned to run just as the woman finished licking the inside of Danny's head clean.

He ran through the aisle toward the sound of the scream, when he saw a young girl. She couldn't have been more than seven or eight, standing with her back pressed against the wall facing her father—the same man Leon had already encountered. He was on his hands and knees pulling on the hem of the girl's dress.

"Hey, hey, leave her alone!" Leon called out. Suddenly the store fell silent. Leon stopped. He and the girl were the only ones left alive.

Every zombie in the store stopped and turned to face Leon. For a heart stopping second he thought there was a chance for escape. They moved in a swarm, bearing down on Leon, and separating him from the girl who had ripped her dress away from her ravenous father and retreated further into the corner. She moved the wrong way, away from the doors. Leon wanted to call out, but a hand clamped down on his shoulder. He spun around, lashing out as he did. He struck the zombie, an old woman, on the top of her head, knocking her backward where she fell to the floor. As the elderly woman fell, three more sets of hungry hands tried to take her place. They grasped only air as Leon had jumped back, putting some distance between himself and the mob. He knew that there was no way he would be able to get to the girl. As if fate had read his mind, Leon's blood ran cold as he heard her young voice call out in agony. He turned and saw her standing in the corner, her dress torn apart, her intestines slowly pulled from their cavity, and sucked into the hungry mouth of the cashier who devoured them as if they were spaghetti.

"I'm sorry," Leon mouthed to the girl whose eyes bored into him with a pain that would haunt him forever.

Growls began to close in on him, and Leon found himself with his back pressed against the door. It would not open. The automatic sensor no longer worked. Panic fueling his every move. He frantically waved his arms and stamped his feet to no avail. A pair of hands suddenly descended on his shoulders. Leon feared the worst, but as he turned, his legs tangled with themselves and he fell, pulling the zombie with him. Lifting his legs, Leon managed to flip the heavyset man over, shattering the glass and pelting him with a rain of razor sharp shards. Ignoring the lacerations in lieu of much larger issues, Leon scrambled to his feet and left the supermarket. The ensuing rush of the walking dead clogged the hole he had created.

Leon knew it would not keep them contained forever. Right on cue a large crack spread across the glass, branching out further and further. Not wanting to be around when it broke, Leon broke into a run.

The wintry wind whipped around him, and Leon realized he had taken his jacket off when he was inside the store. His short sleeve shirt, however, was the least of his problems because the keys to the ambulance were in his jacket. The spare key, a recent standard issue for all teams, was of course in Danny's pocket. Cursing himself, Leon ran for the ambulance, determined to find a way in. The car park was not that full, and the majority of the shoppers were still trapped in the store. It shocked Leon how many shoppers there were, given the warning that played on a looped broadcast on all radio and television frequencies urging people to stay in their homes. A few lone zombies wandered the car park, but they had yet to notice Leon as he sprinted across to the ambulance parked to the immediate left of the main entrance.

The dead in the car park did not take long to turn and start moving toward Leon who had walked around the ambulance trying every door in vain. The sound of the plate glass shattering imbued Leon with a renewed vigor. He could hear the growl of the zombies closing in on him. A quick glance over his shoulder told Leon that his problem was even graver. Behind the charging tide of ravenous cannibals a thick plume of black smoke rose into the sky.

Some held the lead, and others fell behind, absorbed into the group. With nowhere left to turn, Leon hauled himself onto the ambulance's rear bumper and ultimately the roof. The higher ground made Leon feel somewhat more secure. They didn't seem capable of jumping, and even climbing after him seemed to be quite the task. However, what they lacked in smarts, they made up with power—a raw and unrestricted power—which they used to good effect. What began as a few pounding fists soon become a steady hammering, and the ambulance began to rock. The more it rocked, the more agitated the crowd became. They redoubled their frenzied attempts to overturn the vehicle.

Leon struggled to maintain his balance, spurred on by the knowledge that if he fell he was dead. He crouched down and took a firm hold on the light fixed atop the vehicle. The crowd grew thicker and thicker, and in the distance Leon saw them all, the dead, wandering in search of their next meal and the living fleeing in terror.

The reality of his situation hit Leon hard. He became oblivious to the pack of growling monsters that surrounded him five rows deep, their dirty red teeth gnashing in anticipation of his sweet, adrenaline-ripened flesh.

*Lord Jesus, help me,* Leon thought to himself as he rose to his feet. The sound of the growls broke through the mental barrier. Trembling, Leon held his arms out, and sweat dripped from his body, yet he shivered with cold. His heart thundered so fast it felt as if it vibrated rather than beat. He swallowed. His throat was dry and rough, his tongue a sticky mass that sat useless in the base of his lower jaw. One shaky shuffle, and he was on the edge. *Ok Leon, just one more.* He tried to prepare himself, when out of nowhere, a police car with lights and sirens blazing came careening into view. It came in a straight line down Upper Queen Street, the main road that led into the supermarket complex. The car mounted the curb and crashed clumsily into one of the non-shopper, pay and display ticket machines. The sound of the crash caused the entire group to turn. Without so much as a moment's hesitation to ponder the quandary, they set off toward the car. As Leon watched, his head swimming against a black current that threatened to pull him out to sea, he thought for a moment that the zombies moved quicker; that they ran from the supermarket eager to integrate themselves in outside world.

During the scuffle, the creatures had broken both the driver and passenger side windows. Slipping from the roof, Leon lowered himself to the passenger side, keeping himself hidden behind the truck. Leon heard a couple of growls behind him. When he looked, the two walking corpses were some way off—he had time. Sliding his arm through the broken window, he opened the door and climbed inside. Fumbling beneath the steering wheel, Leon ripped open the covering that hid the electronics from view. He struggled to pull a knife from the bag that rested on the floor between the seats. Their emergency kit ensured they were ready for any situation, even the rise of the dead it would seem. With the ignition wire cut through and the ends exposed, Leon closed his eyes and said a silent prayer. He had not hotwired a car since he was a young rebellious teenager. The wires came together, and the engine jumped into life.

Leon exhaled, sat up in the seat, and gasped as his eyes met those of the recently deceased girl from the shop. She had crawled up the front the vehicle and held onto the wipers. Throwing the ambulance into reverse, Leon sped back and screeched to a halt. The monstrous parody of the girl lost its grip and slid to the pavement. Without hesitation, Leon put the ambulance into drive and floored the gas pedal. He felt the bump as he drove over the zombie, and in the rear view mirror saw the flattened torso, while the head seemed to burst like a balloon. Leon knew that it had been a child, but also knew that it was a new world which had begun to bloom. One that embodied the kill or be killed sentiment. He gave a chuckle at the thought, then he laughed until he cried, and then he just cried. Leon drove through a torrent of tears, afraid to stop the vehicle, unable to stop the anguish inside his head.

The real craziness started the moment he left the retail park. Zombies moved in all directions, the pack instinct of the supermarket mob, those who had pulled the unconscious police officer from his car and ripped him apart was gone. Zombies ambled along their own shuffling course in search of the scent of living flesh. Of course, they all turned to look at the speeding ambulance, but Leon did not plan to stop for anybody. He mowed down any creature that got in his way. All around him people were screaming, the echoes of terror creeping through the broken windows and echoing around the ambulance like a cold wind through an old house.

Leon came to a junction of the main road, a crossroads in his journey—in his life. He could see how quickly the dead had spread and how the law and order of civilization crumbled. Every small shop he passed was looted or in the process thereof. Leon witnessed the small Pakistani owner of a corner shop burst through the door after a pair of fleeing youths. His turban had unraveled and dragged behind him, sodden with blood.

Leon knew that he would not be able to rescue both his daughter who was at school, and his wife who was home for the day, preparing their house for a showing. They harbored hopes of completing that sale before the summer, having already bought a newly built home on the outskirts of the city. He had told his wife to keep their daughter home from school, but she had stayed the night with a friend, and they had been unable to contact the parents to discuss it. The school later confirmed that both girls had arrived that morning, and that the quarantine order was in full effect within campus boundaries. Classes had been relocated to the main building wherever possible. There had been a general air of overreaction with regards to the warning. Even Leon had found it somewhat unbelievable…until now.

Leon looked both left and right, debating which way to go. With a heavy heart, he took a deep breath and turned in the direction of the school.

Leon's daughter Keisha went to a private school in a small satellite town. She received a full scholarship to attend; they would never have been able to afford it otherwise. *Maybe it has not reached them*, Leon thought as he sped through the back roads.

The school was a large old family estate with the main house being home to the main teaching area. Three other buildings had been added, or in the case of the sports hall, converted. Two square structures, the science building and the computer lab, stood side by side along the main drive directly before the main house and the car park.

Leon felt his heart sink as he turned into the driveway and immediately ran down a young boy. He could not have been more than twelve, a little older than his daughter, who stood in the middle of the road holding a human arm, munching on the raw flesh without a care in the world.

Leon feared the worst, but continued his drive anyway. The long entrance road that led to the school took him past the two sports fields; one was set as a rugby pitch, the other as a football field. The rugby pitch, which was at the bottom of the drive was empty, the football pitch, however, showed something interesting. The net nearest the road had three zombies trapped in it. The arms and legs caught and twisted into the netting.

*They could not have done that to themselves,* Leon thought. A small ray of hope broke through the cold, suffocating cloud of hopelessness that had enveloped him.

The main school building was a mess. The windows had been smashed, and it looked as though there had been a small fire in one of the classrooms on the second floor of the building. The car park was full, and the large playing field opposite the main building was filled with the undead. At least a hundred students wandered aimlessly in search of their next juicy meal. There were teachers there, too, but when Leon caught sight of Abigail, his daughter's best friend, he slammed his foot on the brakes and brought the ambulance to a sudden stop. The noise attracted some attention, and Leon was not about to wait for another supermarket situation to happen. Leon said a silent prayer for Abigail and started moving again. Rolling along slowly, he tried to make himself as inconspicuous as possible. There was no way he could turn around; he needed to drive the long looping road which would take him to the front of the school into the car park. There was no other choice.

The crowd drew closer, following him like groupies. By the time Leon pulled up in front of the school, the entire population of the playing field had noticed him and had turned his way. Leon was about to drive away when he saw movement coming from inside the school from one of the windows on the upper level. He slowed, leaning forward to gaze up at the building. *It is probably just one of them,* Leon thought. He had scanned the group, looking for his daughter, but out of all of the zombies he had seen, she did not appear to be among them.

The movement came again from the window. It was a man, and he was very much alive. Upon seeing the ambulance, the window opened and a white linen sheet appeared.

"Help us," the plea was weak for fear of attracting even more of the undead, but Leon heard it loud and clear.

For the second time that day, Leon took a dangerous chance. He jumped out of the ambulance and sprinted into the main building, leaving the ambulance running. He closed the door, but doubted the creatures would have the intelligence or the will power to turn away from the prospect of a fresh meal long enough to even try to steal it.

The heavy front door opened with a struggle, and Leon ran in, tripping into the pile of desks and chairs and that been stacked before the door in a crude attempt at a barricade. There were three dead bodies on the floor, zombies, with their heads lined against the opposite wall. Their blood was a thick black jelly that cooled on the heavy natural stone floor. There was a growl at the door, and Leon reacted just in time to slam the door shut, trapping the left hand of the young, newly dead student that was trying to climb through, severing her hand at the base of the finger. What made Leon's stomach churn most of all was that the fingers continued to squirm on the floor like fat maggots.

The school building was quiet. The pounding of hungry fists was a constant beat, but Leon already found himself growing numb to it. He walked over and looked through the window. The ambulance was still there. None of the zombies even paid it any mind. There was a group of about five of them by the front door. One girl, who must have been in her final year, peered through the window, her nose pressed against the glass. Leon recoiled, tripping backward, and falling to the floor.

"It's ok, she can't see you," a voice whispered, eliciting an even greater start from Leon. "It's kind of like one way glass. It has a special coat of some sort of paint. You can only see through if you peer hard. Those things just aren't that smart," the voice continued.

Leon spun around and saw an elderly man standing in what had, until a few moments earlier, been a closed doorway.

"Who are you?" Leon asked, picking himself up from the floor.

"Please, not so loud. If they hear you we are all dead," the man whispered nervously. He glanced around as if uncertain whether the coast was clear. Once he was satisfied, he scurried from the hall, quickly led Leon into the darkness of the room, and quietly shut the door behind them.

The gloom was overwhelming, and Leon began to fear he had made a mistake following the man, when suddenly the lights went on, revealing the full extent of the situation.

The room was a small classroom, probably one of the private study areas that the older kids used in the build up toward exams. There were three desks, and at a quick count, eleven chairs in the room. Leon deduced that they had not all originated from the same place. A student, several of whom were dirty and bruised, occupied each stool. Only one girl was spotless; she had in fact been the girl who saved the teacher who, in turn, saved the students. She had been using the room, as was rightly so, for a study area. When she had heard the screams she went to investigate only to be just in time to see the headmistress eaten alive.

While she had been both directly and indirectly responsible for rescuing the students, she had quickly shut down. She raised her head to study Leon. He saw all of the fear she worked so hard to keep bottled up. As if recognizing this fact, the girl nodded at Leon and returned her gaze to the book which she clasped to as if it were a life preserver.

Leon looked around the room but couldn't see his daughter anywhere. Yet the fact that he had found survivors gave Leon hope.

`Who are you?" the older man asked. When Leon turned to face him he saw that the man held a large carving knife before him, ready to strike if the answer given was not good enough.

"Hey, hey, I'm alive; I'm not going to hurt you." The knife had startled Leon, and it threw his thought process off-track. "I'm looking for my daughter. Keisha, Keisha De Guzman." Leon kept his voice calm but could not take his eyes off the knife. Leon was not afraid of it; he had studied martial arts for a number of years and worked out regularly, unlike the teacher, whose potbelly stretched his shirt buttons. If it came to a fight, Leon could take the knife without problem, but he did not want that. The kids had been through enough.

"It's okay, Mr. Matthews, I know Keisha. We are…were in the same English literature group," one of the girls spoke up.

The teacher looked over at the girl and lowered the knife. "Ok," he said, clearly upset at the arrival of someone else.

Leon turned around to look at the girl. He did not recognize her, but then again, Keisha had many friends. "Have you seen her?" he asked, aware of how pleading his tone was.

The girl, a white girl whose skin was brown with dirt and blood, lowered her eyes to the floor. Her school uniform was filthy, and she had her arms wrapped around herself. "No, sir, I haven't seen her since… since they came." She stumbled over her words, eager to have them spoken so that she could return to silence.

Leon felt his heart sink, and it must have shown on his face.

"There are other groups though," a tall girl spoke up. Her left arm was caked in blood, and she had the beginnings of a good black eye. The swelling occupied the right side of her face, yet a fire burned behind those eyes, a determination that the others noticeably lacked. It was then that Leon realized how, to look at them, the group had already given up hope.

"Where? How many are there?" Leon asked. He was eager to be out of the room. Defeat was contagious, and he had no plans on giving up.

"There is one upstairs on the second floor and another one in the science building," the tall girl answered resolutely. "But you can't reach them. There are too many of those things out there." She spoke about the zombies in a way that sounded cold. She had seen what they did and came to the same conclusion as Leon. Kill first, and ask questions later.

"Well, I have to try," he answered, even attempting to flash a smile as he spoke. It did not work; he thought he probably just looked constipated. "She's my daughter, and if she is alive, I'm getting her out…I'm getting everybody out, somehow." A large rescue operation was not what he wanted, and Leon had no clue as to how he would rescue them all, but the look of hope that spread on their faces told him it was a worthy lie.

"You can't go out there. They will kill you," the clean girl spoke, an action that seemed to shock the rest of the group.

"I understand, but she's my daughter, and I am not going to give up on her." Leon felt the fire in the pit of his stomach begin to grow. "Do you have any weapons? How many of those things are up there?" he asked, eager to know what he would be facing.

"They are all on the first floor. There were four classrooms up there, so I would guess around about fifty, unless some have escaped," the tall girl spoke again, stepping into the middle of the room. "I can show you the best place to go up. I'm fed up with sitting here." She shot a sharp look at the teacher, and Leon felt the strange atmosphere that held the room. He was certain, more than ever, that he needed to leave. Leon's conviction was so strong he offered no resistance to the idea of taking a sixteen-year-old girl with him. Leon simply looked at the girl, nodded to her, and turned to leave. He gave the teacher a long hard look as he left. There was something off about him.

The hallway was deserted, and the girl moved with a sure footedness that Leon lacked. "You didn't have to come with me," he spoke as they neared the main stairs that lead to the second floor. The sound of the zombies stumbling around above their heads echoed through the deserted hall.

"I didn't want to stay there, either." She gave the sort of barbed, curt response that only a teenager could give. It made Leon smile; a slice of normalcy in the middle of a crazy world.

They came to a stop at the bottom of the stairway. Leon felt his body tingle with a mixture of fear and adrenaline. "If you want to kill them, you need to go for the head." The girl offered her advice and started up the stairs.

They made their way up, climbing a few steps before pausing to reassess. The second floor opened into a long hallway with glass doors at either end separating the stairs from the classroom area. The zombies were effectively caged in. "They are pull-doors. They don't seem to have mastered that just yet." The girl heard Leon draw his breath.

As she spoke, the zombies turned around, their mindless shuffling stopped, their minds focused on a joint goal. The sound of their groans also changed. Something about it struck a chord in Leon's mind, and he made a note of it.

It was strange seeing all of the undead students trapped in one space. Leon stared at them; there seemed to be no discernible pattern to it. The only thing he saw was that the level of violence seemed to have either increased or decreased at some point. Those in the best condition had a single wound; a bite wound Leon guessed, remembering the shopping center. Then there were those that had multiple wounds, mainly around the face and neck area. One such student stood closest to the glass. Her face had been eaten on the right hand side. The wet meat beneath had already started to crust over, she walked with a limp, and her left leg jutted at a strange angle from the knee down. Yet it did not seem to impede her progress. The worst cases were the kids who were ripped apart. There were three students that he could see with their flesh torn apart, their bodies picked clean. These three were motionless, yet as Leon watched, they somehow still blinked and hungrily bit at the air; they too could hear the commotion and were just as frenzied by it.

The school was predominantly female in terms of students, with the ratio being about seventy-to-thirty. Looking, Leon did not see a single male student among them all.

"Come on, they calm down when we are not there, but those doors will break sooner or later. Sooner if you just stand there," the girl called from half way to the stairway.

Leon had a second flashback to the store, the glass shattering, and the flood that followed. He shuddered and quickly headed to the second floor.

"How did you get them all trapped there?" Leon asked, impressed by the levelheadedness of the children.

"A lot of kids aren't in school because they're off sick with the flu. Classes had been rescheduled and moved to the second floor. The segregation happened by accident. Downstairs there are also some rooms with them all trapped in. We marked them with a red cross. We killed a few too," she added with a startling nonchalance.

"The flu..." Leon began, pausing to think.

"Haven't you seen the news today? They have as good as confirmed that it is the flu. Anybody who dies from the flu, which is everybody, comes back as one of them... a zombie," the girl explained, mistaking Leon pause in confusion.

"I heard. I was already at work," Leon said. "Besides, I'm a paramedic; our orders were 'business as usual'. The only thing was that we had to try and patch people up at home and to not take them to the local hospitals."

The second floor of the school was much like the first: shut off at either end by heavy glass doors. The main difference was that the upper level was void of zombies and looked for some reason or the other as if it had escaped all of the carnage. It looked utterly deserted, but Leon remembered the flag that he had seen come out of the window on the upper floor, so they pushed on.

"I don't know where they are, but we heard them calling for help." The girl, whose name Leon had yet to obtain, spoke as they opened the heavy glass door. There were three doors on either side of the whitewashed corridor, and the scuff marks on the standard school issue vinyl floor showed that central doors were the most often used.

"I saw something from this room here." Leon walked to the central door that overlooked the front driveway, and knocked.

There were sounds of a scuffle inside, followed by a muffled cry. Without waiting, Leon pulled the door open, ready for anything.

What he found were five boys, all standing in one corner, huddled together. Their faces were etched with an expression of shock, but shock at the interruption. They stood in the corner, hiding something.

"What's going on here?" Leon asked, looking around the room with suspicion. He saw the white sheet that had been held out of the window, and he saw the bloodstains that dotted it; they were red… fresh. He looked back at the boys; none of them appeared injured. The largest of the group fiddled with the zipper of his trousers. It was a small motion, one that Leon saw out of the corner of his eye, but everything then fell into place.

Leon strode into the room and pushed the five boys aside. Behind them, cowered in the corner was a girl, a classmate of theirs. She was naked and had two ties binding her hands and feet. Tears streaked her dirty face while blood decorated the inside of her thighs.

Leon turned his face into an expression of pure rage. "There are no words," he began, his mind consumed by an anger he knew he could not, or rather he would not, allow himself to unleash on children. "Those creatures turned up today, and you are already torturing, abusing… raping." His voice grew louder with each word, until his words were a bellow.

"We…we figured, if we are going to die, we might as well…" the largest of the group began the smirk on his face still evident. His words were cut short as the fist that Leon could no longer keep from throwing collided with his face.

Beneath them, they could hear the zombies become agitated once again. "Please, Mr. De Guzman, you need to keep quiet. Those things will rip us apart if we don't keep quiet," the girl begged.

"It's Leon. Call me Leon," he told her as he reached out and let the terrified young girl take hold of his hand. "As for you five, you are coming with us, and the first place you will be free of me is at the police station, or so help me God, I'll feed your dicks to one of those…things downstairs!" Leon gritted his teeth and spat his words, somehow managing to keep his voice just above a whisper.

The boys said nothing, not even the leader of the pack, whose bloody face stared at Leon with a fiery contempt.

"Leon, we can't get everybody out, that's not possible," the girl spoke. "There's so many of them. We will all die." The girl had begun to look scared. Within the school, with the zombies locked away she was strong, an adult, but outside, surrounded by the undead she was a child."

"Listen, um…"

"Cindy."

"Listen, Cindy, those things down there will escape. It might not be today or tomorrow, but one day they will, and they will come for you. Who knows how many more there will be out there waiting for us then. Besides, I am here looking for my daughter, but I won't leave any of you behind…even you." He stared at the boy he had struck. "Now, you said there was another group in the science building. How can we get there? What is the easiest way?"

Nobody spoke, not at first. The idea of leaving the safety of the school did not sit well with them. "You really don't think those things are going to die?" Cindy asked, her voice changed. If was filled with a vulnerability that could no longer be held beneath the surface.

"They are already dead. This is all new to me, too, but from everything I have seen, these things are hungry. They don't care what happens, they just keep going, crawling if they have to. The only way to stop them is by destroying the head, but there are too many of them. We need to leave, and it is not up for discussion. Now how do we get to the science building?"

Nobody had a chance to answer before the crashing sound of wood splintering came thundering up the stairs. Everybody froze—it did not take long for the screams to start.

"We're moving... now," Leon ordered. He removed the bonds from the abused girl's limbs and handed her back her clothes. She was not yet fully dressed, but there was no time to wait.

"There has to be a back door right?" Leon asked as they swiftly moved down the corridor. The sound of grunts and hungry growls became louder as they reached the stairwell that was on the opposite side to the one Leon and Cindy had used to reach the second floor.

"Yes, if you go down here and just keep going straight, and follow the corridor to the end. Turn...left, yes left, you will come to the side door. You will have to run to the science building though. It's all outside," Cindy spoke, her strength slowly beginning to return.

"Okay. Everybody move quickly, stay with me, and be fucking careful!" Leon stopped a few steps short of the first floor. The doors there still held although the crowd was more agitated than they had been.

They quickly made their way down the stairs, not listening to the trapped crowd as the scent of blood reached their hunger driven minds. "Don't look back," Leon called as the doors began to rattle in their frames.

"What about the others?" Cindy asked as they reached the first floor.

"They're already dead," Leon stated bluntly.

Cindy did not need to ask how Leon knew this because their bodies littered the main hallway. A crowd of zombies that had been trapped in one of the ground floor rooms were gathered around a few of them, hands buried deep inside, yanking handfuls of squishy human goodness from the bodies, and shoveling it into their hungry maws.

They moved quietly, even when the sounded of breaking glass echoed down from the floor above. However, when the young girl they had rescued from the second floor gave a scream upon seeing what Leon thought to be a liver discarded and sliding along the floor like a bloated slug, they were forced to increase their pace.

The entire crowd, seven in all, dropped their feast and turned their heads, their minds in overloaded rapture at the prospect of another live meal.

"Run," Leon ordered as he took off down the hall.

The zombies gave chase, but the group was too fast for them. Leon crashed through the door and out into the fresh winter air. Once everybody was out he closed it and looked around for something that he could use to halt its continued use.

"Right, we need to move. Which way to the science building?" Leon asked.

Cindy pointed down the correct path, and they started off. All but one boy who stood motionless, held in place by a zombie that had come from behind the building and sunk its teeth into his shoulder. He gave a cry of pain. Heat surged through his body, overriding the concept of pain. Inside he burned, and before everything went black he called out his apologies to the young girl he had helped to rape. He got no answer, for the group was already gone.

No order was required. They heard the boy scream and picked up their pace.

The science building was not far, maybe two hundred meters, but by the time they arrived only three of the eight were still alive. Leon was the first to reach the building. He was glad to see someone open the door to meet their arrival. He was an older man, well into his sixties, with white hair, a white beard, and a laboratory jacket. "In here, quickly," he motioned to them. The teacher was a man Leon recognized from his previous visits to the school for parent evenings and other school functions.

Leon stopped by the door and ushered Cindy and the boy whose nose he had broken into the building before entering himself. He had not been aware of how many of their initial group had fallen. The zombies picked off four of the boys relatively quickly after they left the main building. The girl they had rescued had run into a trap; her blood stained legs had attracted the wrong sort of crowd. Leon made to go and rescue her, but the science teacher grabbed his arm and pulled him inside.

"It's too late," he repeated, pulling Leon away from the doors and deeper into the building.

The last time Leon saw her, a small zombie had bitten down on the bloody flesh between her legs. The pack soon descended, but Leon was certain that her suffering was over before they ate her face. She would not be coming back from the dead, that was obvious as the hungry mob stripped her carcass bare before Leon reached the first floor classroom where the other survivors were gathered.

"Daddy," a familiar voice cried out, speaking a word that Leon had not heard spoken in such a tone in several years.

He spun around and felt his heart soar as Keisha ran into his arms. Her embrace was tighter than he had ever felt, and Leon hugged with equal vigor. Both shed tears.

"Daddy, what are you doing here?" the sweet voice of his daughter sang out in his ears.

"I came for you," he replied, his voice muffled against her head.

The pair broke their embrace, and Leon took a glance around. The second floor classrooms were set up for the more theoretical side of the classes. The laboratory areas were on the ground floor. There were seven people including the teacher who had managed to find shelter.

Leon looked out of the window. Judging by the number of zombies shuffling around the science block wearing lab coats and safety goggles, there had been many more when the crisis began.

It did not take long for a large crowd of zombies to congregate around the science building. With everybody up on the first floor they made no real attempt to enter the building, but still they hovered around. It was as if they could sense that fresh meat was in the immediate vicinity.

Leon found himself staring at them. He watched in near fascination as they ambled around, seemingly oblivious to one another. It struck him as strange, for when the need arose, they seemed to work as a rather efficient team.

"Well, looks like we are stuck here," Leon muttered after a few hours had passed, and the crowd had done nothing but increase. He had not counted them head for head, but his guess would have been around two hundred. They meandered around the building; their mere presence reason enough to stay put.

"Give it time, they will grow tired. Their hunger will draw them away at the first sight or scent of anything living," the teacher, Richard Winston, answered. He had joined Leon in staring out of the window. The students, on the other hand, showed no interest in observing the end of the civilized world. Nobody spoke. They sat in silent reflection. Some picked at the bloodstains on their clothes while others just stared into space. The only one that showed any sign of life was Cindy.

"Yeah, I know. I had a close encounter with a group at a Morrison's in the city. They almost got me." Leon did not mention the fact that he came close to giving himself to them, especially as his daughter was seated beside him.

"You mean these things are...everywhere?" Richard spoke up. His tone more of inquiry thank shock.

"Certainly all over the city," Leon answered. "Every channel is broadcasting the same emergency warning message." Leon wondered for the first time just how far-reaching the outbreak was.

"I feared as much." The old teacher nodded his head as he spoke. "Come with me," he whispered to Leon. "This is a conversation we don't need to have in front of the children."

Leon paused. They were all sixteen, some possibly even older than that, but seeing them all sitting there, he understood what the man meant. They were young and lacked the necessary life experience to comprehend what had happened.

The men walked out of the classroom and into the hall. Leon grabbed the boy by the shirt and pulled him out of the room with them. "You're coming with us," he growled as the young man began to protest.

There were four classrooms in the upper level of the building which was a near perfect square, as were the rooms.

"Stay there, I don't want you out of my sight," Leon spat as he and Winston entered the classroom adjacent to the one they had just left.

"What's his story?" Winston asked,

"I caught him and a group of other lads upstairs in the school. They beat and raped the poor girl trapped with them." Leon skipped all forms of verbal nicety. They were both adults, and the situation was no longer one of parent and teacher.

"Jesus! How quick we are to break down in the face of trouble," Winston mused. "I know him. He's a trouble maker, but never figured he would do anything like that," he continued. "Shame really."

"I don't think it will be the worst thing we will ever see. Not if these things really are everywhere. What do you know?" Leon asked eagerly, hoping to discover answers to the plethora of questions swimming in his head.

"Nothing for sure. Just the observations of an old man who has studied science his entire life," Winston spoke not to boast.

Leon nodded, acknowledging Winston's background and reasoning. "I'm listening," Leon answered as he slipped on to one of the stools tucked beneath the desk.

Richard Winston took a deep breath, removed and cleaned his glasses, and then settled them back onto his nose before continuing. "This whole thing started with the flu. People got sick; very sick, very fast, and then they died. The say that the first ones to rise were the ones that died from the fever, right?" Leon nodded, his mind already starting to make possible connections. "Isn't it funny that people got sick for two days and then died? Now, two days after the first ones started to turn, or so I figure judging by what I saw on the news this morning, the flu just disappears; nobody seems to be getting sick anymore." The old man held his tongue, allowing Leon enough time to either catch up or clarify his thoughts.

"I don't follow, how do you know people aren't getting sick?" Leon asked, puzzled.

"None of this is certain. All I can tell you is on Monday I had a class of eighteen kids. The next day all but five of them were home sick, and a further two went home sick Tuesday afternoon. Now, here we are with ten people, and there is not as much as a sniffle between us."

Leon cast his mind to the people had had met in the school. None of those had so much as a watery eye, either. "So what are you saying?" Leon queried.

Below them came the ever increasingly familiar cry of a human in excruciating pain. Both men ran to look out of the window. It overlooked the playing fields where they saw a group of four zombies surround a student that had evidently been hiding in the tall grasses that bordered the school grounds. They wondered for a moment what had startled him out of hiding, until they saw the nearly legless zombie come creeping out of the field; its remaining lower limb hung on by a thread, and a meaty stump was all that remained of the other.

"What I'm trying to say is, I believe there is a link between the flu and the zombies. You told me once before you are a medical man, a paramedic, correct?" The old man surprised Leon by demonstrating his sharp mind, no doubt a small attempt to show that his brain still operated at a sane level.

"Yes, that's right," Leon answered, staring at the creeping zombie. It had reached the fallen student whose eviscerated body was torn open from its groin to its throat. The zombie, seemingly disinterested in its own condition, started chewing on the arm of the boy, tearing large chunks of rare flesh straight from the bone. *How did it get out here in that condition?* Leon wondered, making a note to ask Winston's thoughts on the matter.

"Then tell me, how often have you seen a bout of flu so virulent that it kills people so quickly, only to have it disappear within forty-eight hours? Think about it, Leon. Doesn't that seem rather strange to you?"

Richard believed in what he said, and Leon, when he ran through things in his own head, could see why. The man made a very good point. "You really believe that this was...an attack?" Leon asked. However convincing it all sounded in his head, saying it aloud was an altogether different story.

"Yes, albeit unintentionally. I do not think the living dead were the plan. The virus, however,—just think about it for a second. You are at war, you drop in a virus that wipes out the majority of the population within forty-eight hours and then disappears, not even leaving a trace. You can just waltz right in and clean up Dodge," Richard stopped. Something had caught his attention, but he did not know what.

"So this was an attack...but why Norwich of all the damned places?" Leon offered up a counterpoint, but he also found his subconscious focusing on something else.

"It is probably everywhere," Richard offered, his gaze moving away from his conversational partner to stare out of the window. The zombies had eaten their fill of the boy and left, leaving him to flop around on his back on the turf, unable to roll himself over. His arms and legs were no longer attached; they lay on the ground around him, eaten to varying degrees.

"No, that's just the thing," Leon answered. "We spent yesterday running a taxi service for people with the virus, they were collected and brought to hospitals out of the city, and one crew was even sent out of the county at the end of the afternoon. The infection started here." Leon turned to look out of the window. He understood what it was that held his attention now. It was a steady, deep hum, like a heavy vehicle. Both men stared, and it was Leon who saw it first, with the connection being the legless zombie that just crawled from the field.

"Well, one thing is for sure, if you took people out of the county, the zombies have damned sure spread out now," Richard offered, as he too saw the source of his intrigue.

"Yeah, well, at least it looks like we are saved," Leon offered as the large combine harvester crested the hill of the field.

"For now..." Richard added with a somewhat ominous tone.

# CHAPTER 6 – MINDLESS FOOLS

"That is pretty much it as far as my story goes," said Leon. "We managed to attract the attention of the farmer. The science building had a flat roof, so Richard and I went up and started signaling. The farmer had been chasing zombies out of his field all afternoon. He had been coming to check the school for any survivors, and he took us back to his farm where we stayed for about a week." We would still be there if that damned storm hadn't hit. Anyway, we had to leave after the zombies got in. Only Richard, Cindy, Keisha, and I got away. The rest fell behind on the outskirts of town. We came across a huge group of them... a herd is what they are calling it. There must have been three maybe four hundred of them at the edge of the city." Leon paused, taking a moment to calm himself. He had hardly stopped during his narrative.

Paul was glad for the respite, for his wrist ached from taking notes.

"Where are Richard and Cindy now?" Jessica inquired. She sat upright, listening intently to the tale as it unfolded. There was a sense of urgency in her eyes; an air of expectancy.

"Cindy was on another plane. They separated us when we arrived at the airport. A military convoy came through the housing estate we had holed up in. We had hung white banners from the two upper windows. They arrived all guns blazing, clearing the streets, and whisked us away just before dawn," Leon answered. He lowered his head as if in prayer, taking a moment before answering the second part of the question.

"Richard didn't make it. He got bit one evening while he was having a smoke. He almost got away, but the damned thing nipped the tip of his finger off.  He begged me to do it," Leon added, as if their silence at his minute paused in narrative was some form of holy condemnation.

"Do what?" Jessica questioned.

"Kill him," Paul answered for the man whose eyes had started to fill with tears as he recalled the memory. "You killed him so that he wouldn't come back as one of them," Paul revealed to Jessica, while leaving Leon the chance to continue. Paul had a strange fluttering in his gut that told him there was more Leon wanted to divulge.

"Yes, but it was strange," Leon paused, trying to find the correct words. "All of the things I have seen, the change is almost instant. One of those things bites you, and it is game over. Not with Richard, he took two full days to turn."

"Two days? Did he get sick?" Jessica interrupted.

"Yes, but not in the way you think. He fought it; his body fought against the...whatever it is that causes people to change. The bite was not too bad, and so it gave him the chance to fight it. You know what that means, right?" Leon hinted, hoping they would answer the question with the same confidence he did the night Richard posed it to him.

"There might be a cure," Jessica whispered, half talking to herself.

"Exactly." Leon let out a relieved breath. He had not mentioned Richard's death to anybody. Not even the military which had thoroughly interrogated him after his rescue. They seemed especially interested in his relationship with the two young girls with whom he cohabitated.

"Do you really think it is possible?" Paul challenged. "I mean, I spent a long time surrounded by those damned things, and all I saw were brainless monsters. There didn't seem to be anything left that could be saved." Paul was aware how cold he sounded, but after killing nonstop for two weeks, a new attitude toward life and redemption was a pre-requisite.

"I like to think so. I mean, I'm not a scientist, but medically, it could be plausible, especially if it is true that it was a biological attack," Leon added, as if any of them were likely to forget such a controversial theory.

While the two men were chatting, Jessica got to her feet. Her legs were shaky, and she was still lightheaded from the blood loss, but when the men moved to help her, she waved them away. "I need to give the captain an update on the flight; maybe find out where we are going," she stuttered unconvincingly and walked away.

"I don't buy it, man. I as good as lived among those things. They are mindless fools, slaves to their hunger," Paul reaffirmed. A cure of being undead just did not sit with him; at least a cure that was not death...again, that was.

"You're wrong, man," a new voice spoke up from further down the cabin. A young man, not long out of his teens, stood up. "They are not mindless. At least, not all in the same way."

"What do you mean?" Paul appealed, stealing the words from Leon's mouth.

The young man walked toward him with a profound limp, but looked as though he had survived relatively well; he had a healthy color to him.

"What I mean is...well, you said they are mindless animals, slaves to their hunger. You're right, but they are all different. Some of them have a hunger for something else entirely." He looked around for the best place to sit. He chose the row of seats in front of Leon, diagonally across from Paul and Jessica, who returned close behind him.

"Tell me everything," Paul solicited, eagerly flipping to a fresh page.

"Ok, but please, don't judge me..."

# CHAPTER 7 — DON'T JUDGE ME

"Don't judge me, okay?" the young man repeated as he settled down and fastened his seatbelt. He left enough room to allow himself the room to turn around and face his newfound scribe.

The plane bounced through another patch of turbulence, and the man closed his eyes and gripped the seat handle at the first little bump.

"You don't like flying?" Paul asked, once again taking control of the conversation.

"You noticed, hey," the younger man snapped. His eyes sprang open, and a flash of fire shone within them. He caught his words and reeled his temper back in. "I'm sorry, I haven't…never mind, it's gonna make me sound like someone I'm not," he corrected himself.

"It's okay; we are all open minds here. No judging, I promise." Paul flashed the young man a smile and offered him the pack of cigarettes. He took one and appeared to calm almost immediately.

Further down the body of the plane somebody coughed, the throat tickled by the smoke, or rather the smell of the smoke, for the air filtration system in the plane was state of the art, a little something extra added by the military the first time Jessica had landed and unloaded the passengers. They stood up, ready to make their protest. One look at the bloodied group at the back of the aircraft and the worn out looks on their faces was enough to make the man sit back down.

"I still can't believe any of this is happening, can you?" he stalled. "I used to love those fucking films man—all that zombie shit." He gave a slight chuckle as he exhaled a stream of smoke. "Me and the guys would sit around the dorms all day long watching them. We would joke about how we would do it differently; how we would kick zombie ass all day long and be treated like kings for saving the world." He gave another laugh which sounded more like a cry at the end. He fidgeted in his seat, and his breaths came quicker and quicker. He pinched his eyes closed and slammed his head back into his seat. "What a fucking joke. What tough guys we were." He spat out another burst of crying laughter and took a deep drag on the cigarette. "We were going to have all the women begging to stay with us; we would keep them safe. HA! What a joke that was. Sure, we got women, oh, they got all the women they wanted, but like that…no, not me…I wasn't going do anything like that. You need to understand…I didn't…" the young man spat his words so fast they came out without pause or breaks, and it was the best Paul, Leon, and Jessica could do to separate them where they could and fill in the necessary blanks.

"Listen kid, calm down…take deep breaths. Come on, do it with me, let's breathe." Leon had risen from his seat and crouched in the aisle before the kid; tears streaked his face, cutting tracks through the grime.

It took a while, but Leon managed to talk the man down off the emotional ledge. "We are all in this together. We all have blood on our hands." Leon looked right into the young man's eyes, and said, "Trust me on that."

The kid nodded, and sat back up in his seat, wiping his eyes on the back of his hand. "Ok, but I heard your story, and trust me, those things are more than just brain dead monsters." He took one final pull on the cigarette and stubbed it out on the armrest of the seat.

Nobody said anything about it.

"What's your name?" Paul asked after having counted to ten in his head, wanting not to appear too forceful.

"Robert…Robert Wise." He held out his hand and offered it toward Paul who for a moment stared at it before grasping it in his own. The handshake was firm, and Paul understood. This story would be something else entirely.

"Well, Robert, just relax, and tell me what happened."

# CHAPTER 8 – ROBERT WISE

When Robert first woke, the pounding in his head was so loud that until the haze of slumber lifted from his mind, he thought the music still played from the speakers in the living room. When the full force of the hangover hit him a few minutes after getting up, he immediately ran to the bathroom and vomited a noxious combination of spirits, cannabis, Jell-O, and pizza. The stench alone caused a secondary regurgitation before he had the chance to flush the toilet and clear the air a little.

Robert wandered back into the bedroom. He was lucky. He had been one of the first people to arrive at the dorms on the first day of school, and he had snagged himself one of the three rooms with an en-suite bathroom. Not that it meant anything. He would regularly find other people either using it or having left evidence of its recent use.

Robert stepped over the three passed out forms, taking a moment to enjoy the view offered by the naked girl that lay between his two best friends, Dan and Mark. He grabbed his clothes from the floor beside his bed. Giving them a sniff, he deemed that they were a clean set and pulled them on.

The dorm rooms where he and the other students lived were nothing more than a large house on the edge of the university campus. It was privately owned but rented exclusively to students via the university. The three floors of the house had been divided into two floors of sleeping areas with eight double-bedrooms and two singles. There was a landing between the first and second floor that was home to one single room, and then a small single on the upper floor squeezed between the two largest double rooms. It was on that floor, in the larger of the two doubles, that Robert lived, while his best friends occupied the second double. Roberts's roommate, Charles Knight, was a nice person, but not a close friend. He had a girlfriend who rented a place on her own a little deeper in the city. She had entered the final year of her course and, therefore, no longer had any entitlement to university housing. Most nights he stayed with her, and it suited Robert and his friends down to the ground.

His head pounded even harder by the time he reached the ground floor of the house, which was somewhat worse for wear following the end of their two-day bender celebrating the end of the winter exam period. Much of the previous two days was a blur. Several large blocks of time were lost altogether from his memory.

A number of passed out bodies littered the floor of the living room, and even more spread over the three large sofas that came with the property. In total, there must have been at least twenty-five people on the ground and top floor alone. Robert did not want to chance a guess at how many were crammed into the six bedrooms on the first floor.

A recent outbreak of the flu had seen a number of students either headed home, or in some cases, into the hospital for treatment. Their house had not been hit too badly, probably given to the party more study less attitude of the majority of its inhabitants.

Nobody else was awake, and given the ginger condition that they were all likely to be in, Robert decided against turning on any lights. The one from the refrigerator was bad enough. He opened the door and had to shield his eyes like a vampire walking into sunlight. He grabbed a carton of orange juice and cleared some space on the side to allow him to reach the coffee machine.

With the juice in his stomach, and the smell of coffee gently caressing his senses, Robert found the haze began to lift. The handful of Paracetamol he had dry swallowed played a part. Only once his coffee mug had been filled and that first warming gulp had simultaneously burned his tongue and heated his soul, did Robert pay any attention to the floor. It was warm and wet. Not that he gave it much thought. After a party they had been known to find a great many inexplicable things in all manner of places, including an incident that seemed to involve a two liter carton of olive oil, a golf club, and two pairs of rubber gloves. Nobody ever came forward or ever seemed to recall that moment.

It was only when he went to walk away and almost slipped that Robert paid it some mind. The floor was dark; it looked black. He bent down and dipped his fingers into the puddle that he saw covered nearly the entire kitchen floor. Standing back up, Robert had no option but to turn the light on in order to see what had been spilled.

Robert's scream was the loudest of them all when the light finally flickered into life. The kitchen floor was covered in thick scarlet blood, the walls were smeared with it, and bloody handprints looked as though whoever had been the victim put up a good fight before they died.

"Keep it down man, fuck!" a groggy voice came from the living room, followed by the sounds of shuffling footsteps. Kurt Von Trail moved beside Robert and made his way into the kitchen; he still had his eyes closed, and his movements were driven out of pure coffee scented instinct. His feet skidded on the floor and he fell with a crash. "What the... oh, holy Jesus fuck!" He screamed when he saw what had caused him to slip. He tried to scramble to his feet but did nothing but spin himself around on the floor. When he fell for the second time, it was face first. He stood back up and spat out a lump of flesh. "What the…" Kurt began, but was cut short as a blood-encrusted hand grabbed him by the throat. The sound of sharpened nails piercing his flesh sounded just like the opening of a tube of Pringles: crisp and sharp. The hand disappeared again, ripping Kurt's throat away. The large well-muscled figure fell to the floor with a wet rush of expelled breath. His hands moved to try to stem the flow of blood that was projecting from the gaping wound with large arching spurts. Robert felt his bladder let loose as a warm jet splattered his white t-shirt with gore.

Robert stared with open eyes at the young, naked girl who stood opposite him, her mouth chewing furiously the on the flesh she had crammed into it. While her jaws worked on the flesh, her free hands massaged her breasts and her crotch with a similar fervor. Fingers from her right hand slapped noisily as they entered her, blood dribbling from both north and south holes as she continued her quest for successful self-pleasure.

Robert backed out of the kitchen, his body unable to turn away from the scene before him. All around, the screams began to resound. Finally, the hold was broken, and Robert spun around just in time to see another similarly dead figure make a grab for him; this one a male. Not just a male, but Todd, the man who had moved into the dorm house the same day Robert had. He had a two gaping holes gouged into his flesh, one on the side of his neck, and the other in his flank. Both showed the clear indentation of teeth marks.

"No, no nonono! This can't be! " Robert cried out as the reality of the situation dawned on him.

"Todd," he called out as the male zombie fell on him. His teeth snapped closer and closer, searching for the sweet taste of fresh meat, while his hips thrust with an unknown fury. His stiff member probed and prodded Robert's crotch. With a firm push, Robert managed to dislodge the much lighter man and scramble to his feet. Blood hovered in the air like a mist as he saw four of those… zombies tear chunks of flesh from the bones of his friends and their female companions. As he watched, Todd got back to his feet and grabbed a naked screaming girl from behind; falling into the sofa, she was pinned beneath him. Impaled on his penis, she screamed and lashed out, but could not dislodge him. Todd gave a growl as he buried himself deep inside her while simultaneously ripping deep chunks of skin from her back and shoulders. The blood flowed down her spine and slapped noisily with each undead thrust.

"Open the door! Rob, open the Goddamned door!" a strained voice echoed in Robert's ears. It sounded as though it came from miles away; shouted from a distant place.

Robert turned his head and saw the source was indeed much closer than it had sounded. The whole world had become a dull throb in his ears. The only thing he could hear with any certainly was the frantic thundering of his heart. Mike McMullen ran toward him, his arms wrapped around another one of the creatures.

"The door," Mike called again. Without thinking, Robert spun around and pulled open the front door. A few seconds later, Mike barreled past him and out into the cold early morning air. He wore nothing but his boxer shorts and an odd pair of socks. With a grunt, he threw the zombie that he had been manhandling down the small flight of concrete steps that led up to the front door of the house. It landed in a heap on the floor, its thighbone snapping with a loud crunch.

Mike did not stop to celebrate his victory; he just turned and ran inside, slamming the door shut behind him.

"What the fuck is happening, dude?" Mike asked, his eyes wide with fright. I smoked some shit last night, but tell me this isn't happening." He nearly begged as a new woman fell into his arms. She wore a red lingerie set; or rather, it was a white set stained red thanks to the hole in the side of her head. Her attacker had pulled her hair back so fiercely while she attempted to flee that she had been nearly scalped. The zombie had been in such a rush to consume her active body that it had bitten on the side of her face. It had removed her ear and a good portion of her left cheek. As she stood, grasping for both Mike's neck and his crotch, her arousal forever linked with her more literal hunger for the flesh, her hair flopped around like a bad toupee. It was this that Robert grabbed hold of, pulling her back just as her teeth began to pinch the flesh of Mike's neck. The yank was hard enough to rip the scalp away from the head and gave Mike the chance to strike out. He punched the zombie woman in the face, snapping her head back with the sound of crunching bone. She lunged forward once more, but Mike sidestepped her advance, dipped his knees, and drove forward with his shoulder. He hit her in the stomach and doubled the zombie over. He pulled back and gave a sharp double-handed shove. With Robert's expert door wielding skills once again shining through, the horny women fell over the threshold and into the waiting arms of the previously expelled houseguest. Unlike his sexually charged companion, the other zombie seemed more intent on swaying and staggering around drunk, barely able to hold himself up. He vomited, and a thick trail of dark blood spilled from his mouth, showering the female that stood next to him, groaning at the way the night air teased her dead flesh.

Mike slammed the door shut once more, and the pair turned to face the room. The floor was strewn with seven zombies and six fresh corpses. Those that had managed to escape either hurried up the stairs where they met the descending crowd that that been woken by the screams or had escaped through the back door. Their cries of terror echoed down the street.

"What do we do, man?" Mike whispered. Six of the remaining zombies were fully engrossed by then in the feast of flesh before them. Todd was still in the throes of lust with his victim. The girl Robert had first seen was crouched on the floor, grinding her bloodied crotch in Kurt's face while she had eaten his genitals and was busy filling her stomach with chunks of leg meat.

"We need to get out of here. That's what," Robert said, and yanking the door open, he ran into the street. He leaped past the two zombies who turned to face him. The girl was significantly more alert than the male who stumbled in a drunken advance, his broken leg further hampering his forward momentum. The girl gave a low screech as she gave chase. Robert made to flee, but stopped. He looked around and saw that the dead littered the street, and the sound of growling zombies caused the ground to shake as if Robert stood near active power cables.

"Rob, behind you!" Mike's voice called out just as the female zombie pounced. She forced Robert to the floor, and although he could turn himself just in time, her dead weight was heavy against his tired limbs. The initial adrenaline rush provoked by Todd's attack had worn off.

The woman's body was cold, her touches anything but gentle as she forced herself upon Robert. He held her at bay with stiff arms, and just as his strength began to give, her head exploded, showering him with blood and shards of bone. Robert looked around and saw Mike standing holding a cricket bat against his shoulder. Blood smeared the flat face of the bat, and a long crack ran through the wood from the impact.

Robert scrambled to his feet and followed Mike back inside as the herd of zombies that had gathered in the streets descended on them in a rush.

Mike bounded up to the front door, while Robert stopped. He stood beside the drunken zombie whose head was flattened on one side. He found it oddly fascinating to see how the creature refused to give up on his undead existence. It tried to snap its shattered jaws at Roberts's ankles. Another stream of sour smelling vomit bubbled through its shattered windpipe and covered what remained of its face in thick yellow bile.

"Come on man, they're gaining on us," Mike called from the doorway. His face wore an expression of disbelief. He watched as Robert removed his shirt and started beating his chest in the street like some kind of animal.

"Hey... hey, over here, come and get me," he roared toward the house, screaming his voice hoarse.

"Rob..." Mike began, but as the first zombie appeared in the doorway, its wide eyes a held a strangely vacant look, and the smell of cannabis seemed to seep from its clothes, the masterstroke of Robert's plan dawned on him. With a shove, Mike grabbed the zombie and threw it to the floor, striking out with the bat. The connection was not powerful enough to kill it, but enough to ensure it stayed down for a little while longer.

Mike started shouting and banging on the door. He pulled his shirt over his head and slapped himself hard enough to leave a red print on each side of his chest. The plan seemed to work, because Mike came running down the steps toward Robert with a group of about seven zombies in close pursuit. "Run man. We'll need to double back." Mike didn't slow down as he ran, even though they could have out maneuvered the crowd at a steady walk.

Robert followed suit, and together they drew the pack of six zombies out of the house and into the street where they met the oncoming crowd. Upon later, closer inspection, the dead were comprised predominantly of lecturers and students.

The boys ran a few hundred meters down the street—enough to keep the zombies interested in them—and Robert and Mike made a sharp left hand turn, running down a small side street that would bring them to the back garden of the property. They could hop the fence if it was not already open and sneak in through the back. They started down the side street but stopped when they came face-to-face with a large blood soaked creature. His jaw hung loosely as if dislocated on the left side, and his ankle was folded double with the sole of the foot horizontal to the floor. It gave a growl, and its demeanor changed in a flash. It moved for Mike who was the closest to him.

Mike managed to avoid the thing's grasp by stepping to one side, but the street was narrow, more of an alleyway than an actual road, even if it did have a name.

"It's too narrow, man. If we meet another one of these things, we are done for," Mike called as he shoved the zombie head first into the wall. It slid to the floor, a disgusting trail of blood left behind.

"We don't have a choice; just leg it." Robert looked over his shoulder and saw the first of the chasing pack had reached the road's entrance.

"Shit," both said in near perfect unisons as they broke into a sprint.

The pair charged down the alley and hurdled the body of a former student whose broken, glass-encrusted form had been forced to creep on its belly following a fall from the top floor window of one of the neighboring houses. They made it to the street that ran behind the property and stopped. The newly undead were everywhere, milling around, oblivious to their presence.

"Keep quiet and keep low," Robert whispered. He had seen enough movies to know how it worked. Even if the zombies in them were never sex crazed or drunk, he still hoped that the same basic rules applied.

They crept along the wall and breathed a sigh of relief when they saw that the gate was open. Slipping inside, they closed it and turned to face the house. All of the lights were on, and the blood stained kitchen windows created a strange orange glow. A pounding at the gate told them that their disappearance had not gone unnoticed. Both men jumped as the gate shook on its hinges.

"We need to get inside." Mike moved away from the gate as he spoke and moved toward the house. Robert followed him. They opened the kitchen door, and a shower of warm blood sprayed into Robert's face, blinding him. He heard Mike scream, a sound he had never expected from a man built like Mike. The scream defied description. Its pitch was high enough to cause Robert's ears to ring even after he was inside. Moving quickly, he jumped inside and slammed the door as Mike's gargled pleas for aid went unanswered. Robert wiped a clean spot on the window and looked out. His friend lay on the floor, a bite had been taken out of his face, and his right eye had burst. Then the zombie headed south in search of a juicier morsel and now shoved a steaming pile of fresh human offal into her ravenous mouth.

A hand fell on Robert's shoulder and he spun around, arms flailing in defense. His target never stood a chance. Its head snapped back, and lips were split open. With a gargled cry of surprise and pain the young girl fell to the floor. The fact that she was *not* a zombie dawned on Robert a few moments later when she started crying.

"Oh fuck! Shit! I'm sorry, I'm so sorry. Here, let me help you." He reached out and helped the girl to her feet. "Shit, let me take a look." He pulled her hands away from her face and grimaced when he saw the bloody split that ran the width of her mouth.

"What's happening?" she cried, showering yet more blood into Robert's face.

"They are all zombies. I don't know how or why but…wait a second, are they all gone?" Robert stopped talking when he heard growls coming from the living room.

He walked out of the kitchen, and the girl grabbed him by the hand as he went. The living room looked as though a small incendiary device had exploded in it. Blood covered almost every surface. The furniture was smashed and the sofas tipped over. From what Robert could see, there were three zombies left. Todd and his conquest continued to fuck their way through death. Her back had been picked clean down to the bone, and Todd's bloodied face was buried in her upper arm. A third lay on the floor impaled on numerous bits of broken furniture. Four men, all college friends, stood huddled in the corner taking turns trying to stop the creeping zombie by stabbing at it.

"It's not a fucking vampire, guys!" Robert called out, startling them all. He walked over to the group, taking a wide berth around the zombie, and took a large piece of wood—a table leg—out of the hands of Darren, the newest member of their house. With a big swing, Robert crashed the leg down on the zombie's skull. It took two more strikes before the creature fell still.

A loud noise from behind him alerted Robert to the fact that Todd had finally disengaged himself from his conquest. Turning, it was clear to see that his lust was far from over. He moved toward the young girl, attracted by the scent of her bloodied face and tasty cunt. She screamed, and Robert stepped in swinging the table leg like a baseball bat, and he hit Todd square in the face. His nose crunched loudly, and the table leg when pulled back had opened a deep, wedge shaped gash. Todd fell to the floor. Thick black blood fell from the wound which had removed both of his eyes, or rather covered them with flayed skin. Still he crawled, inching his way forward, his tongue hanging out of his mouth like a dog on a summer's day. Robert bludgeoned the thing with a frenzy of blows, not stopping until globs of bloody brain covered the end of the table leg, and his friend's face resembled nothing more than roadkill.

Robert dropped the weapon and fell to the floor. He was exhausted and could not stop the darkness from over-taking him.

Robert gradually rose from the emptiness that had enveloped him to a world that seemed filled with a heavy banging. He opened his eyes. He lay on the floor in the same place he had fallen. The thudding sound invaded his senses. He closed his eyes; it wasn't a hangover… Then he remembered the blood, the zombies. He sat bolt upright, convinced that they surrounded him, only to find the room was empty… and dark. Wood and all manner of objects were crudely fastened over the windows blocking out all but the smallest views of the street. The bodies were also gone. The smears on the blood-crusted floor showed that they had been dragged outside.

Robert climbed to his feet. His legs screamed in agonized revolt as he moved. The pain from his aching joints seared through his nerves. His left side felt as though it was on fire. Robert pulled up his shirt, worried that he had been bitten; he saw a large bruise that ran almost the length of his torso, but no blood.

"Oh, thank God you're awake. I couldn't take having to throw you out there too," Mark exclaimed, seizing him in a bear hug.

"Mark, where is Dan, did he get…"

"No man, he's upstairs securing the door to your room against the window. I tried to tell him those things don't climb, but he just said…" Mark began.

"I said those things don't fuck either, but Todd sure did give it a good go. We're not in a movie here. Who knows what those bastards can do in the real world?" Dan stated as he walked down the stairs. Dan was an annoyingly upbeat person; the glass was not just half full with him, but overflowing. He tried to see the fun in everything, even the rising of the dead. "I'm glad you're up, man; I didn't fancy having to kick you out," Dan echoed Mark's sentiments.

"How long was I out?" Robert asked, twisting from side to side in an attempt to work the stiffness out of his joints.

"A while. You just dropped," a female voice spoke up. Robert turned around and winced when he saw the young blonde girl sporting a large, swollen set of purple lips. "I took one of your shirts while I was upstairs; I hope you don't mind." She tried to smile, but the pain in her mouth stopped her at a grimace.

"It's fine. I'm really sorry about that," Robert started.

"It's nothing. I shouldn't have snuck up on you like that. Besides, I took a hockey stick to the head last year. Now that made a real mess of me," she joked, and a light shone in her eyes, and that told Robert she meant it.

"Robert." He held his hand out, much to the entertainment of his two friends. "What?" he asked, turning to face the grinning pair.

"We've met, two days ago when you invited me here to the party… I… um… we slept together last night… I was still in your bed this morning when you woke up," the girl answered. "Nathalie," she prompted, smiling at the group.

"Oh yeah…" Robert began to make excuses when a deep growl silenced them. A number of frame splintering blows that pounded against the door followed it. Had it not been reinforced with the dining room table there was every chance that it would have yielded under the torrent of abuse.

"It's getting dark out." Mark had walked to the window and peered through the barricade. "They seem to be more active in the dark."

"Then we should probably head upstairs and maybe block it with something," Nathalie offered.

"Good idea. If we keep all the lights turned off they should leave us alone. I mean, there are plenty of other places…" Dan caught wind of how callous his words sounded and stopped himself. "You know what I mean."

On the first floor of the dorm house, Robert got introduced to the remaining survivors, people he had not thought about until he saw them. Glenn and Matt were the only two from the dorm that seemed to have survived, and they each had a woman with them. The girls introduced themselves as Rebecca and Danielle; they were also students at the university. Robert even had a couple of English classes with Rebecca; not that they ever hung out beyond the odd accidental meeting on campus.

"Dude, do you think getting plastered is the right thing to do?" Robert asked as he saw Glenn open up a fresh can of beer and take a deep gulp.

"Why not, man, what else is there to do? There are too many of them for us to leave, and if they come in, hell, I would rather be drunk and not see it coming than anything else."

"He's got a point, man. Besides, what else can we do? The TV is off-air; they're just showing this damned alert message and recording the whole time," Dan agreed as he grabbed a beer and emptied half the can.

"I just think we should keep our heads, that's all," he offered. Yet when a beer was slid into his hands, Robert found it empty before he could remember taking the first sip.

As night began to fall the party resumed. After, a while, Robert took Nathalie by the hand and led her back up to his room. It was cold in the house. The heating had broken and the winter weather made the air electric on their naked bodies. They fell to the bed, their bodies entwined. Robert winced at the pain in his side, yet as Nathalie slipped on top of him, her warm skin pressing gently against his own, he forgot all about it. They toppled over the edge of the abyss together and fell into carnal darkness, enveloped by the beast with two backs which moved through the shadows and engulfed them both within his dripping maw.

By the time they surfaced it was morning, and the barricades held firm.

As he had done the previous day, Robert slipped out of bed while Nathalie still slept, although this time he remembered who she was and found his hangover to be non-existent. Instead of rushing to the bathroom Robert crept to the window. He pulled the curtains to one side and peered through a gap between the wood.

Robert's room looked out over the rear of the property. There had been a heavy frost, and the ground held that white shine which only a crisp winter morning can create. There were a few zombies that wandered along the street, but not as many as he had feared. As they had expected, with the lights turned out and the house secured, the Zombies had grown bored and wandered off in search of fresh meat.

Out of the number of creatures that dotted the street that ran behind the house, Robert could see a few people he knew…or rather, used to know. Surveying the damage, he noticed that the majority of the zombies had not merely been bitten, but ravaged. Their bodies were torn and broken in ways he had not ever seen in movies. As he stared, a fat man walked past wearing nothing but a dressing gown and slippers. He appeared fresher than the rest because his organs which hung from the wound in his flank still smeared the street with gore as he walked, dragging them behind him. Robert watched him move, shuffling aimlessly in whatever direction he faced. His intestines stretched the longest, of course, and when the end came in sight, there was a dead dog attached to them, hungrily chewing his way through the heavily flavored meal without hesitation.

What is going on out there?" Nathalie whispered, slipping her arms around Roberts's waist. They were both naked, and the warmth felt good.

"Nothing," he answered quickly, dropping the curtain back into place. After everything that had happened the previous day, there were still some things that were best left unseen. "Just a boat load of nothing," he lied, and Nathalie knew it, but she let him have it. He did it to be nice.

"So, what is the plan?" Nathalie asked, sitting on the bed as if the pending discussion was a trite affair, like what to eat for dinner or where to hold a birthday party.

"Don't die," Robert answered as he sat beside her on the bed. The simplicity of the answer and the way it was delivered caused them both to giggle and became a fit which spread through their bodies like a warm drink on a cold day, and soon had them lying on the bed in a burst of hysterics. Both had tears in their eyes by the time the laughter passed, and the reality of it all sank in. "No more drinking. We can't drink and expect to survive. I've seen enough of these movies to know how quickly it spreads, and how important it is to be prepared." Robert tried to sound as authoritative as he could.

"Agreed. I don't want to be…eaten by one of those things," Nathalie confirmed.

"In any meaning of the word," Robert added without thinking, referencing the seemingly horny mindset of some of the zombies. Nathalie looked at Robert, and when she realized he had meant it in jest, she smiled, and another bout of laughter ensued.

"If someone could train them I wouldn't need a vibrator anymore," she joked.

"True, and you would save a fortune on batteries," Robert continued to joke, and both laughed so hard that at first they did not hear the calls coming from the first floor. They both dressed still shaking with laughter.

When they did hear the calls, however, both fled the room at a run, their jovial-in-the-face-of-adversity mood shattered and their game faces set.

The cries came from Glenn's room which was on the opposite side of the house. The room looked out over the residential area in front of the house. In the background the main office blocks of the City center could be seen on a clear day.

"What's wrong?" Robert called as they burst through the door. Nathalie was close on his heels, and behind them, clearly the worse for wear, came Dan, Mark and Rebecca, each in various stages of undress.

"You've got to see this." Glenn stood by the window while Danielle lay in the bed with the covers pulled up to her chin, seemingly unfazed by the crowd in the room.

Robert, Mark, and Dan quickly headed to the window, eager to see what had gotten Glenn so worked up. The girls hung back at the door. Danielle jumped out of bed and pulled on some clothes while the boys had their attention diverted. She was unsteady on her feet from the alcohol that still coursed through her body.

"Sweet crap on a cracker," Mark whistled. The sky was a beautiful blue, and the sun had already risen high, which told them all they had slept until well on toward the middle of the day. The only clouds in the sky were the plumes of black smoke that rose at a distance. It looked as if the city were burning. For the source of the smoke was a wide strip that encompassed the area where the tall buildings of the business sector once dominated the skyline. "What caused it?" Mark asked once the initial impression faded.

"I would guess an explosion or a fire, but who would do something like that?" Glenn asked, unable to take his eyes away from the scene.

"It's panic, man," Robert answered. "People are fucking scared. Just look down there." He pointed to the far right of their field of view. The large crossroad was the scourge of intercity commuters. It was a mass of cars, but not neatly queued and waiting for the lights to change, but rather piled up and broken. A handful of zombies stood around the mess, the majority searching for the flesh of the dead that lay trapped inside. While a few, having been found before the release of death could hit, re-emerged into the world.

"Shit... I kind of hoped it had all been a dream or something." Dan spoke under his breath. He didn't want the girls to hear.

The others gave no answer, but nodded their heads and cleared their throats in agreement.

The front of the house was more active than the rear. Zombies filled the street. They wandered up and down, no focus to their movements, yet when they reached the end of the road, most simply turned around and ambled back again.

"Do you recognize anybody?" Robert whispered as he saw the faces of the three people he had been playing darts within the campus bar just a few nights before.

"Yeah, it seems like most of the ones out there are students," Dan answered, while Glenn offered a similar response. Mark was quiet, his face pale.

"It's unreal, man," he whispered, his voice breaking.

The sound of an approaching car reached their ears, and a few moments later an old Volvo Estate came crashing into view. It careered straight through three zombies, sending two over the top of the car to land on the pavement behind. The first landed head first, its skull popping like an overinflated balloon. The second landed softer, its legs broken. The bones protruded just below the kneecap on each leg. Immediately, the creature began to writhe on the ground, twisting itself over onto its belly, whereupon it resumed its back and forth pacing and inching its way along the road, a thick smear of fecal matter tailed behind it from where its exposed bowel had ruptured as a result of the impact.

The car, having survived the initial impact of the bodies, swerved at the wrong moment, mounted the pavement, and crashed into a tree. Blood covered the windshield, and while the wipers worked at full speed, the last round of collisions had bent them to an angle that rendered them useless.

The zombies descended en masse. Seeing how quickly they transitioned from aimless stumbling to intentional stalking at the first scent of a new meal chilled them each to the bone.

The car doors opened and three men tumbled to the ground. Each was armed and fired several rounds into the approaching zombies. Several fell. A star shaped wound appeared in each of their foreheads as the bullets found their mark. These, at least, would not rise again. Most were merely winged, so continued their advance. Rather than running away, the three men backed themselves up against the car.

"Oh god, they're going to…" Rebecca began. The sound of gunshots had brought the three women to the second window in the room where they stood with slack-jawed horror as the three men were overrun by the sheer numbers of the group.

The sound of the gunshots was a dinner bell to the undead ears. All within sight had turned and readjusted their trajectory to bring them over to the car.

"Shit! They´ve just attracted half the fucking city to this street. Idiots," Glenn growled.

As a fellow zombie enthusiast, Robert nodded his agreement, but did not give voice to them.

"There are still people in the car," Danielle called as the zombies fell into three squirming piles. Fresh rivulets of blood flowed into the street, and through the single glazed windows the squishy sounds of human organs being snacked upon didn't fail to turn the stomachs of all seven onlookers.

"She's right, look." Robert pointed to the car where a woman and two children were trapped inside. Their attempts to escape from the rear door without attracting any unwanted attention had proved to be a labored affair.

"We have to help them." Robert and Dan both took off, running down the stairs without a thought as to what they would do.

They freed the door from its reinforcements—a little too easily—they reasoned as an afterthought. Robert ran into the street, waving his arms in a frantic attempt to get the attention of the women.

A growl from behind him made Robert jump and fall. The naked woman from the kitchen was once again behind him, her fingers still buried deep within herself. The blood encrusted pubic hair had dried to resemble a giant scab which flaked away with each cold thrust her fingers made. She reached forward for Robert with the other hand, but stopped when Dan stepped in from the side and blindsided her with a shot to the face with what looked like the leg of a bar stool.

"Thanks," Robert said to his friend as he scrambled to his feet. He turned back to the woman just as the first child was ripped from her arms. Two zombies argued over the small body which tore apart under the pressure. Each undead monster ended up holding a severed arm, while blood fountained into the street. The child's cry was overpowered by the mother's agonized wail.

"Come on, lady," Robert and Dan screamed as she ran down the steps and into the descending crowd of the undead.

"My baby!" The woman had turned white and could barely support herself. The other child, who must have been about nine, stood frozen with fear between the convulsing body of his brutalized younger sister and his mother.

"Mummy," the small boy cried as the monsters encircled him. They closed in on the kid just as the mother looked around in answer to her child's call.

"No," the mother shrieked as she changed direction to charge after her son. Dan reached out and grabbed the woman, pulling her back toward the house. Robert knew he should have turned back, but he had to at least try to rescue the child.

Robert grabbed the nearest zombie to him by the back of the shirt. He pulled with as much strength as he could find, and the creature flew free. Robert stopped and howled in horror when he saw the face that stared back at him. The skin of the boy´s face peeled away in one thick strip, including his eyebrows, lids, and lips. Tears dripped from the exposed white eyeballs as three zombies continued to feast on the tender flesh.

"Leave him man, leave him. It's too late," Dan called as he continued dragging the mother inside. Robert pivoted and ran, leaping up the steps and slamming the door shut behind him.

Robert turned and leaned against the door but did not have the chance to breathe before the mother was upon him, beating him with a flurry of slaps and scratches. Her wails so loud they made his ears ring. As quickly as they could, Dan and Mark pulled the mother away, while Nathalie appeared at Robert's side, eager to help him to his feet. He shrugged her away, tears stinging his eyes as his mind overloaded. He could not hold it back anymore; the child's mutilated face was burned into his mind.

"Let me go, I want to go outside to my babies. My babies need me. Please." The mother collapsed to her knees on the floor, her torment writ upon her face. Her pleading sobs echoed in Robert's head.

"I'm sorry, but they'll kill you." Glenn tried to reason with the woman who was in her mid-thirties, a few strands of grey beginning to mar the thick raven colored locks.

"I don't care," she growled. The knife came from nowhere, pulled from the waistband of her trousers before anybody could even register it. The women swiped out at Glenn, plunging the knife into his chest. She pulled it out and held the weapon before her, a wild and crazy look in her eyes. The last spark of her sanity was extinguished; it had died with the agonized screams of her children. "Now open the door, and let me walk away," she spoke through clenched teeth; the act of violence she had committed had yet to register with her.

None of the group paid her further mind as they rushed to aid their stricken friend. The woman opened the door and ran wailing into the street, swallowed by a host of the undead.

It was only as the first zombie crossed the threshold that the group realized two things: One - Glenn was dead, his blood no longer flowed from the wound in his chest; Two - the door had been left open, and the dead had queued up for their turn at the buffet.

Everybody moved in an instant, by impulse rather than actual decision. Rebecca and Danielle began flailing away with whatever they could find, screaming with exertion as the first of the assailants approached. He was an older, heavyset man, who used his bulk to walk through whatever stood in his way.

Robert and Dan grappled with a pair of zombies, trying to force them out of the open door and back into the masses.

A cry rang out as Rebecca pulled her arm away from the man, the floor already crimson from both the wound and the gaping mouth lunching on her flesh. The zombie, with one arm free, struck out at Rebecca, punching her in the face hard enough to cause her to lose her grip.

The menacing creature growled as it stood to full height, ready to claim its conquest.

"Die bitch!" Nathalie screamed, appearing from the kitchen with a canister of hair spray and a cigarette lighter. Without a moment's hesitation, she flicked the wheel. On the third attempt the lighter sprang into action with a tall flame. The zombie showed no signs of stopping. Nathalie sent a jet of hairspray through the flame and watched with amazement at the speed with which the man caught fire.

Flames savaged the flesh as if it were a pile of dried out twigs. The zombie screamed, or rather, gave a high pitch groan. Robert never knew if they could feel pain, but that sound the creature made as he burned made him certain they could on some level.

Thinking quickly, Mark jumped up from beside Glenn and grabbed a large sofa cushion from the floor. Using it as a shield, he shoved the zombie backward, guiding him through the open door and into the crowd. The flames spread, and within seconds of closing the door, seven of them were consumed in the blaze.

"Fuck me! That was too close." Mark breathed a heavy sigh of relief as he slid down the door, coming to rest with his knees pulled toward his chest and his head resting in the groove between them.

"Too close," Dan agreed.

"What should we do with Glenn?" Dan motioned to the newest body in the house's history. He lay on the floor, his eyes closed, at peace. "We can't leave him here, and I am sure not about to throw a friend of mine out to them," he continued, stamping his foot on the floor for added emphasis.

"We will put him upstairs for now. We can rest him in Phillips room." It was only a small room on the mezzanine floor that divided the house into a marketable three story property, and that meant that the body was above them, and they wouldn't have to walk past it every day.

The body was heavy. It was with weary limbs that the three men carried their friend up the stairs. The door to Philip's room was closed. Nobody had seen what happened to him, but Phillip was a wild one, and the craziest of the group. For him to disappear was normalcy.

"You get the door, Rob, we've got him," Mark grunted.

Robert released his hold on the body and turned to open the door. He did and screamed. The others took a single look and screamed. They dropped the body which landed with a heavy thump onto the floor.

"Philip, what the fuck man?" Glenn cried out after his brain had allowed him to piece together the scene.

"Dude, you need to try this," Philip's voice came from the room. The stench of alcohol and cannabis flowed out of the room like a rolling mist and made them all cough. "This girl's always fucking horny, dude. It's awesome." Philip howled like a lunatic and resumed his wild pounding into the raised rear of the zombie he had tied to the bed. She lay on her stomach, but from the way her restraints crossed each other, it was clear that she spent most of her time looking at the ceiling. Her mouth was open and chomped at the air, her tongue darting from between the bloodied mess that had been her mouth like a snake's tasting the air for the food she knew was close by. It was then that they saw Philip had removed all of her teeth. They lay in a pile on the floor beside of pair of pliers.

Philip pumped a few more time, and then gave a groan of satisfaction before falling back onto the bed, laughter erupting with his every breath.

"Come on, dude, climb on this bitch. She loves it." He sat up, and they could see in his eyes that he had gone quite mad. "Watch." He sat up and rolled the undead woman over. The hole in her neck had already dried which told them how long the two of them had been locked in the room.

The moment the zombie was on her back, she began to grind her hips in the air, and when Philip released the bond that held her left hand to the bed, rather than search for his neck, it searched for the dried out spot between her legs.

"I'm going to be sick." Mark retched and spun away just as a shower of vomit erupted from his mouth. He fell to his knees and called at the approaching girls to stay where they were.

"Phil, man, you need help. Come here, man, and we'll take care of her; you get dressed and go grab something to eat," Robert offered.

Though it had only been a few days, there was a strangely emaciated look to his friend, a pale sickly pallor to his skin.

"No! Just leave us alone, it's our honeymoon." Philip screeched at them, his hand reaching out to squeeze the hardened tits of his stone cold lover. It was then that they saw the wound on his left forearm. It was not a bite but rather what appeared to be a deep scratch, for it ran through his flesh for several inches.

Moving quickly, Robert and Dan jumped back and pulled the door closed.

"We can't leave him there; he is sick, it is only a matter of time before he turns into a fucking zombie." Nobody laughed at the double entendre of Dan's statement. All five of the remaining houseguests sat together in the Glenn's bedroom. The girls had not seen Philip but had heard enough to consider themselves up to speed.

"So what, we just throw them both out there?" Robert pointed out of the window.

"What choice do we have? We can't just leave them in there to fuck for the rest of our lives," Dan responded.

"What is that all about anyway?" Rebecca asked. "I thought that zombies were just hungry for…flesh and brains." She cringed as she spoke the words. All of the sights and sounds of the previous few days played out in her mind.

"I don't know. This is real life, and there are zombies. I don't think movie rules apply anymore. My guess is that if you died with certain…cravings or urges, then you kept it when you came back," Robert mused, watching their faces to see how they would react. It was something he had been thinking of ever since he met the first corpse finger banging herself in the kitchen. Had she not been so preoccupied, he would have been dead too. Of that, he was certain. "If they were strong enough, that is."

"It can't be, man," Mark scoffed, unable to think of anything more fitting.

Robert rose from the floor and walked to the window. "Oh no? Take a look at this." He pulled the curtain to one side and stared at the gathered crowd. "You see down there…watch. Drunk, drunk, horny," he pointed to three zombies, all of whom had been at their party the night everything started. "But over there, you have a group of hungry zombies, and look, there is the woman that we tried to save." He pointed to the bloodied form of the mother that had killed Glenn. She stumbled around, her hands out before her, a cry etched on her face. Her abdomen had been ripped open and an indeterminate organ— it looked like her kidney—hung from the hole, bouncing around like a macabre yo-yo.

"Don't you see it, Mark? Being a zombie fills you will hunger, but if you had a desire for something else when you died, that must stay in your brain too; the prefrontal cortex or whatever part it is that controls such things."

Though they were all convinced by the points Robert made, there was no time for anyone to speak. There was a loud scream and a crash from the bedroom on the half-floor.

Moving quickly, the group, including the girls, who did not want to be left alone, made their way back to the bedroom. The female zombie was still half tied to the bed, and her other hand still buried between her legs. Philip lay on the floor, his body convulsing as the last pulses of life fired out into the world.

"Looks like we don't have a choice anymore." Mark was the first to speak.

They closed the door and stood on the landing in silence, nobody daring to voice the only real option they had.

"Who's going to do it?" Rebecca asked, and the silence had made her whole body itch.

"We'll do it together," Robert answered, looking at his two friends.

"Yeah, ladies, why don't you go wait in the room? There is no need for you to see any of this." Mark offered them the chance to walk away, but they did not move.

"We are all involved. If we're going to survive this, we all need to carry our own weight. We can't hide in here forever," Danielle offered in a surprising display of defiance.

"Ok, well, let's do her first, and hope that Philip doesn't wake up before we get done," Robert suggested while they waited for Mark to return with the right tools to conduct their business with. He came back with a kitchen knife, a pair of scissors, and three chair legs.

"I don't know what I'm doing here, man," he apologized as he handed out the weapons with trembling arms.

"None of us do, dude. These will be fine." Robert patted his friend on the shoulder. "We'll go in on three. One… two…"

* * *

With the deed done, they sat in a sort of comfortable silence. The bodies had been disposed of, and from the sounds that came beyond the door, the zombies had picked their bones clean; especially Philip, who had been the fresher of the two.

Night fell, and the group slept. They moved as a single unit: if one went downstairs for a snack, they all went; everything became one fluid motion. Even toilet trips followed the same routine, although privacy was still granted when called for. No chances were taken, and the house was searched at regular times throughout the day, not just for signs of intrusion, but for possible weak points and escape routes should that be necessary.

The food and drink were in ample supply, and after three days when the electricity went out, they had cleaned out all of the fresh food and drunk all of the beer so paid it little mind.

"Hey, look," Mark whispered to Robert, who sat perched on the edge of the bed. The two of them had been on the night shift and now, just as the day began to dawn, Mark looked out into the street to find it almost empty.

"They're getting bored. They're moving away," Robert whispered with a smile on his face. It was a little too early to get excited.

"Shall we tell the others?" Mark asked.

"Why wake them? We can't go anywhere; or rather, we have nowhere to go. We'll have to move soon, but not now," Robert answered, looking up and down the street. Something didn't feel right about it.

Two days later, as they shared the last can of soup in the cupboard, they made the decision to move. The road had been relatively quiet for forty-eight hours, and while the odd zombie strolled past, the men were confident in their ability to take their shots and keep the group mobile.

"Worst comes to worst, we flame thrower them and duck for cover in a house. We will keep to the residential areas as long as possible. Make our way out of the city." Robert outlined their plan. He knew it was shaky and a foolish idea to suggest charging into a house without checking it out first, but this was their emergency contingency plan after all; desperate times always called for desperate measures.

"Why out of the city? Surely help will be in the city," Rebecca replied as she swirled the last mouthful of soup in her cup.

"I doubt it," Robert began, not understanding that every word he spoke increased his standing as the leader of the group. "The zombies will be at their heaviest in the city center. I mean that it will be the most heavily populated area. We need to head out of town into the rural areas. Once we get there, we can plan where to go. I think we should avoid the densely populated areas."

"We should try to find a military base," Dan offered.

"Marham is the nearest base to here. It's an RAF base…" Mark began but was cut off by Nathalie.

"Marham is too far away, we'd never make it, not if those things really are everywhere. Our best bet is to head up to Coltishall. They closed it back in '06, but I heard that everything was still there. It is the perfect place. If the military were going to set up an additional base of operations, as they're bound to do, that would be their ideal place. They would just need to send people, no additional work required." She stopped talking when she noticed every face at the kitchen table staring at her in wide-eyed astonishment. "What? My dad was in the RAF. I know all about that stuff," she added as if it was common knowledge. It was easy to forget that they had only really known each other a few days.

"Where is that?" Robert asked. He was not from the area, and while he had lived his whole life not too far away, the geography of towns and places was Greek to him.

"We head north out of the city, past the airport. Head east toward the coast, follow the A140, and then the B1354, I think. 54 or the 56, I always get them confused. Anyway, it's a lot closer than Marham and our best bet out of the city," Nathalie continued.

"Then it's settled," said Robert "One more night here and then we will leave early, just as the sun comes up. That seems to be when the streets are quietest." Robert rounded off the meeting, which had begun as a discussion about making a supply run to the Texaco garage two streets over for toilet paper and chocolate bars.

None of the group slept much that night. When the time came to open the front door and head out into the world, all fatigue was forgotten, and a strange excitement hung over them.

# CHAPTER 9 – THEY CAME FROM OUTSIDE

"We didn't make it more than three miles before we lost our first member. We rounded a corner and walked right into a cluster of about a dozen zombies. They had just ripped open the chest of some random guy. His screams were still in the air. We turned around to move away, but Rebecca tripped and turned her ankle. We tried to carry her, but it was too late. They tore her from my grip and ripped her apart." Robert's eyes had welled with tears as one by one he recounted the deaths of his friends.

"It's okay, Robert, I've got enough here," Paul interrupted, taking the moment to wipe the sweat from his brow.

"We made it out of the city onto the ring road. It was freaky man. The cars had all been moved to the side of the road and parked in long neat lines. The army did it, I guess, because they picked us up as we drew close to the airport but…but…" A tear rolled down Robert's cheek as he fought the memory.

"What was it, Rob?" Leon gently pushed.

"They took the time to move the cars, line them up nice and tight, but they left the dead sitting in them. After everything that I saw in that house, after having watched my best friends ripped apart, that was still the worst. Seeing those cars filled with corpses was the worst." Robert dissolved into sobs. He clenched his jaw and screamed into his pursed lips, slapping himself in the forehead as he did so.

"Easy man, take it slow." Both Leon and Paul moved toward him, but the young man calmed down quickly and looked at them.

"I've been at the airport for three days now standing outside in a fucking queue. I haven't seen Nathalie since I arrived. They separated us at the cleaning stations, and we just kind of entered different flows. I hope she is okay." Robert spoke the last half sentence in a hushed voice, addressing himself.

"I'm sure she made it out alive. There was a second plane being loaded on the other side of the terminal," Jessica offered. Rising, she fetched a small bottle of whiskey and offered it to Robert.

"Thanks." He twisted the cap and downed the miniature's contents in one swift gulp.

Silence fell over the cabin, and the gentle rock of the plane helped soothe jittery nerves, while darkness comforted them all. Strange given the creatures that walked below them were most active in the night, but still, none could deny the feeling of calm that washed over them.

"So… So far we think that it was a biological attack—a toxin or something unleashed into the air? The flu was the main idea, and the zombies came along as a nasty after effect, right?" Paul was the first to speak as he flipped through his notes. The book was already more than half filled with his cryptic, homemade version of shorthand.

"Plus, emotions play a part. Any strong emotion you felt the moment you died following contact with a zombie, was brought back with you," Jessica added, mulling the theory over in her head as she spoke. She had not seen any such activity, but her rescue had come on the first day.

Leon was clearly impressed. "So the virus, or agent, whatever you want to call it, attacks the brain. It had to be. Smart really. Then couple it with the fast acting nature of the agent, a short half-life that threw doctors off the scent by causing them to treat a smoke screen illness."

"It had to be terrorists, right?" Robert asked. The alcohol had returned the color to his cheeks.

"That would be my guess, but why attack Norwich? Delia's cooking isn't that bad. Other than insurance and mustard, there isn't much going for the place," Paul mused.

"Early TV reports and NHS warnings confirmed that the outbreak, as they called it, was centralized in the city."

The group fell silent, their brains tying together everything they had heard, hoping for an answer to appear. Another new voice broke the silence.

"It didn't come from within the city; it came from the outside," a middle-aged black woman spoke as she walked toward them. Her left arm was cradled in a sling and she had a deep half-healed gash that ran along her forehead.

"But reports confirmed that Norwich was the source," Jessica shot back before the woman had a chance to introduce herself.

"Maybe, honey, but it wasn't in the city. It started on the outskirts," she added again, her words not cruel or barbed, but firm.

"How do you know, if I may ask?" Paul spoke up, instinctively turning to a fresh page in his notebook.

"I worked in the city center. We got emails from our head office in London advising us to close the building down. They hit the center in a giant herd. Plus, the satellite companies we worked with fell before we even saw the first one of those things." With that, she sat down and offered her hand to Paul. "Monique Jones."

Paul took the hand and shook it, introducing himself and then the others as a natural response. "So Monique, where does your story start?"

# CHAPTER 10 — A TRIP DOWNTOWN

Monique sat down and straightened out her bloodstained skirt, ignoring how the dried blood had starched the creases into it. For a while she did not speak or even look around to face the group. She sat on the opposite side of the cabin to the others. She didn't choose the aisle seat next to Jessica, but rather the one before that in the same row as Robert.

"Would you like a cigarette?" Paul asked, having noted that all of the conversations had begun with a ceremonial smoke.

"No thank you, honey. I survived hell. I don't fancy ruining that with cancer." Her reply was tart, her words hard and easy to misinterpret.

"Ok, well, just take your time, alright? There is no pressure." Paul spoke with a soothing voice.

Monique opened her mouth to speak, but instead she gave a loud sigh. Paul wasn't certain if it was because of everything that had happened or because he annoyed her.

"I just told you, I work in the City Center. I mean that literally; my office is as central as you can get." She seemed keen to stress the location, so all four listeners offered an understanding head nod.

"Yes, you said that those things came into the city, and no offense, but how could you know that?" Jessica asked. Her interest in how everything started, and subsequently broke down did not surprise Paul. She had been working the evacuation flights non-stop. She probably had no idea about how bad it was outside the safety of her plane.

"Don't take me for a liar. I would not even consider wasting your time. I think a written record is just what we need. Once this is all over, and we have beaten this plague, we can look back, and with the help of this sort of book, educate others." Monique sat rigid in her chair and turned her head rather than her entire body when she spoke to them.

"I apologize, Monique. I mean no offence." Paul adjusted his approach with the smooth fluidity of a professional journalist.

Jessica stared at him, puzzled at how someone with such ability could get stuck working for a tabloid paper.

"Thank you, honey. I know I'm a bitch, so don't worry, you won't be the only one who thinks that way of me."

Paul wasn't sure she had made a joke or not, so he opted for the professional approach: silence.

The turbulence had passed, and the cabin thrummed with the hum of the engines. The white noise, coupled with the exhaustion most people felt, led to a deep sleep. Paul, too, gave a yawn and cracked his spine as he stretched.

"Hey, Jessica, I know this isn't a commercial flight, but do you have any coffee back there?" Paul hoped so. Coffee was his lifeblood. Even during his time in hiding, he would take the chance to make coffee at every possible opportunity.

"Um…sure, I think there is some back there. I mean, I know there should be, but maybe the pilots have drunk it all. This is the last flight of the day." With that, Jessica rose from her seat and disappeared into the rear galley.

Paul scooted over into her seat and leaned forward. He placed his hand on Monique's arm. Her skin was cool, but his touch seemed to make her recoil. In that moment Paul understood some of the horror that Monique had endured. Knew that writing her story would be a less than enjoyable experience.

"I understand, and if you're not ready, you skip any parts you want. This isn't therapy. We're just trying to get to the bottom of what caused this and where it came from."  His words had the desired effect. Monique relaxed in her chair, and after a few deep breaths, she turned to face Paul.

"Alright, I'm ready." Monique had her eyes closed, and when she opened them, rather than tears, Paul saw strength.

"Well, then, Monique, tell me where it began…"

# CHAPTER 11 – MONIQUE JONES

"Danny, I will need those quarterly figures on my desk by the end of the day. The regional meeting is tomorrow, and they are keen to see what sort of progress we've made in the last period," Monique said as she popped her head into the small office space of her assistant, Danny Williams.

Danny was a young guy, ambitious and eager to climb the corporate ladder. He had quickly risen from temp, to clerk, to office manager, and now to the position of assistant to the regional Head of Logistics and planning for the Medicines and Healthcare products Regulatory Agency (MHRA). Danny planned to continue his climb outside of the office. His sights were set on the main branch of the MHRA in London.

"That won't be a problem. I need to work out the final few details, but you will have them before lunch." Danny looked up from the mound of paperwork on his desk and flashed Monique his best smile. She knew he hated her, but he knew how to play the game.

"Thanks, Danny, you're the best." Monique accepted his smile and gave a rare compliment. She meant it too. Danny was the best assistant she had ever had, and while she knew he would not stay around forever, she hoped that he would remain long enough for her to seal the promotion she had been chasing. She wanted to head back to London, to the big city. Norwich was a nice enough place, but it wasn't London. She missed the hustle and bustle, the action and adventure that hung in the air. She had volunteered to move when the promotion to Region Head opened up, and she didn't regret doing so. However, after five years she was ready for a new challenge. The desire to be closer to her family was also a big factor behind her motivation to relocate. Monique was a single woman hovering on the abyss of her forties. She had no real desire for children of her own. That ship had sailed in her early twenties when doctors gave her the news that natural pregnancy would not be possible. A husband would be nice although far from a requirement. She had a dog at home, Max, a German shepherd, and he was all the company Monique needed.

From her top floor office, Monique could sit in the chair and peer out over the city center from eight stories up. The office was not the tallest in the city, but it was the dominant figure in their area. It took up an entire corner of town. Four main entrances—one on each side—made the building an impressive sight. With over 300 employees, including the large postal department that occupied the two lower floors, the office was always busy, with people streaming in and out on a regular basis. The street was also home to two offices of a large insurance company as well as a multi-company office complex. All three buildings combined ensured for an active street. However, as Monique sipped at her coffee there was not a single person in sight. The day before almost half of her workforce had called in sick. At first, Monique had thought it a trick of some sort, but as the news started throwing out warnings of a pandemic, and an advisory caution regarding infected individuals, she understood that it was serious.

A figure appeared at the end of the street that spilled into the top of the high street and main entrance to the large, state-of-the-art mall that had reopened after refurbishment work. Ordinarily, this went unnoticed. Monique had more to do than just stare at the world as it went by. However, the staff shortages had spread across the country and reached a point that the workloads were close to non-existent. The company, and even the government, was at a standstill.

Monique watched as what looked like a woman stumbled down the street. Her gait was a strange shuffle. Her left leg dragged behind rather than lifted and placed. It was a strange sight, and given the emptiness of the street, it was downright creepy. As she watched, Monique felt the temperature in her office decrease.

The world was still. Even the wintery, windy, and infrequent sleet flurries had abated following the appearance of the lone figure. The only thing that Monique heard was the slow rhythmic pulse of her own heart. She listened to it as the figure limped down the street. It shambled down the center of the road, swaying this way and that. The more Monique watched, the more of the figure she saw, and the more her heartbeat pulled her into a trance.

It was a young woman, possibly in her early twenties. She was covered in filth and grime. Her clothes were sodden with mud. In the midpoint of the street, the figure stopped and looked up at Monique's office, or so it seemed to her. A shrill ping from the computer broke the haze that had settled around Monique. A new email had arrived. A quick glance at the flagged email made Monique's blood run cold. The title was a single word...Lockdown.

Her hands trembled as she opened the message. As she read it, a strange static sound began to fill her ears. The email had come from the head office. It advised all staff in the Norwich office to lock the floors down and to close the main entrance. It had been copied to each of the branch officers and affiliated as well.

A scream shattered her thoughts. Monique jumped, knocking her coffee onto the floor. The cream-colored carpet soaked the warm drink up in an instant, much to Monique's disdain. Monique turned to grab the tissues that stood on the windowsill. Once more she saw the figure still standing there. She looked closely and felt the scream build in her throat as she realized it was not mud that covered the woman's clothes…but blood.

Monique scrambled to open the office window, to call out to the woman, but the moment the outside air entered the office, it brought with it the sounds of a city in agony. The cacophonous wave of anguish flooded through the small opening. Monique felt a shiver chase its way up her spine. She swallowed hard as the woman in the road opened her mouth and uttered a long, deep growl.

A few moments later a second figure appeared. It walked at a slow pace, and had the same hesitant gait as the woman. The two offered not even the slightest hint of recognition. A third soon followed. Monique intently studied each of them. Blood covered all three bodies, and the third had it smeared over its face. The sound of static grew louder and gradually overpowered the screams. The street began to fill, not with the usual lunchtime crowd, but with a lumbering mass of the dead. They moved in a wave. The sound of their shuffled, dragging feet was the cause of the static sound that had burrowed beneath Monique's skin. There was no end to their ranks. Monique found herself watching the scene unfold with a strange feeling of anticipation building in her stomach.

*It's one of those flash mobs just like that stunt in Belgium a few months ago.* She thought back to the You-Tube video she had seen. She looked at the crowd again, and saw the pattern in their look and mannerisms. They were zombies. *I bet they are doing Thriller.* Monique smiled at the thought. As a lifetime Michael Jackson fan it was a performance she was bound to enjoy.

The large glass entrance doors to the multi-company office opened and the crowd turned to face them. The sudden unity of their actions only served to enthrall Monique further. *Here it comes.* She edged closer to the window.

The mob faced the doors, and a groan erupted as two figures walked into the street. Monique watched as they descended upon them. She felt her anticipation evolve into horror as the screams began and blood flowed over the slate entrance floor. *What are they? Oh my God!* Monique screamed as she saw a severed human leg tossed through the air into the crowd where it was fought over like a wedding bouquet. The door to the office was open, and the group moved as one toward the door. At her office window Monique stood in frozen shock as all hell broke loose.

As the undulating mob entered the main doors, people streamed out of the small emergency exit of the company that rented the first two floors. The workers ran into the street and tried to scatter, but the dead were upon them too fast. Monique knew she was powerless. She could only watch as the people filed out of the building and into the waiting arms of the rapacious multitude. The street was a river of blood, and even the air seemed filled with scarlet mist.

Several windows in the office block opposite her smashed. As more of the undead forced their way inside, more people tried to escape by climbing from the lower floor windows. They would rather take their chance with the crowd outside than avoid them on the inside.

One man did well. He landed on his feet after leaping from a first floor window. He ran the instant his feet hit the ground and zigzagged through the crowd. He came close to making it before the crowd swarmed him. Monique felt her world being to spin as she saw one of the people sink their teeth into the man's throat and rip away a large chunk of flesh.

The screams inside the building increased, and the sound of panic began to echo through the halls. She watched as staff began to flee every building on the street; panic driving their every action.

"Get back inside!" Monique screamed. She knew it was useless, but repeated her warning all the same.

Her computer chimed repeatedly as a flurry of mails, some from the head office and others from people within the building, flooded in. Monique opened a few. The first one advised them once again to lock all doors, and barricade the buildings as best as possible. Rioters had broken loose and headed toward the city center in a wave. *Rioters my ass,* Monique thought. The next email echoed her sentiments insofar as it stated in no uncertain terms how far from the truth the previous message was.

One email from a junior clerk on Secondment just outside of the city was a goodbye note to his family. He described how he was the last one alive, how the dead had risen, and anybody bitten would come back too. Zombies! He wrote the word several times.

He had a separate message for his daughter, Imogen, and reading it made Monique's heart break. She grabbed the phone from her desk and dialed the number to the satellite office, but the line was dead. She then phoned down to the reception area. The guard answered on the seventh ring.

"Yes ma'am, everybody is to remain upstairs. The barricades are in place, but I don't know how long it's going to hold. Yes, I can take the elevators to the top floor and shut them down. However, if I do, the only way out will be the stairs. Ok, Ma'am. If you insist," Trevor, the long serving security guard spoke with a steady voice, even though both he and Monique knew that his day would not last much longer. "I'm sending the elevators up right now. God speed Monique." He spoke before the phone clattered to the desk. "You can't go out there. No, it's not safe. We need to stay inside…no, don't touch that…" Trevor's frantic voice carried down the line and led with the sound of splintering glass and the resultant screams of whoever tried to escape.

Monique jumped from behind her desk and ran into the hallway. People scrambled this way and that in a blind panic. Others had slumped to the floor in either prayer or defeat. It was hard to tell the two apart.

"Monique, what is going on?" Rebecca, a long-term temp ran down the hall, her long blond hair disheveled while her eyes held an oddly feral look.

"I don't know, but whatever they are, they have gotten into the building. I have ordered the elevators to be disabled, but the stairwell is still open. We need to block it off somehow." Monique thought practically, and broke everything down into precise steps. It calmed her and focused her thoughts.

At that moment, Danny and two others walked passed. She grabbed Danny by the arm and gave him the same advice about blocking the stairs.

"What about the other floors?" Rebecca asked as she helped to push one of the desks over to the door where Danny and Walter Clapham, a middle-aged man who had worked for in the same government position most of his career, stood waiting to erect the damn to stem the flow of the undead.

"We will get the message to them," Monique offered, "but now just help me push this."

With three desks and six chairs, the men got to work blocking off the doors on both sides. While they worked on the fortifications, Monique and Rebecca began calling the other floors.

The lower two gave no answers. The frantic mix of screams, growls, and wet slapping noises that reverberated up the stairs were answer enough. Floors three to seven were about to be breached. The third floor, the first real office work level, was already overrun. The manager, a good man by the name of Rupert Duncan, had locked himself in his office. Before their phone conversation could reach a natural conclusion, the door splintered, and Rupert screamed his goodbyes.

By the time the last floor had been called, the zombies were everywhere. The barricade held firm, however, and as the day wore on, their pounding became less. The screams of those less fortunate still pierced their ears four hours later. Those who had hidden were discovered; losers in a deadly game.

"The streets don't look as crowded anymore," Monique relayed as she peered through the closed blinds down at the street below.

"What good is that going to do us? We're trapped up here. The building is still full of those things," Walter answered in response.

"Those aren't rioters! Why would Head Office lie to us like that?" Rebecca had not realized that she had voiced her thoughts aloud until an answer came back.

"They are zombies. According to the news, the fucking dead have risen. Can you believe that?" Scott, another young member of staff, spoke from behind his computer.

"Do you believe everything you read on the internet?" Monique asked. She refused to accept the obvious fact: that the world was ending, and the dead had taken control.

Scott looked up from his screen, the fear of his boss dissipated in light of external developments. "I do when it is on every site, yes." The whole room felt the sting in his barbed retort.

"Dear God, help us," Monique whispered as she made the sign of the cross on her torso.

The eighth floor of the MHRA office was a large square, and with only eight employees on the floor. Each warranted the luxury of a small office. Monique had the largest, while Danny had the small solo room adjoined to Monique's via a connecting doorway.

The other three offices were shared, with a third desk set up for any visitors. The offices were set around the perimeter and offered a view of the city in all directions. The rest of the floor was set up in much the same style as a hotel foyer. There was a reception desk, where the receptionist greeted all visitors. The elegant lobby contained a high end coffee machine and a refrigerator well stocked with soft drinks and juices. The large flat screen television mounted on the wall had been programmed to show various news channels at certain times of the day. The five of them sat on the chairs. Monique had returned from her trip to the window and sat beside Rebecca, while the men had adjusted the chairs so that they sat on either side of the sofa. They all watched the screen, reading and re-reading the message that was being broadcast. They all resisted the growing temptation of a chortle at the promise of help being on the way.

In the street, they heard sporadic bursts of gunfire, but the predominant sound was the monotonous growl of the creatures that stood in wait. With their attentions no longer focused on the people in the buildings, the majority of the herd—for that was exactly what it looked like to Monique: a herd of wandering cattle—wandered aimlessly through the street, showing no interest in those of their own kind.

The sun began to set, and the group shared out the contents of the fridge. Despite the circumstances, the sound of helicopters overhead, and a more profound rally of gunfire had raised their spirits. Even the pounding at the doors had ceased, although they could still hear the creatures on the stairs as every so often one would turn and tumble to the landing. Their undead brains seemed to have mastered the art of ascent, but lacked even the most basic comprehension of descent.

The group laughed and joked. Even Monique felt herself unwind a little; something she rarely did in the company of others. As the night wore on, the activity in the street increased once more. Looking out, Monique understood why.

"It's the lights. They attract their attention. Turn everything off, now," Monique whispered her barked order.

"What?" Danny flashed a strained look at Monique. "I'm not turning the lights off. If those things get in here, I want to be able to see what I'm fighting." He stood up from the group, and a strange weight filled the air. Monique walked away, and without saying a word, turned off the lights, one office at a time.

"Hey," Danny called out, striding towards Monique. "This is the real world now. Things have changed out here. You're not the boss anymore," he spat. The stress of the day, and his dislike for his boss festered in his words.

"Maybe not, but take a look." She took Danny by the hand, but before she could move, he snatched it away.

"I'm not a fucking child, Monique! You don't have to lead me by the hand," he snarled.

Monique paid him no mind. She walked to the window and waited for Danny to join her. "Do you see all of those… things? Look at them, Danny. Tell me, what are they all looking at?" She spoke with the sharp skills most teachers possess. It only served to infuriate Danny even further.

"I see that, but they can't get it in here, we made sure of that. We need to see what we are doing, trust me." Danny stood firm. The pair had moved into Monique's office, but with the door open, everybody overheard their increasingly heated words.

"Maybe not at the moment, but look at how many are out there now. Their numbers have tripled in the last hour alone. What if they never leave? We cannot sit here forever, you know. We have eaten most of the food already. Think Danny," Monique implored.

"Fine, but I still think it is a bad idea. If those things grab us in the night, I sure as hell won't slow down to save you." Danny glared before he strode out of the office.

A few moments later, the lights went out. Monique stayed where she was, the comfort of her own surroundings appealed to her more than the need for companionship. Sitting in her chair, she swiveled and looked at the night sky. The street lamps were on, but their floor was above them. The view of the stars was extraordinary.

A strange shuffling noise ripped Monique out of her sleep. Somebody was outside her office door. She sat up in her chair, wide-awake, all thoughts of sleep purged from her system. An unusual calm wrapped around her. Monique found it smooth and oddly relaxing. The initial desire to call out abated as a level-headedness settled. Monique rose from the desk and inched her way toward the door. She froze when the shuffling started again. She caught her breath. The footsteps drew closer to the door. The door's handle began to move, the action slow and smooth. It drew a slight gasp from Monique, who leaned over and held her hand against the handle, holding it in place. It was possible to lock the door, but lack of motion seemed to be enough for whatever was on the other side. She heard it shuffle away with a growl of discontent.

Monique fell into her chair, her body shaking as adrenaline surged through her veins. She cried silent tears as she waited for the screams that never came. At some point in time, she fell asleep. Before she knew it, the sun had begun to caress the horizon behind the buildings.

She jumped from the chair and stared down at the street. It was too dark to see clearly, but the fading moonlight offered enough to deflate the hope that had risen during the night.

Monique's mind circled back to her visitor in the night. Had it eaten the others? Were they all like them? Were they sick with the flu? A multitude of questions flooded her brain as she searched for a weapon. In the top drawer of her desk she found her letter opener. It had been a gift from her parents during one of their many elderly globetrotting adventures. The blade was approximately six inches long. It was her only option.

The hallway was quiet as Monique slunk out of the room, closing the door behind her. The lack of lighting turned things in her favor. The shadows seemed to envelop her, to pull her to safety as she made her way into the room. She could make out the sofas and chairs and could see the bodies that lay on them. Monique's mouth was dry as she clutched the letter opener in her fist. The blade was raised to her shoulder, ready to strike if needed, when a snort from the chair closest to her broke the silence.

"Who's there?" a voice shouted out as the figure in the chair sprung to life. It was Danny. He too clutched a knife in his hands; a bread knife found in the drawer of the kitchen area.

"Danny it's me, Monique," she whispered, raising her hands in surrender; an automatic reaction.

"Good God, you scared the crap out of me. What are you doing creeping around in the dark?" he asked without lowering the knife.

"Quiet, I think one of those things is in here. I heard it creeping around; it was at my office door," Monique whispered.

"Shit."

"We need to check everybody," Monique continued, her voice calm and steady, while on the inside her heart ran at a gallop.

Danny turned his back for a few seconds, and when he turned back to face Monique, he held a flashlight. "I found this in Alan's desk drawer." He referred to Alan Parker, the first person on their floor to call in sick with the flu.

"It was his first day sick in almost twenty years. I guess I should have known it was serious," Monique whispered as Danny flicked the switch and hoped the light was not too bright.

"Maybe so, but I mean zombies—who would ever predict that fucking zombies would walk down Main Street?" Danny whispered as he and Monique lit up each member of their group in turn, checking for bites. "Everybody's clean."

"I know I heard something. Let's check the rest of the floor." Monique nudged Danny to indicate the direction she wanted to head first.

Together they checked the entire floor, moving from office to office. The silence between them was not borne from animosity, but necessity. There was nothing. By the time they fell into the chairs once more the others had started to stir, while outside, so had the zombies.

"Take a look at this," Monique called over to the group.

"What is it?" Rebecca asked

They moved to the window and stared down into the street. Even though the winter sun was not yet over the horizon, dawn was certainly upon them. The zombies stood in the street, and it took a moment for them to see what Monique had.

"They're asleep." It was Walter that first saw it.

The zombies were still; they swayed back and forth but took no real steps. They all stood with bowed heads. The static sound of their growls had been replaced by a strange, hushed murmur. A few of the creatures had woken, their heads raised to the sky, and as they started moving, the rest of the herd woke to another day.

The sky was grey, and a light wintery rain fell. The walking corpses in the street didn't seem to notice. They flowed through the street; a never-ending river of the damned. There seemed no end to their ranks. It was almost midday before the first burst of gunfire reached their ears. All it succeeded in doing was speeding up the flow of the masses in the street.

"I always thought they were slow," Rebecca whispered as he and Monique looked down into the street. "You know, like in the movies."

"This is reality, kid," Walter spoke as he moved to join them. The crowd had responded to a second, longer burst of fire, and moved through the street at the stumbled equivalent of a brisk walk. Their arms flapped around them as they moved at a speed that seemed too much for their basic levels of coordination.

"What are we going to do?" Rebecca asked, looking at Monique for answers. Rebecca was only twenty-two, and this had been her first job out of university. Monique often forgot that beneath her professional exterior was a naivety that would only disappear with age.

"For the time being…nothing. We are stuck. We can't go out there with that many of them around." Monique stared through the glass as she spoke, a distant, thousand-yard stare in her eyes.

"We still need to come up with a plan." Danny strode to the glass. "We can't just sit here and wait to die," he added.

"We can't leave with that many of them out there. You saw how they wiped out an entire office." Monique countered, "We have to wait for them to move on."

"Those have moved on Monique; it is just that more of the fuckers take their place," Danny spat. "We have no food. We will need to get going eventually, so I say we make a plan. Be prepared." Danny was right, and Monique knew it. She nodded in agreement, and with that, the reins were snatched and Danny straightened up to take the control he so craved.

The day passed, and the first signs of a rift began to show. Danny and Walter stood together in private conversations, while Scott, who was always the shy and reserved member of the team, sat and watched the news. He hadn't spoken a word since it happened. His pale face and clammy skin told them that he was in shock. He had a young baby at home, and he had not been able to get hold of his wife when he called. Monique and Rebecca sat quietly talking about life, their past; they bonded.

"I'm so hungry," Rebecca rubbed her stomach as they settled onto the sofas once again.

"We all are," Danny replied. "I haven't heard anything banging at the door today, so tomorrow we will try to go down to the lower floors, see what food we can find."

"Do you think that's wise?" Monique asked.

"Do you want to starve to death? I'm saying we are going, but don't worry, Walt and I will go. You ladies don't need to get involved." The words sounded tainted, not because of what he said, but by the manner in which he said them.

Monique knew better than to cause a fight. Everybody was tired and hungry; arguing was not the answer, so she let the remark slide.

Night fell, and Monique stood watching the crowd. There were fewer zombies now, maybe fifty in total standing in the street, too many for her liking. What scared her even more was the notion that Danny may decide to make a move in the daylight. The sounds of slumber echoed from the center of the room, and Monique once again moved back to her office. She couldn't sleep and wanted to see if the Internet still worked. It took several attempts, but she managed to connect to the network. She didn't know what she was looking for, so started with the basics: Zombies. She read about the genre, the obsession the world had with the living dead, and watched several short films and clips. The recurring themes were that headshots killed them, or fire, and that even a scratch was enough to spell the end. The more she read, the more she learned, but at the same time, Monique realized she was re-reading the same material, phrased differently. Nowhere did she find a common description as to what caused the problem. Even in fiction it appeared that the cause was never truly known.

Monique searched the Internet until the early hours of the morning. Fighting sleep, she made her way from site-to-site, doing all of the things she should have done before. She created a Facebook account and tried to find her friends, sobbing at the thought of each old acquaintance she came across, wondering if they were dead or stuck walking away as a reanimated corpse. She cried at the years she had lost, hiding from the world and the relationships that she had never allowed to develop.

Monique felt her grip begin to slip. The cracks that had surrounded her sanity had spread further and now threatened to break her completely. The only thing that saved her was the return of the shuffled footsteps from the other side of her door. Monique quickly turned her computer screen off and jumped up from behind the desk. She went to reach for the letter opener, but it wasn't there. She had left it on the sofa. The shuffling figure on the other side of the door drew closer and stopped outside of Monique's door. The handle jiggled again, but stopped. A thump from the stairwell side of the main door caused

Monique to scream and sent the figure scurrying away. Within a few seconds, all of the lights on the floor came on. At the same moment, a growl spread through the crowd outside who woke from their quasi-slumber the instant the light appeared.

Monique ran out of her office and straight into Danny who stood before her door, reaching for the handle. Monique shoved him away with as much force as she could. "You stay away from me," she spat, her mind caught between fear and anger. The overwhelming sadness that had consumed her moments before was gone, pushed back deep inside, behind the crumbling walls.

"What?" Danny asked as she sprinted past him. The door to the floor was ajar, but the zombie on the other side was stuck on the barricade. Its arms reached through the gap, clawing frantically at the air the moment the group came close.

Rebecca started to cry. "Get rid of it," she squealed as the creature's head appeared through the gap.

Thinking fast, Danny kicked out and the door slammed against the arm, splitting the soft skin that ran along the length of the forearm. The zombie however, didn't notice. Thick dark blood spurted from the wound and covered the walls.

"Do something else!" Rebecca screamed, slapping Danny on the back, pushing him closer to the door. "Stab it," Rebecca called as the head appeared again. The lips pulled back into a snarl, and the bloodshot eyes stared at the group. Danny struck, stabbing with Monique's letter opener. The knife pierced the skull just above the left eye. The creature gave a gargled groan and fell backward into the barricade.

"Help me close the door," Danny called, looking around at Monique who stood closest to him.

Monique stared at him. The image of her letter opener in his hand, the creeping figure by the door, the hateful look in his eye, combined with his lust for power made her shiver. Monique offered no answer. Instead, she turned around and walked away.

Danny and Walter remained standing by the door waiting for any others that may happen upon them. They had closed the door, but the lock was broken from the recent, sudden impact.

"We can't stay here." Scott whispered his first words in three days as he sat on the sofa with the two women. He turned to face them, but his eyes refused to focus.

"I know. We're not safe here," Monique answered, although neither Scott nor Rebecca understood what she was talking about, or saw the way she stared at Danny, watching his every move.

Monique got up from the sofa and walked away, moving past the reception desk into the office that overlooked the main high street. It was one street over. Their office overlooked both a Starbucks and Pizza Hut. The Surrey House—every building in the street had a similar name—employees were responsible for a large portion of the daily trade in both establishments. They had even managed to talk their way into a specialty corporate rate. Monique stared at the two premises, their smashed front windows looked like ravenous mouths with shards of glass for teeth, ready to tear into the flesh of whoever dared enter. A zombie appeared in the Pizza Hut window, its uniform ripped apart but still identifiable. Half of its face was missing, as was an arm. Injuries serious enough to prevent it from climbing through the blood streaked glass, but not enough to kill it for good.

"I don't want to become one of them," Scott spoke up from behind Monique, who jumped at the sound of his voice.

"Scott," she said, her breath robbed from her lungs. "I didn't see you there."

"Sorry. It's sad isn't it? That this is what we have all become? I mean, look at them." He pointed to the street where a crowd of close to fifty milled around the street. It was then that Monique saw the two busses stranded in the street. With the doors locked, the dead found themselves trapped inside, much like the Pizza Hut employee Monique had seen.

"I try not to think about it," Monique said. "It is what it is, Scott. I am sure that one day this will all be over. It will become another part of history, like the Black Death in London, SARS, or that Mexican Flu. It isn't the first time mankind has been killed off, and it won't be the last." Monique tried hard to keep her words uplifting, while the entire time her eyes were focused on the bus, wondering if they would just sit there forever, trapped like her and the others; a stalemate between two clueless sides.

"What if it isn't?" Scott asked as he turned and walked away.

Monique's mind whirred, overloaded with thoughts and images. She was certain, now more than ever, that they would have to move on; escape the office somehow.

A scream brought her thoughts to a sudden halt, and as the mental ball dropped, it shattered into tiny pieces which scattered through Monique's mind. She was hungry, tired, and a little disoriented. Her body moved through the office before her brain had recognized the movement. Rebecca was ahead of her, staring into what used to be Danny's office. From the opposite side of the floor, Danny and Walter also rushed to see the source of the commotion.

"I won't become one of them!" Scott's scream somehow found a way through the haze, burning a path into Monique's brain.

The group came together at the same moment, but too late to stop Scott from plunging from the open office window. The windows opened inward with the hinge in the base. They didn't normally open more than a few inches, but Scott had somehow managed to pull the entire window from its frame. The rush of winter air and the hungry drone of those below overpowered them. Monique and Danny ran to the window, an instinctive reaction rather than anything with purpose. Scott's plummeting body hit the ground with a dull thud and his head cracked open. Blood and brain spread out beneath him like an egg dropped on the kitchen tile. The crowd descended on him in a rush, hiding him from view. The noise of their greedy champing covered Monique in goose bumps.

"We need to move out of here," Monique whispered, more to herself than anyone else.

"I know. We'll think of something," Danny answered. Until then, she hadn't noticed he was there, and upon seeing him, Monique quickly turned and strode away.

"What's your problem?" Danny called, but Monique offered no answer.

Danny did his best to fix the window back into its frame. He stood his desk—which they had not needed for the door barricade—on end, resting against the glass.

"I think the best thing for us to do is to try going down one floor at a time," Danny began as they sat to have their first discussion about leaving the office. "I think we should head down one level, look around, and then come back here. There will certainly be something to drink down there that we can bring back. If the coast is clear, we regroup here, and then head down again.

"What if we see any of those...things?" Rebecca asked.

"We kill them," Walter spoke up.

"We take care of them," Danny overruled. "Let's hope we don't meet any more, but if we do, we should try and leave. We can trap them on the floor, and then move onto the next one. Killing them is a last resort." Danny looked at Walter, but couldn't shake Monique's accusing gaze. Her eyes bored holes through his chest and threw his mind off track.

"When do we go?" Monique asked. Her eyes refused to blink while they locked onto Danny.

"You don't. Walter and I will do it. We will check the floor, and then we all move down together. I don't want to hear any feminist bollocks here either. We have the only two real weapons, and we're stronger. It´s that simple." He rose from his chair and ended their meeting before another word could be spoken.

The men readied themselves with lightning speed and were out of the door within thirty minutes of their meeting. They did not exchange goodbyes with one another.

The sun soon began to set. This was something their plan had failed to take into account. The darkness of the building would only act as a hindrance to their progress should they be delayed at all. This would mean either a midnight relocation, or a second scouting trip the next morning ahead of an afternoon move. "Fools," Monique uttered beneath her breath.

"Do you think they will come back?" Rebecca asked as she turned off the large reception area television. The emergency broadcasts still played, although several channels had shut down completely. They tried the TV three times a day, hoping for something else.

"I don't care. I don't trust Danny," Monique let it slip. It was just her and Rebecca, who was younger and much more attractive than she was. "You need to watch out for him."

"Why?" Rebecca turned to face Monique.

Monique explained all about the two previous evenings, and how she had thought it was a zombie. She watched Rebecca's eyes widen when she told her about her letter opener and how Danny had been right by her door that morning.

"But he was always so nice," Rebecca began.

"He's ambitious, and in this new world, he sees power there for the taking." Monique was quick to point out the difference between being nice or evil as opposed to powerful.

They sat in silence, listening for the sounds of either retreat or return. Nothing was forthcoming, and after a while they both found themselves staring out of the window, across the city. Smoke rose in several places as invisible fires raged.

"I'm so hungry." Rebecca steadied herself against the glass as a fresh wave of lightheadedness washed over her.

"I'm sure they will be back soon with some supplies." Monique placed a hand on the young girls shoulder.

"But then what? Where are we going to go? Those things are everywhere." Rebecca shook, and Monique pulled her close to her. It was an unnatural act for her, but it felt good.

"Let's just take it one step at a time. There are people out there, and they are fighting back. If it is the army or whatever, then we just need to get to them," Monique soothed the young woman.

An awkward but not all together unwelcome silence fell over the floor as the women waited for the others to return. When the door finally opened, only Walter crossed the threshold. Bruises dominated his face, and his left eye was swollen shut. He walked with a limp and had the bloody letter opener tucked into his belt.

"What happened to Danny?" Rebecca asked when after a few moments he didn't come through door.

"We…um…there were zombies. He got bit," Walter answered, his demeanor different to the laid-back style he had in the office. His eyes had turned cold, like those of a shark.

"How many were there?" Monique asked.

"Just the one. It got him and almost took me down too." Walter pointed to his face which struck Monique as strange, as from what she had seen of the creatures, hand-to-hand melees were not their style. They ripped and devoured.

Walter removed the letter opener from his belt; it was dripping bright red blood as opposed to the blackened syrup the previous zombie had ejected from its body. Walter saw Monique looking at the blade. "Danny fought back, he got away from the zombie, and I killed it. But he'd been bitten. He begged me to end it before he turned. I had to do it." Walter's voice never faltered; his tone was flat, devoid of all emotion.

"Did you find any supplies?' Rebecca asked, looking around for the bag the men had taken with them.

Walter shook his head and looked at the floor. "No, there was nothing like that. We found two bodies, both suicides, but that was it. The flu wiped out the floor, I guess. It looked as though they were the only people working today. Good news is, I had a quick look around the stairwell, and it looks like the building is empty. It doesn't smell too fresh, but hey, none of us do." He flashed a smile, but it felt strange, as if the atmosphere on the floor had darkened in some way.

"When do we leave?" Monique asked, the closeness of the walls suddenly something she longed to be rid of.

"Not until morning," Walter spoke, the same slimy smirk on his face. Moving in the dark won't help us. We'll stay here tonight, and then look to make a move. I figure we can stay on the ground floor a day, and then head out, up the street toward the council building.

"Then what?" Rebecca asked with a deflated tone.

"I don't know," Walter snapped, his temperament changing in a heartbeat.

"Come with me Rebecca," Monique said. "We'll stay in my office, sleep there. Walter, if you take first watch then later we can swap and I'll take over. With the door and window broken I don't trust not having someone awake out here." Monique replaced her arm around Rebecca's shoulder and led her away.

Night fell, and while Rebecca fell into a deep sleep, Monique sat looking at the stars. The heating in the building had stopped working, as had the power. Monique closed her eyes, but her hunger made the world spin every time she shut them for more than a few minutes. She was pleased that they would make a move once the sun had risen. The outside world seemed like a distant paradise from their caged position, and zombies or not, she longed for freedom.

Monique slipped into a doze. Before she knew it, something sharp was pressed into her throat, and a hand clamped over her mouth.

"Make a sound, and I'll slit your throat you black bitch!" Walter spat. Burning spittle peppered Monique's face. The scream that had built in her lungs froze, and she swallowed it back down.

Walter moved his hand from Monique's mouth and slid it down her body, slipping it under her shirt. When she flinched, he pressed the tip of the knife even further into her throat. "No, no, no, love. That's not how we play anymore. I'm in charge now. I give the orders. The world as we knew it has ended, and only the strong will rise to take power," he sneered as he squeezed her breast. It took everything Monique had not to fight. "Your tits feel good. Now get on your knees. I've got something for you."

Tears stung Monique's eyes and streamed down her cheeks as her mouth was filled. Walter smiled down at her, and his black shark eyes shimmered in the night like the moon on a lake.

With his height reached, Walter turned and walked away without saying a word. While Monique fell back onto her chair with tears burning the back of her throat.

She once again fell into a turbulent sleep. She was falling, and below her was a crowd of zombies, each one a clone of Walter. The more she struggled, the quicker she fell, plummeting into the outstretched arms, embraced by their hungry growls. She woke with a start and immediately shielded her eyes. The sun had already risen in the cloudless sky, and the thick frost from the night before had started to thaw.

Monique rose, wincing at her stiff joints. She coughed to try to remove the lingering taste of her assault.

Rebecca woke not long after, and when they went to leave the office, she was surprised to find the door opened fully, without any hindrance.

"Walter," Monique called. The name tasted foul, even worse than the gift he had given her the night before, but she didn't want Rebecca to find out. She didn't want anybody to find out.

No answer came. As they walked through the office, it soon became apparent that Walter had left them behind.

"Look." Rebecca pointed at the empty soda cans that stood on the sofa. "I thought he said they hadn't found anything," Rebecca gasped, shocked.

"I guess he lied. It looks like he left us behind." Monique pointed to the open door as she spoke.

"So we are alone?" Rebecca couldn't hide the panic in her voice.

"I think so, but you know what? I think it is better that way. Nobody to slow us down," Monique answered, as the tears once again threatened to break the surface.

Rebecca didn't seem as convinced, and collapsed into the sofa with a despondent groan. "Why would he leave?" she asked

"Walter wasn't who you thought he was, Rebecca. Trust me on that, and if you ask me, I think he murdered Danny yesterday." With the words spoken, Monique felt a wave of guilt rush over her at the way she had treated her former assistant.

Rebecca didn't say anything. She picked up each can in turn and shook it, but they were all empty. In a movement so sudden it made Monique gasp, Rebecca snatched up a can and threw it across the office, screaming as she threw. One by one in quick succession, she snatched up each can and launched it. When she was done, Rebecca turned around, her eyes red with tears. "Where do we have to go?"

"Well, I don't know if you were copied in on all of the email, but the talk at…the end was that it came from outside of the city. The flu started all of it right?" Rebecca nodded her silent agreement. "Well, think about this floor; the first people to call in sick were those that lived furthest away. The outskirts also reported the first zombie activity, too. Remember those early news broadcasts?" Monique once again made Rebecca work a little in their conversation, for the young girl's face had begun to assume the same distant expression that Scott had worn. Rebecca nodded again. "The day the zombies arrived there were a few live news reports sent out before the emergency broadcast became the only show on TV. There were images of the streets on the outskirts of town, and the main residential areas by the ring road which were completely over-run by the undead."

"I don't remember; it's all just a blur. Do you ever think about your family?" Rebecca asked, changing the direction of the conversation. It was a conversation they had purposefully avoided and for good reason. It was a topic that could rapidly develop into an obsession.

"My family is in London. I don't know if it has gotten there… yet," Monique answered truthfully. "I like to think that it has been stopped."

"But what if it started there?" Tears streaked Rebecca's cheeks.

"It didn't. Headquarters sent me an email saying that something had happened in this area, and that we were all to stay indoors. It started here." Monique knew that her answers were not answers, but avenues to further questions. It was the best she could do. "I'll tell you what, if we get out of here, then we will find your family. Rebecca, you need to listen to me now. Don't think about them, not yet. We need to focus on getting out of here. The first thing we need is food. We need to head into town, find something to eat, a place to sleep. We can make our way slowly—"

"...where?" Rebecca interrupted.

"I don't know. There must be a military base or something around here," Monique began. "They would have set something up within the city. If we can find that, then we can see where we need to go."

Rebecca nodded, but said nothing. "I don't want to go out there...with them," she whispered in a cracked voice after a prolonged period of silence.

"If we stay here, then we die." Monique was frank and to the point.

"When?"

"Now," Monique answered, her mind committed to getting out. In secret, part of her wanted to find Walter and feed him to the dead.

The women stood and hugged each other, enjoying one final moment of peace before they walked to the door.

"We should stop on the floor below. If Walter lied about having food, maybe there are still some supplies down there." She left the next thought unspoken. *Maybe we can find out what really happened to Danny.*

Between each floor were two small flights of stairs that were opposite each other, with a small square landing which served as the connection point. The wall by each landing was decorated with the floor number, the department name, and the name of the respective managers. Monique paused for a second to look at her name on the board. Something had smeared it with blood. It looked as though someone had stroked it, for the smears were single tracks, and the relative width of a finger.

The door to the seventh floor was glass. It saw a lot of visitors, both corporate and public, so held a much more businesslike appearance than the eighth. Dried blood clouded the glass. The door was open. The electronics had shut off, so Danny and Walter had forced it open. The odor of death seeped through the doors.

"I don't need to look in there, let's just keep moving," Rebecca whispered.

"I need to check something. Wait here if you want." Monique walked toward the door. Her head was giddy from hunger, the world around her a queasy sea as a result of the meaty stench.

Creeping closer, Monique checked the door. It was heavy, but she felt it would move if she pushed hard enough. A growl from the other side stayed her hand. Monique stifled a gasp and went to pull away, but she had a burning need within her to see for herself what had happened to Danny. She was sure that it was latent guilt. The gap between the doors was large enough for Monique to peer through. The moment she pushed her head between the two doors she saw the problem. Danny was dead, but it had not been from a zombie bite. Walter had slit his throat. The growl had come from the zombie that had since buried its face in Danny's stomach. It had ripped Danny's abdomen open. Half-chewed clumps of flesh and torn organs bubbled from the gash as the zombies swallowed mouthfuls of cold, jellied innards. Monique felt her gorge rise, but swallowed everything back down. She pulled her head from the gap and turned to Rebecca.

"Come on, there's nothing there." She controlled herself. There was no need to scare the girl any more than she already was.

They made an uneventful trip down to the third floor. Most people had been home sick on the day it started—or were already dead. Monique was painfully aware of the irony of it all. As they descended the first flight of stairs leading to the second floor, they stopped. Rebecca saw it first. A zombie lay on the steps. It wore a bloodstained suit. Monique was sure that had it been a whole face it would have been familiar to her. The pair froze, but it was too late, the thing had seen them and started trying to claw its way up the stairs. It was then that Monique noticed its legs. They were broken, the ankles, too, judging by the fact that they were twisted almost one hundred and eighty degrees.

"It must have fallen...he must have fallen... before he became one of those things." Monique stared at the creeping form. She watched as it inched its way closer to them, one step at a time. Its neck craned to face them. The lower jaw was caked with dried blood that fell away in thick flakes, revealing that what lay beneath was raw meat. The bone had been ripped away during that first feed. "He can't hurt us. He's got no mouth left." Monique felt sorry for the creature.

"What do we do?" Rebecca had frozen, her back pressed firmly against the wall.

"We put him out of his misery." Monique answered. She pulled the knife from behind her back, the one Danny had found on the first day. "Wait here," she advised Rebecca as she walked down to meet the zombie. She crouched down and pushed away its feeble, off balance swipe at her, and then plunged the knife through the top of the dead man's skull.

The act of killing her first zombie signified a change in Monique. She felt the life leave the animated corpse, and it was powerful. She pulled the knife free and wiped it on the corpse's shirt before sliding it into the belt of her suit skirt.

"Come on. We need to keep moving," Monique called back to Rebecca.

"I don't...is it really dead?" Rebecca stammered, nervous about having to get so close to a dead body, even one that wasn't going to stand up.

"As a doornail, Rebecca. Now come on!" Monique ordered the girl and smiled when she saw her move away from the wall.

Monique paused by the main entrance to the office. She had expected there to be bodies, but the sheer number shocked her. None of them were alive, but the small wave of relief was lost when the stench hit her. The large windows and glass entrance door were no more. Their broken shards littered the floor, crunching and grating under their every step.

"Wait here." Monique motioned to Rebecca as she stepped through the shattered windowpane.

After having been locked inside and above the city for so long, it felt strange being in the open. Monique felt intimidated. The tall office buildings of this street and the two behind it were powerful objects. The open space and fresh air were awe-inspiring. For a few seconds, it was too much for Monique. She forgot about the undead that milled around them.

When her senses returned, Monique looked around and quickly ducked back inside.

"The street is pretty empty. A few zombies here and there, but in general the coast looks clear," Monique whispered.

"I don't think...just give me a second," Rebecca stalled, but Monique was not in the mood to play games.

"No! We move now. Follow me. We head to the right. That will bring us onto St. Stephen's. We follow it along to Castle Street." Monique ran through the route she had planned in her head the previous day. It was a small street filled with several off licensees and a small series of deli restaurants. There would be their best chance of finding an immediate meal...if the looters had not already struck.

Monique heard Rebecca gasp as she stepped into the street. The thing that struck Monique this time was the silence. The city was still. Their footsteps echoed down the street, and the empty office blocks loomed over them.

At the end of the street, the road branched off in either direction. A left-turn led straight to the ring road, passing alongside the large cathedral which was one of the city's major landmarks. The right turn the women had planned to follow would take them to the entrance of the high street, and ultimately, the castle.

However, they never made it that far…

# CHAPTER 12 – SURVIVAL OF THE FITTEST

"We turned right onto St. Stephen's Street and…I just didn't think. It was just second nature. I was so naïve." Monique bowed her eyes and wiped her eyes.

"What happened?" Paul asked, once again enthralled by the tale of survival. Yet at the same time he found himself appalled at the speed with which society, in particular the male gender, regressed to the most base level.

"We rounded the corner, and there they were. There must have been about a hundred of them, maybe more. I don't know. They just stood there… waiting. We came around the corner, and I remember they just turned around in one fluid movement. In that second, they were no longer individuals, but a single entity, bonded by their hunger. They moved toward us, and we…I ran. Rebecca, she…she was scared and did not move. She screamed at me to help her, but I just kept running. They were on my heels the whole way. I never looked back, not at them, and not at Rebecca. They came from everywhere: out of houses, from behind cars, inside cars. They were down all of the side streets. It was like a flood. You remember that tsunami in Asia? Yeah, it was like that. They just came from nowhere and destroyed everything that got in their way. The ground shook as their footsteps pounded on the pavement behind me." Monique paused to refocus herself.

"I know what you mean," Robert spoke. "When those things chased me, it was…I don't know if there is any way to describe how that feels."

"Then you get it more than the rest," Monique answered. "I wanted to reach the Cathedral…I don't know why. Maybe I hoped God would protect me. Stupid, I know. But there were too many of them. I turned a corner, and there was another group. I turned and ran back, but a third cluster appeared. They surrounded me. That was when I saw him…Walter. He had crawled under a car. I saw him looking at me. He still had that dark look in his eyes, but his face told me he was afraid." Monique raised her head to gaze at the plane's ceiling. She took a series of deep breaths, while her hands fidgeted nervously, washing themselves like Lady Macbeth. "I ran over to the car. He waved frantically at me, trying to get me to stop." Monique spoke in short, broken sentences, pausing between each one. "I didn't listen. I ran around the far side of the car, dropped to the floor, and rolled beside him. He stared at me, and

I have never seen a look of hatred so strong before. At that moment, he hated me more than I hated him…more than I hate myself now."

Another deep breath. Nobody said a word…there was no need.

"There wasn't much room under the car, and both of us knew it. I did what I had to do to survive. I understood it when I killed that zombie. I guess I learned it when Walter raped me, too. It is all a matter of survival of the fittest." Monique didn't need to say anymore; they all understood that she had stabbed Walter and used him as bait to escape the chasing pack.

"With the zombies distracted by fresh meat, I managed to get away and up to the cathedral. The doors were open, and as I ran in an army team all turned around and aimed their weapons at me. If it wasn't for the quick reactions of their commanding officer, I would have been put down." Monique gave a strained laugh as she recalled how close she came to dying.

"That was a close call." Paul nodded to himself as he spoke.

"I know, right? A few of them still wanted to shoot me even after the order to lower their arms, and I can't blame them. As we made our way back to the airport, we came across another large herd of zombies. All students from a local prep school. A gang of survivors opened fire on the trucks as we turned a corner. The car in front of us lost two men. The survivors sat in a small office building. The gunfight was horrible. I never want to be involved in something like that again. We didn't have a choice." Monique spoke the last sentence aloud, but it was only intended for her ears. She needed to convince herself that the bloodshed between two surviving parties had been a necessity.

A silence fell over the cabin. Paul realized that more and more people had turned around or had their ears pricked, listening to the tales being told. He suspected that everybody had something to contribute; some small item that could help shed light on the plight of the world. It took a while for him to realize that Monique had finished her tale.

"I find it strange that you worked for a central government agency, and that they, too, didn't say anything until it was too late," Leon began, but stopped when he saw Monique's face flash with rage. Her head snapped around to face the paramedic who had risked it all to rescue his daughter. Lucky for them both, Paul had regained his senses and reasserted himself back into the conversation with the smooth ease that only a real journalist can possess.

"He means that it must have taken our government by surprise; that they didn't even have a chance to warn their own people, not that you have lied to us. Right, Leon?" Paul looked at the paramedic, who nodded gratefully.

"Of course! I wasn't about to suggest you were a liar." Leon looked at Monique and loosed a sigh of mild relief when he saw the anger dissipate.

"Do you really think it was terrorism? I mean, why like this? Why Norwich, of all places?" Monique began.

"We think that the flu was the actual weapon. The zombies are just a...side effect." Paul recapped what they had already discussed. "Now we know that the government never saw it coming, yet they had troops responding pretty quickly, so they were ready for it." Paul began to put the pieces of the articles together, to dissect them, to extract the horror from the truth, and then sift it down even further to the clues.

"The only thing is a double where and why issue. Why Norwich? Why the outskirts, and not the center? Where did it all start—the precise location? Maybe that is the clue we need," Leon spoke, staring at Paul for any signs that he had overstepped his boundaries as storyteller.

"My best guess is that it was an error; a misfire or something like that. London had to be the target. Something just didn't work as it was supposed to. It would fit and tie everything together." Paul turned the page of his notebook again, checking that he hadn't missed anything obvious. He was about to speak again when an inebrious grunt cut him off.

"You make me laugh. All this talk about why, and who dunnit. It doesn't damn well matter now, does it? We survived. That is all we needed to do. Wondering about it all will only cause more problems than it solves. I know that much for damned sure." There was a slight slur to the words, and the belch that ended it was enough for them to know that the man had found the liquor supply in the galley.

"I'm sorry you feel that way. Some people find comfort in answers and in knowing the truth," Paul offered, hoping that he could engage the man in conversation. Unlike the rest of them, there was a wild look in his eyes. Paul's gut told him that the drunkard's story was one he absolutely must hear.

"Why? You want to write a story about me; make me some hero because I fought back?" The man seemed to see a hidden threat beneath anything.

"If you don't ask any questions, you never get any answers now do you? Maybe you are right. Maybe there is no point to all of this. It happened, and we should adjust, but hey, there is no movie on this flight anyway. So humor us," Paul joked, and was relieved to see the man smile in return before he collapsed into the row of seats before Paul.

"Ok, that sounds fair...I like you...Peter..."

"Paul."

"Paul…Peter, Paul, George, what's in a name, right?" the man continued. His breath was redolent with rum and whisky. Each breath hung in the air long after the words that the expulsion had created were gone.

"I don't know. Why don't you tell me?"

"Tim. Tim Dunn, and alright, I'll play along, but know this: how to kill those sons of bitches is the only thing we ever need to know."

"That might well be, Tim, but humor me. Tell me you story." Paul spoke as he once more flipped for a new page in his notebook.

# CHAPTER 13 – DO WHAT YOU NEED TO

Tim looked none of them in the eye as he spoke. Despite being unsteady on his feet, he refused to take a seat. "There isn't really that much to tell. I mean, you do what you need to do in order to survive. You get from the start of a day to the end in one piece. The world has changed. It isn't like what it used to be. Our values have had to change, too. Survival. That is what it is all about."

"I agree with you, Tim. How did you change? What did you do to survive?" Paul asked, hoping to get the conversation into a flow as soon as possible. The man was drunk and seemed more interested in playing the tough guy than offering anything constructive.

"You'd love to know that, wouldn't you? You all want to know how Tim survived. Well, none of you wanted to know about me before it happened. I wasn't fucking good enough!" He slurred his words and fell suddenly silent. His eyes took on a distant, glassy look. For a moment, Paul was certain that Tim's role in his story had already reached its conclusion. Then with a wet belch, consciousness returned, and Tim resumed his story. "You all looked down on me before the zombies arrived. Never gave old Tim a chance, did you? Now look who is coming crawling back looking for answers." His voice rose with each sentence uttered, and one by one the other passengers turned their heads to stare his way; an act that only seemed to enrage him further.

"I have never met you before, Tim. I do not know you, nor do I judge you. Please, have a seat and tell me your story. How did you survive out there?" Paul kept his voice emotionless, but his tone sincere. Tim stared at him, his face a deep shade of red. He gave a sigh and collapsed into the seat beside Jessica. She gave a quiet groan—which only Paul heard—and adjusted her position in the chair.

"Fine, I'll tell you anything thing want to know. You want to hear all the gory details? I mean, I didn't fuck any of them, like this schoolboy here." He pointed with an unsteady finger toward Robert. "My dick would have been colder than their cunts at the thought of it." He made no attempt to hide his lecherous gaze that rested on Jessica.

Jessica, who no longer saw the need to stand on professional ceremony, rose from her chair with a disgusted look and stepped over Paul to take the spare seat on the other side. Paul couldn't help but smell her perfume, Chanel No.5. It had been his wife's favorite also. "I'll get him some coffee," she growled when Tim shot her a grin that made his

DIARIES OF THE DAMNED

glance seem almost suave. "And I might just throw it over him," she grunted in an angry whisper that only Paul and Leon heard.

"Where do you want me to start then, hey? I can tell you all about how I busted their heads open, or about how...they ate my wife." The emotion in his voice changed from anger to pain midsentence. "Is that what you want to hear, Mr. Writer?" Anger once again flashed in Tim's eyes, and Paul realized, as he had done when he leaned in to reassure Monique, the intense trauma the man had been through.

"Start wherever you think is the important place to start. This is your tale to tell." Paul knew he would have to be patient with Tim, but it didn't bother him.

# CHAPTER 14 – TIM DUNN

"I can't believe this flu," Mary Dunn sighed as she set the phone down on the kitchen worktop.

"What's happened?" asked Tim, her husband of fifteen years. He sat at the dining table which was in the center of their open kitchen-cum-dining area. His face was a picture of concentration as he scoured the wanted advertisements for any job he could find.

"The hospital just called. There are only two nurses on duty tonight. The rest have all called in sick, and they need me to go back in right away," she answered him as she cast a glance over her shoulder at the meal she had been working on all afternoon. "I know it's our anniversary, but they didn't give me a choice." She began to sob. Tim rose and embraced his wife, kissing her on the top of her head. "It's okay. I'll love you even more tomorrow, so we can celebrate then instead." He took her face in his hands and tilted her head so that she looked into his eyes. "Go save lives, honey. I love you." He kissed her and tasted her tears.

Mary turned and instructed Tim on how to finish cooking the meal, and made him promise to serve himself up a plate so that it didn't go to waste. She then went upstairs to change, and Tim returned to his job hunt. He had worked for the same electronics company since he left school and had worked his way up to being a regional store manager. Three weeks ago he had arrived to open up the store only to find a paper notice taped to the window advising all staff that the company had gone bankrupt overnight, and that all of their positions had been terminated, with immediate effect. Since that morning, Tim had applied for more than fifty jobs, had been invited for three interviews, one of which was given to a potential candidate before he even got the chance to answer any questions.

"I don't know when I will be home. They said it would be open shifts until this flu passes, or the staff numbers get back up again. I'll call you from the hospital the moment I know more," Mary called as she grabbed her coat from the rack by the door. Her phone was vibrating in her pocket, advising her of the five missed calls she had received from the hospital. Her mind was occupied with all manner of things, so the fact that there was a figure on the other side of the door didn't even register. It was only when she walked into it that she noticed it was there.

She gasped, but stifled her scream the moment she saw that it was their neighbor, Russell Bishop. He stood still and didn't make a sound. He stared at Mary, his eyes sunken and dark. His face was pale, and he was dressed in nothing but a t-shirt and his underwear. Before Mary could do so much as express her concern at his lack of dress in the freezing wintery air, he attacked. Russell was a sixty-year-old, lifelong accountant who had lost his wife to cancer two years ago. Yet as his hands clamped down on Mary's arms, his grip felt like a vice. His hands were cold, like stone, and the speed with which he moved had a graceless, jerky quality to it. Before Mary could scream, her mouth filled with hot, coppery blood, and she was drowning. The pain didn't register until the heat subsided. Russell gave a growl and shook his head like a dog with a new toy. Mary's skin tore away and sent thick arcs of blood pumping into the air. The strength left her body immediately. It was all she could do to raise her bare hands to her throat before she hit the floor. As Russell stood over her, Mary remembered he had been sick the day before, and could see in his lifeless eyes that he was as dead as she soon would be. She tried to call out, but all that escaped her lips was a rushed gargle of air. She closed her eyes, waiting for Russell to move in once more, but he didn't. A scream from out in the street caught his attention. He sniffed the air like a predator, his mouth still full with flesh cleaved from Mary's neck. He swallowed it, turned, and then walked away in pursuit of a new kill.

Mary tried to move, she tried to inch herself into the kitchen, but the floor was slick with her blood, and her old tennis shoes slipped without gaining any traction. With her body in mid twist, her head craned back in search of her husband, Mary felt her body grow cold. A convulsion rocked her entire frame, followed by a burning cramp which moved like a wave and ushered in the inevitable darkness of death.

Tim had not heard the scuffle between his wife and neighbor. The entire encounter had lasted but a few seconds, and he had once again immersed himself in the job sections of the local paper. A chill wind swept into the kitchen and rustled the paper on the table. Tim looked up and felt the change in room temperature. He rose, checked the pans on the stove, and turned them off as instructed.

With no idea as to what awaited, Tim walked into the living room in search of the reason for the draft. He saw the front door was open, and for the first few steps he took, that was all he saw wrong with the room. The moment he saw his wife, the way her body laid still and twisted on the floor surrounded by a sea of congealing blood, he collapsed. The tears were instant, they burned his cheeks the same way the rising vomit burned his throat.

"Mary," he called, as he crawled over the floor toward her.

Tim could see the wound in her neck and the look in her eyes. Her upper body had turned while her legs remained flat, an image reminiscent of a baby during their first attempts to turn.

"Mary," Tim called again. The room began to spin. Another gust of cold wind ran down the street and into the house, bringing with it the echo of a multitude of screams; a wailing anguish that surely contributed to the cold feel of the evening.

For Tim, time stopped. All he knew was that his wife was dead beside him. He did not even entertain the notion that the killer might still be in the house. It didn't bother him. The haze that had gripped his mind like a cold fever dulled everything to a strange pulsating nothingness. This was a sensation Tim would happily live with for the rest of his life if it kept grief at bay. Only when he heard a deep, foreign growl did he move his gaze from the ceiling. He turned his head and noticed immediately that Mary had moved. Her body was no longer twisted. Her arms reached out in search of solace no more. She lay on her front, and her hands were flat on the floor besides her shoulders. It was Mary that had voiced the growl. As Tim watched, the muscles in her arms twitched, and she pushed herself from the floor. The blood she had lain in had congealed and dropped from her rising body like a jelly. Tim sat in silent incredulity as Mary got to her feet. Her white nurse's uniform was stained a violent red. Loose shards of flesh around the wound in her neck billowed like flags in the wind. She gave another growl and moved toward Tim.

"Mary…you're alive!" Tim scrambled to his feet, not to flee, but to embrace his wife. They had been friends before lovers and remained both long after marriage. Tears filled his eyes once more, but the joy in his heart cooled them.

Mary took slow and unsteady steps, her balance all but gone. Her feet shuffled along the floor rather than lifted. "We need to call you an ambulance. Come here." He held out his arms, and Mary moved in close to him.

She gave another growl, and as Tim wrapped his arms around her, he felt how cold and stiff her body was. He pulled her close to him and felt her draw no breath. His brain made the connection long before his heart would admit it. Even as her grip tightened and her head moved in toward his neck with her jaw stretched wide, Tim refused to accept any thought other than his wife had somehow survived the unsurvivable.

*She survived death…death, coming back, she came back to me…from the dead…the dead are rising…zombies…FUCK!* The thoughts hit Tim in a rush as he felt his wife's teeth graze his neck. "No!" he yelled, pushing his wife away with a strength that surprised him.

Mary stumbled backward, her jaws gnashing in hunger-fuelled fury. Her face was white from blood loss; her eyes sunken pits of darkness. This told Tim all he needed to know. Whatever it was that caused his wife to get back up, life wasn't it, and what had returned resembled his wife in body alone.

Another growl came from Mary's throat. She moved forward once more, her hands reaching out not in search of comfort, but nourishment.

Tim sidestepped her advance with ease and ran from the hall into the living room. Mary followed as he expected. The living room was small and filled with two sofas, a coffee table, and a dresser unit. A quick lap of the room and Tim was standing by the kitchen while Mary was struggling to maneuver around the coffee table.

"I'm sorry, my love," he whispered as he closed the door. The sound of pounding fists came not too long after the door closed. With no lock on it, Tim knew it would only be a matter of time before his dead wife either figured it out or broke through the cheap wood.

Tim's mind charged at a mile a minute; his breaths coming quick and deep. He was close to hyperventilating, and his vision was dull and blurred. Tim stumbled into the kitchen with the grace of a drunk on Saturday night. He opened the cupboard beside the oven and grabbed the first bottle from the shelf. He opened it and drank deeply. The fire of the alcohol burned through the fog and brought with it a sense of clarity. There was a crash from the hallway, and Tim remembered that the front door was still open. Grabbing the kitchen knife from the counter, Tim moved into the hallway, uncertain of what lay in wait. The screams from elsewhere in the street were enough to tell Tim that something was wrong. He tightened his grip on the blade and moved toward the door. The source of the crash had been a fight between three neighborhood cats who now all sat side by side lapping up the cooling pool of blood. They looked up at Tim as he approached, their eyes wide and dark. All three growled at him, their claws at the ready.

"Scat." Time clapped his hands and stamped on the floor. The animals moved, but did not run. They backed away, keeping low to the ground, their ears flat against their heads. Tim knew that they were afraid and so tried a different tactic. He crouched down and called them to him. "Come on, it's ok, come here." He rubbed his fingers together and tapped his nails on the floor, but the animals backed even further away. They were half way out of the door when the first one pricked its ears up and ran away. The other two felines attempted the same evasive maneuver, but stopped when a pair of undead hands clamped around their middles. Tim jumped as Russell appeared in the doorway. His face and chest were stained with blood. He had a large gash on his flank, which had been the cause of his demise. He held a cat in each hand and squeezed. The animals cried and twisted their flexible bodies in an attempt to break free, but were unsuccessful. They moved in a flash of teeth and claws, but the injuries they inflicted were ignored. Russell's grip tightened, the muscles on his forearms bulged—solid from years of golf and country club tennis—until one of the beasts also began to bleed. Blood spat from its lips as it hissed and growled at the man that held it. Russell shook the creature until it fell silent, not dead but dazed. He raised it to his mouth, and before Tim could move either in defense of the creature or retreat, teeth had sunk through the fur and pierced the skin beneath. Blood spurted from the wound and ran down Russell's hungry face. As he tore the flesh away from the animal's body, the cat let out a cry that was beyond description. A high-pitched wail that sounded human.

Russell spat out the mouthful of fur and grabbed the dying animal with both hands. His other captive fell to the floor immobile, its spine broken by the powerful grip. Its head thrashed on the floor while urine and fecal matter flowed from its rear the way blood flowed from its then deceased friend. Russell buried his face in the animals flank and gobbled down the bite-sized organs with a satisfied growl.

A crash from behind him told him that his wife had made inroads to her escape also. Seeing no other option than to fight or flee, he charged at his dead neighbor, plunging the large knife into his chest. It slid through the man's flesh with a slick ease. Tim released his grip and stepped back. His hands shook, and his jaw dropped as the man he had comforted after the death of his wife stared at the blade and proceeded to amble toward him as if nothing had happened.

"Russell. Hey neighbor, it's me… Tim."

The zombie showed no interest in conversation. His mouth moved but only with hunger. Strips of cat flesh hung from his teeth while blood had painted his lips a deep burgundy.

"Shit!" Tim cursed as the door to the living room cracked down the middle, only to be forced open by Russell who had mistaken the occupant for being alive. It gave Tim a window, however, and he took it. He ran through the house, into the kitchen where he slammed the door closed, and pushed the dining table against it.

With no time to collapse into the shock that tempted him so delightfully, Tim grabbed the bottle of drink and took another long, throat-scorching gulp. He followed this up with two more.

By the time fists began to pound on the kitchen door, Tim was long gone. He vanished into the world, leaving behind a half empty bottle of liquor and a knife rack that was missing two blades.

Tim and Mary lived in a cozy cul-de-sac in a small town just outside of the city. When they had bought their house, it had been a small rural community. As the years passed, the farmland that had separated them from the city was replaced by housing estates and promises of planned development. The road through their town filtered directly onto the ring road. It was there that Tim headed, panic and alcohol fuelling his movements. He gave no thoughts to whether others had experienced similar fates, at either end of life's spectrum.

Tim vaulted over the fence at the end of his garden, landed on his feet on the pavement that ringed the cul-de-sac, and ran head first into a stumbling, bleeding figure.

"Help me," the man gargled, showering Tim with a fine mist of blood. A large gash ran the length of his forehead, and a rapidly spreading stain drenched the center of the man's shirt. Before the man could say anything else, he collapsed to his knees, falling face first to the ground.

Tim looked around and saw a car had crashed into the brick wall of the house three doors up from where he stood. The driver's side door was open. The accident explained the wound on the man's head. The stumbling, growling figure explained the gaping wound that ran down the man's spine, effectively filleting him.

Reeling backward, his feet leaden, Tim turned to move and saw that the things were all around him.

"Sweet shit heaps!" he cried aloud. The road was relatively empty. Three cars had crashed into one another on the other side of the street, and the crowd of five zombies that headed toward Tim told him enough about what had happened to them. One man walked with a heavy limp, his left leg buckling beneath him every time he placed his weight upon the limb, yet he showed no signs of stopping.

In the distance, the sound of a police siren wailed, and all of the…things in the street turned their heads and watched as the car sped down the street toward them. The officer behind the wheel hit the brakes when he saw the crowd in the street and swerved hard the moment he saw he could not stop in time. His car mounted the curb and ploughed into another creature that was approaching Tim from the rear. Her body bounced on the hood of the car, crumbling in on itself, and sliding up the window with all its limbs flailing in a rare moment of grace before it landed on the roof, shattering the lighting rig. It had until that moment continued to flash before finally crashing onto the road in a heap. Bone had pierced the skin of both legs just below the kneecap, and the body lay twisted in a fashion that could only be the result of a broken spine.

The car door opened, and the police officer half-climbed, half-fell out of his vehicle. His face was white as a sheet as he looked at the trail of clotted blood that created a racing stripe on his car.

"She…It…I didn't…the officer stammered as he stared at Tim who, in all fairness, returned the stare with an equally blank look. "Oh Christ!" He raised his hands and ran his fingers through his hair. As if the act had focused his mind, when the officer lowered his hands his face had a determined look set onto it. "Ma'am? Ma'am, can you hear me? I'm going to call an ambulance, just try not to move," the officer called out while he fumbled with his radio.

At the sound of the man's voice, the body on the floor snapped its head around and stared at both Tim and the officer. The jaw had been broken and hung from one joint. Skin peeled away from the body; before or after death, Tim could not be certain.

"What the…" the police officer began as the female corpse began to drag herself along the road, creeping ever closer to them. A deep growl came from her throat as her jaw wagged, gnashing at the air as if their very scent offered some form of sustenance. "It can't…there's no way," the officer stammered again, as he looked back at Tim in search of validation of the scenes occurrence.

"Don't look at me," Tim offered with a shrug of the shoulder.

"Behind you," the officer shouted, as another figure appeared behind Tim.

Tim spun and dove out of the way just as the pair of strong arms swung to catch him. Tim's spin brought him into the middle of the road with his back to the scene. Moving down the road were several more of those monsters. Screams hung in the air.

"We need to get out…" Tim called as he turned, but his words were a waste. The police officer was no longer able to hear him, for his head no longer sat atop his shoulders. The large zombie that had swiped at Tim had caught the officer. He had tried to use his Pepper Spray on the creature, but with little effect. The zombie held the head up before him, inspecting it the way you check a melon for ripeness. It then took a big bite from the cheek, tearing away a patch of flesh that stretched from ear to mouth. The crawling zombie had reached the officer's foot and torn a hole in his trousers. With vicious greed, she bit down into the leg, wrenching it with her head to tear the final stretch of muscle from the bone.

The sound of their hunger made Tim queasy. It was a raw, wet sound, which made him think of eating celery.

Screams echoed louder as more people fled into the street. The housing estate they lived in was an upmarket area. To see the locals in such a sense of panic was almost more alarming than that fact that the dead had come to life.

The small group of zombies that had made their way across the road toward Tim stopped at the sound of the screams. When the small crowd appeared in the street, closely followed by an equally sized group of the undead, they altered their course and flanked the fleeing banquet.

Tim took the opportunity and ran around the feasting pair who had broken into the officer's chest and stuffed their faces with all manner of juicy morsels. The police car was still running, and despite one flat tire and a crumbled hood, it still drove when Tim threw it into reverse and pulled out into the street.

Blood smeared the windscreen, and when Tim tried the wipers they did nothing but spread the gore. "Shit," Tim growled at himself. There was a bottle of water on the passenger seat. Tim grabbed it and emptied it onto the windscreen as he drove. Somehow, he managed not to cut his wrists open on the jagged glass of the shattered driver's side window. The blades swept furiously managing to clear a small patch of everything but a light pink haze. It gave Tim enough room to see by. The faster the car went, the slower his heart and mind went.

Tim didn't get to drive very far. The ring road was filled with cars, the aftermath from an accident further up. He could see the lights of the emergency vehicles flashing down the road. Everybody stared at him; the wrecked car, the blood smeared windscreen—it drew attention.

Tim stopped the car, looking this way and that in search of a way through the mess, when the passenger door to car opened and a police officer fell into the seat.

"Drive Harry, drive!" The man was out of breath, and bloody. "You're not Harry. Where is he?" The officer was remarkably calm at finding a stranger driving his partner's car.

"D… Dead," Tim stuttered.

"Fuck! Then drive, whoever you are. Get the fuck out of here! Those things are everywhere!" The officer clutched his hand which Tim saw was bleeding. He said nothing, afraid to speak too much in case the officer smelled the alcohol on his breath, even though fear had sobered him in an instant.

Tim floored the car, feeling more confident having an officer beside him.

"What the crap is going on?" Tim asked shortly after narrowly missing a group of people in mid retreat from a group of three blood soaked walking corpses.

"No fucking clue! I heard all manner of things. The flu—they say it's the flu that started it, but those things, the ones back there weren't sick. It looked as though they had been—"

"Bitten," Tim interrupted the officer.

"Yeah. They were dead when we arrived. Take a left here. They were fucking dead. Then one of 'em gets up, starts biting people. Then more get up, and all hell broke loose. One even bit me. Took my finger clean off." As if he were proud of his wound, the officer showed Tim his mangled hand. The index finger was missing at the palm, and the middle finger hung on a thread. The sight caused Tim to swerve the car and crash into a group of bodies. The world went black before he had time to question their life status.

Tim came too with a heavy head and a left eye that refused to offer a clear image. The police officer that had sat beside him was gone, and a large bloodied hole in the windscreen told of his exit route. The body spread across the hood confirmed his final destination. All around him Tim heard the cries of the wounded… of the people he had hit.

"Jesus…" he whispered as the memory of the crowd he had mown down came back to him. He tried the door, and after fighting to release the seatbelt, Tim stepped out into the road. There were at least seven people strewn across the road. One was dead—scalped. If the messy smear of blood and hair on the road was accurate, Tim had been the cause.

"Help me," a young woman called, as she grabbed hold of Tim's leg and tugged at it. "Help me, they're coming!" she wailed.

The others, who seemed more panicked by what chased them than their injuries, echoed her sentiments. Tim saw three broken limbs and numerous lacerations that would require hospital treatment, yet they all ignored them.

Tim didn't need to ask what they were running from, for the growl preceded the arrival of the ravenous pack and set Tim's nerves on edge. A quartet of zombies appeared, and then he understood that was what they were. Each had a similar wound in their necks, although the smallest of the group appeared to have had his entire throat ripped out. Blood still dripped from the wound, and its head lolled from side to side with each stumbled step it made.

"Help us," the pleas began again.

A groan behind Tim caught his attention. He turned and saw that police officer had begun to stir. Somehow, he had survived the crash. Tim ran over to him, and bent down to… he didn't know what he was going to do. The officer gave another groan, a deeper, longer sound, something guttural. Tim realized that it was a growl just before he reached the crouched point of no return. The officer twisted its head and snapped its jaws shut, narrowly missing the same two fingers on Tim's hand that had caused his own transformation.

The growls grew closer. A glance over his shoulder told Tim that he didn't have long before they were upon him. He looked down at the people he had injured, and with a pang of guilt he turned and ran, hurdling the rising, undead police officer as he did.

They had followed the ring road, but there were plenty of houses in the area. Tim ran until he saw an open door. He bounded up the steps and charged over the threshold, doing his best to shut out the screams of those he left behind and the wet ripping sound of their bodies being torn apart.

Only the officer followed, crashing into the door a few moments after Tim had slammed it shut. The door withheld the initial impact, but Tim knew he needed to do something to keep himself safe long-term. Looking around, he saw the house was modern and well kept. The hallway led directly onto the stairs with what looked at first glance to be the living room off to his immediate left. To the right was a door opening onto a small toilet. Between the door and the foot of the stairs was a heavy pine cabinet which could have had many uses, from bookcase to shoe cabinet, but it appeared to have been used as a little bit of everything. Unbothered by the contents of the cupboard, Tim ran and heaved the heavy cupboard over to the door. It was heavier that it looked, and by the time he had it in place, the pounding had ceased. Moving carefully, Tim crept into the living room, checking to see if anybody or anything lay in wait. The ground floor was deserted. The overturned dining table and chairs, along with half-eaten meals and blaring television, was evidence of a hasty departure.

The evening sky was beginning to darken. Tim knew he needed to hide from the undead monsters that filled the street. He could hear the TV playing some sort of warning, begging people to keep calm. Tim couldn't help but give an angry, coughed laugh before silencing the set. He also, after trying all three switches, managed to turn the lights off in the house. With the Venetian blinds closed, the darkness was disorienting. The layout of the room was foreign to him, and it took a while for Tim's night vision to kick in.

He moved slowly through the ground floor and into the kitchen. The door was closed and locked, the key missing. With the ground floor locked up and secure, Tim made his way back into the living room and peered through the blinds. The officer stood before the door, staring at it. He didn't move. Behind him in the street the carcasses of those that he had left to die had begun to stir.

Within a few moments, five of the seven stood and sniffed hungrily at the air. They ambled up and down the street, stiff and disjointed. Even in the light of the rising moon, their injuries were clear. Three walked on broken legs. The protruding bones caused them to move with a severe limp, but failed to stop them. Another walked with their intestines hanging between their legs like a long link of sausages. Every few steps, it would stumble over the hanging entrails and further pull them from their natural location. The fifth walked with the shoulder dislocated and their head twisted on an angle that looked as though they were holding a mobile phone to their ear. Two other figures lay still. Seeing as how their limbs lay separated from their bodies, Tim assumed that they were stuck there at the very least.

Pulling away from the window, he checked the upper level of the house. It was empty. There was a pool of bloody vomit on the floor and walls of one of the bedrooms. Judging by the decorations and the toys, it had belonged to a small boy. Tim didn't need any more information to understand the tragedy of what had happened in the house, so he went back downstairs.

He moved with the aid of the light on his phone. The police officer had moved away from the door and entered the current of undead that now filtered down the street. A few people ran by, and every now and then a car, but it was all in vain. Inevitably, a scream would come. By the time the complete darkness of night fell, Tim was glad to have his vision obscured. He fell onto the sofa, and the paralyzing acceptance of his new reality set in. He felt the darkness draw around him, he heard their stumbled footsteps and growls, the cries of those they caught. His breathing became a battle, each lungful of air was a fight to take and a war to expel. Pressure crushed his chest. Tim couldn't breathe. He stumbled into the kitchen, stubbing his toe in the darkness. The pain brought a scream to his lips, but he silenced it; swallowed it back down. He rummaged through the fridge. While a meal had recently been cooked and plated, the general supplies were low. He grabbed a can of beer, opened it, and took a drink. The effect wasn't instant, but by the time Tim had finished the can, his breathing had relaxed. By the time he threw the sixth can onto the floor he had blocked out the sounds of the real world, and with a self-satisfied smile, collapsed onto the sofa and tumbled into a fitful sleep.

Tim woke to the sound of shattering glass. His legs trembled beneath him, their power gone. It was dark, and his head swam with the lingering images of the bad dream that had gripped him, while the room spun from the alcohol that still buzzed in his system.

He looked around, momentarily lost. "Mary?" he called out for his wife. Then the memory came back. The dream was real—his wife was dead. She had come back a zombie, and he had left her. A scream pierced the night and pulled Tim over to the window. He stumbled as he walked and almost pulled the entire blind from the fixture. He peered through and saw that the zombies had all gathered around a house in which a light shone on the ground. It had drawn them all like a swarm of deadly moths. He watched as they shattered the main front window and clambered through the broken pane, ignoring the glass shards which ripped chunks of flesh from their frames.

Tim felt sick. He saw a small face appear in the upper window. A child, whose bad dreams and pleas for his parents had caused them to turn on the light through sheer force of habit. Tim stared as the child pounded the glass and then suddenly disappeared from view. A few moments later, blood splattered against the window, mercifully obscuring everything that followed from view.

Tim collapsed to the floor. Screams echoed in his mind as he recalled the accident: the cop, his broken face, partially skinned from his ejection through the windscreen. He heard their pleas for help. They were so loud that for a moment Tim thought that somebody else was in the house with him.

A zombie moved past the window, its frame brushing against the glass as it limped along. Tim gave a yell of surprise and the creature spun with lightning quick reactions. Tim jumped back from the blind and stumbled backward through the room. His heart thundered as he waited for the glass to break. When the thump came, it didn't shatter the glass, but came close. Tim jumped, he turned to run, tripped over the rug that lay on the floor and fell head first into the dining room table. His world fell black before he realized what had happened.

Morning sunlight shone across Tim's face. When he opened his eyes the world screamed at him. His head felt as though someone had put his eyes and brain through a cheese grater. His stomach cramped, and his eyes stung. He got to his feet, his balance broken. The table steadied him. He looked around, lost. The living room he was in was nothing like he had believed it to be when he arrived the previous evening. Children's toys dominated the house. Two clothes racks stood in the far corner, piled high with ironing that would never be completed.

There was a mirror on the wall behind the dining table. With trepidation, Tim looked at his reflection. One eye was swollen shut from the accident. The skin was an intoxicating mixture of blue and purple, shades he didn't think actually had a name, but thoroughly deserved ones. There was also a large swelling above his eye from where he had fallen against the table. It looked as though he were growing a horn.

It hurt to look at his image, but the faces that stared back at him from the mirror made him soon forget his own problems. He spun around, but there was nobody.

"Who's there?" Tim called out. The sound of his voice brought with it another crash at the window. The sound of splintering glass followed a second assault.

Tim looked around the room, his ears deaf to the zombie that was close to breaking his meager defenses. The room was empty. He was alone. He looked back at the mirror but saw their faces still. They had gathered around him, their skin pale and white, eyes sunken and black. Blood covered their flesh, and open sores cut deep into the meat beneath.

"Help us..." their cry echoed in his mind. Tim knew who they were. He didn't need to see their walking forms outside the house to remember their faces.

"Leave me alone!" he roared at the mirror, grabbing the fruit bowl from the center of the dining table and launching it into their pleading faces. The mirror shattered, showering the floor with razor sharp shards. The sound also muffled the shattering of the window. The first Tim knew of the zombie was when he was thrust to the floor. Spinning himself around as he fell, an instinctive reaction above all else, he managed to raise an arm in self-defense and push the snapping jaws away just before they bit down on his face. The hot, rancid breath of the zombie hit Tim in the face and caused him to gag. The blood-crusted face stared at him with a wild fury.

The creature showed no sign of letting go and was stronger than Tim had realized. It was only a matter of time before he ran out of resistance. With his left arm free, he felt along the floor, his fingers brushing over a long shard of broken mirror. An ironic twist of good luck he would later think to himself on one drunken night. He slid the shard into his hand and without hesitation slammed it into the ribcage of the zombie. The creature roared, but refused to back down, and if anything, the rage seemed to increase. With the glass slick with blood, Tim struggled for purchase when he tried to retrieve the weapon.

The zombie's head inched forward. The snapping teeth creating a rush of air that dried out Tim's eyes. As his strength began to fail, Tim found purchase on the blade and pulled it out with a wet sucking noise. Striking quickly, he stabbed upward. The shard entered the back of the creatures head and split the softened bone. With a deep growl, the zombie gave a series of jerks and fell to the floor beside Tim, dead for a second time. For a while they lay together, and neither moved. The sound of other zombies out in the street, attracted by the noise of their scuffle no doubt, dragged him to his feet. He checked his hand for injuries, and saw that somehow he had escaped even the slightest nick from the razor sharp shard he had used to defend himself.

Three more undead began to climb through the jagged entrance. He looked around the floor, seeking another weapon, but all he saw in each reflective shard was the face of one of the people he had run down and left to die. Their screams echoed in his head louder than the approaching zombies. Tim turned and ran through the house. The kitchen was large and gave him enough room to breathe; to escape the closed walls of the dining room. There were two doors in the kitchen, one that led into the garden, and another that led into the type of garage extension that had been so popular a few years earlier.

The zombies drew closer, their clumsy footsteps crushing the glass shards that littered the floor. Thinking fast, Tim turned and headed for the door that led to the garden. He grabbed a knife from the rack as he passed, and he promised himself that he wouldn't lose it as he had the previous two.

* * *

He yanked open the door and felt the cold morning air wrap its icy fingers around him. The door to the kitchen burst open just as Tim closed the door behind him. He pressed his back against the wall in an attempt to make himself as small as possible. He closed his eyes and held his breath. His heart slowed down to a sedate pulse. His life had come down to one of two possible outcomes, and Tim knew it.

The growls told him the dead were close. The creak of the kitchen door that had not fully closed drew a slight gasp from him. Their hungry shouts covered the sound as they discovered a trail of blood that led them out into the garden. He hadn't known that they would follow his blood, but the fake trail he'd created was his only chance of getting rid of them.

The moment they had all left the kitchen, Tim threw open the garage door, and locked the one the led to the garden. After a quick check of the house, which told him that he was once again alone, he grabbed a towel and wrapped his injured hand.

The house was a wreck. Tim knew he couldn't stay there, but he needed shelter and a plan. He made his way upstairs, taking the bottle of liquor he had found with him. He hurried through the living room, eager to avoid any contact with the hundreds of screaming faces that glared at him from the glass littered floor.

Tim locked himself into the master bedroom and pushed the bed against the door. He sat on the bed and closed his eyes. His hand throbbed, and his head ached. The beers from the previous night had given birth to a bastard ache in his skull which seemed to pulse in alternating synchronicity with his hand.

The world was silent. When Tim looked out of the bedroom window, he saw why. The street was deserted. Blood greased the tarmac, and bodies littered the view in all directions. Cars stood bumper to bumper on the ring road. Wafting above the houses on the other side of the street in the direction of the city center, tendrils of thick black smoke rose into the air. As Tim watched, three helicopters flew over the rooftops low enough for Tim to feel the rush of air from their rotors.

The noise of their passing seemed to bring the street to life. Bodies that Tim had thought to be dead rose to their feet while others appeared from within houses or from behind cars. The street went from abandoned to thriving in a matter of minutes. With the dead woken for the day, Tim felt his hopes at escape sink. There were too many of them. He understood that he couldn't outrun them. This fact was demonstrated by a small group that descended on a scared Border Collie spooked from its hiding place by the helicopters' low-level passage. They ripped the animal apart before he had a chance to utter the start of a yelp.

Tim sat back on the bed and opened the bottle of drink. The growling sound of the horde outside the house grew denser rather than louder. It became a noise like the static back in the day when the television shut down at midnight. The alcohol drowned out the thrum. By the time Tim had finished the bottle, he no longer heard anything.

The next thing Tim knew, it was evening. He was lying curled up in the corner of the room, the liquor bottle clutched in his hands like a club. The end had been smashed, and Tim had a gash on his forearm to match the wound on his hand. He couldn't remember what had happened, but the sun had descended behind the houses and painted the skyline a warm orange. For a second he thought that the city was ablaze.

Tim's stomach churned and rumbled. He was hungry and queasy in one confusing combination. Holding the bottle as a weapon, and having once again lost the knife he had taken, he headed downstairs. In the kitchen, he found some food in the refrigerator, and made himself a few sandwiches. He moved as quietly as he could because the sound of the shuffling undead in the street echoed through the house. As he was leaving, he noticed another bottle of alcohol in the cupboard. He stared at it; it was some sickeningly sweet and flavored crap according to the bottle. Yet he took it, for while his head throbbed, it was silent. The screams of those he had hit, the mental sensation of the car hitting them, rolling over their limbs, condemning them to their deaths, were gone; blocked out by the numbness that only alcohol can offer.

Tim made it back to the bedroom, and ate the food he had made while staring out of the window again. He watched the dead limp around. He thought of his wife. Was she still out there, walking the streets...killing...eating? His skin shrank around his frame at the thought. He tried to push it from his mind, but what replaced it was an image of the car he had crashed into the crowd. He saw the two limbless corpses lying there. He stared at them, and before he knew it, the sugary alcohol had replaced his bread as the main form of sustenance.

He stared at the bodies as the drunken, vision-clouding wave rolled over him. One had been ripped open; his torso a dark maw destined to cry out for eternity. The other, however, was alive. In spite of its limbless condition, the head thrashed, and as Tim listened, the faint cries of hunger reached his ears. The body rocked as the bloodied stumps that had once been arms and legs twitched in attempted movement.

Tim drank the bottle empty and collapsed to the floor. When he woke again, his head was heavier. The sun streamed onto his face, and the growls of the undead echoed in his ears.

Tim's eye snapped open, and with a burst of pain in his skull, he sat up. The door to the bedroom crashed in its frame and opened part of the way. Upon returning from his trip to the kitchen the previous night, Tim had neglected to push the bed against the door again. The gap was too small for the zombie to fit through, but it afforded him a view of Tim. That meant he would not leave voluntarily.

Time looked around for the broken bottle. It lay on the bed. He moved to grab it, trying his best to ignore the screaming ache inside his skull.

The zombie had an arm through the door, and grabbed at Tim as he approached. The flesh hung from its elbow in a long strand, stripped down close to the bone. Tim grabbed the bottle and slashed at the arm. The jagged edge of the bottle sliced the rotting flesh, but Tim knew what he needed to do. He waited for the right moment, then struck out with the bottle, thrusting it forwards into the face of the creature. One long glass shard slid through the dead eyeball, popping it like the yolk of a fried egg, and disappeared into the skull. The creature roared, and pulled backward, yanking the bottle from Tim's hand. It stood for a few moments before it collapsed.

Tim waited to be sure that the creature was indeed dead before he left the room.

The house was no longer safe, he knew that, but the street was also crawling with the dead. Left with no choice, Tim watched the street and slid outside. There were two zombies in the distance milling around an overgrown garden. Their heads rose and snapped toward Tim the moment he came into view. Tim saw them and turned to run, but something stopped him. The zombies were making their way toward him but they moved slowly. They were handcuffed, together. Tim moved toward the police car he had crashed, and cast a quick glance for the knife he had dropped. It was on the floor in the passenger side foot well.

He opened the door and grabbed the knife. The two zombies were still some way off, and another three shambled along behind them. Hurrying, he turned to leave, but caught sight of the flapping form of the woman he had hit first, the same woman had called to him for help; that had begged him with such pain in her eyes. Tim moved over to her and crouched down. Her head snapped to one side, her body straining to reach the sweet meat of the living.

"I'm sorry," Tim spoke to her, holding back the tears that wanted to fall. He felt sick from the drink, but vomited because of the guilt.

The zombie snapped noisily at him. Her perfect white teeth crashed together with a loud snap. Tim clutched the knife. Time had run short on him. The secondary line of the dead moved faster than the bound couple and was almost upon him.

"I had to," Tim whispered again before he stabbed the body through the head. The bone was just as softened as that of the creature he had killed with the mirror shard. The zombie fell still, with her eyes open. They stared at Tim, no longer pleading, but with an untamable anger.

Rising, Tim turned and moved quickly down the street, putting as much distance between himself and the pursuing group as he could. He followed the main road and kept his head down. The silence was horrendous. The long line of abandoned cars, so neatly in line, waiting for the lights of forever to change once more and allow the living to continue their journey unimpeded. He passed a handful of zombies, but no survivors. One house he came to had smoke rising from the chimney and a crowd of six hungry zombies pounding at the walls. Tim didn't slow down; there was no saving them. He could not beat them all, so told himself he would not try.

The continuous drone the zombies made alerted Tim to their presence and gave him time to seek shelter from the approaching crowd. A good thing, too, for when they passed, he estimated their numbers to be close to fifty. They moved in a group but showed no visible signs of attachment to one another. Tim hid in the garden of a house under whose shadow he had retreated. He sat against the gate, his feet drawn up to his chest, eyes closed. He waited until the sound of their shuffles began to diminish. Once he was sure they had passed, he rose and looked for a way into the house. The back door was open, so he went inside. This house, unlike the previous one, was tidy to a degree. The shelves in the living room and dining room—two separate areas in this abode—stood filled with knick-knacks - clocks and figurines. He moved quickly, eager to ensure that he was alone. He didn't even flinch when he found the bodies in the living room. It was a fact which sickened him more than anything else he had seen until that point. The elderly couple had killed themselves; there was no question about that. They had slit their wrists. Tim looked at them and saw his wife. He heard her, felt her hot breath on his neck. He remembered the touch of her fingers as they traced their way over his body as they lay in bed. He recalled the painful pinch of her strong arms as she tried to eat his face. The hole in her neck glistened in his memory of her as if encrusted with tiny jewels; romanticized to avoid the painful truth.

"Help me," she whispered in his ear. That whisper was so real he had to turn around. They all stood there: his wife, the people he had run down, and the faceless bodies of the family whose house he had walked past.

"Leave me alone," he called, as he swiped at the air. The figures stared at him but made no sound. "You're not real!" he shouted. "There wasn't time! I couldn't save you! They would have killed me too, and I'm not ready to die!" He felt the tears begin to fall. Of course, his wife's face held his gaze with the look of sadness in her eyes. It was that sadness that cut him to the bone because he knew that was not who she was…not any more. She was a machine; her mind set on one thing— death. Hunger had consumed her, and unless someone put a bullet in her head, she would continue for…who knew how long those things could live for? Tim broke down. He collapsed to his knees. He had condemned thirteen people to death. While he may not have been able to save any of them, he had not even tried. It broke his heart, grabbed his spirit, and choked him until his heart and lungs burned. He didn't realize that he had been holding his breath until he began to grow woozy from the oxygen deprivation.

He looked around, eyes blurred and burned by tears. He was alone save for the dead lovers.

Tim found two bottles of expensive liquor in the dresser and promptly opened them both. He started drinking them with gusto and carried on until he no longer recognized the world he lived in. He did not forget about the dead that wandered the earth, it was merely that he no longer cared. He drank, stared at the elderly couple, then drank some more. What began as warmth in his belly soon consumed him. It swallowed the hangover that had started to settle inside his skull and buried it deep back inside. Fire spread through his entire body until he was an inferno. His skin tingled and burned to the touch. The feel of the carpet against his skin, his clothes, excited him and took his befuddled delight even higher. With one bottle finished and the second half empty, all concepts of time and space lost to him, Tim rose.

He staggered to the door, falling into the lap of the now decomposing corpses. The days had ticked past that much Tim was certain of. For it was raining when he threw the door to the property open and bellowed into the street.

"Fuckers!" He roared, before throwing up in the bushes. He replenished the lost fluid with a double helping of liquor from the second bottle, and then wandered into the garden.

The dead stirred, although their numbers were significantly depleted since his arrival.

"Come on," Tim slurred his words and staggered into the street. A zombie approached him. Its lower jaw was missing. The tongue dangled from the hole that had been its mouth like a flaccid penis. Tim saw several of them, and launched the bottle he held at the central figure of the bunch. He hit the creature and sent it to the floor. Not that it bought him any time. Others were upon him. Three came from behind, while several appeared to flank him. One even emerged from the garden of the house he had left.

Tim collapsed to his knees, his arms out to one side in surrender.

"Mary!" he screamed as he closed his eyes and waited for the end…

# CHAPTER 15 – HOLDING ONTO HOPE

"I was ready to die," Tim told them. During the telling of his tale, the shake in his limbs had lessened, and his speech had lost the slur it had held when he made his first introduction to the group. "I mean, we do what we have to do to survive, right? Well, I'm done surviving." Emotion poured from his mouth in a torrent. He was powerless to stop it.

"You would become one of them? A monster? I don't get it. Why not…" Leon began but stopped himself short of suggesting suicide as a viable option. He looked over at Jessica who lowered her gaze the instant their eyes met.

"No, my wife is one of them. When I saw that old couple sitting together, I knew. I should never have left; I should have let her kill me." There was an eerie finality to Tim's words. They created a sense of hopelessness. Nothing they could say or do would change his mind.

"Don't think like that, Tim. She isn't your wife anymore," Jessica began. She spoke from behind Paul, for there was still something dark about Tim that she didn't trust.

"What would you know about it? You took the easy way out too. You don't have the right to sit there and condemn my decisions," Tim spat.

Paul interrupted. "Hey, let's keep it calm okay? There's no need for things to get ugly. We're just talking here." He felt Jessica stiffen beside him, ready for a fight.

"It's so easy for you all, isn't it? To sit here, above the world, safe and sound. Looking back, it is always different. We romanticize the bits we want to remember, twist them into something less to make ourselves feel better about our actions, or in this case, to allow ourselves the freedom to say that we survived; to talk about hope. Bollocks to it. I won't change my view." Tim poked at the air as he spoke, yet his fiery gaze never left Paul.

Paul shifted in his seat and set down his pen. The story was over; there was no need to note the rest. He took a sip of the coffee Jessica had given him when she returned from the galley and waited before he answered. A fight was not what he needed. It was not what any of them needed.

"I'm not asking you to change your view, Tim. You sat to talk with me. Sometimes voicing our stories is as all we can do." He realized that it sounded rather bleak, but he hoped that the others would understand his tactful approach.

Leon spoke up. "He's right. Talking won't bring back my wife—nothing will. Landing at the airport, wherever the hell it is they are taking us, won't magically reassemble our lives. Everything has changed, Tim—everything. Talking is all we have left. It will unite us; bring us closer together. I mean, like it or not, we survived, and I dare say once we land we will be kept together for a while until our ultimate destination has been decided." Leon showed Paul that he understood precisely what he was trying to do with the emotional man.

"Then you are all fucking fools. I was ready to fucking die, to be with my wife, and those army assholes come riding in to grab me and piss me off again! I didn't ask to be rescued." The tears had started to form in Tim's eyes. "Where were they when the people I hit with the car needed help? They begged to be fucking saved, but nobody came!" he started to yell.

"You were there. You didn't help," Robert added. He spoke without thinking, with the quick-footed, narrow sighted enthusiasm of youth.

"Go fuck yourself, kid. If I wanted the advice of a child, it wouldn't be you I would turn to," Tim spat and slammed both fists into his thighs.

"There is no need for that now, Tim. We've all been through hell. We've all lost people. Turning on each other serves no purpose." Paul's words fell still as an image flashed before his eyes. It was his wife. She screamed and begged for help as the zombies tore her from his grasp. His children were asleep. They never got the chance to say goodbye to their mother. She turned quickly and came at Paul like a heat-seeking missile. He wondered if they were somehow drawn to their own family more than to strangers. He had killed her, and it broke his heart. "Now, I am sorry for the loss of your wife, but believe me, becoming one of those things isn't the answer." Paul felt his hand start to shake. The tears he had for so long managed to avoid were slowly rising to the surface.

"So what, I should just carry on as though nothing happened? Forget?" Tim gave an anguished sigh. He leaned back in his chair and stared at the underside of the baggage rack above his head until he closed his eyes and covered his face with his hands.

"We never forget, Tim. We just move on. Things have happened that none of us could have ever foreseen. We have to adapt—to carry on. Live for your wife. She wouldn't want you to become one of those things. She wouldn't even remember you." Paul raised the armrest and slid one seat further over toward Tim who still hid behind his hands. "I know it's tough, but you did the right thing. You said it yourself: The world is now a question of survival of the fittest."

Tim didn't speak but uncovered his face. He turned and looked at Paul, his eyes red with tears. The stench of alcohol that came from his body was strong, but only served to heighten the helpless air that hung about him. He looked at Paul. The two didn't speak, not aloud. Their conversation took place within the eyes; a silent confirmation of deeds done, a shared pain, a common grief.

"You're wife turned, too, didn't she?" Tim spoke after a while.

Tears had formed in Paul's eyes, and when he nodded his head, they rolled down his cheeks. He wiped his eyes and forced them back down. Now was not the time. "Yes, she got bit on the first day it all happened. My kids …they were…" Two more tears fell. "They were sick in bed; both had the flu. When my wife changed, she came for me, and…I did what I had to do," Paul stumbled over his words, unable to speak of the act he committed, however justified it may have been. He swallowed the lump that had formed in his throat and began once more. "I killed her, and believe you me, Tim, that hurts more than I can imagine. Every damned day I think about doing it differently. About leaving her alive, locking her away somewhere, but I can't change it. Any decision we made would be wrong. Normal rules no longer count," he continued, feeling a sudden weight lift from his shoulder and admitting his pain.

"What happened to your kids?" Jessica cut in. It was an act she regretted when she saw the color drain from Paul's face. He looked as though death had brushed him with the dull edge of his scythe, a forewarning of what lay ahead for all of them.

"They…they died. I…" Paul stammered. His hands twitched and buzzed at the memory of holding their heads below the surface of the water. Their weakened struggles, and the image of their still frames bent over the bathtub. He felt scalding tears burn his cheeks as the recalled their peaceful faces tucked up in bed. "I made the right choice," he said in self-reassurance.

Tim stared at them as the aircraft bounced around in another small patch of turbulence. He didn't know what to say. The anger he felt still raged below the surface. He wished he had died, but none of that was their fault. They had all survived, and hearing their tales had only served to make him feel worse about his actions.

"I was a coward. I took the easy way out," he spoke after a silence had descended over the swelling group. "Why did I deserve to be saved?" He looked at them, questioningly.

For a while, nobody spoke. It was a new voice that finally answered the question.

"Everybody deserves the chance to be saved. You will have a role to play in the future.

That's just how it works," a young female spoke. She sat three rows in front of them.

"Do you really believe that?" Tim asked, his need for validation partially met.

The girl turned around. She was young—a few years younger than Jessica—and her light brown hair had been cut brutally short by what seemed to be an unsteady hand with a pair of kitchen scissors. Yet none could deny that the haphazard hairstyle did nothing to detract from her fine featured beauty. Her skin was a delicate cream. The light sprinkling of pale freckles over her nose took even more years from her appearance. Had she introduced herself as being in school still, they may well have believed her. The girl tried to turn around to face them, but in the end stood up from her seat. They soon saw the reason for her difficulty in rotating herself in the cramped seats. Her belly was swollen, and the child that dwelled within it was certainly close to making its entry into the world.

Paul's first thought upon seeing her was about the safety of air travel at such a late stage of pregnancy. He opened his mouth, but Leon cut him off.

"Tracey, you need to rest. Sit down," he spoke in a friendly yet demanding tone.

"Sorry, Leon, but I have been listening to what you all have to say, and just...well, I think it is important that we don't give up hope. Without hope we are no better than those creatures we have run away from." She addressed the group as a whole, looking at each face in turn.

Everybody thought about what she had said. It wasn't until the man she was travelling with, her husband, stood up and started talking that they realized how silent they had all fallen.

"You have said it yourself, these creatures, they are not like in the movies. They retain certain characteristics. I...we," he took Tracey by the hand and gave it a squeeze, "have seen it for ourselves. We have a chance. We have options. Whatever is waiting for us when we land, as long as we can hang onto hope, we can get through anything." He smiled at them.

Paul had already reached for his notepad and pen the moment Tracey first stood. As he turned to a fresh page, the tears in his eyes dried. Their talk of hope struck a chord. He was not an overly religious man, but hope; that was something he liked to believe in. He raised his eyes from the page and looked at them; a happy couple. He thought of their baby, and instead of seeing the possibility of dark times ahead, he saw light. He saw hope, and it made him smile.

# CHAPTER 16 – A LITTLE BUNDLE OF JOY

"If you don't mind me asking, how far along are you?" Paul asked, looking at both Leon and Tracey, for they seemed to know each other.

"I'm thirty-two and a half weeks. Don't worry. I'm not going to burst on you." She flashed a smile—a genuine smile—at Paul. She looked across to Leon also. "Leon took good care of me. He checked me out and said I was fine." Another flash of white teeth, and the entire world seemed to lighten just a little in the presence of such vibrant good cheer.

"She's telling the truth. That one there is as fit as a fiddle," Leon spoke up. "We were stuck in the same holding area. I gave her the basic check-up and monitored her every day. The military even gave me a few basic medical supplies and ran some blood work. I'm not too happy with her flying, but under the circumstances, we didn't really have a choice." Leon looked at Paul as he spoke. "I'm only a paramedic, but I've delivered my fair share of babies." He smiled; an act that was infectious.

"That's good enough for me," Paul answered, finding that without even making any effort, the corners of his mouth had begun to curl upward.

"What are you having?" Jessica asked as the young couple took their seats. Robert rose and allowed them to take his seat, while he moved to sit in the row directly before Paul and Jessica who had rapidly become the central point of the group.

"A boy. A baby boy." Tracey beamed, unable to hide her delight. "A real bundle of joy." She gleamed at the merest mention of her unborn child.

"Aren't you afraid of…?" Jessica began, but stopped the moment the smile began to fade from Tracey's face.

"We try not to think about it. I mean, there were always bad things in the world. This is just one more thing for the list. Besides, we're being rescued—a fresh start. What better place to raise a new life?" Tracy rested her hands on her stomach and gently drummed her fingertips over her body's extended curve.

"Excuse me one second." Jessica rose and walked down the cabin toward the cockpit door. She knocked three times in quick succession. Paul watched while listening to the conversation that had started between Robert and Alan. The door to the cockpit opened, and with a look over her shoulder, Jessica disappeared. The expression that Paul had seen on her face troubled him, but in the low light and with the gentle shake of the cabin a seemingly constant companion, he wrote it off as being nothing. She was still weak from her suicide attempt, after all.

"I must admit, it is refreshing to hear people being so positive. I have to ask…I mean, with you being pregnant, Tracey, your…um, mobility is somewhat reduced?" Paul thought carefully of his words, remembering how easily his wife misinterpreted his words during her pregnancies. He found himself tense, waiting for the explosion, the accusations of insensitivity. None came.

"We survived. The same as everybody else did. But…" She began but stopped herself, her eyes turning down to stare at her lap.

"What?" Paul prompted. His grip on the pen tightened, His fingers began to tingle.

"Well, something strange happened, but it was probably nothing…" Tracey looked at Paul, and he nodded at her.

"Go on, tell me."

# CHAPTER 17 – TRACEY AND ALAN ROBERTS

"Honey, where are the plates?" Tracey called from the kitchen. She had four pans cooking on the stove, and found herself crouched down, as best she could, sorting through the array of large moving boxes that littered the kitchen.

"Um, I think they are in the box marked china and breakables," Alan called back from the living room, where he was also sorting through a selection of boxes marked DVD's / Vinyl.

"I'm looking in that one, but it is filled with bed linen," Tracey called back. "I think I saw some paper plates from the barbeque last summer lying around. Do you mind eating off a paper plate?" she asked as she drifted through the foreign kitchen, opening every cupboard in the place until she found what she was looking for.

"Fine by me," Alan called as he slipped the last few DVDs from the box onto the shelf.

They had been moving all week, slowly bringing stuff across from the small flat they had lived in. The new furniture they had bought arrived first. Due to Tracey's pregnancy, they decided to take it slow. It was to be their first night in the new house. The move had gone smoothly—too smoothly—Alan had been saying. No arguments. Not that they ever really argued. There were no lost or badly damaged items save for a cup that Alan broke when packing.

"It feels like we should be doing this differently. You know, making a bigger deal out of it," Tracey said as she twisted the pasta strands around her fork.

"Yeah, but we can have some people round for dinner next week or something. Give us time to settle in and get everything settled. It will give this flu that's going around the chance to pass through also." Alan slurped a long, sauce-covered strand into his mouth. It flicked and whipped like a snake's tail as if it was resisting its fate.

"Yeah, I just hope we don't get it. It sounds bad. My aunt came down with it two days ago, and they took her into the hospital." Tracey laid her fork on her plate and pushed it into the center of the table. "I'm stuffed. Besides, I bought a chocolate lava cake for us." She smiled.

"You do realize the contradiction there, right?" Alan laughed playfully at his wife.

"Hey, chocolate doesn't count! There is always room for chocolate!" Tracey joined his laughter, and the sound of it filled the house which had been empty for some time before they purchased it. Everything about the move, the moment, even the timing, felt right.

They had drawn several funny looks, moving so late in the pregnancy. Both argued it was easier than moving with a newborn baby, and the flat they had lived in was just too small.

After their meal, with the dishes left for the morning, the couple headed up the stairs to bed. They were exhausted, but the moment they slipped between the sheets and their warm flesh connected, passions grew, and feelings stirred. They melted into one another and away from the world around them. Engulfed by their passion, they made love and fell asleep in one another's arms.

The cool air of early morning woke them, and as was so often their way, they made love again. The cries of their ecstasy mirrored the agony felt in the house beside them, where the neighbor they had yet to meet had been ripped apart from the belly up by her young child.

With his mother eaten, her hollowed out carcass strewn on the bed, the child headed out into the world in search of fresh meat, its hunger uncontrollable. He could smell the lovers from outside of the property, as could the others that stumbled into the streets, their stiff, clumsy frames coated with fresh gore.

"I'm in the mood for breakfast," Tracey spoke once her breathing had returned to normal. "Pancakes." She smiled.

"I thought those sort of cravings were only at the start of pregnancy." Alan smiled at her. Tracey had spent a large portion of her childhood in the United States, and pancakes for breakfast were one of the few things she still insisted upon from time to time.

"You stay here. I'll make them. You always make them too thin." Tracey stuck her tongue out in jest as she rose. Her naked body shivered in the cool room.

Alan threw out a wolf whistle as she got dressed, which received him another smile and cheeky tongue flash.

Tracey headed downstairs, allowing herself a moment to enjoy the large house; the space from wall to wall and floor to ceiling. Everything felt open and wonderful. She loved her kitchen, and busied herself with making breakfast and washing up the pans from the night before.

Her mind was wandering the avenues of its own existence, following a merry path through fields of happy memories, when a knock at the door pulled Tracy back to reality. It was not so much a knock, as a crash. Tracey jumped, and gave a scream when she saw the dirty child's face by the door. Being a Primary school teacher, Tracey was no stranger to seeing children with cuts and bruises, so even with the quantity of blood that was on the child, she remained calm.

Above her, she heard Alan call out. Obviously, he too had heard the crash against the door.

"It's fine, honey. It's a kid, but I think he's hurt," she called out as she moved toward the door, simultaneously thinking about where she had packed the first aid kit.

"Tracey…wait…don't open the…" Alan raced down the stairs, his footfalls heavy slaps against the wooden flooring. He sprinted into the kitchen with his sentence half finished, but he was too late. Tracey had opened the door, and the child, whose blood encrusted face had appeared before the door so suddenly, charged. He lunged at Tracy, his jaws snapping. She gave a scream and jumped backward. The child entered the house and gazed at Tracey. It took one look at her and stopped. Its eyes moved up and down her body, then its attention turned away, and his gaze fell upon Alan who was in the background. Tracey fell away from the child's vision, and it went directly for Alan.

The child was across the kitchen before Tracey had time to think about what had happened. Alan, on the other hand, reacted quicker. He had seen the others from the bedroom window. He had seen a man rip the arm off another man only to start eating the dripping, raw flesh straight from the bone. He had watched a group of adults shovel the juicy innards of a fat man into their salivating jowls. Another woman, a young single mother he had been chatting to the day before about baby care products, came running out of her house. He knew it was her from the clothes she wore rather than anything else. She was missing her face, and it had been ripped clean from her skull, leaving nothing but the denuded flesh beneath. She ran a few meters into the street, her screams a sound akin to fingers on a blackboard in the way they made Alan's skin tingle. Her lidless eyes were a bright white against the red backdrop, until she finally fell, landing on her face in the street.

Alan sidestepped the charging child and kicked out at it. The small legs buckled and the kid fell to the floor with a grunt. Scrambling over to his wife, Alan turned around just as the child got back to its feet. It charged again, stumbled left and right as it moved, but never was there any doubt about it making the journey across the room.

"Alan, what's wrong…why did you…why is it?" Tracey screamed.

"You need to stay calm, Tracey. Just don't worry about this," Alan answered as he took a step closer to the child. "Look away, baby," he instructed as the child lunged for him. Alan threw a punch. Something he was not used to doing; certainly not toward a child. His fist connected, and he felt the juvenile jaw pop from of the impact. The kid tumbled to the floor again, and Alan kicked out, forcing him to stay on the floor. With a final stamp on the child's spine, the body fell still. While it still rasped for air, Alan grabbed the back of its shirt and trousers, and heaved the surprisingly heavy body out the door. With the kitchen door locked, he barely had time to turn toward Tracey before the creature was back, clawing at the door like an irate pet.

"Tracey, we need to get upstairs, now," Alan whispered as he took his wife by the hand.

"Why, what's going on?" Tracey cried, her mind overflowing with emotions and images that she could not interpret or place.

"I don't know, but people are all killing one another. Come on! We need to get upstairs. Just don't look at anything, ok?" Alan made her promise, countering his own haste by refusing to move until she promised. "You don't need to see what I have seen. We just need to get upstairs and wait for the police to arrive. They will sort it out." The words he spoke seemed to lose their confidence in transition from mind to mouth.

The couple moved swiftly up into the bedroom. Tracey collapsed onto the bed. Though she couldn't see anything, the agonized screams of terror were impossible to block out. The terror, the pain, it was an orchestrated score of anguish that cut through the walls, through the windows, and pierced the mind without hesitation.

"What's happening?" Tracey cried as a high-pitched cry rang out and cut off soon after into a gargle.

"I...I don't know. People have gone mad," Alan stuttered as he moved away the window, his face ashen.

Tracey rose from the bed, but Alan laid his hands on her shoulder to stop her. "Don't," he spoke, but didn't look at her. Instead, his gaze looked through her, and it gave Tracey the chills.

"Let's put the news on, honey. Maybe it's like those riots in London the other year." Tracey tried to be rational, but the gentle cramp in her stomach—of nausea rather than labor—made it next to impossible.

They sat on the bed together and watched in horror as one by one the channels turned off, and a recorded message that advised everybody to keep inside and to remain calm replaced the live feed.

"I don't understand..." Tracey began as the last channel they had found with a live feed showed a reporter surrounded by a group of people. They were clawing at her. They had ripped her shirt open exposing her breasts to the camera. She screamed and tried to get away, but she couldn't move. The feed died just as one of the people bit down on her left breast and removed a large chunk of flesh above the nipple. She disappeared in a shower of blood and a sea of hungry hands. The same error message then came on screen as all of the other channels, and with it, ended all lines of media communication.

"We just need to sit tight. The police or military will be along soon to sort it all out." Alan slipped an arm around his wife and pulled her close to him.

"What if they don't?" Tracey pushed. "I mean, we don't have any food in the cupboard and nothing to drink. Everything is empty." They had planned to do all of their shopping today and had bought only the essentials for dinner the night before.

"We'll cross that bridge when we get to it," Alan replied. An undertone of doubt shadowed his words.

They spent the day in their room, only venturing as far as the toilet when required. Alan regularly checked the streets, and was horrified to see that some of the bodies he had seen torn apart earlier were now back on their feet and stumbling through the streets. There was even a creature, for it no longer bore resemblance to a human being, crawling along the road, a few shredded strands of flesh dragging behind it where legs had once sprouted. The image chilled Alan to the core.

The night brought with it a series of chilling sounds which appeared to move in waves. Growls and shuffling feet, a crash followed by screams. Then silence; a painful silence, punctuated only on occasion by the sound of wet, smacking mouths greedily shoveling flesh down hungry gullets.

Tracey and Alan lay on their bed, the covers pulled around them. They lay arm in arm, their bodies curled as small as they could make them. Neither dared talk…move…even breathing caused their hearts to flurry.

When the sun rose the next morning, Alan once again chanced a look out into the street. There were several cars parked in different haphazard positions. Suitcases and personal belongings lay strewn in the street. One suitcase in particular still had the owner's arm attached to the handle. The rest of the body was nowhere to be seen. A handful of the dead roamed the street, but not as many as Alan had been expecting. One shuffled toward their house, moving on a meandering path between a series of five cars which seemed to have all tried to leave their drives at the same moment, and succeeding in crashing into each other in various ways as a result.

Alan watched as Tracey's peaceful, slumbered breaths continued in the background. A crowd of birds took flight as the creature drew near, an event that infuriated the woman—Alan could see that it had been a woman—and saw her snatch angrily at the air, growing ever more frustrated with each feathered body that escaped her grasp. Finally she caught one, and while its black wings beat against her face, she forced it against her mouth and bit down with an explosion of blood that ran down her chin. She dropped what remained of the carcass, clearly less than impressed with the taste of crow. Her pale face was a bright red from the bird's blood which had applied itself to her skin in such a fashion that it created an evil smirk on her face.

Behind him, Alan heard Tracey stir. "What's going on? Is it all under control?" she asked in a sleepy voice. She half-hoped that it had been nothing more than a bad dream.

"No, it's not over. However, it looks quiet out there. Most of them seem to have moved on," Alan told her honestly. He heard the rustle of bed covers, and even with her pregnant stomach slowing her down, Tracey was by the window before Alan had the chance to interject.

"I need to see, Alan. If we are going to survive this, then I need to see it," she told him when he turned to move between her and the window.

Reluctantly, Alan stepped to one side. He stood with his eyes closed and waited for what he knew would come. Tracey gave a stifled cry, retched, and then buried her head into Alan's neck where her silent tears burned them both.

"They're zombies, aren't they?" Tracey spoke once her tears no longer stung her eyes. "I was thinking about it last night. What you said, what I heard…there isn't anything else they could be."

Alan didn't answer. There was no need. He simply hugged Tracey tighter and kissed the top of her head.

"We can't stay, Alan. We need to move somewhere else," Tracey said as they sat in the kitchen. The child they had first encountered had gone—crawled away, enticed by the sound of a different meal.

"I don't think we should. You're pregnant. What if you stayed here and I went out…you know…looking for some supplies. It happened quickly, so maybe there is still plenty of stuff around." Alan thought of the local corner shop. It was two streets over and would have everything they could ever need.

"No! I'm not letting you go out there alone, Alan. If something happens and you never come back, I would really be screwed." Her voice was strict and hard. A tone Alan had not heard before, but somewhere deep in the back of his mind he found it to be rather appealing.

"I don't…" Alan began.

"We are safer in numbers. If not you, then me. What if one of those things attacks the house while you are gone?" Tracey interrupted him, and wore an expression on her face that Alan knew well enough to understand that he would not be able to talk her out of it. She was a stubborn woman; at times impossibly so. Her strong will was one of the main things that had attracted him to her.

"Fine, but we will have to be quiet and prepared. If any of those things comes at us, we will have to fight back...to kill them," Alan stressed the final word in a last ditch attempt to convince her to stay home.

"I agree. But we should do it quietly. If we make too much noise then maybe it will attract more of them." Tracey provided a thoughtful answer, which had not been the intended outcome of the conversation.

"There is an axe and some fire tools in the living room. I saw them tucked away in the corner when we were bringing all the boxes in yesterday," Alan told her, accepting defeat before an argument could brew. They didn't argue much, but when they did, Tracey won, so Alan understood there was no point. Not just because of tears either. She always posed a good argument and had debated a lot through school.

"Grab them, but let's try not to kill anybody while getting the groceries, okay?" She smiled at him, and her face lit up. Alan returned the smile and felt the oppressive nature of the room begin to lift. They were in a bad situation, there could be no denying, but they were together, and that was the main thing.

They grabbed the weapons and donned as many layers of clothes as they could force on. The basis of their logic being that the more layers, the more chance they had to surviving should a zombie chomp down on them.

With themselves wrapped up and a promise of no tears, Alan cracked open the front door and peered into the street. It was relatively empty. Alan saw the woman who had eaten the crow wandering in the distance. She had somehow turned around and found herself stuck in the maze of cars. Something held her attention, for her head darted from side to side. Alan hoped it was another bird, or even a cat, rather than another human being.

"Ok, come on. Try to be as quiet as possible," Alan whispered before he opened the door, and they walked out into the street.

The silence was the first thing they both felt. The absence of sound, of life, had become something physical. There was no traffic, no birds chirping—nothing. All background noise was removed. The world was set on mute. Every footstep rang out and echoed through the streets. Both Alan and Tracey found themselves holding their breath until their lungs burned in an attempt to make as little sound as was possible. The row of cars parked along the street gave them enough cover as the three zombies they could see wandered down the road as if using the white stripes that dissected it as a navigation point. It was also a stark realization for them, as under normal circumstances the street would have been empty, with the cars sitting stationary on the motorway heading in to work.

The only break was a space where two cars had collided. From the debris that lay in the street, the impact had been at a higher speed than the larger accident.

They reached it and paused behind a tall van giving them enough cover to stand upright and assess their options.

"Wait here," Alan whispered as he poked his head around the front of the van. They had passed the first couple of zombies, and the ones they saw shuffling back and forth in the distance were far enough away to discount them as a direct threat for a moment.

"If we move quickly, we should be fine. I'll move first  then wave you across once the coast is clear. No arguments," he added when he saw Tracey open her mouth to speak. She closed it again and offered no further resistance.

Alan moved quickly and kept himself as low to the ground as possible. He stopped in the mid-point to regroup. The car that had been the faster moving source of the impact had flipped onto its roof and spun across the tarmac. It ran close to parallel with the road. Alan paused, took a deep breath, and went to move, but couldn't. Something held him in place. The growl that sounded made him gasp. The tug on his leg knocked him off balance, and he fell to the ground. Twisting, he kicked out in an instinctive reaction. The arm that held him broke, for it was stuck between his foot and the small gap in the twisted metal frame that had one been the rear door. The face that peered out at him was only half-visible. The rest was a meaty mess peppered with glass and small shards of metal. The seatbelt still held the creature—another child—in place and saved Alan's life. The broken arm reached limply, the bone jutting through the skin, yet not quick enough to penetrate the surface. Tracey had moved from cover the moment she head Alan's gasp, and had given a scream of her own when she saw what clung to his foot. She had stifled herself as soon as possible, but it was too late. Attention had been garnered. The three zombies they had crept past all turned and headed their way. Alan was on his feet quickly, but the first one was too close for them to safely flee, for it would follow them and lead others to their door.

They stopped, and Alan turned, his axe raised high. Tracey stood by his side and pushed his arm away when he tried to move her to safety.

The zombie drew closer, and Alan began to tremble. The creature stared at him, and then one-step further its gaze was lost. Diverted to Tracey, its dead eyes gave the impression of focus, the head tilted down.

It stared at her swollen belly. The zombie stopped its advance and stared at the baby bump. It gave a growl, a strange semi-muted growl, and raised its arms as if in gesticulation. Alan wasted no time; he raised the axe above his head and swung. His eyes closed at the last moment, and he missed the target. The blade buried itself deep in the zombie's shoulder. It gave a loud roar and spun back to face Alan. The movement caused the weapon to tear free. Alan waited. The zombie took another step, and that was when Alan swung the axe once more. The blade split the skull and formed a crack which ran down the bridge of the nose and into the upper lip. The zombie gave a series of short, sharp jerks and fell to the ground. Alan stared at it with a mixture of emotions and sensations swirling inside his mind and gut. His legs buckled, and he vomited what was left of the meal from the night before over the second-time dead torso.

"Did you see that…it looked at the ba…I mean…it stopped," Tracey stuttered, unsure as to the significance of the event. There was no time for further conversation, however. The two remaining zombies and the group that had been in the distance were all on their way, having heard the screams and the struggle.

"We need to move!" Alan fought for his breath as he scrambled back to his feet, taking Tracey by the hand and pulling her along the street. "Down here," Alan called as they reached an alleyway. He pulled Tracey along, although there was no need. Her survival instinct told her where they needed to go before Alan gave it a voice.

They ran down the alleyway and then darted into the first garden they came to with a gate and fence that offered them a place to hide. They closed the gate and slipped down to the ground, their back against it. Together, with their hands interlocked, they sat and waited.

It didn't take long for the first footsteps to shuffle past the gate. Tracey gave a squeak and Alan pressed his hand over her mouth. His finger to his lips, he bade her be quiet. Tracey nodded, tears filling her eyes.

They remained where they were for fifteen minutes after the footsteps had ceased. It was just long enough for Tracey to calm herself and for Alan to think of a way to tell her that something was watching them from the house's dark interior.

The face that gazed at them from the window was eyeing them with a nervous curiosity, a trepidation that Alan recognized as being dangerous. With no interest in a protracted standoff, Alan made his move. He got to his feet, walked toward the house, his hand open, and out to one side. "Let us in," he asked in a whisper. He knew they heard him, for the figure twitched at the sound of his voice. "Please, my wife is pregnant."

Alan's voice increased a little, and he motioned to Tracey. The figure in the window was unmoved, and after a few moments the old man, for Alan could see him clearer as the inched his way closer to the house, reached out and snapped the blinds closed.

"Come on," Alan grunted under his breath. "We need to keep moving. The shop isn't far away. If we can get inside we will have supplies and a chance to rest." Alan began, pushing the old man out of his mind.

"Who was in there? Why won't they let us in?" Tracey asked, her voice little more than a whisper.

"They're scared." Alan gave her the simple answer as he opened the gate and looked down the alley. The coast was clear. "Come on; let's get moving before they come back." He put his arm around Tracey, and they left the garden. Alan made sure he closed the gate properly before they set off.

The sky was grey and overcast. The cold air still found a way to seep through their multiple layers of clothing and freeze them to the core. It was the steam from a bulk exhalation that alerted them to the group hiding behind the car on the other side of the street. There was something about the way they hid that made Alan feel uneasy. He increased his pace and alertness. It was only when they got level with the car, and the road branched off to the left, that they saw the reason for the group's hiding place.

A crowd of seven zombies stood gathered around the front of the store. A set of brutally dissected remains lay scattered around the pavement, and blood smeared the windows.

"Get back," Alan whispered hurriedly when he saw the group. He and Tracey ducked back around the corner and down beside a parked car. Alan heard the hushed whispers of the group opposite them. He wondered what they were planning and did not have to wait long to see it for himself.

A tin can flew into the air and clattered on the ground by Alan's feet. The clattering noise was like a mortar blast.

"What are you doing?" Alan stood and growled across the road.

"Surviving man, no hard feelings," a man in his early twenties answered. He slammed his hand down on the roof of the car, and one of his unseen friends launched a new attention-seeking missile across the road.

The sound of shattering glass was unmistakable, as too was the sound of approaching zombies.

"What…why did they throw that at us?" Tracey asked as the shards of shattered glass spread around them.

"They want to get to the shop too. They want to use us as bait," Alan told her directly. There was no time for niceties.

"Why would they do that? We are all in this together." Tracey fought back the tears.

"I think things are breaking down faster than expected. They have their own group and want to survive at all costs," Alan answered. There was a tin can and small piece of wood by his feet. He could have risen and thrown it at the group, but something stopped him. It wasn't right to condemn them to death.

"We need to move back, find another way," Alan whispered, but Tracey stood firm. The zombies drew ever closer.

"No. We need to get to that shop, Alan. We have as much right as they do. We can work together. We just need to show them we aren't a threat."

The first zombie shuffled around the corner and was immediately on the same side of the road as Alan and Tracey. Retreat was no longer an option. Alan adjusted his grip on the axe which was covered with semi-congealed brain clumps.

"We'll never be able to take them all, Tracey. Come on, we need to move," Alan implored, but Tracey didn't listen. She stared at the approaching zombie.

It was a woman—or at least had been. Her body was filthy, her skin pale. Dark black rings circled her eyes, and blood stained her face. Her clothes were ripped and torn. Her left shoulder hung at a strange angle to the rest of her body. There was no visible sign of a bite wound or any injury. Tracey thought of the news reports; how people with the flu had started dying. The rest fell into place relatively quickly. Then a mad notion crept into her mind. She didn't have time to discuss it with Alan. She wouldn't have in any case. She knew it was madness...suicidal even. Most importantly, she knew Alan would try to stop her.

Tracey rose to her feet, quickly crossing behind the car and into the middle of the street. She said nothing, but stood still and watched as the zombie's attention snapped her way.

"Hey! Hey you, crazy chick! Get the fuck down! Run away! Those things will kill you," the now panicked voice of the young man that had launched the bottle at them spoke up. He turned and rose into a crouch, only to be pulled back down by his friends.

"Tracey!" Alan shouted, his position forgotten. He sprang to his feet and ran to his wife, but she hushed him with a raised hand and forced him to stand behind her.

The approaching zombie took several steps closer to Tracey and then paused. The others had joined and stopped in the same position a few meters away from Alan and Tracey. They all stared at Tracey's swollen belly. It held them transfixed.

A small, squeaky noise came from behind the car as one of the women in their opposing group tried to stifle their cries. Tracey never broke her gaze on the zombies, but Alan chanced a glance and saw that they had all turned around to stare at the unfolding scene.

The sound of the suppressed cry caught the attention of the group which swiveled like a marching platoon and descended upon the car, leaving Tracey and Alan behind them. The group did not stand a chance once the zombies heard them. In a flurry of kicks and screams, the massacre began. Blood sprayed into their air like the release of a series of hell geysers and rained down onto the car. The sound of ripping flesh and hungry growls filled the street. The agonized cries of the group made Tracey vomit. It was a sound that she found indescribable. Not just for the pain that was expressed in that person's final cry, but because of the simplistic, crisp sound with which the skin tore apart; a fragility that had never occurred to her before that moment.

"Tracey, we need to run, now!" Alan grabbed his wife by the hand and together they sprinted, as best as their respective physiques would allow, to the shop. The door opened as they drew near, and a Pakistani man appeared.

"Hurry," he called to them.

Alan reached the shop half a step ahead of Tracey but stopped, waiting for her to cross the threshold ahead of him.

It was dark in the shop, and Alan soon saw why. The quantity of shed blood, both inside and out, staggered his mind.

"Quick, get away from the door. Please, sit. Sit, here." The owner of the store scurried around in the dim light and came back with an old, beat-up computer chair which he insisted Tracey sit on. She didn't argue.

Alan stood staring at his wife, a mixture of anger and despair sloshed through his mind. "You could have been killed," he spoke after a time, only realizing once he had finished how obvious the statement actually was.

"I remembered the way the boy looked at me, and then the other zombie, the one you killed. They all seemed to stop when they saw I was pregnant. It was the only way...but oh God, those people." Tracey clapped her hands over her mouth as a tremor worked its way through her body. Suddenly the sound of their raw flesh being consumed by the undead echoed in her ears, and there was nothing she could do to silence it.

"They were trying to get us killed. You didn't mean for that to happen." Alan wrapped his arm around his weeping wife and pulled her close to him. As he held her, he looked over at the store owner and mouthed his thanks.

"Those bitches tried to break in, to steal my stuff. They've been watching me for hours now. I won't miss them," he spoke with a second-generation accent.

"Thank you for letting us inside. We appreciate it," Alan answered as Tracey pushed herself away from his embrace and sat under her own power. The tears had subsided, but she knew they would not be the last.

The store was deserted save for the bloody puddles which were all that remained of several customers who had been doing their shopping at the time of the outbreak.

"Where are the bodies?" Tracey asked. Alan hadn't even seen the way she sat staring at the blood. Her face was pale, and it shocked him.

"You need to eat. Please, do you have anything? I don't have any money with me," Alan began, but the shopkeeper waved his hands.

"Please, take anything you need. My shop is closed. Take all you need." He turned away from them and moved to stand by the door. He had a shotgun leaning against the wall where he stood. Alan assumed it was loaded given the open box of shells on the counter top.

Alan had frequented the shop on many occasions and knew his way around the shelves. He quickly grabbed a sandwich for his wife and a Cornish pasty for himself, as well as two bags of crisps, and some bottled water.

"Here, eat this. You'll feel better," he said as he handed the food to Tracey. She took it without comment and began to eat.

Alan opened his own and walked over to the door to stand beside the owner. "How many of them are out there?" he asked, his voice a forced whisper. The group that had attacked the other party had moved on. Their feeding was over, and the momentum had been set on course.

"Three new ones. No idea where they came from. I don't recognize them," the man answered without breaking his watchful gaze.

"It's the flu. People started dying and came back as…well, zombies," Alan explained, unsure if he was talking sense or boring the man with information he already knew.

"The world is ending. They predicted it would." The man wore a pendant around his neck which he clasped in one fist. Every so often, he would close his eyes and mumbled to himself, as if in silent prayer.

Alan stood in silence. The weight of the man's words fell heavy on his ears.

"What's the plan now?" Tracey asked when Alan had rejoined her. She had finished her sandwich and was munching her way through the second bag of crisps. The color had already begun to return to her cheeks.

"First, you are going to rest. Don't forget, you're pregnant. We need to take things slow no matter what is happening out there." Alan looked around, surveying the store. There was a fire exit in the rear right corner, and a large cooler / freezer unit in the center of the rear wall. "We seem to be secure here. As long as we keep quiet, I don't see why we can't just wait it out." Alan continued, "The army or somebody will come along looking for survivors. They will have to," he added, as if in an attempt to convince himself.

"I hope so," Tracey answered, rising from the stool. "That thing is more uncomfortable than standing," she whispered.

As the time began to tick by, the silence in the shop began to grow oppressive. Their host never moved from his post by the door. Not even to shift his weight. He seemed uninterested in their company yet had seemed rather insistent that they stay. Something about it didn't sit right with Alan. He mulled it over repeatedly in his mind, trying to find the cypher that hung before his nose yet somehow eluded him.

He moved away from Tracey and walked back to shopkeeper. "My name's Alan," he offered his hand to the man who refused to acknowledge the offered appendage, but gave his name in response. "Vijay...Vijay Patel."

"Thank you for saving us." Alan tried to get a conversation going with Vijay, while behind him, Tracey stood studying a pool of blood and wondering where the smeared trail led.

Tracey heard the two men and their staccato conversation, but as she stared at the bloody trail that ran through the store, she found that their voices faded into the background. She followed the trail that led off from one a large pool—there were several areas of blood loss throughout the store—but this was by far the largest. The smear ran through the aisle but in the wrong direction to the one Tracey would have expected. They all ran toward the back of the building. Following the smear through the aisle filled with breakfast cereals and hot beverages, Tracey began to shiver. The air seemed to have grown suddenly colder as she approached the rear. *Knock it off Tracey* she chided herself and carried out.

The bloody trail led right to the door of the freezer / chiller unit. The blood that had gathered by the door was not what Tracey would call a pool, but certainly it showed her where the bodies had been dragged and then left. *Maybe they became zombies, and he led them out of the front door,* she reasoned with herself.

While Tracey was following the red scab road through the store, Alan continued to push Vijay into a conversation. The more the man refused, the more certain he became that there was something else afoot.

"Why did you save us? It strikes me as weird. I mean, if you wouldn't help those others…" Alan tried again to dig for the information, and this time, unlike the previous seven times he had tried, Vijay gave a sigh and turned his attention away from the world outside.

"You seemed like nice people," Vijay answered, but Alan could tell the words were false. His accent could not hide the lie.

"Okay, but you couldn't tell. Those others there, they looked decent too. Young kids, alone, scared." Alan pushed, but something resonated in his head like a gong struck in just the correct spot.

"They were trouble." Vijay had grown nervous. He turned his attention back to the window, but was not the same statue-like figure. He struggled to get into any position that he could hold for more than a few second.

It also became clear that he had nothing else to say, so Alan turned around and looked for Tracey. He didn't see her at first, and the panic in his voice when he called for her made Vijay spin around. It was then that the pieces came together for Alan.

"It's my wife isn't it? You saw how those things left her alone because she was pregnant. You just plan on using us to keep yourself safe." Alan stepped back, away from the man, for he had grabbed his shotgun as he turned.

"Where is she?" Vijay asked in an accusatory tone.

"She must have gone to get something else to eat. You know how pregnant women are," Alan answered, his eyes focused on the barrel of the shotgun.

Tracey picked that very moment to both call out to Alan and give a startled cry of alarm, one following the other in a smooth flow of sound.

Alan ran after the voice which had come from the back of the store, closely followed by Vijay.

"Tracey! Tracey where are you?" he called, but before she could answer, he spotted her standing at the rear of the shop against the freezer door. She was trying to open it.

"No, get away from there!" Vijay shouted, his accent heavier than ever. Tracey heard him, but it was too late to stop. She had turned the lock and pushed the handle down past the point of no return.

Alan was a few feet away from his wife, when the door to the freezer burst open, and five bloodied zombies stumbled out of the dark with a rush of frozen air.

Alan jumped to the side the moment he saw the first shadow pushed against the dark doorway. He grabbed Tracey and held her tight. Vijay, however, was not so quick on his feet. The years of working in a small shop had made him somewhat portly. He gave nothing more than an angry howl as the first zombie stumbled into him. A deafening blast rang out as Vijay pulled the trigger on his shotgun. In a shower of innards and blood, a hole appeared in the chest of the lead zombie and managed to injure the next in line. Yet both continued, unaffected. Alan saw Vijay through the hole in the creature's chest, but as the group descended, only his screams told of his presence.

"We need to run! Here, use this door." Alan grabbed his wife and hurried her through the fire exit. As they moved past the row of breads and sandwiches which occupied the rear corner, Alan grabbed an armful of whatever he could carry and followed Tracey out into the world.

They closed the door and stood with their backs against the wall. The alley was empty, but the same could not be said for the streets at either end.

"We should have helped him. He saved us," Tracey stumbled over her words. Everything had happened so fast, her brain and body had yet to catch up.

"He only saved us to save himself. He saw how those things ignore you, I guess because of the baby, and he wanted to use you for his protection," Alan answered. While he did not know it for certain, the actions of the man, and the fact that he had zombies trapped in the store with him, added up and pointed toward but one theory.

Tracey said nothing, and when Alan looked at her, he saw that she was trying hard to hold back the tears which he could clearly see were burning her eyes.

"We just need to keep moving. We will find an empty place and settle down. We can wait it out for a while. We have some food, so we can make it a day or so. I mean, a house would have some food in it, too." Alan gave his wife a kiss and then studied the alley. "We came from this way, and we know that there are several zombies standing around out there. So I guess we should try this way." He pointed to the left. I think that's the road we take to get to our street. If so, we can skip around to the right, follow the road, and try to find something in the older houses around the football stadium." Alan wasn't a sports fan, but even he thought it was interesting to live so close to the local stadium. He knew that the team was in the top league. Whether they were any good or not, he had no clue, but the idea of going to watch the odd game didn't strike him as being anything unbearable.

Tracey understood that they needed to get off the streets. Her back ached, and her ankles had started to swell. She could feel them straining against the side of the trainers she wore.

They emerged from the alleyway onto a deserted road. Once again, all of the cars sat neatly in their spaces. They made quick progress through the once busy street. Tracey only stopped once to rest but got moving quickly thereafter, when she looked through the window of the car she had chosen to lean against, and saw two blood soaked children's seats strapped into the back seat, including a baby carrier. The windows were broken, and the jagged tips stained with dark crimson highlights. A child's stuffed toy, a pudgy faced doll, lay by her feet. It, too, was covered in a scab of dried blood. Tears burned her eyes and throat as she forced them back.

"Why can't we just stay here?" Tracey asked. The street was still empty, and the houses loomed large over them. They were old buildings. Most had four floors with the majority being divided into two-story apartments.

"It's too close to the road. Plus look at all the damage," Alan pointed to the open doors, broken windows, and blood stained brickwork. "Who knows what is waiting inside? I want to get away from the road, a few streets in. If we can find a place that looks untouched, we'll stop there." He stopped as they came to a fork in the road. Opposite them was a small park, and in the center of it, a small children's playground. It was fenced off and gated to allow the youngsters freedom to roam and had acted as a perfect containment area. Seven zombies had somehow been corralled into the area, and the gate was not only locked but blocked shut by the wooden boards of a park bench which had been ripped apart for that very purpose. The metal frame of the bench still sat in its concrete fittings, naked and alone. At the sight of the two figures entering the street, the zombies, who had been docile until that point, became as agitated as a tank of piranhas at feeding time.

"We need to get off the street," Alan called as he ran his eyes over the houses. He didn't want to be that close to the road, but if they could move through a house and into the street that ran behind, then they should be out of the way of any large groups that may happen to come through. He watched *The Walking Dead*. He understood how things worked.

When Tracey gave no answer, Alan spun around, and was surprised to see that the street behind him was empty. "Tracey," he called out, further enraging the locked up crowd. Alan looked in their direction, his heart in his throat, and gave a startled cry when he saw Tracey walking toward them. He ran after her, but she turned around and told him to stop.

"Trust me," she called back. With every sinew in his body set on edge, an electric buzz covering his skin at the thought of his unborn child being in danger, Alan waited. He forced himself to stand still, even to retreat.

Seeing her husband listen to her request, Tracey turned back to the zombies. Their eyes were set on her, but once again, they stared at her stomach, a look of intent in their eyes. Something about it suppressed their hunger—all but one of them.

One, a large, heavyset man with a long beard gelled to a fine point by blood, paid the rounded belly no notice. He snarled, and clawed at the air. It was almost comical to see such a large man, easily close to six-feet-six tall, struggling to overcome a three-foot high fence.

Tracey stood opposite the group, unsure of what her next action was to be. Her initial intention was lost, wiped from her mind by the fear that now held her still. She watched as the group slowly began to regain their aggressive nature. The snarls started, like those of a cornered dog: a gentle warning, followed by a bark and ultimately…a bite. By the time all seven zombies were snapping and swiping at the air, Tracey was back at the house.

"What was that?" Alan asked the moment they had shut the tall front door. They had tried six houses before finding one that was unlocked. A body greeted them the moment they stepped into the living room, the only room that sprung from the small square hallway which led directly onto the staircase. The owners of the house, a husband, wife, and presumably an adult child or lodger, had suspended themselves from the oak beams that were to be found in all of the properties on the road. Their faces were purple; their bodies already starting to bloat.

"Keep moving. I want us to head out the back and find another place out there. We will be hidden from the road but close enough to run for help if it comes through," Alan spoke, whispering in case anything else lurked in the shadows of the house. The curtains were drawn. The final act of a respectable family, hiding the shame of suicide even when convinced that it was their last available option. The electric wheelchair in the corner of the room told Alan a little more about their lives, and ultimately, their decision.

He shuddered when he realized that already, after but a day or two, he was neither fazed by death nor could he feel the loss and grief which hung in the air like smog.

"I can't go on any more, Alan. I need to stop." Tracey held her belly in both hands, cradling it as she planned to cradle the child when it arrived.

Alan looked at his wife and saw how exhausted she was. Her skin was clammy, her face drawn, eyes sunken. It looked as though she had aged a decade or two in the few hours they had been away from their marital home.

"Okay, we can rest up her for a few minutes, but we really need to find a new place to stay before it gets dark." Alan comforted her.

While Tracey rested in the kitchen, having no desire to sit in the living room with the rotting chandeliers, Alan checked the rest of the house. He was gone a long time. Tracey was beginning to get worried, but just before she stood up and went to look for him, Alan returned.

"The house is empty. We're safe for now. So why don't I go and see if I can't rustle up something to eat?" Alan clapped his hands together, his demeanor somewhat changed since his departure.

"Why? I thought you wanted to move somewhere else. What changed?" Tracey asked, skeptical of her husband, who at times could be as stubborn as they come.

"Nothing," Alan answered quickly, turning his back on Tracey so she would not see the fear in his eyes.

"Alan, tell me the truth. I can tell when you are lying." Tracey rose, but sat back down as a cramp seized her lower back rendering her temporarily immobile.

"Fine, we're trapped here. I was up on the top floor. I looked out of the window, and all I saw was them...the zombies. Not a whole city, but hundreds, and they are moving together like a wave. If we move now and run into them, we wouldn't stand a chance." Alan watched the words sink in as Tracey's face went through a number of expressions before settling on one that he guessed to be defiance.

"Fine, we wait here. We're safe and warm. We can wait them out." She rose and hugged Alan tight.

"I hope you're right," Alan whispered.

"How far away are they?" Tracey felt the sudden compulsion to ask. She felt Alan stiffen against her, and knew the answer before he whispered it to her.

"They're here."

The first few zombies moved past the window. The shadows were long, twisted images; misrepresentations of their true form. They soon disappeared, however, replaced by the mass as it swept down the street. Car alarms sounded and startled the herd. A strangely unified growl filled the air as they all turned in search of what made the noise. With their attention diverted, the group's momentum was lost and their progress stalled, leaving the house surrounded.

"If they are here, can't we go out through the back?" Tracey asked, ensuring that she kept her voice to little more than a gentle exhalation.

"I won't risk it," Alan answered.

A scream rang out from outside. It was joined by several others a few moments later. Everything fell silent not long after as the group descended. Their growls and sheer number overrode the sounds of death, and for that, Tracey was grateful.

"I'm going to check the window. Stay here," Alan whispered to his wife. His hands rested on the curve of her stomach, and for one moment he felt the baby push toward his hands. It wasn't a kick. It seemed as if his child was reaching out to him for comfort.

"No! They will see you." Tracey had felt it too, and the tears came in a flood. Much like the zombies, they could not be stopped.

"It's okay, honey. There is a hole in the blinds. I can look through without them ever knowing," Alan whispered as he stepped away, walking backward, waiting for Tracey's approval or continued resistance.

He bumped into the leg of the older man who hung from the ceiling. It made him jump, but somehow he stifled the gasp that leapt into his throat. That was until the corpse began to struggle and snatch at him. Cold, dead hands settled on his head and grabbed at his hair.

Alan could not help but shout. He unlocked his knees and sunk to the ground before jumping out of the way. He ripped several large chunks of hair from his head, and could feel small rivulets of blood flow from the wounds on his scalp. Terror soon overrode the pain, however, for all three figures had come to life. They growled, scratched and kicked at the air, while the rope that cut into their flesh choked their cries to an extent. Alan's gasp had been more than enough to alert the herd that waited outside. They pressed against the house, and the main front window began to creak. They hammered against the door which shook and splintered in its frame. The house began to shake from their frenzied advance.

"What do we do?" Tracey screamed. All need for quiet was long past.

"Run...out the back. That group was smaller. Maybe they haven't gotten into the side street yet.

The pair sped through the house, leaving the three dangling zombies behind them. If felt as though the temperature had dropped even further as they left the house and entered the deep garden. The property was well kept, and they both saw the gate at the far end which would lead them to the street. Unlike their previous two accommodations, it was not an alley that ran behind the house, but another, albeit smaller, road. Houses lined the street in semi-detached pairs. Finding shelter in one of those was their best bet, and it was that incentive which Alan used to power him forward.

They opened the gate as they heard the shattering of glass coming from the house behind them. The herd had found their entry point.

"Go! Stay against the wall. Move left, alright? When I saw them, they were coming from this direction." Alan pointed to the right as if his words needed an explanation.

Tracey merely nodded, and moved in the direction Alan shoved her. The street was far from empty, but the smaller group that Alan had seen was still some way off.

"Move! Move now!" Alan urged as they fled down the street. One of the houses had thick black smoke coming from inside, and the smell of the flames was unmistakable.

"Where are we going?" Tracey screamed as the herd began to close ground.

"We need to put some distance between us all. If they see what house we enter, we are doomed." Alan was by her side and held her hand. A double-sided action, for it allowed him to comfort her while simultaneously forcing her along at a pace quicker than she would have been able to maintain alone. "Lean on me. It's fine. I can take it," he spoke as he felt Tracey begin to struggle.

They reached the end of the street with the gap between them and their pursuers lengthened. The large herd still had, for the most part, their attentions drawn to the house, car alarms, and second group of survivors their presence had spooked out of hiding.

"Here! Down here," Alan called. They turned onto the dissecting road and moved back toward the busy road they had tried so hard to avoid. Moving as quickly as possible, Alan chanced a look over his shoulder at the very same moment three large zombies appeared from behind a white panel van. Their mechanics overalls were stained with grease and blood. One was missing his left arm. The other two had multiple bite wounds to their neck and shoulders. All were missing fingers and had clearly put up a good fight.

One of the men reached out and grabbed Alan with a hand as large as a shovel. The power in the grip made light work of the multiple layers which at that moment only served to limit Alan's mobility.

Tracey screamed, and the three looked at her, but none made a move. Alan gave a cry as hungry mouths closed in on him. Their rancid breath had a meaty stink to it, and it made him gag.

Tracey cried, but her fear held her immobile. She could hear the groups coming up behind them and could do nothing to help Alan. The three zombies engulfed Alan until one by one their heads exploded in a mist of blood and brain globules. The blood splatter painted the side of the van, adding a splash of color to its finish.

More shots rang out, and the sound of an engine—a heavy, powerful engine—made the street shake. Tracey's legs buckled. She fell to the ground hard, landing on her side. She grabbed her belly and hoped that her death would be swift.

The last thing she remembered before everything went black were voices…several voices; frantic shouts…orders, followed by the sensation of being lifted from the ground.

# CHAPTER 18 – SMARTER THAN THE AVERAGE CORPSE

"It turned out that there was an army group following the large herd. They were trying to lead them into an area they had picked out to try to kill them all in one fell swoop. They saw the commotion by the house and followed up," Tracey told the group, her tale almost told.

"If they hadn't taken those shots when they did, I wouldn't have made it. Those things had me good," Alan confirmed. His eyes took on a distant, hazy look as he recalled the events in his mind.

"Well, thank God they managed to save you. That baby is going to need a daddy," Monique spoke, drawing a look from everybody.

"I wish I knew how we are going to handle all of this," Alan said, his response encompassing everything from life and the baby, to the unknown that lay ahead for all of them.

"It sounds like you handled everything just fine," Paul commented. He had been silent until that moment as he hurriedly finished his notes and read the questions he had scribbled in the margin, as was his way.

"Thanks, but I didn't do anything more than the rest of you. Besides, Tracey saved us a few times along the way." Alan gave her a look. They were both young and still had the look of a schoolchild with a crush whenever they looked at one another. It was something that could not fail to touch the soul of anybody lucky enough to witness them together.

"Yes, that is something new to the puzzle," Paul mused. He spoke to himself, or so they all thought, for he appeared engrossed in his own scribblings. "It certainly lends credence to the theory that it was an agent of some kind rather than a natural occurrence." He raised his eyes and looked at the group who sat gathered around him as if he was their minister and they his flock in search of salvation.

"There is something else going on here, though," Alan offered. "I haven't heard all of your stories, but I've read a lot of zombie books and watched a lot of movies, but until two weeks ago I didn't believe zombies existed, either. They shouldn't care about a pregnant woman." Alan stopped talking, hoping that someone could shed some light on the matter.

"The professor I was with told me he believed it to be a biological agent or something like that. He thinks the flu was an attack of some sort. The zombies are a side effect. It explains a lot, like the short half-life of the infection. If you think about it, it makes sense then that people retain parts of their humanity. What if the bite doesn't actually kill them, but mutates them?" Leon mused aloud.

"I could buy that if those things were bitten once and carried on walking. But we saw them get ripped in half, shot, stabbed, you name it. People did it to 'em, all but shove a firecracker up their backside and light it up." Robert took his turn to speak. How could they keep coming if they weren't dead?" he asked Leon directly.

"I don't know. Maybe they are dead, but the infection does something...it keeps them alive, somehow. In their brains." Leon threw it out there, but nobody dared to argue with it, because it was the closest thing they had to an answer, and worst of all, made a modicum of sense.

"So what we are saying is that these things are still alive...on some level." Paul scribbled again without looking down at the paper. He knew instinctively where he was and when to turn to a fresh page.

"Then that means we could cure them," Jessica spoke up with a hopeful tone. "Maybe this could be cured." She pushed, eager to hear more, but unsure as to what she could contribute.

"Well, if we theorize along that line, I would say maybe. Those too badly injured would die, and those that have not sustained enough nutrition would also probably die. Then there is disease. I mean, these people are, let's be honest here, eating raw flesh." Leon paused, a final hypothesis floating in his mind. "If they were still alive, and if they could be cured, then I think the cure would kill them." He sat back and ran his hands over his face, grating his thumb and forefinger against the thick stubble that adorned his face.

"But it would stop it from spreading. We could beat it," Jessica pushed, "if they are alive."

"Oh, they are alive, kid. I'm sure of it," a new and aged voice spoke up, "and I'll tell you one thing. They are evolving... learning." The voice spoke again, but nobody saw where it came from.

"I don't understand," Tracey spoke, and jumped when the man appeared above the seat in front of her.

He had a flock of unruly white hair and a mass of white stubble that covered the lower half of his face like a moss.

"If you put a rat in a maze and electrocute the walls, after a while he will learn. So do those creatures. If you watch them long enough, you will see if for yourself like I did," he continued. "Brian Crawshank." He extended his hand to Tracey who shook it without hesitation.

"How do you know?" Paul asked, finding himself excited by the prospect of another tale. He no longer thought about the book he had planned to write, the tales of the survivors. Writing about the cause of the zombies themselves was far more interesting.

"I know because I saw it with my own eyes. Holed up in my own home the whole time, I saw them change…grow." He nodded his head as he spoke as if his words needed an additional emphasis.

Paul felt his heart rate increase, and anybody who looked at him would have surely noticed the way his eyes lit up. He squeezed his pen and tried hard to keep the smile out of his voice. "Do tell."

# CHAPTER 19 – RATS IN A MAZE

Brian Crawshank addressed them all as he spoke, and they all listened to him. Their bond had grown, and with it, their desire for answers.

They had slowly started to piece things together. The virus was a biological weapon. They had been attacked by terrorists—or so they assumed. The initial flu virus had been the weapon, but it had mutated somehow, or at least it reacted differently to what had been planned, because anybody who died from the flu rose up as a zombie and set everything in motion. One by one they had all told their story, and each time learned something new, either about the zombies or the world around them. When Brian rose and offered his assurances that the zombies were smarter than people took them for, they all snapped to attention. Their desire for knowledge burned inside them with the same lustfulness that the zombies had for flesh.

"You see, everybody thinks those things are brainless. Nothing more than dead husks hell-bent on consuming every living thing they come into contact with." Brian spoke with the flair of a man used to addressing a crowd. "Sure, those things are dead. There is no bringing them back, that's for damned sure. But dumb? Hell no! If you would have seen what I have seen, you would understand that these things aren't dumb. They're smart. It may take them a while… like rats in a freaking maze or something, but they get it." He spoke to the group, and ensured that each one received eye contact from him. It was a small detail but something that struck all of them. Until then, most of the people had looked at the floor or their own hands while talking. Only Leon and Tracey had looked directly at Paul the whole time.

"Would you care to tell us about it?" Paul asked hopefully.

Jessica fidgeted nervously beside him, crossing her legs one way and then the other in search of a comfortable sitting position.

"Are you alright?" Paul asked her. Jessica looked pale, and the bandages around her wrist had started to stain a little. "your wrists are bleeding," he noted.

"No, they are just leaking a little," Leon answered for her. "It's the altitude. "You really should keep your arms elevated a little more, Jessica. Try putting them on the top of the seat in front of you. That should help. If you feel as though you're going to pass out, give me a sign, okay?" Leon had placed his hands in the same position he advised

Jessica to adopt. He only lowered his once she had copied his instruction to the letter.

"I'll be fine," she whispered, her voice a little distant…weaker. Paul had almost forgotten in the buzz of things that she had slit her wrists but a few hours before.

Once Paul was certain that Jessica wasn't going to pass out on them, he redirected his attention to Brian who was staring at Jessica with a strange look in his eyes. There was something behind the gaze, something that troubled Paul, but he wasn't sure what it was. It was as though there was something trapped within him, some second part of the man that wanted to break free. It had forced its way to the surface, and when Brian noticed Paul staring at him, he closed his eyes and shook his head, hiding his face within his hands. When he pulled them away, the look was gone, forced back below the surface.

"As I was saying," Paul continued, unable to shift his gaze from Brian's face. He did his best to adjust the expression he wore as a counter measure. "You say these…things, can learn. I'd very much like to hear about that." He flipped once more to a fresh page in his notebook and began to write in his own form of shorthand.

Brian paused for a second, and for most people, Paul understood that they were searching for the right place to start their tale. With this man, however, Paul got the distinct impression that he was not thinking about where to start, but rather about what bits he should tell and which should be omitted. Paul didn't like it. Something about the man made Paul feel uneasy, but Brian had gotten through the quarantine just like the rest of them. Plenty hadn't, so he was probably just over reacting.

# CHAPTER 20 – BRIAN CRAWSHANK

The creatures that wandered the streets were a strange sight for Brian Crawshank when he woke late one afternoon. After a particularly problematic midnight shift he had marked the start of his week vacation by treating himself to a six-pack of beer and a pizza. He had passed out midway through the sixth beer just as the sun was starting to rise. He was surprised to see that his mobile had no missed calls. The workforce was operating on a skeleton staff after a bad flu outbreak had stripped them down to below regulation numbers. He had pulled three double shifts in a row that week.

A strange growl rang up from the streets. With a dull ache in his head, Brian opened the curtain and winced at the bright grey light that assaulted his eyes, increasing the ache from dull to moderate in a fraction of a second.

The streets were filled with people ambling in all directions. They were covered with blood. Several were limping down the road with broken legs, and in one case, a partially severed leg dragging behind them.

"What the hell?" Brian called out, but his house was empty. His wife was out of town helping her mother move into a nursing home. It was a choice that had been hard on her, but her mother's rapidly failing health and her reluctance to move closer to her only daughter made it a choice of practicality.

A more focused look out of the window showed a car wreck further up the road, but it didn't look like anything major. Certainly not large enough to result in the number of injured out there. An image flashed in Brian's mind. He saw a plane crash; a broken wreck lying in a burned out field. Debris was scattered everywhere, and the survivors and those injured on the ground were walking the streets in the state of shock. *It would explain their pale faces* he thought to himself.

A pregnant woman came into view, stumbling down the road. Her face was covered with blood, and she clutched at her swollen belly as she walked. As she walked through Brian's line of vision, he saw the large knife that jutted from between her shoulder blades. He was on the move and charging down the stairs before he knew what was going on.

He lived in a small semi-suburban area on the outskirts of town. He was on the wrong side of the ring road for it to be considered country, but the properties were large and the streets quiet enough for someone not to guess the actual location on a map. It was a quiet neighborhood. Most of the people had lived there a long time. The woman was foreign to the street, for none of Brian's immediate neighbors were still of child bearing age… at least not naturally.

"Miss…. Hey, Miss, wait, let me help you," Brian called as he sprinted into the street. The woman turned around as everybody seemed to do upon hearing his voice.

The moment Brian saw the woman from close range he knew something was wrong. Her skin was not pale or sickly, but deathly white. Her features were not contorted in pain as he had first thought, but into something else. She reached out for him, growling.

A voice called out to him, but he heard it too late. "Get away from them…"

The woman was upon him; her teeth snapping closed a split second after Brian instinctively pushed her away. The stench that she gave off was another pungent indicator as to her condition. It was the stench of illness…an odor of death.

"Get away…" the same distant voice called.

Brian turned and saw a young man, probably in his mid-twenties, running down the street toward him. He was covered in blood, but there was something fluid about his movements which, in the presence of the disjointed, lumbering bodies that surrounded them, seemed somewhat surreal.

Brian opened his mouth to call out, but the man was grabbed by another figure that appeared from behind a white work van. The younger man fell to the ground. When the new arrival hauled him back onto his feet, Brian's blood ran cold as he saw the blood erupt from the young man's throat. The body dropped to the road in a powerful rainbow of arterial spray. His conqueror stood above the body, chewing on the chunk of meat it had ripped away. On the pavement, the body jerked and twisted as life flooded from the wound. It fell still just before a group of three others arrived, drawn by the scent of the blood. They all fell to their knees, and in a scene that strongly reminded Brian of an Animal Planet documentary of lions lunching on a felled zebra, they began to tear away chunks of clothing and flesh. The man's torso ripped open, and a burst of steam erupted as the warm organs spilled into the cool wintery air, and were shoveled into the hungry mouths of the undead.

Brian felt his world begin to spin. He had forgotten about the woman he had pushed away. She wrapped her arms around him, breaking the trance he had fallen into. The only thing that saved his neck from meeting a similar fate as the younger man was the protruding belly of the woman which kept her from getting a good grip on Brian and meant her salivating mouth could not get close enough to clamp down on anything.

Brian spun around and pushed out, once again acting on instinct. The woman gave a howl and fell to the floor. It was then that Brian saw she was still wearing what appeared to be either a nightdress or a hospital gown.

In any case, as she fell the loosely fitting clothing rode up and exposed her crotch to the world, and what Brian saw would haunt his dreams until the day he died. The woman had fallen with her legs spread, and between the nest of scabby hair, a tiny misshapen head peered through the blood-encrusted lips. Its mouth was a toothless snarl, while its body was forever encapsulated within its mother's cunt.

Brian stumbled backward, his world alternating from light to dark, as if the sun had become a celestial strobe light. Growls echoed around him as every zombie in the street bore down on him. Brian spun around. Only the zombies seemed to have any color of definition. The rest of the world was matte black. A woman drew close to him. Her shoulder was dislocated, and her neck twisted sharply to the left. She had five deep gouges running down the side of her face and neck. The slits opened and closed like gills as she limped toward her prey—toward him. Brian understood that she meant to eat him. He turned to flee, but the gap was closing fast. He sprinted between the zombies who grabbed at him and ripped his clothes. Brian pushed his way through their ranks, and upon breaking through found himself on the wrong side of the group to his house. There was no time for him to regroup, however, for they were closing in on him. Their lumbering gait had lulled Brian into a false belief that they were slow. In reality, their walking speed when blood was in the air reached a speed that bordered on swift.

The pounding in his head thumped in near perfect synchronicity with the slapping of his feet against the damp tarmac as Brian sprinted down Costello Drive. He ran with no purpose, no direction. His mind was a sea of black; his conscious brain working hard to hide the events he had witnessed from his mind.

He had to keep going, to stay away from the group that pursued him. Their numbers had swollen. The undead appeared in doorways and from behind cars. From behind each new obstacle he passed, a new snarling face emerged, each hungry for blood and closing the gap between him and his demise.

Brian lived two miles from the city's main hospital. He knew that his physical condition—even with the heavy head—was more than able to complete the run. So it was there that he aimed himself. The simple logic being used was that something was wrong. People were sick and dying. A hospital seemed like the sensible choice.

By the time Brian reach the junction of Costello Drive and Main Street West, the road that led to and then past the hospital, he had a group of around fifty zombies lumbering after him, including one in what looked to be military attire with a rifle slung over its shoulders. The weapon bounced against the dead man's torso like an oversized necklace.

At the junction Brian emerged onto a busier road. For the first time he could see the extent of the problem. Cars stood abandoned in the road. Bodies littered the street. The echo of emergency service sirens hung in the air like a music score. Slowly his focus returned. He saw people—living people—being pulled down and torn apart by the undead. Tears streamed from his eyes as he ran through a cloud of pain. A family sat trapped in their car while a child lunged from the backseat and removed the passenger's throats with the brutality of a wild animal.

A car sped down the street and ploughed through the group that was chasing Brian. Their bodies fell like Skittles in an alley. Their skin split from the impact and peppered the air with thick, semi-congealed blood globules. Bodies and assorted loose parts rained down with wet smacks as Brian pushed himself onward. The car, having pushed through the crowd, sped around the corner and out of view. It, too, was headed in the direction of the hospital.

Half a mile further up the road, a few hundred meters before the hospital driveway began, Brian came across the car. Its front end had been crumpled, the roof flattened. He found the radiator first, and was shocked to see the shift in structure of the vehicle. The driver lay on the hood, having been thrown through the window upon impact. His shirt had been torn, and the glass had raked deep gouges into his flesh. The rear of his skull was also missing, exposing what remained of the man's brain. In the passenger seat, and doubtlessly the cause of the crash, sat a young woman whose face was the very picture of pestilence: gaunt and pasty, with a decidedly green hue. Her eyes had sunken into deep pits while her body emitted a stench that was overpowering. Part of the meaty aroma came from her sizzling lap as it roasted beneath the hot motor that had landed there. Had it not been for the way she still snarled and growled at Brian, her arms reaching for him, oblivious to the way the flesh on her legs bubbled and melted beneath the engine, he would have felt sorry for her at having met such a grizzly end. Ultimately, all he felt was relief; relief that she was pinned down and that her seatbelt was also still intact to hold her in place. He slammed the door of the car and ran onward toward the hospital, his heart sinking further every second as more and more of the undead appeared around him. They came across the grass fields that stood before the famous old building and through the wooded thicket that acted as the right side boundary of the grounds. On the other side was the old college building which was now used exclusively by medical students. The zombies came in droves and forced Brian to abandon his plans to find shelter in the hospital. Instead, he turned around and headed back toward the residential area.

The zombie pack that had been chasing him had dispersed. The litter of emptied out corpses, their freshly opened torso's still steaming, told of the distraction that had ultimately saved him.

The houses that ran along the main street were old but sturdy. Many of them were abandoned, their doors left open, the occupants scattered to the wind. It was one of these empty looking houses that Brian fled to. He slammed the front door closed and collapsed to the floor. His legs became jelly, and his lungs burned. He took in deep gulps of air, closing his eyes as a series of tremors shook his body.

There was no time to relax, however, as his undead groupies collided with the door and sent Brian spilling into the hallway. The door splintered from the frame, and the dead spilled into the house.

"Come on, give me a break!" Brian cried as they crashed to the floor. The bottleneck created by the narrow door opening gave him the second lucky break of the afternoon. He turned and ran through the house, into the kitchen, and into the garden. Being terraced houses, it was easy for Brian to jump over the fence and the three that followed until he landed in an overgrown garden filled with weeds and all manner of oversized vegetation. The For Sale board that had been attached to the rear wall of the property told Brian all he needed to know. He sprinted through the garden, moving so fast that he collided with the rear door of the property. To his relief it was unlocked. Brian slipped inside, pulled the door closed, and sunk into the darkness.

All of the curtains in the property had been not just closed, but pinned together, cutting off all light from the outside world.

The air in the house was stale. It had been empty for some time. A thick layer of dust covered everything. It tickled Brian's throat and irritated his eyes. He fought against the desire to sneeze. He did not want to attract any of those creatures to him.

Moving slowly, he crept through the dark house and peered through the front window, rubbing a small viewing space for himself on the grimy glass.

The street was no longer teeming with the undead. The ones that Brian did see appeared to be moving, constantly roaming the streets, rather than hunting for anything they couldn't see. Brian breathed a sigh of relief. As his eyes slowly adjusted to the darkness, he saw that the house still contained a few meager furnishings. A small table, two chairs, and a camping bed. It actually looked as though somebody had been living there. Fast food wrappers and beer cans covered the floor. In the kitchen, the debris that Brian found in the sink confirmed his suspicion. The water in the property had been turned off, and there was no light for the bulbs had all been removed.

There was an upstairs portion of the house, but Brian didn't have the energy to go and explore. The stairs were guarded top and bottom by an old baby gate. Brian decided to sit down for a few minutes first and then plan his next move. The camping bed creaked beneath his weight as he sank onto it. He leaned back against the wall and closed his eyes. The sounds of the undead shuffling through the street, the cries of the living as they were discovered and eaten alive, seeped into the house in a macabre lullaby. Brian felt the world around him begin to blur. The edges of reality softened, and the dream world broke through. Before he knew it, Brian was asleep.

He woke with a jolt; one of those inexplicable jolts that jerked him into the conscious world with such speed, that he didn't realize he was awake. The streets had darkened. The shadows lengthened. The flames engulfing a house a few streets away gave the night a surreal, orange glow. A handful of zombies roamed the street, but their numbers seemed to be thinning. In the distance, Brian thought he heard the echo of gunfire.

*We're winning*, Brian thought to himself as he sat back on the bed. The darkness of the house, coupled with the lack of anything to keep him occupied, soon lulled him back into an uneasy sleep. It seemed only seconds before the heavy footsteps of the house's other occupant punctured his doze.

Brian opened his eyes to a new day. Confusion at his unfamiliar surroundings enveloped him until the reality of the previous night broke through. He sprang out of the camping bed, hoping to see that the military had reclaimed the streets and stopped the zombies before the problem grew out of control. Brian thrust the curtains aside ready to greet the day, but froze when he saw the street filled with the undead. Their numbers had increased over night, and they moved through the street in a procession of death, spreading their message to every living soul they found.

It was then that Brian heard the shuffling footsteps coming from the hallway of the house. He jumped. His blood froze in his veins. He felt vulnerable and exposed. He had no means of self-defense, and there was nothing to stop the dead from forcing their way into the house to take him.

Brian eyed the door, waiting for the end to come. After five minutes, nothing had emerged through the door, and his nerves settled. The creature was upstairs. He heard that now in the way the boarding above his head creaked. *Has it been there all along?* Brian thought to himself. He then remembered the stair gates that had been put in place, he presumed by the previous owners, in an attempt to keep their child away from harm. Who knew it would also one day protect a stranger from the hungry gullet of a reanimated corpse.

Brian moved carefully, slowly, into the hallway. Every nerve ending in his body tingled. Every muscle screamed at him to flee. He knew he could not stay there. He needed to find a new place to shelter down—to fortify. Still, something inside him had to see. His presence in the hallway excited the creature on the first floor. It appeared behind the bars, dragging itself on all fours. Its head appeared a few inches above the ground and caused Brian to stagger backward. The zombie could not have been more than six months old. Its body propelled forward with uncoordinated grasps. Not even a crawl. The small blood stained mouth showed it had just two freshly sprouted teeth. The infant gave a growl which reminded Brian of a Jack Russell terrier in the way it sounded much meaner than it appeared.

Unable to help himself, Brian opened the gate and ventured upstairs. The baby was clearly not the one the gate was intended for, but its presence did account for the camping bed and rickety dining table.

The infant began to bang its head against the bars as Brian drew ever closer.

"Easy, kid, I'm not dinner," he spoke to it as he reached the top step. A small arm found its way through the bars; the tiny hands grasping in the air.

With a quick movement, Brian opened the gate and the infant zombie was swept to one side. Stepping over the dazed form, Brian moved onto the landing. Behind him the creature began to turn, but it did not get far. Feeling confident, Brian turned to look at the rest of the property. A scream erupted from him as the mother and father zombies appeared out of the master bedroom a few meters from where he stood. Their movements were not only more forceful, but more successful. The mother was first. She was shirtless, and missing her left breast. Brian didn't need a second look at her decaying tit to understand she had been breastfeeding at the time of the child's death. Her husband had no visible injuries, though he had the same sickly pallor as some of the other zombies Brian had encountered the day before. Whipping around, Brian sprinted down the stairs, remembering to lock the lower gate.

He ran out of the house through the back door, remembering at the last moment the dangers that lay beyond the front door.

Leaping over the fence into the neighboring garden, Brian was greeted by a dog which charged at him with salivating jowls and evil eyes. He didn't spend enough time there to ponder the question as to whether the dog was alive or not.

Jumping the fence once more, Brian found himself on the street, having reached the end terrace property without realizing it. In a lull of activity, the street was next to empty. By the time the air was flavored with his scent, he was out of sight; vanished into the shadows. Brian moved quickly, entering the first decent looking house he could find. His mind was reeling, but he made sure that he moved quietly, locking the front door behind him. He didn't stop to rest until he had searched the entire house and double-checked that all of the doors were locked.

Once assured of his security, Brian moved a heavy dresser unit to block off the door, sealing himself inside. The window was a deep bay and could not be blocked easily. Brian reasoned that if he stayed quiet and remained upstairs as much as possible, he could keep himself hidden well enough until he figured out a way to block the windows and further secure the property.

The first night was the worst. Not long after midnight, gunfire erupted in the neighborhood, wrenching him from sleep. The noise was deafening. While it raged for but a few minutes, the impact lasted for days. The military unit that had initiated the skirmish was overrun by the undead whose bullet-ridden bodies advanced on them with no regard to the assault they came under. The sounds of their screams chilled Brian more than the sound of their weapons. The noise of the attack attracted even more creatures searching for another meal. It only worsened when the freshly risen military troops made their appearance. Three of them still clutched their rifles. As they walked, their decaying fingers would twitch and fire off an occasional shot. One even blew out the back of a passing zombie's head.

It took two full days for the zombie herd to thin out enough for Brian to even consider moving from the top floor of the house. He was weak with hunger and dehydrated but had not been discovered; a fact that encouraged him.

The perishable food had spoiled, but there were tinned vegetables and soups aplenty. While he couldn't bring himself to heat them, the cold food perked him up and improved his spirits.

The boost he got from the food was eliminated, however, when he looked out of the window in the kitchen located at the rear of the property. At some point, he presumed in the period between the first zombie waking up and his arrival, the fence at the rear of the property had been smashed through by a car which sat abandoned in the middle of the small garden.

Zombies wandered through the grass, not in search of him, but rather funneled that way as they tried to find a way around the roadblock which had been the reason for the car to swerve from the road in the first place. A quick count put four zombies in the small back yard. While they did not make any direct moves, they all showed signs of a heightened alertness the moment Brian appeared before the window.

He retreated back into the shadows, his options limited. He was surrounded on all sides, and running had already proven to be a pointless exercise. He was exhausted and wouldn't make it far even if he tried. So he stood and watched them. They stumbled back and forth; some in an endless loop around the car, while others came and went. A few returned, but most were replaced by others. Men, women, even children. There was no difference between them all. They had become one and the same.

Time sped by him unnoticed as he watched them. It was like staring at a fish tank. With his presence removed from the window, the undead paid no attention to the house and once again resumed their pacing.

The close proximity to the house made it a risk, and Brian knew that he could not stay there indefinitely. He raided the cupboards and gathered all of the supplies he could find. He split the pile into the things he would take, and the things he would leave. There was enough food to last him several days—maybe even a week if he was careful. So he allowed himself the luxury of a second large meal before he prepared to leave the house.

As he packed, Brian heard another crashing sound. Running up to the master bedroom, Brian looked out and saw a group of fifteen zombies trying to force their way into a house at the end of the street. A fresh body, the head roughly wrenched from the shoulders lay in the street, while a raggedy looking zombie with wild hair crouched beside it, scooping the fresh contents out of the inverted skull. At that moment Brian understood. He would not be able to stay in one place. He would need to keep mobile, and be prepared. Luck would not keep him alive for long.

With the food packed, Brian added a rack of kitchen knives to the backpack he had found, as well as a cricket bat from one of the upstairs bedrooms. The roads around the house were as empty as could be expected, so once more Brian left a home behind him and scurried out into the night.

He only made it two streets before he needed to find shelter. Jumping into an open garage, he crawled beneath the car parked there. He watched as a group of zombies passed along the street, pausing to sniff the air as they neared the open door.

Brian held his breath and waited. The group moved on. As Brian hauled himself out from beneath the car, he realized that no matter where he went they would always be there. The military could not stop them. It was up to him to survive, and without a place to call home, he would be useless. He needed to find a place out of the way. A property separated from the roads and out of the city. In the few seconds it took him to crawl from under the car his mind conjured up the image of a house in the country, walled off and secure. He saw himself and others. They all stood gathered around him, looking up to him. He was their leader, and they listened to his every word. He was important. He was somebody. A smile stretched across his face as he left the garage and hit the streets at a brisk pace. On the other side of the hospital grounds was the countryside. Fields and farmland for the most part, peppered with houses, barns, and plenty of open space.

It took the better part of two days for Brian to reach the farmhouse, with zombies forcing him to find shelter in three different homes in one day. The very first farmhouse he found seemed perfect right off the bat. It was empty of zombies, but in the kitchen he found the sad remains of two more souls that had opted for suicide. During his trek into the countryside he had seen plenty of suicides; the majority from within the secured walls of the hospital. Doctors and nurses had hung themselves on whatever they could find that projected from the building. Three hung from the flagpole, which raised the question of how three people made it that far in order to hang themselves without wrenching the pole from its fixtures. As Brian watched, the pole bent and tumbled to the ground, and a horde of hungry monsters descended on the meat. Even though it was not the freshest of cuts, the juicy center was still damp enough to satiate their hunger for a few moments.

The hospital had been secured from the inside and had trapped a large majority of the zombies within the walls. As Brain came close to the mesh fence that ran around a section of the perimeter, they charged at him, pushing against the fence with their combined weight. They would escape. It was only a matter of time.

This is what kept Brian walking another day; choosing to head as far away from the hospital as possible.

With a callousness that accompanied the rising of the dead, Brian collected the bodies and moved them into the fields. He would find a shovel and bury them, but first he needed to make sure the perimeter was secure.

The farmhouse and the surrounding fields had three security measures in place. There was a fence that ran past the outer edge of the property. From the looks of the barns behind the house and the lack of any large vehicles, it had been a livestock farm.

Having started to secure the house, Brian ensured that he was alone, and that it would stay that way. He installed a trip wire made from rope. It was hardly sophisticated, but good enough to stop the walking dead. He secured it at waist height on every door. Next he checked the fence that separated the farmhouse and personal land from the business section. The fence was intact and a large gate secured the driveway. During his check of the surrounding fields, Brian found six zombies, all moving alone. Had they been in a group he would have been dead. By the time he had dispatched the fifth body, he had learned that headshots killed them. Anything else just pissed them off. It took the best part of the day to check the outer hedge, with the farm being in the center of five large fields. Four surrounded the property and another lay to the south of the house. A rolling hill hid the field from view. There were several lone zombies in the field, but Brian's first goal was to find any weaknesses in the fence. Where were they coming from? He found the gap in the third field. A gate had been opened, knocked open by a speeding pickup truck. The truck sat in the field, the occupants nowhere to be seen, and its interior was covered with blood. Brian didn't need to look any closer. Closing the gate sapped what little strength he still had. He was about to head back to the house, eager to see if there was a meal that he could rustle up, when a strange, deep groan rang out. Something about the cry drew Brian to it even though the light was fast fading. The air changed and the sound grew as he drew closer to its source. It became heavy, meaty. As Brian crested the hill, an image formulated in his mind of what he expected to see. The reality, however, was far more chilling.

The field below the hill, easily twice the size of the others, was home to the cows. In the near corner was what Brian assumed to be the milking shed.

There looked to be around one hundred and fifty cows in the field, each with a distinct black and red color with gaping holes in their flanks. The field was also crawling with zombies. It was the mixture of their hungry growls and the pain filled cry of the dying cattle that created the wail on the wind.

Offal littered the ground. Thick strands of bovine intestine spilled from the opened carcasses like the arms of Cthulhu. Brian had no concept of how long he stood watching the feast, but before he realized it the sun was setting behind him, and the downed cattle at the end of the field had fallen victim to the encroaching eve.

Brian hurried back to the farmhouse. A check of the house told him it was clear. He closed the doors and settled down to another bowl of hot soup, courtesy of a wood burning stove and a healthy stockpile of fuel piled beside it. There was also an assortment of crackers and biscuits. It was the best meal Brian had eaten in days.

That night he dreamed of his wife. It wasn't a happy dream. They never were. They had argued all the time and rarely shared even a meal together. Her visit to her mother was a journey taken all too eagerly, and a break that they both welcomed. Yet when Brian wrenched awake, upright in his bed, sweat coating his body in a chilling blanket, the tears in his eyes were real.

The silence of the countryside somehow seemed to amplify the growls of the zombies. The cows had fallen silent, but their conquerors remained. They were all trapped inside the field, unable to master the fence that held them captive. Brian lay in the soft double bed of the master bedroom and waited for the sun to rise. He was lost in his fantasy again; his empire built around him, a harem filled with women grateful to him, their rescuer.

With the rising of the sun, Brian got to work. Having worked in construction most of his life—until the recession had cost him his career and relegated him to a factory position—he was more than capable of doing what was necessary to fortify his new refuge. He knew that the women would not come to him without proof of their security, so after a hearty breakfast of semi stale bread and jam, he got to work digging a trench that ran along the field where the zombies were corralled. The cattle had been further stripped of their hides, though it appeared that their juicy centers were the main ingredient to a zombie meal. The trench did not need to be very deep nor wide. By the time the sun had moved above his head, Brian had dug the basic trench from one corner of the field to the gate which rested at just past the central point. It was here that he came to the iron grate that stopped the cattle escaping should the gate be opened by some force or another. His work had attracted the attention of the zombies who lined the fence and grabbed at the man whose musky aroma overrode their senses.

The fence held their weight, but the wood strained and groaned in places. After lunch, Brian decided that fortification was in order. Having found rolls of barbed wire in one of the large barns behind the house, he quickly got to work attaching it to the fence post. He worked quickly, in random stages to keep himself one step ahead of the undead that followed his every move. Their frenzy grew with every passing minute. While adding the fourth section of coiled razor wire, Brian cut his hand when his footing slipped on the edge of the trench he had dug. The zombies turned in unison at the scent of blood. Brian jumped out of their way and continued working on the opposite end of the fence. The creatures, so tantalized by the smell of fresh blood, began biting down onto the barbed wire, their heads getting stuck within the twisting coil.

By the time the day was done, Brian stood shirtless. His body was caked with dirt and dripping with sweat in spite of the cold wintery air. The trench was dug, and the depth would be completed the following day, while the barbed wire held firm. One of them had torn itself free while two others struggled against the wire, only succeeding to embed themselves further. Brian drove a screwdriver through their heads as he walked back to the house.

After boiling water on the wood stove in two large pans, Brian treated himself to a small bath, and crept into bed. He smiled as the dreams came, for with them came more visions of his future, and more ways to prove his strength. Once he got his art perfected, they would come. They would seek him out.

The days came and went in a blur. Brian cut away every second rung on the iron grate, changing it from a cattle guard to a zombie guard. The invention pleased him. It would be the first place he would bring the ladies when they arrived.

On the third day, as Brian arrived to start embedding the disjointed gridirons into the shallow trench he had dug, sticking them at alternating angles to one another, he noticed that none of the zombies had gotten stuck. It was the first time, and Brian felt disappointed. He tried to get down to business, but something kept gnawing at him, and it would not let up. Brian walked to the fence and stood opposite the zombies, who kept their distance from the wire. The closest was a large man, clearly a farmhand or some other manual laborer. It was a zombie that Brian had seen every day. Many of the others were new. The undead came and went like migrant workers at harvest time through the gap in the fence.

Brian stared at the zombie; its teeth were bared and thick spittle hung from his lips as if it were under some great internal struggle to keep from charging the barbed wire and ripping itself to pieces in an attempt to claim the fresh meat that taunted it.

Brian pulled a Stanley knife from his back pocket and drew the blade across his palm. He smeared the blood across the wire, the whole time staring at the big zombie. Its body shook as it resisted its natural urges. Ultimately, it lost, and descended on the barbed wire, snarling and salivating. It bit into the wire with such ferocity that it severed its tongue lapping up the blood it had been given. Brian executed it and finished planting the spikes, but it was with an uneasy feeling that he headed back to the farmhouse.

As he enjoyed a meal of tinned spaghetti, scrambled eggs, and baked potato, Brian thought back, realizing that the whole incident had lasted only a matter of minutes. It had seemed worse at the time, but the fact that the zombie had resisted its nature had him confused. Besides, how would the women feel safe with him if the zombies didn't stay put? As Brian filled the pipe he found in the living room cabinet, he thought through his options, and came to the only possible conclusion: In the morning, he would set up some additional traps and run a few tests. He needed to know just what their limits were. Then he would go looking for the women.

He slept fitfully that night, waking several times to the sound of screams cutting through the night. Once they were his own.

His fifth day on the farm, Brian woke feeling tired. His joints ached and his head was heavy. He made a coffee and took it outside. He sat in the cold morning air and stuffed the pipe. He took it everywhere with him now. He smoked and drank his coffee while opposite him, the zombie crowd gathered. They glared at him with undead eyes while Brian smiled at them. He looked them over, waiting to see if any more offered resistance. Five were trapped, impaled on the blood-smeared barbed wire, but Brian needed more. Besides, his harem would need entertainment. They could not live in the throes of passion forever. Even Brian accepted that.

With his coffee gone, Brian clenched the pipe between his teeth and crossed the modified cattle grid. He picked up one of the grid sections he had not embedded in the trench. Holding it like a staff, Brian unlocked the gate and jumped back across the grid. Zombies piled through the opening and fell between the gaps of the grid. Their legs snapped as the pressure of bodies behind them increased. Several of them spilled over the pile and fell onto the spikes, sealing off all possible escape. The undead thrashed and growled in spite of their positions. Brian leaned in close, just beyond the reach of their swiping arms. Their hunger controlled them…drove them. It was clear to him now that they held no other interest than flesh.

"We are too dissimilar, you and me," Brian whispered to the zombie closest to him moments before he drove his trusted screwdriver through the thing's forehead.

The zombie fell still. After using the iron pole to finish off the remaining trapped zombies, Brian reached under the chair and pulled out the rabbit carcass he had found in the barn. He tossed it into the field and watched those gathered by the gate turn and descend upon it. The body was devoured in no time flat, but it gave Brian enough time to close the gate.

The trials, as Brian liked to call them, were repeated throughout the day with the same result. The creatures piled onto the spears and charged over the grid without as much as a second thought. After two further days of similar results, Brian decided that it was time to take things to the next level. He had found a journal and started keeping notes. He spent most of his days watching and taunting the zombies in the field. Each creature was carefully noted, for when the women arrived he would handpick the creatures and fight them. He would show them all how much of a man he was. He would prove it to them on the battlefield and in the bedroom.

On the morning of the eighth day, after two days of rain, Brian drew up to his arena in the grounds behind the house. It was a square arena, the size of two boxing rings. He dug a trench and filled it with wooden spikes which he had fashioned himself from the walls of a crumbling shed that stood to the west of the house. He angled the poles so that they all faced the arena, decreasing the surface area and ensuring that things swayed in his favor. He would keep the women inside and coat the wood with blood. He would strike fast, and kill without mercy. Smiling, he dropped the pole and grabbed the notepad from his pocket to scribble down another detail of his master plan. He then buried three knives under the ground, marking each with a series of stones. With his battle lines drawn, Brian knew he needed one final test before he opened his doors to the women. He was sure that the news of his fortified farmhouse had started to spread. Sanctuaries such as the one he had created always generated gossip. Someone would have seen it, he just knew.

Brian stood in the dark outside of the house, listening to the growl of the zombies in the field. He prodded the pipe that fit his mouth so perfectly and shifted his weight from one foot to the other. Above his head, the sky was clear, and the stars shone down upon him. He focused on Orion, the mighty hunter that dominated the sky. Brian stood tall and beat his chest in the moonlight. He let the robe he wore fall from his shoulders and strode into the field. The air refused to touch his naked body as he strode over grass and across the iron grid that lay before the gate to the zombie paddock. A scrawny zombie in a torn football shirt snapped its teeth and lunged at the gate. Brian opened the latch and watched as the creature spilled forward, falling through the grid. Brian slammed the gate closed and grabbed the trapped zombie by the arm. Holding it in a straight arm bar and using the creature's own lunges to move forward, he led it to the ring he had created. Releasing it, he waited. The zombie was one that had been in the field since the beginning, and Brian had watched it watching him.

"You think you can win?" Brian screamed at it as the zombie lunged for him. Brian sidestepped the attack, and the zombie impaled itself one of the spikes. It pierced the thing's chest and drove through its back. The creature groaned. Brian, lost in the euphoria of his victory, decided to leave it where it was, skewered like a rat in a trap, until the morning. He would keep it as a pet until the women arrived. He would honor their arrival with its slaughter.

The next day when Brian woke, he found the zombie standing free in the center of the ring. It paced back and forth, stopping before the spikes each time. For a while Brian stood and watched, noting everything down in the dog-cared notebook. He was still naked, his body covered with zombie blood. He wrote furiously and felt his anger rise accordingly. He finished his coffee and his breakfast and then strode out to the ring. The zombie turned on him the moment he entered the ring. Brian sidestepped again, anticipating the same result, but the zombie stopped its advance short of the spike. It spun, locking Brian in the stare of its cold, heartless, dead eyes. Again the zombie made the first move. Brian sidestepped it, and once again it stopped before impaling itself on the spike.

Annoyed, Brian charged. He ran at the creature, throwing it onto the spikes. He lifted his shoulder and deposited the creature in such a fashion that the wood pierced its abdomen and emerged through the navel. He thrust the football player further and further onto the spike, laughing as he did. Spittle flew from his mouth as he forced the zombie further and further onto the skewer.

"You will fall for my traps! You will not make a fool of me! They are coming, and I will be their god! We will repopulate the earth, me and my women!" Brian unleashed a volley of kicks and punches which rained down on the adolescent zombie who never once stopped snapping at the appendages thrown its way.

Finally, once his torture was complete, Brian grabbed one of the knives from under the ground and crouched besides the zombie. The stench that came from it was repugnant, but as Brian had given up bathing and sleeping, he too smelled like something that had been evicted through the puckered anus of a demon and left to float through the sewers before being deposited in the fresh air that escalated quickly. Brian held the knife and drew the blade across the zombie's throat. It was impaled in such a way that its head was titled backward, and once the skins barrier was broken, gravity did the rest and ripped a large secondary smile onto the creatures face. Thick coagulated blood as black as crude oil fell from the wound with the consistency of milk left out in the sun for too long. Brian watched in amazement as the creature continued to snarl, even when its head was as good as severed from its shoulders. In a final act, he drove the knife through the zombies head, missing the forehead, but instead entering through the eye socket. The result was the same: the zombie was finished.

Standing up again, Brian went inside, dressed himself, grabbed the notebook from the kitchen side where he had left it beside his coffee, and headed back to the arena.

He had lost track of the number of days he had been on the farm. It no longer mattered. Time meant nothing any more. He had all the time in the world.

Brian approached the zombie. It seemed that it had started to decay at an accelerated rate since its second death. The body was coated in a layer of early putrefaction. Brian wrenched the head from the shoulders, and with it clutched in one hand, strode toward the field with the head raised above his own. He screamed as he tossed it into the crowd of gathered zombies.

"You see that? Do you see that? I am the master here, and you are mine!" Brian beat his chest and roared at them until his throat was raw. He took out his notebook, made a new entry, and promptly collapsed into the grass.

When he came to, there were three women standing around him. All three had hazel eyes and matching hair. Two had theirs pulled back into a simple ponytail—his favorite—and the third had hers loose. Behind them, the sky was a cloudless blue, and the sun lit them up like the angels he knew them to be. He reached out and stroked the face of the woman with the loose hair. He ran his hand down the side of her face and groaned with pleasure at how smooth her skin was. His fingertips brushed over her lips, and as his hand moved down her body he opened his mouth to speak.

"Welcome home. I am your savior." His hand reached the woman's chest. Before he could realize what he felt were flash bang grenades strapped to a flak jacket and not the mammary joys he had been fantasizing about, the butt of a rifle separated him from consciousness.

"What a fucking weirdo," one of the soldiers remarked as they hauled the half-naked man to his feet. They motioned to the three armored cars that sat in the field surrounded by the fallen bodies of bullet-ridden zombies. The three male soldiers they were travelling with had unloaded several clips of ammunition into the small herd the moment they entered the paddock. None had seen the crazy man until he the crowd of zombies by the gate had been felled. The women went to check on the survivor while the men dispatched the undead with their bayonets.

# CHAPTER 21 – MAD AS A HATTER

As Brian told his tale, he became more and more agitated. His eyes moved from Jessica to Monique and back again. He spoke not as if he were talking of survival, but with the wild abandon of a man no longer in his right mind.

Paul made the notes nonetheless, figuring that an account of someone who survives the rising of the dead with his sanity in tatters was also a good idea, a counterbalance of sorts; a chapter to prove wrong all the romantics that survived.

'Troubling times will break even the toughest soul' was the comment Paul had made in the margin of his rapidly filling notebook.

"They were angels gathered around me. I rescued them from the jaws of the undead. Killed them all myself, and they loved me for it. We loved each other. You…and you, would both have fitted in fine. We could have had fun, the six of…" Brian's words fell away as his body began to shake and spasm. Thick white spittle flew from his lips as his eyes rolled into the back of his head, and he collapsed to the floor.

The large figure holding the Taser had been listening to the story with as much interest as the others, amazed at the level of insanity that could be reached in a short period of time. Paul had seen him and the weapon he had drawn. Hence his willingness to allow Brian to spin his tale; to play his crazy part in the writing of a new history.

"It's ok folks, he's not dangerous. Just crazy as a loon, that's all," the man spoke as he disconnected the Taser cartridge and holstered the weapon.

"He seemed so normal at the beginning," Monique spoke with a calm voice. All of them were dulled from the harshness of their new reality.

None of them could deny the truth in what she had said. Brian had been a little off when he first stood up, but as he talked he gathered speed and came unwound.

"He had a bad time of it," Paul spoke with a wise head, looking not at the man on the floor but at the picture he had painted. "It could have happened to any of us," he added, looking at each one of them in turn.

"If you knew he was crazy, why did you let him speak?" Robert asked, his youth and naivety shining through the mature head he wore.

"Just because he was crazy, didn't mean he had nothing to contribute. Besides, maybe he is telling the truth. We know jack shit about those creatures, and everybody should be given a chance to explain what they saw. That was the point of starting this in the first place." Paul hadn't noticed that his writing had become some political statement for the future, but when he heard the answer he gave, he understood exactly what it was they were doing…all of them.

"If you knew he was crazy, why is he not restrained?" Tracey called to the man with the gun. He was checking the unconscious Brian, ensuring that nothing serious kept him immobile.

"He was in the same convoy that I was in. When we found him he was passed out in a field. Mad as a hatter he was. But we didn't think he was dangerous…not to us at least." The man stood back up to his full height. He was a large man, in all dimensions.

"You're military then?" Paul asked, his interest piqued.

"No, not exactly. I worked on a military base on the outskirts of the city. We were rescued and met this guy as we travelled back to the airport. His farmhouse was about to be overrun. That clown shoved a handful of metal poles into the ground and cut up a zombie he had skewered around the back of the house. The military guys I was with took out the zombies, while the three female soldiers grabbed him and brought him back. The whole trip back he kept jabbering on about his women, his girls that were waiting for him back at the farmhouse." The man stopped speaking as Brian began to stir on the floor. He gave a groan and rolled onto his back. Around them, the plane pitched forward as it lowered in altitude in preparation for landing.

"So was he lying about it all?" Jessica eyed the man with a suspicious glare that Paul could not escape noticing.

"Someone's lying, that's for sure," the answer was curt and to the point.

"We can't trust a damned word he has said," Leon answered, frustrated at the wasted time.

"He was talking out of his ass. That farmhouse was broken down. He sure as hell wasn't staying inside it, because it was all boarded up. He was half dead from exposure and hadn't slept in weeks." The man hauled Brian to his feet and strapped him into a window seat a few aisles ahead of them. The plane pitched forward even more as they began their final descent.

"Maybe so, but let's be honest. We don't know anything about these things. But if we take what he said as being true, at least in some way, and accept that they can learn or at least become familiar with the same trick after repeat exposure, it would fit with the thinking that this was some biological attack side effect that means not all of the brain is dead. I mean, who ever heard about randy zombies before…not me. I never saw it in any film," Paul reasoned with them all. He felt sorry for Brian.

The man did not strike him as dangerous, and while he could very well be wrong, he trusted his own instinct more than many other people he had met in his life.

"Okay, say it's true. It doesn't really matter anyway. I mean…we're clearly coming in to land. Freedom is a few minutes away, and we can start to rebuild our lives. I don't think we will ever understand what happened," Alan spoke, his voice was weak and cracked as if he were suffering from the tail end of a nasty head cold.

"I don't know about that. Sure, we are almost at the end of this trip, but it is only the beginning of the journey. We've learned a lot, and who knows how many more people are waiting down there for us to talk to," Paul answered, not noticing his use of the group pronoun when referencing their future.

"Us…" Jessica answered, stealing the response from Leon's lips.

Caught off-guard, Paul looked at her and smiled. "Why not? We've been through so much. We could stick together; rebuild. Actually help each other. Maybe we could piece together the rest of the puzzle."

"Why? What would be the point?" the new man asked. Brian was fully secured in his chair and sleeping once again.

"Why not? We survived something horrible. We have a right to know what happened. There might not be many people left to tell us, but we seem to be getting pretty close to it," Paul shot back, feeling the weight of the eyes of the group upon him.

"Right. A terrorist attack, that's it right?" the new man scoffed.

"Do you know something we don't? Working on a military base, but not a soldier…you're clearly an educated man, and armed with a weapon like that I doubt you were a cleaner," Paul prodded, looking for a reaction of some kind.

"You're a sharp bastard." The man paused. He smiled at Paul, showing his comment was not meant as a threat, and then his face cleared of expression. He was caught in a thoughtful dilemma, and it tore him apart to have to choose.

Beside Paul, Jessica shifted in her seat. "I think we are getting ready to land. Everybody should take their seats." She interrupted the conversation, and went to stand.

"You'd like that wouldn't you? Well, maybe you're right…"He looked at Paul, trying to remember his name.

"Paul."

"Maybe you're right, Paul. Maybe I do have a story to tell. But if I do, I want you all to be ready for the consequences." His tone was serious, his eyes burned with a dark focus.

Jessica moved to interrupt him again, and he silenced her with a fiery glare, moving his hand down to the holster of his Taser. It was an act that many did not notice, for they were looking at Paul, waiting for his answer.

"What do you mean?" he asked, fathoming his way around the new intriguing moment of their escape.

"You're getting pretty close. I'm impressed. Really I am. But I know the truth. I was there. I know the what, when, and why of it all." He paused, and the atmosphere in the plane turned heavy, as if someone had sucked the air out of the room. They all gasped, yet nobody dared speak.

"Why did you not say anything before now?" Paul pushed, choosing a simple question so as not to lose the man, but also to buy himself some time to think.

"The same reason I am reluctant to tell you now," he answered.

"And that is…"

"The truth. If you know it, you cannot un-know it. When I say I know the truth, I mean not just about the attacks, but also our destination." He looked at the ground, fearful for the first time that he may turn the group against him.

"But by that measure, you are also heading the same way," Paul continued to find his way.

"Yes, that was also part of the problem. I didn't want to admit it to myself."

"What is your name?" Paul asked, finally turning to the fresh page in his notepad.

"Neil, Neil Mayberry," the man answered.

"I don't think we have time for this, Paul," Jessica pushed once more, but Paul looked her in the eyes, and she saw the look on his face.

"This man knows the truth. Aren't you interested in knowing that? We have time to hear his story." Paul would not budge, and the rest of the group voiced a supporting murmur. Jessica sighed and sat back in the chair. Her face, still pale from the blood loss, Paul reasoned, looked sunken and tired.

"Neil, take a seat, and please, tell us your story."

# CHAPTER 22 – WE ARE ALL DAMNED

Neil Mayberry felt the weight of nine pairs of expectant eyes boring into his soul. His claim to know the truth had roused them. He sat, his heart pounding in his chest. He did know the truth, and he would tell them, but at his tempo. He would not be rushed, for to miss even the smallest of details could end up with him looking like an accomplice rather than a victim.

"Well, Neil, you certainly have our attention," Paul started, his pens clamped between two fingers. He gripped them so hard, both digits had turned white from the pressure they exerted. "If you knew the truth all along, why have you not said anything until now?" Paul asked, spitting his first question out before this interviewee had truly settled. He couldn't help it, he needed to know.

"I don't know. Fear, I guess. Not everybody on this flight is who they appear to be," he stated cryptically.

"Like you, you mean?" Jessica piped up, a tone of spite flashed in her words.

"No, not like me. I am innocent in all of this. There are others on this plane that know the truth; that are behind it all." He stopped talking. His face glistened with a sheen of sweat.

"Then why stand up now?" Jessica continued. She sat rigid in her stool beside Paul and never once broke her gaze upon Neil.

"Well, I've listened to everything you have all said, and I must say, you have gotten very close. The final detail however, that one key bit to the puzzle is something you will never guess…not in time at least." He looked from Paul to Jessica. While the others all listened, it was these two, the ones that had started it all, that received all the true attention.

"Okay, but I still don't understand why you chose now to stand up. If you know the truth and are so afraid of their reactions, what has changed?" Paul asked, shaking his pen several times. It was almost empty…typical.

"Well, I'm on this flight, aren't I? Us, all of us, we're all damned. I haven't got anything left to lose. If I am going to end this day queuing up at the gates of heaven, I want to do it with a clean conscience and untroubled soul."

Paul nodded. "I understand what you mean. Why are we all damned, what is going on?"

"More than you know." There was a clear tone of fear in Neil's voice.

A nervous clamor went around the stuffy inside of the now rapidly descending aircraft. One by one the word of their new predicament had spread, and more eyes than ever turned their attention on the group.

"Then please share it with us, for we are at a loss. You said that we are pretty close, so I take it that it was a biological attack of some kind. We were right about the flu, right? The zombies were unplanned, just like Leon said." Paul pushed a little harder, aware that their time ran short.

Neil looked down at his hands and started to pick at his fingernails. For a while he didn't speak. When he looked up again, his eyes were burned a pale pink by the tears he fought hard not to shed. "Yes." It was a small answer, but it meant so much to them.

"Neil, what did you do for the army? How would a security guard know the truth of something like this? Isn't it classified or something?" Paul could sense that the tale was close to starting.

"Exactly. I may have just been a security guard, but I wasn't sitting behind the front desk checking ID badges and ordering pizza. I joined the military fresh out of school," Neil began. The talk about his life before the outbreak seemed to come at a more natural pace. "I spent seven years in the military before an injury to my leg during a training exercise forced me to retire." He placed the final word in air-quotes.

"Okay, and then you joined a security force?" Leon couldn't help but jump in. Paul didn't mind. He liked Leon.

"No, I was at home, mulling over my options. My wife and I had gotten divorced. After I lost my job I kind of lost myself too. In the seven months it took between me being discharged and taken on again, my life kind of crumbled around me." Neil paused, focusing his mind and to wipe away a tear. "They came to my house late one night—my old sergeant and the commander-in-chief at the base I used to be stationed at. They told me they had a job for me. Gave me the details and left. It was all very secretive, and I never saw them again. I turned up for the meeting and was transferred over to Norwich the very next day." Paul stopped, feeling his background was not sufficiently told.

"There are no army bases in Norwich; not like the ones you are referring to," Robert began, remembering the conversation he had had around the dinner table of his zombie infested frat house.

"Not the kind you are thinking of, but this base…it was underground. Secretive sort of stuff; experiments and the like. The place was manned by more scientists than soldiers. It was underneath some big farmhouse just outside of the city—not the same one Brian here found himself at, but similar." Neil paused, hoping that they would fill in the blanks for themselves. He had made peace with what had happened, but still, saying it out loud was a different matter entirely.

"Are you trying to tell us that this was an accident? That this virus simply escaped or some crap like that?" Robert jumped in again.

"Are you not breaking some non-disclosure order or whatever? Surely you have to sign something like that to work for the government," Jessica interrupted the interruption. Her eyes bored into Neil, who held her gaze and smiled.

"I'm on this flight, aren't I, love?" Neil reiterated. "My fate is sealed. It doesn't matter what I say or do anymore." Neil moved his attention toward Robert and the others. He took a deep breath before speaking. "It wasn't an accident. I wish it had been as simple as that. The truth is a far more disturbing tale than any imagination could weave. But let me tell it right; it is important that you all know the truth."

# CHAPTER 23 — NEIL MAYBERRY

Neil Mayberry arrived, walking up the long flight of stairs, humming a jaunty tune, eagerly anticipating his first cigarette of the day. He had tried to quit on numerous occasions, and had managed it twice…for a month at least, but sooner or later the pressure of his job got to him, and the smokes were the first thing he reached for. Alcohol was banned on the base, one small mercy he was thankful for. Had it been permitted, or even possible to bring such contraband inside the perimeter, he would have happily drunk himself into a coma whenever he was off duty.

The morning was cool. A frost had settled on the fields coating everything with an icy finish. His breath left his body in dense clouds, and as Neil exhaled after a long drag, he closed his eyes and allowed his mind to wander. He had not left the base for more than a week at a time in seven years, and even then he was under close observation. He longed for the day that retirement would come his way; if they ever allowed him to retire, that was. Being the oldest active officer on site (only being surpassed by three of the scientists—one of whom was pushing eighty) the whole retirement process was a great unknown.

Before he had gotten half way through the first of the two cigarettes he allowed himself before a shift, Neil was distracted by a frantic call coming through his radio. With a sigh he picked it up and headed inside, flicking his cigarette into a bucket of rainwater that stood by the door. It made a small hiss of disapproval and then died.

Neil was at the end of the long flight of stairs that led to the underground laboratory when another burst of chatter came through. This time the sound was a scream, and it ended with a burst of gunfire. Neil broke into a run. Only he and the other guards were supposed to be carrying firearms, but the shots that sounded over the radio were not from the automatic rifle they carried. It was a series of single shots, most likely from the pistol that was kept in a locked security box within the laboratory. The scientists were kept separated from the military personnel during work hours; a must, given the materials that they worked with.

Neil arrived at the laboratory to find the long window of his station was covered with blood. A coating so thick that all events on the inside of the lab were hidden from him. He stood and hesitated. They were forbidden to enter the laboratory, but there were always extenuating circumstances. Another shot rang out, and Neil moved. He slammed his first through the protective casing and pulled the lever that powered up the high-powered air filtration unit and ran around to the laboratory's main entrance. The carnage inside the lab was obscured by a pink mist, and it was not until Neil crossed the threshold that he came face to face with the cause.

The scientists worked in three teams of seven, and at a quick count, Neil noted five bodies on the floor, although it was hard to tell who the scientists were. They had been turned inside out and their organs spread around the room.

From the corner of the room, behind the door he had come in from, Neil heard a strange squishing sound. He turned as a blood-covered figure leaped at him. The body collided with a heavy force and knocked Neil from his feet. They collapsed to the floor, tipping over the one remaining table, sending a shower of instruments and beakers tumbling to the floor. Neil recognized his attacker, but only just. Dr. Deborah Jennings, normally a reserved and mild-mannered woman in her mid-forties, was naked and covered in blood. Her grip was like a vice as she crushed Neil's arms. She growled and spat at him, her snapping teeth inching ever closer to his neck. Neil tried to resist, but he was powerless, pinned to the floor by the woman he had often fantasized about being with.

When the gunshot rang out, Neil though he had died, it was so loud, magnified by the stainless steel surroundings. Dr. Jennings's head exploded with a meaty pop, like a water-balloon. A mist of blood, brain, and skull filled the air and added to the already heady aroma of gore. An eyeball landed on the floor besides Neil and stared at him, the hatred still beaming through its unseeing pupil.

Neil looked around for his rifle which he had dropped when he fell. Grabbing it, he turned as Dr. Walter George limped toward him. The doctor was in pain, his right ear was missing, and it looked as if someone had taken a bite out of his neck. When he brought his hand away from the wound, blood spurted in thick jets. Neil saw he had also lost the first three fingers of his right hand.

"Dr. George…what the fuck is going on?" Neil asked, sweeping his eyes around the lab. There was nobody else left alive.

"Move! You need to leave, now—and lock the door behind you," the scientist whispered, his voice hoarse.

"No, don't be stupid. You need help…your hur…" Neil began, but stopped when he saw a change come over the doctor's face. It was a fleeting glimpse, but it looked as though a flash of anger so intense took hold of him that it made his soul scream.

"This was a test. We knew what we were doing. You need to leave now. Everything is chronicled for the following team. They know what they must do." The scientist inched his way closer to Neil, and when he reached out for him, the strength in his grip did not match his weakened condition.

"I don't understand... you did this to yourself?" Neil's head spun, and he felt giddy from the death fumes that surrounded him.

"You don't want to. Now go! I cannot be allowed to leave this place." With a shove, the lead scientist of the base forced Neil out of the door. He entered a code on the keypad and locked the door from the inside. The last thing Neil heard as he was taken through the two cleansing chambers that removed all traces of whatever it was they were working on from his body, was a gunshot. The next time he saw the lab it had been cleaned up, and the incident was never spoken of. Two weeks later, the announcement was made that Dr. George had retired, and his team had transferred to another facility to start working on a new project.

Neil never spoke a word about what he saw. That just wasn't how things worked in the military.

* * *

**Three Years Later...**

Neil stood in the open field that bordered the farm smoking his third morning cigarette. He knew he should stop, or at least try to cut down. Ever since his encounter with Dr. George and his team, smoking was the only thing left in Neil's life that made him feel. He had slowly become numb to the world, to himself. It was not that he was depressed—far from it. He could laugh, cry, perform all of his normal duties, and mean the emotions he displayed. He just didn't feel them anymore.

Dragging the cigarette until the flame lit the filter, Neil released the smoke with a sigh. He flicked the butt to the floor where it fizzed in the thick layer of frost that had settled during the midnight hours.

Turning, he headed back into the abandoned barn, whereupon he lifted up a false crate and exposed the staircase that would lead him back to the labyrinth. That was what he had christened his place of employment. He found it apt, given the meandering corridors and the numerous laboratories that branched off each passageway. The living quarters were just as complicated to access, with keycard operated doors every few hundred meters, and an iris scanner at the final entrance to each lab and living zone. After eleven years in the same location, Neil had forgotten everything else. This was his world, and he loved it.

The facility was abuzz as Neil reached the center. The scientists had been preparing for something. He didn't ask...not anymore. He knew that they worked with diseases and various other aggressive biological agents, but the details were of no interest to him.

"Hey! Hey, Neil, can you give me a hand with this?" a young scientist called out. He had been at the compound since the day he left university, which was coincidentally the same day Neil had joined. The two had become close, but not quite friends. The unspoken knowledge of what went on within the labs stopped them from become anything more than acquaintances.

"Sure. What is it?" Neil turned before he got the answer.

"Just a couple of crates. They need to go to the surface. I can do it, but it would be easier with two of us to lift." Charlie Clogger gave a smile, and his thick glasses slipped down his nose. They were poorly adjusted, so Neil assumed, because they never appeared to remain in place for more than a few moments.

"What the crap do you have in here? It weighs a ton," Neil huffed as he struggled to adjust his grip on the crates. They didn't look strong enough to hold anything that heavy.

"Come on, Neil, you know that I can't tell you something like that. Not yet at least."

The answer was not the one Neil had been expecting. He knew the protocol directed people toward non-disclosure, but something so simple as a couple of crates being taken to the surface; normally it meant throwing away old equipment.

"Fine, man, fine. I'm not going to push." Neil further adjusted his grip, and they resumed their ascent. Charlie was right. They had a trolley that allowed them to climb the stairs with a heavy load, but it was awkward and cumbersome. The old-fashioned approach was always the best. "Why is this junk not going through the services elevator?" Neil asked, unable to stop himself.

"Because it isn't junk. It's a test." The word echoed in Neil's head. He froze and almost dropped his end. In that instant he saw his (almost) friend's face change from a healthy natural color to bleached in an instant.

"Watch out! Jesus Christ! If you drop that stuff in here…we are all fucked." Charlie tried his best to control his anger. "Sorry, I mean… just… be careful," he stuttered.

Once on the surface again, they carried the crates out of the barn and placed them on the ground. None of it felt right to Neil. The crates were being left out in the open but not in the regular pick up location.

He had a bad feeling about everything. It tickled the back of his neck and made his body shudder.

"Thanks, man. I've got it from here. I think you are needed by the main lab," Charlie called, his voice nervous. He was clearly lying.

Neil turned to leave but walked only a few steps before he ducked into the barn. He turned to his right and hid in the shadows. Neil peered through a crack in the warped wooden side and waited.

A chill ran through him as he saw Charlie open both crates and crouch down onto his haunches. He reached into the box and pulled out a large canister. Setting it on the ground, he worked hurriedly to unscrew the cap. Neil wanted to call out, but he knew that whatever it was, it could not be stopped anymore. He had a flashback to Dr. George and his team: The blood, the body parts strewn about the place, and then the cover-up—retirement. The memories returned in a flood.

With trembling hands, Charlie reached inside the canister. It looked as though he were unscrewing a secondary cap. Vapor rose from the container while Charlie's hand was still inside. He jerked backward, screaming as he did.

Neil reacted without thinking and ran over to his friend. The steam continued to escape the canister.

"Charlie, get back," Neil called, unsure as to how the canister would react.

"Neil...what are you...get away from me. Stop, it's too dangerous!" Charlie screamed, the force of his words enough to stop Neil dead in his tracks.

"What do you mean?" Neil asked, holding his breath as soon as he had finished talking. Images of three years ago played in his mind like a flashback sequence in a bad movie.

Charlie didn't answer. He had turned his back and was once again kneeling over the canister. His hand disappeared inside the vapor cloud. It appeared to be translucent, but Neil couldn't see Charlie's arm through it. It was as though the light was refracted around any object that it came into contact with. After a few moments the vapor disappeared, and Charlie withdrew his hand. He collapsed to the floor.

Neil made to move toward him, but his friend shouted, in a much-weakened voice that he needed to stay away. Charlie rose into a seated position. This simple movement seemed to take all of his concentration and effort. His face was pasty; his eyes red and weeping. He looked sick. "Stay back man, get inside," Charlie insisted, his voice growing weaker by the second.

"Call Dr. Templeman. Tell him there is a problem... a leak. Too much escaped. Go, get inside, now!" Charlie's strength was failing him.

Neil was caught, trapped between a feeling of moral obligation to help Charlie, and to listen to him; to get inside and raise the alarm. While he dithered, Charlie pulled out his revolver and raised it to his head with a trembling hand. He fired one shot, but his strength failed at the last second. His hand fell and the bullet ripped through his throat. It entered just above his shoulder and blew a gaping hole on the other side. Blood sprayed from the wound and with a rush of air, Charlie died.

Neil turned and ran into the barn, bounding down the steps at a speed that hovered on the edge of his control. Twice he felt his balance leave him. His legs were moving too fast. He caught himself at the last moment on the handrail, yet he refused to let his pace slow. He needed to report what had happened. He needed to speak with Dr. Templeman. He needed answers.

The alarm was raised, and Neil was pulled into the laboratory where his blood was taken for tests, and not in small quantities either. He was left feeling dizzy and drained. He fell asleep and woke in one of the sleeping quarters. The room was not even his own. All possessions had been removed leaving him with bare walls and a bare bed. A woolen blanket lay folded in the center of the mattress, and a chamber pot had been thrown into the far corner of the room. He was fed at irregular intervals, and all of his demands for answers were met with the same response. "Dr. Templeman will be with you the moment your test results are confirmed."

After four days, nobody had been to see him. While there was no window or way to tell the time, for his watch had been taken along with his recently issued revolver, Neil was certain that he'd had no food for at least twenty-four hours.

Neil lay back down and felt his consciousness begin to fade in and out. He didn't know how long he was unconscious for, but when he woke up again his body was stiff from the strange position in which he landed on the bed. There was no sign of any meal having been delivered, and the hallways had fallen oddly silent. The lights had gone out in the hallway. Only a small naked bulb in his room still glowed, and even that seemed to have lost some of its power.

"Hello?" Neil called. The only answer he received was his own echo and what he believed to be the faint sound of gunfire.

Panic began to set in. Neil understood where they were; how deeply under the ground they were buried. Something had happened, and he had been part of it—a witness. Neil felt his heart begin to race. He had been working in the Labyrinth for eleven years. His own sleeping quarters were not much larger than this room, but suddenly the walls felt much closer, as though they were creeping ever closer to him.

His self-control began to wane. He jumped as a burst of gunfire echoed through the corridor to his room. The burst was quick, and no further sounds followed it, but Neil didn't care. He pounded on the door and called out until his throat was hoarse.

From the other side of the door a strange, deep growling sound called out. Neil stood with a sudden a renewed strength and called out again and again. The growling grew closer, and before long the hammering on the other side overpowered Neil's own clubbed blows. Confused, he stepped away from the door as it began to rattle and then splinter in its frame from the force of the blows. The growls had increased until they were as ferocious as a wild animal. Alarm bells buzzed inside his head as the sound of the cries echoed in the bare room. Neil had heard growling of a similar ferocity once before, when he had been attacked by Dr. Jennings. Shrinking backward, Neil instinctively began to search for something he could use to protect himself. The only thing in the room was the bed. Within a few moments, Neil had wrenched one of the metal legs from the low cost frame, and wielded it like a baseball bat. There was nothing to do but wait.

It didn't take long.

The first creature that burst through the door created a hole with its fist, but was driven wild by the aroma of fresh meat, so it abandoned its approach, and instead forced its head through the gap. Jagged splinters dug into the creatures flesh and ripped deep gouges in the man's face. It didn't seem to realize. Even when the blood that ran from the wounds blinded it, it continued to snarl and snap its jaws like some primitive beast. Neil thought he recognized the man; he was sure of it. There were not that many people working beneath the surface. During his eleven years of service, he had certainly met and built up a basic relationship with people. Yet there was something different about the face—other than the bleeding lacerations—that made it unrecognizable. Inhuman was the word the came to Neil's mind as he watched the man struggle against the door which held him prisoner.

Neil had no idea what had happened, but he was certain that it had something to do with the canister Charlie had opened. Charlie. It was the first time he had thought about him since it had all happened. While Neil lost himself in dangerous reminiscence, the zombie in the door continued to force his way through, splitting the wood further and further. There were clearly others that stood behind the door, but the over-exuberance of the first creature had blocked the passage for the rest.

It bought Neil some time. He knew what he had to do, and his grip on the metal bed leg tightened until a cramp burned in his forearm. Before Neil could take a swing, however, the zombie stopped its struggles. Its eyes widened, and then a split-second later its head exploded, bursting like a water balloon. The stench which emanated from the hollowed out skull was enough to make Neil gag.

Three more shots rang out, and Neil once again found himself bordering on panic. Was this gunman his rescuer or his executioner?

Time froze, and Neil held his breath. He waited, his body trembling with anticipation. The growls had gone. They were all dead. Of that he was certain. The body had disappeared; pulled free from the door. The door rattled in the frame once more, but this time the handle also jiggled up and down.

"Hello, is anybody in there?" a scratched and broken voice whispered. It was barely audible.

Neil held his tongue, caught in a quandary. He needed to get out of the room, and to do that he needed help…friend or foe.

"Hello," the voice called again. It was only when he heard the footsteps begin to shuffle down the corridor that Neil responded.

"I'm trapped. Please, tell me what is going on?" Neil was shocked at how meek his words sounded.

"Neil… Neil, is that you?" the voice called back, a change in the tone revealing the owner.

"Jack! Jesus Christ, man! What is going on? Help get me out of here," Neil called out to Jack Porterfield. He was the lead scientist at the compound. He and Neil had often spent time together talking about various daily activities around the complex. Betting on anything from who will sneeze first during the flu season to what the weather was going to be like on a given date. The wager was usually cigarettes, but on rare occasions, they would up the stakes and use shifts. One year a particularly late end of winter had cost Neil two double shifts; anything to pass the boring off-duty hours.

The door rattled and then, following a solid kick from the other side, flew open, breaking from the hinges it fell into the room. "Neil… they told me you were dead." Jack ran up to him and embraced him in a strong hug; a gesture that had never been part of their previous greetings.

"Jack, what happened? Who told you that? What was wrong with that man…? I mean...I saw Charlie and…it was just like a few years ago…" Neil started to speak, and everything came out in a nonsensical rush. Oddly enough, Jack seemed to understand every word.

"Man, the whole world has gone to shit. Did you see what happened to Charlie? We can't stay here. We need to move. More of them will be coming. The gunshots only attract them." Jack started walking out of the room before he had finished speaking, his initial question also seemingly forgotten.

In the hallway everything was pitch black. Only the emergency lighting shone in the main branches, and even those were low wattage bulbs spaced at intervals that left long stretches of darkness to be navigated.

"Be careful. Those fuckers can be everywhere. Don't let them bite you." Jack spoke as he walked. He never looked back, but had swung the rifle over his shoulder. Instead, he held a large hunting knife. It was the standard issue given to guards. Neil knew it wasn't the right time to ask how he acquired it but understood that it signified something bad.

"What are you talking about?" Neil asked, afraid to hear the answer, but at the same time he knew that he needed to know.

"Zombies! We started the zombie apocalypse, man. Now come on, we need to head back to the main lab." Jack quickened his pace, and Neil did likewise.

"Is that where everybody is, at the lab?" Neil asked, his breathing labored. His condition had deteriorated with a few days of no food or water.

"We *are* everybody, man." Jack's response was cold and delivered just as they entered another patch of darkness.

"What do you mean? Where is everybody?" Neil pushed on, ignoring the pain that had started to dig into his side.

"Dead...or at least, they *were* dead...now they are walking around here, looking for us. They're hungry, and nothing will stop them besides a shot to the head." Jack stopped walking for a moment and turned to look at the man who, while not yet given the official title, was as close to a friend as Neil had. "God help us... what have we done?" With nothing further to add, he turned around again and took off at an even brisker pace. Neil had to run to keep up with him.

By the time they reached the main laboratory, Neil was starkly aware of the fact that they were indeed alone. The presence of a pile of half-rotted corpses piled up in the hallway that brought them to the lab was evidence enough to know the state of their facility.

"What happened?" Neil asked, as he stopped to stare at the bodies. They were all people that he recognized. Their bodies were withered and distorted by death; their features warped and twisted into a hungry grimace. A bullet hole between each pair of eyes showed how they had been finished off.

"There is no time," Jack called back to Neil, and continued his pace which had increased to a jog. Behind him, the lights from the laboratory came on and bathed him in a bright light. "They're coming," Jack whispered, his voice impatient.

"Who's coming? I thought you said we were alone?" Neil made the mistake of asking. Before he received an answer from Jack, the hungry growls of the approaching horde of the undead gave him the only response he needed.

Neil broke into a run and reached the laboratory just as the doors began to close. Jack had no plans to wait for him.

A group of around a dozen zombies appeared out of the darkness, their growling faces covered in dried blood. Three were missing half of their faces, and their heads lolled to one side from the wedge of flesh missing in their necks. Several others were limping or sporting other visible injuries. Two of them had severe wounds in their torsos; gaping, festering wounds that oozed thin pus colored liquid. Jack explained with an eerie nonchalance that they had been the last two to die. They had, along with Jack, been trapped in one of the smaller labs. They had been searching for supplies when a group had surprised them. Jack had escaped, but the other two, Phillip Wilson and Alok Punjesh, had been overwhelmed. They were ripped apart by the group. Had an explosion from somewhere else in the compound not distracted them all, there would have been nothing left of the two men to return.

"I think it is time that you tell me what the hell is going on," said Neil. "No lies; no bullshit. I saw something happen in this very lab a few years ago. Dr. George didn't retire. His team didn't move on to something new. They died. Dr. Jennings killed them, and Dr. George shot her and then himself. I was there. I know. That canister, whatever it was that Charlie let out, that was the same thing, right? It was the same stuff that killed the others." Neil knew he should stop talking and allow the Jack a chance to answer him, but he found his mouth no longer listened to the commands his brain gave.

Jack removed the rifle from his shoulder and placed the hunting knife on the countertop beside the firearm. He had his back to Neil and seemed unconcerned by the pounding of the undead against the glass, the only barrier that separated them all.

"You need to understand, what happened to Jennings and her team was an accident. They were not supposed to die. However, it did give us a glimpse at a problem we had overlooked. We thought we had resolved it. All of our tests had yielded positive results. It is us…humans. We are the cause of the mutation. We start it, and then…once they bite anything, any living creature, the hunger spreads." Jack turned around and looked at Neil. His face was ashen. He looked as though he were about to pass out.

"Did Charlie know what he was getting himself into? Was he under orders to release that stuff?" Neil felt his emotions begin to settle. A blurred image was forming in his mind, but it was too obscure to see clearly. He already understood, however, that he wanted no part of it. Anger became his driving emotion.

"He knew, but it went wrong. It wasn't supposed to react so quickly. It should have had a dispersal time. He was supposed to get away from it." Jack ran his hands through his hair, his eyes wide and bulging.

"What are you fucking talking about?" Neil roared, throwing a beaker against the window where it didn't simply break or shatter, but rather it disintegrated into nothing more than a sandy powder.

The agent reacted quicker in the open air that we had anticipated in the trials," Jack continued, his eyes finally locking on Neil's. "I don't know what happened, but the genetic make-up of it all changed."

"What agent? Jack, give me a straight, no-bollocks answer for crying out loud." Neil's anger had reached a level he didn't know resided within him.

"This is the military, Neil. What do you think I mean?" Jacks words were cold. It was a side Neil had never seen. Off-duty he was a jovial sort of fellow who enjoyed a laugh and the odd drink.

Neil stood for a second, the constant groan and pounding of the zombies breaking his concentration. His weakened state of mind increased his level of confusion. Looking over his shoulder, Neil saw that while blood smeared the glass from the outside, it showed no signs of any damage.

"Don't worry about them. Nothing could get through the glass. We are safe. You need to get your head wrapped around the situation, buddy." Jack tried hard to explain everything to Neil, while at the same time not breaking protocol too directly.

Neil looked at him, and it was as if his head had been dunked in a bucket of ice water after a night of drinking. Everything cleared, his mind settled, and the picture came into a sharp and startling focus.

"It was a weapon. You have been creating a biological weapon. Charlie was supposed to launch it, quietly, without attention, but it went wrong. But why? Who...I mean, who were you attacking. Why create zombies if you can't control them? I don't understand," Neil stuttered. Having served his time in the military, he had been on many exercises and a couple of real life scenarios where a threat was expected. That had taught him all he needed to know about biological warfare.

"The zombies were not our plan. The agent is a fast acting flu that incapacitates anybody it comes into contact with, killing them within two days. That is at the more diluted end of the exposure spectrum. Don't give me that look." Jack stopped his tale to admonish Neil for something he did not know he was doing. "That holier than thou shit."

"You would kill millions; women, children. When did the military get involved in slaughter?" Neil stood his ground.

"You reaction is fair, but let me finish my tale before making your judgment. Although…" Jack paused and lowered his gaze for a moment. "The agent was easy to create. The trick was stopping it from spreading; removing the contagion. It infects whoever it comes into contact with, but has no contagious properties once it has been activated… once it has come into contact with a host. The virus dies within two days. It would be dropped on an area, a military compound for example, and then within 48 hours our military would walk through and stake their claim for victory." Jack smiled a little. While he did not approve the methods, he was a scientist. What he (and the team under his control) had managed to create was something fabulous.

"So what went wrong?" Neil asked, forcing himself to focus on the conversation at hand and not the half-dressed female scientist who stood with breasts pressed against the glass, writhing and rubbing her body over the cold glass as if she could feel the pleasure it caused.

"By suppressing the contagious nature of the disease, we changed something on a molecular lever, and that didn't react well to the death of the host. We should have seen it. But hell, fucking zombies!" Jack shifted his gaze over Neil's shoulder. Neil knew what he was looking at. The woman's rack was incredible, dead or not.

"Then who was the target? North Korea, Iraq…Germany?" Neil felt compelled to ask. Not only did he find it important to know, but it bought more time before they started discussing things like consequences and escape from the underground prison.

"You don't want to know that, man. It isn't important," Jack shied away from the questions.

"Tell me Jack, I need to know everything." Neil took a large step forward. The movement startled Jack and seemed to excite the undead crowd.

"Norwich was the target, man… Norwich." Jack lowered his gaze, and took a deep shuddering breath.

Neil stood in a stunned silence. At first he was certain that he had heard Jack wrong. Yet when he replayed the conversation in his mind, the answer was the same each time, and it was not one that gave much room for misinterpretation.

"You are talking terrorism. You guys are terrorists or something?" Neil automatically reached for the gun he normally had on his hip. He found it was missing, and the memory of its removal coming soon after, but the action itself was enough to scare Jack.

"No, no – not at all. We are employees, Jack. We do as we are told, and we are rewarded very well for our efforts. When we started, we didn't know their plan. We were just told to create the virus. Then each time we presented our findings we were told to tweak it slightly." Jack spoke quickly, eager to state his case. Around them, a handful of new arrivals had formed a second group—half a dozen at most—on the glass wall opposite the main branch of their small underground herd.

"Then why Norwich? Why attack innocent people? Why did you attack a city… wait," Neil tripped over his own words, his thoughts changed with such speed. "Are you telling me that those things are everywhere out there? That Norwich is a city of the dead? How could you?" Neil was not a religious man, but even he believed that there would be eternal consequences for such an act.

"It wasn't supposed to go down like that, Neil. We planned to release a very small test sample; it would be enough to infect two, maybe three people. We didn't want to see its destruction but rather the speed with which it died." There was clear emotion in Jack's voice, his words spoke of hurt and an internal anguish that would never leave.

"Innocent people! That's fucking terrorism. Were they really your orders?" Neil jumped forward, much to the arousal of the hungry crowd, and snatched the rifle from the table. He pointed the muzzle at Jack's chest and let his finger gently brush the trigger.

"Jesus, Neil, put that fucking thing down. No, I mean…Yes, they were our orders, but it isn't terrorism. It is war. We are at war, man, and somebody needed to do something to escalate things." Jack had his hands raised in surrender, and from the look on his face and the aroma that wafted on the recycled air a moment later, he had also urinated.

"What do you mean? We're not at war," Neil began.

"We are always at war. There is always a threat, but you can never make a move. You don't want to be the aggressor…" Jack stopped talking. He knew he had said too much.

"You crazy fucks." Neil took a step away from the man he had known for so many year, as if his mindset was contagious.

"Come on, Neil. You were regular military before you came here. You know how it is." Jack smiled now as the power of the conversation turned in his favor once more.

"Besides, it would not have been as bad as it sounds. We were always working on a vaccine, one that could be administered in the same way. We always had a 'get out clause' if things went sour."

"Always," Neil interrupted, patting his rifle as if to add extra emphasis.

"We are working on something, or at least…we were, until they all turned. Nobody could have predicted zombies, Neil." Jack continued to defend his actions.

"You planned to launch a biological strike on our own people just to blame some foreign country and justify going to war. Surely at some point before fucking zombies you would have questioned the validity of what you are doing." Neil refused to believe that there was any logic in their actions.

"Don't be so naïve," Jack spat, turning away from Neil to stare at the zombies. "Besides, it is too late now."

"Why don't you release the antidote?" Neil wasn't done with his side of the conversation, and was determined to get more answers.

"It was too late. The virus is already dead. It worked exactly as it was supposed to in that respect." Jack walked closer to the main group of zombies; a mixture of soldiers and scientists, and started to gather all manner of vials and containers from the chilled storage unit.

"What are you doing?" Neil asked, shocked at the level headedness of the man and the way he coldly turned his back on the conversation.

"Well, if you kill me now, I'll die and stay dead. If you put the gun down, we are stuck here surrounded by the undead. So until we run out of air and supplies, I intend to keep working on a cure. So you can either put the gun down and help me, or for the love of Christ, put a bullet between my eyes. I really don't care which. It's your choice."

Neil stared at Jack and saw the strain in his face. He followed his orders, and while doing so had forced himself to make peace with the eventual result.

"Fine," Neil placed the rifle back on the countertop. "But tell me one thing. Why? Why did you start this?" He understood how orders worked, but failed to see how common sense had been so easily and convincingly overridden.

"Leverage." The answer shocked him, as did the falter in the voice that spoke it. "We are trapped down here, our families aren't." Jack spoke more with what he didn't say than what he did, and suddenly Neil saw the situation in a different light.

"They blackmailed you…threatened you. Our government…what the…" Neil started, but stopped when a collection of glass beakers were placed in his hands.

"I need you to fill these with Calcium Chloride, Albumin, and Potassium Chloride," Jack interrupted and spoke as though he had not been listening to Neil in the first place.

"I have no idea what they are," Neil stammered.

"It doesn't matter, Neil, I just need you to shut the fuck up," Jack shot back, and gave him a wry smile.

"I understand, but man, this is big news. Our government has effectively held you prisoner and launched a domestic terrorist attack to finance a war. To top it all off, it backfired, and now our country is filled with fucking zombies!" Neil blurted it all out, aware that he was repeating himself. He hoped that by saying it often enough, he would start to understand it or that it would at least stop sounding so absurd.

"Yeah, well, none of that is happening now. I guess you can't help but think maybe this is just some sort of karmic justice." Jack took a few moments to ponder his thought, stroking the thick stubble on his chin as he did so. He then turned and busied himself with his work.

Neil wandered around the lab looking at each zombie in turn. He recognized them all, knew their names, yet already he no longer associated the names with the faces. It was the eyes more than their other physical changes. The eyes were dead. They did not even reflect the light of the lab. As he moved, Neil could not help but pause at the semi-naked woman whose breasts were still pressed against the glass. Her nipples were inverted by the pressure of the rest of the group clambering to get as close as possible to the glass.

"Do you really think that you can cure it?" Neil asked, speaking aloud and breaking the silence that had fallen. He heard Jack jump, and while the scientist recovered quickly from the shock, he stumbled over his words.

"I don't know," said Jack "The flu, yes. We had the cure before Charlie…well, it was nobody's fault." Jack paused, his face set in a strange expression. It was as if he was lost, not just in thought, but in terms of where he was.

"Charlie didn't die did he?" Neil found the question spring from his lips before had had a chance to even consider it.

"No, he was the first to come back. He bit the two guards that were carrying him down to the lab, and well, things just snowballed from there.

The pounding on the glass had taken on a strangely rhythmic quality. That or it was the result of Neil's natural desire to find a rhythm in things, however small. Whichever it was, the result was a growing headache and a strange distant sensation, like the state one hovers between when drinking: to stop would kill the buzz, but to take one more sip would remove all events from memory.

At that moment, Neil saw another figure shift in the shadows. At first he thought it was nothing, a trick of his eyes, yet he found himself drawn to it. Behind him, in the background, Neil heard Jack talking to him. No doubt it was a further attempt at justification. *What's done is done,* thought Neil as he continued to watch the shadows for further movement. He was about to turn away when the figure appeared.

"Charlie…" Neil gasped as the figure limped into view. He didn't need to have a face in order for Neil to recognize him. The bullet had ripped a hole through his throat moving in an upwards trajectory, and the blast from the close proximity of the shot had burnt the flesh around the wound which had resulted in the skin tearing under the chin. Over time, and as a result of many hungry jolts from within the group, the skin had been worked up over the face and sat piled on the top of his head like a macabre skin-turban. The raw meat beneath had begun to dry and around the edges had taken on a hardened, leathery appearance. Coupled with the red, wet center, his face reminded Neil of a perfectly cooked piece of roast beef.

With a shake of his head, Neil turned his attention back to Jack. He was furiously scribbling in his notes. The table he now stood before was filled with charts and pads of paper, yet what he wrote in was an old, leather bound journal, the kind most people would use for keeping a diary.

Jack was muttering to himself, but Neil picked up a few words, the only important ones as far as he was concerned: human trials, a moderate success, further work needed.

"How are we going to get out of here?" The thought hadn't crossed his mind until that moment.

"How hard can these things be to kill? We take them out with the rifle and head up to the open. Surely the military has started fighting back." Neil waited for Jack to answer him, and when nothing came, he grabbed the scientist and spun him around. "I asked you a question. After everything you have done, the least you could do is give me a fucking answer!" He felt rage begin to bubble beneath the surface; years of pent up anger at what he had first witnessed with Dr. Jennings.

"You don't get it, do you, Neil? Without a cure, there is no point in going up there. They know we are here. We have contact. A limited form of contact, but we have something. They will come for us. Until then, we need to keep working. Now take a seat because what I am going to ask of you next might…" Jack stopped talking and his eyes once again took on the vacant stare of a man confronted with the ghost of his past. "It can't be," he stammered.

"What?" Neil asked, turning around to look in the direction the lead scientist was facing. "Don't try and get out of this, man." Neil no longer knew if he could still trust the people he had spent the most of adult life with or not.

Jack raised an arm; a trembling limb that shook with more than age or nerves. "Him...that zombie there, he...I um...he should be dead." The words were stuttered and varied in pitch as if the older man had hit a second round of puberty.

Neil studied the crowd, and saw nothing but the undead, their bloody bodies twisted and broken, yet somehow still moving forward. They no longer stood gathered in one spot but circled the glass, like animals. They could sense the fear in the air and knew that it would only be a matter of time.

"It is as if they are looking for a weak point," Neil mused aloud, unaware that he had done so until Jack answered him.

"Don't be stupid, they are brainless monsters. All of them," Jack said. His voice had regained a level of composure, but it was not the same collected speech of the rational man he had been a few moments before.

"Yeah, well," Neil spat, giving Jack the evil eye. "Even the walls of Jericho fell eventually, and I don't think there is a God here still willing to save this place."

Jack said nothing. He didn't even hear the remark. His attention was held by the tall, gangly body of the young scientist he had injected with his most recent strain of a potential cure. He had been returning from his quest for a suitable candidate when he had happened across Neil.

"Hey, is it me, or does that zombie seem to have more of a purpose to it than the others?" Neil asked after having followed Jack's gaze for a time.

"You saw that too, huh?" the scientist turned and grabbed his notebook. He began to scribble frantically, talking to himself as he wrote.

"Yeah, I saw it, Jack, but you did first. You know what is going on. I told you I wanted to know what was going on. Don't keep lying to me, Jack." The name was expelled with a venomous barb attached.

"I found him just before I found you. He was alone in one of the hallways, and I injected him with a cure I had been working on. It was strain number 13. He had the same reaction as the rest: seizures, bleeding, and death... again."

"Well, he looks pretty alive to me—or well, undead." Neil paused to consider that correct wording. While he pondered, the zombie walked to the main entrance of the lab and reached for the handle. Its movements were uncoordinated yet effective, for after a few moments it held the cold metal handle in both hands and had started to jiggle the doors this way and that.

"What the hell?" Neil asked, watching the scene unfold with no thought to the implications of such a change. "You cured it." He looked over at Jack, expecting to find a relieved figure. Instead, he saw a ghost.

A figure so pale he could have passed for one of the dead. "What's wrong? You said it yourself, you gave him the cure. Maybe he just needs a bigger dosage or something like that," Neil offered his opinion.

Jack said nothing, but stood in stunned silence as slowly the outer doors began to open. He moved quickly, opening a cupboard he pulled out a lockbox. With fear fuelled fingers he struggled to enter the key code, but on the fourth attempt, he heard a faint click, and wrenched the box open. Inside was a fully loaded pistol; nothing fancy, but enough to stop even that hardiest of human beings.

"What's wrong? I thought they couldn't get through?" Neil asked, amazed at how quickly even he had been comforted by the concept of safety.

"The outer walls no, but none of them have ever tried the fucking door before." Jack's answer was absurd.

"You never locked the door?" Neil found it beyond comical.

"No, this place is secured from the outside in. This lab is designed to keep bacteria inside should something happen, not keep people out."

"Okay, that's fine. So what is the plan? Where is your escape route?" Neil asked, falling back on his army training which had always taught him to have a secondary way out of any situation he may be in.

"There isn't one. Not here anyway. The lab is sealed; one way in, one way out," Jack answered as he slammed the magazine into place and flicked the safety off. He grabbed five boxes of ammunition and put them into his lab coat's two side pockets.

"What if we let him in?" Neil answered, spitting the idea out. It left a sour taste in his mouth to just suggest it.

"What do you…?" Jack began, but stopped when he realized what Neil meant. "The others will never get the door open. If we can separate him from the rest…that might just work. But who is going to go let him in?" he asked, with a tone that was more hinting that really questioning.

"I'll do it, but if you get the chance, take the shot." Neil handed the scientist the rifle. "Use this," he said as he released his grip on the rifle. He grabbed the knife in addition to the forty-five automatic handgun.

The reanimated body of a soldier formerly known as Philip Gentry met Neil at the inner door. He had five deep gouges running down one side of his face and a large hole in his neck. He growled and groaned, becoming more agitated the closer Neil got. Behind him, the outer doors were still open. With the power out, and the lab running on a subterranean generator, all unnecessary electrical equipment had been disabled, including the doors.

"Great," Neil whispered under his breath.

"What is it?" Jack asked, having seen the drop in Neil's shoulders more than he heard the sigh and whispered words.

"The outer door is still open. I'll close it quickly once we have taken care of this guy," Neil answered, sure that his response was the same order Jack was about to give him.

"No," Jack bellowed, a deep, booming roar of emotion. "Don't open the door," he began, but it was too late.

Neil had released the internally operated pressure valve that held the door closed. The glass doors – already cracked from the zombies blows, slid apart and the undead corpse of Philip Gentry lunged into the lab.

The thing that struck Neil first, even before the clubbing blow from the once young soldier, was the smell. The entire facility stunk of death, and when the seal was broken, the heady aromas of decaying meat and spilled blood flooded into the small space. Neil couldn't help but gag, the wall of odor was so intense.

"Neil, move!" Jack called from behind him, although to Neil, he could have been on the other side of the complex. He saw and heard nothing but the zombie before him and the hammering of his own heart. A shot rang out, but it sounded no worse than the release of the vacuum when opening a jar for the first time. Philip Gentry's head exploded as the rifle round tore through his softened skin and bone. The bullet passed through his skull and through the open doorway before hitting the concrete wall with an echoing ting that caught the attention of every zombie that had surrounded them so patiently.

"Christ, Neil, move…you need to move," Jack called, but once again Neil heard a distant whisper. He watched as the body remained standing for a moment, as if deciding whether or not this death would be the final one. A thick blood oozed from the meaty mess that had once been its head. It bubbled to the surface, its viscosity not comparable to the blood Neil felt coursing through his veins at the moment.

It didn't take long—thirty seconds at the most—for the first zombie to find the opening in the lab's defenses and force their way through.

"No, Neil. You need to hold them off. Kill them all. The cure, I've almost found it. We need to save the lab," Jack called as he fired another round into the head of the next zombie. The weight of the crowd behind it pushed the body forward in a fashion not dissimilar to the way riot police storm a building with their long shields held before them.

Jack fired a burst of gunfire into the crowd, and while every bullet tore through the flesh it came into the contact with, his nervous hands caused his aim to lessen, and so he did nothing more than add an extra wound or two to their approaching bodies.

Neil felt his consciousness clear, and with quick reflexes he raised his pistol and fired off several rounds into the head of the first three zombies he saw.

While not quick creatures, the way they moved with such unfaltering fearlessness served as an equally overwhelming ability. Their numbers seemed much thicker than they were, and soon the lab was filled with the zombies. Neil emptied the clip of handgun as he retreated deeper into the lab. His shots echoed around the enclosed space, and when he turned around, having run out of room to retreat into, he saw that he had dropped three of them. Another sported a gaping hole in the center of its throat where a wayward bullet had torn the flesh apart, burrowing a channel through and out the back of the zombies throat.

"Jack, Jack, help!" Neil yelled as the zombies continued to close in on him.

"I can't, the fucking thing is jammed!" Jack screamed his answer with the same frantic voice of a man who was on the cusp of his own existence.

Neil looked, but couldn't see the scientist. He was hidden behind a wall of the undead. An undead hand clamped on Neil's shoulder. He looked to his right and saw a face void of flesh, a red meaty mass with a chomping center leaning in for a taste of his flesh. Neil struck out, punching the zombie straight on. The blow was a forceful one, and snapped the head of the creature backward, but it did little more than buy Neil a few moments.

Panicked and out of ammo, for Jack still held the spare magazines, Neil dropped the handgun as he remembered the hunting knife he had in his belt. With a lunging stabbing motion, Neil slid the knife with a sickening ease through the face of the zombie which had regained its footing and moved in for a second attempt. It gave a gargle which Neil thought had a tone of surprise to it, and then it fell still. It fell to the floor, sliding from the knife with a wet, sucking sound. The blade was covered in thick black blood, but there was no time to examine anything, for with one zombie felled, two more appeared to take its place.

Neil slashed and stabbed with wild abandon, and before long he had slain six of the crowd that filled the lab. Turning, he made his way toward Jack who had barricaded himself behind a stainless steel gurney. The gurney was one of several in the lab, and they had restraints in each corner, almost as if they had been designed to hold a human being in an exposed and vulnerable position. Neil put the image out of his mind. He would ask later, but only if they both survived. With their backs to him, Neil made quick work of four zombies before his presence was smelled. The remaining seven creatures turned, their dead eyes like cold spotlights, chilling the air around whatever it was that fell under their gaze. Neil felt his skin shrink, but through the gap he saw Jack, and in his arms he cradled several beakers filled with a milky liquid. It gave Neil a second wind, and he retreated, drawing the creatures away from Jack and the supposed cure, but also into an area that was less crowded with the dead—the unmoving kind. The zombies descended in one unit yet without any coherence, and so each blocked the other more than they aided either. The confusion bought Neil time to strike out, slide his knife through the skulls of two zombies, and further reduce the numbers of the opposition.

"Neil, draw them out of the lab. Lose them in the tunnels," Jack called out, distracting the savages and thus enabling Neil to stab another three, one of which took several attempts. Weak from hunger and dehydration, it hadn't dawned on Neil that he had still yet to drink anything since his rescue, his arm was wracked with cramping and refused to fully obey the commands of his brain. He stabbed the creature once in the shoulder, the blow being intended for the apex of the bald, egg shaped head that sat on the zombies shoulders. The second attempt had been more of a thrust, but found the mouth and not the brain.

"Come on, we need to move," Neil wheezed. He was covered from head to toe in a foul smelling blood which could only be described as putrefaction. His vision blurred, and his knees buckled, but he forced himself to remain standing.

"No, we need to stay, Neil. We need to fix this," Jack started to protest, but the final two zombies had split, and one bore down on Jack while the other remained focused on Neil.

With his strength failing him, Neil was driven backward by the zombie, where they collided with the wall of the lab. Raising his arm, Neil slipped the knife beneath the creature's chin and held the salivating mouth away from his throat, while he fumbled with his grip on the knife in his other hand. Unable to reach the creature's head, Neil sliced through the abdomen, cutting with furious abandon. He only stopped when he felt the cold mass of internal organs spilling onto the floor. Even that did nothing to stop the zombie's hunger, but the sudden change in its center of gravity gave Neil the edge and he drove the knife through the creatures face, puncturing the eyeball and burying the blade to the hilt. The creature fell to the floor just as a scream rang out from across the lab. In a shower of glass and broken vials, Jack flew through the air, launched inadvertently by the zombie he was trying to avoid. The milky liquid splattered the floor and cabinets, and for a moment, Neil thought he caught a faint orange scent wash through the room.

"No," Jack cried as he scrambled to his feet, knocking over several stools in the process. The zombie was upon him soon after, its bare feet crushing the glass shards without second thought.

Neil jumped across the room. Adrenaline fueling his actions, he leapt with the knife raised above his head and stabbed downward through the back of the creature's neck. The spine snapped with an audible and brittle sounding crack. The creature—for Neil no longer associated any of the names his brain threw at him with the creatures he saw—fell to the floor, the knife still protruding from its back. Reaching out, Neil grabbed the blade and watched in horror as the creature whose arms and legs had been rendered useless continued to snap at the ground, snarling like a cornered dog.

Neil watched fascinated by the creature and the change that had come over it. He took the knife and paused. What would be the purpose of killing it? Surely it would die of its own accord. He withdrew and turned away.

"I guess we don't have any reason to stay now," he spoke to Jack as he walked away.

Neil flinched when he heard the sound of the zombies head exploding as Jack stamped it to bloody pulp, roaring with savage triumph while globs of grey brain jelly splattered the floor. He did jump, however, when he turned around after a hundred meters and saw that Jack had not left the lab. He had taken a seat with his back to Neil and leaned on a countertop with his head in his hands.

"Jack, come on man. What are you waiting for?" Neil called. He was overly aware of the way his voice echoed through the passageway.

"No, I can't leave," Jack called back, his words muffled by his hands.

Neil stood, looked in all directions, and with a heavy sigh moved back toward the lab.

"Fuck the cure, man. I am not leaving you behind. You found the secret. Great. Tell that to the boys topside, and they will give you everything you need. Do you really think this is the only facility like this?" Neil urged. He paused at the entrance to the lab.

"It's not about the cure, Neil. Go, get to the top, and seal it off." Jack stood clumsily, knocking his stool to the floor. He turned around, his balance already failing.

"Jack, quit playing, there's bound to be more of those things down here…" Neil's words caught in his throat when he saw the blood. Jack was missing three fingers on his left hand. They had been bitten off just above the palm.

"Neil, leave, now!" Jack ordered. The power of his statement was clear even though the strength of his voice was failing him.

Even as Jack spoke, the color drained from his face. His eyes sunk, and he found himself fighting a consuming rage that had developed within him. He saw Neil, he knew his name, but hardly recognized him.

Neil was saying something, but he couldn't hear. The words were foreign to his ears, like static.

Neil reached out to grab the scientist, determined to pull him to safety. He had read plenty of zombie books to know that sometimes people were immune. As someone who had worked on the cure, Jack had surely been exposed to more than enough to help him fight it off.

Jack growled as Neil touched him, his head thrust forward, and his jaw clamped shut, nearly trapping its prize. Neil gave a surprised yell and pulled his arm away. Jack had narrowly missed his skin, instead biting into the sleeve of his shirt.

"Jack, come on, it's me. You can beat this thing. Nobody else knows the cure. Otherwise, tell me, show me your notes." Neil looked over the fresh zombie's shoulder at the pile of notebooks and scribbles upon loose sheets of paper.

Jack lunged forward again, his stumbled steps creating an illusion of lost balance. Neil was forced to jump backward once more. He jumped into the glass refrigerator unit, which had already been knocked off balance by the previous wave of the undead, and he sent it crashing to the floor with a cacophonous crash that surely alerted any remaining zombies to his presence. Jack continued to move, and while Neil pushed him out of the way, the message was not received, and he strode forward once more.

Back pedaling, Neil knew what he had to do. With a drop of his shoulder, he threw his weight in one direction, pushed back again with the other foot, and with a second dip ducked underneath Zombie Jack's outstretched arms. Neil planted his feet, twisted his body, and forced the knife through the back of Jack's skull. Having only just turned, the skin and bone had yet to soften, and so the blade refused to withdraw. Neil left it behind, quickly filling his arms with as many books and pieces of paper as he could find before running out of the lab and up to the surface.

He dropped three books as he ran, but refused to stop, for his mind made him believe that he was being followed. Neil burst from the underground facility, bolted from the barn, and into the fields that surrounded them, knocking over three army personnel before finally losing his balance… and almost his head. The rifle that was fired adjusted its aim the same time the trigger was depressed, and as a result the bullet merely clipped Neil's shoulder.

# CHAPTER 24 – IS IT EVER TOO LATE FOR REDEMPTION?

Neil stopped talking. His chest was tight to the point of being painful. He felt the weight of their collective gaze and the heavy air that had fallen over the cabin. For a while nobody spoke, and Neil found himself beginning to tremble.

"Do you really expect us to believe you? To believe that our own government planned to attack us just to start a war with another country? I mean who? North Korea, Iraq… China?" Jessica spoke, her voice stronger than at any point in the flight thus far.

"Really, that's rich coming from you," Neil spat.

"Shut up, soldier," Jessica snapped, her façade slipping.

"Paul, you wrote down everything that people have told you. So tell me, what was her reason for slicing her wrists?" Neil turned away from Jessica who stared at him with her jaw clenched.

Paul flipped through his notes, reading and re-reading his coded scribbles.

"Save it, because whatever she told you was a lie. She slit her wrists because she wanted the easy way out. She couldn't cope with the knowledge of where we are really going," Neil had started to shout. His face darkened as anger took over his emotions.

The plane continued its descent, a steeped event that most had previously experienced. "I should probably go check with the pilots." Jessica had regained her mild natured tone of voice.

"Save it, Captain," Neil spat. "Or whatever rank it is you managed to fuck your way into. You forget I know where this goddamned plane is going. I've got nothing left to loose. That's why you cut your wrists. I tell you what. Give me a knife, and I'll finish the job for you." Neil had lost all control. His emotions came in a rush.

"Hey, hey, Neil, calm things down. Leave Jessica alone. You've been through something shitty. We all have, but there is no reason to turn on each other. Now Jessica told us about the army, how they conscripted her to fly these planes. She is bringing us to safety and has been flying back into Hell every night for weeks. So why don't you sit down, and start telling us the truth." Paul, usually cool and in control of himself, could no longer hold his tongue. After the crazy story spun by Brian, he had had enough of being lied to and played for the fool.

"I am telling you the truth. She's no stewardess. She was born into the army. Her father, probably even her grandfather. She was an officer before she even fucking signed her papers."

"Shut up," Jessica snapped.

"Make me!" Neil roared. "Go ahead, kill me now, save them the satisfaction," Neil roared as spittle flew from his lips.

Paul sprang to his feet, followed by Leon. Everybody else shrank away.

"Okay, everybody calm down. Jessica, what the hell is he talking about?" Paul looked from Jessica to Neil.

"I don't know. He must have seen me at the airport. That General followed us around; me and the team that put these flights together. I was there when they brought him in. I heard what he had been through. Don't blame him. He's been through enough. He was trapped under the ground for a week or more without food. Waiting for a court martial, that's what I heard. He's lucky to be getting a second chance." Jessica rose, smiling at Paul, scowling at Neil. "Now, we're coming in to land. I need to talk to the pilot." She stepped over Paul and placed a hand on Leon's shoulder, easing him back into his seat. "You should all sit down. I have no idea how bumpy this is going to be."

"Wait just one second," Paul spoke up. "Look at me, Jessica. Look at me. Tell me the truth," Paul urged.

"Yeah, tell him, Jessica," Neil jabbed, much to Paul's annoyance.

"I don't have time for this, Paul. I told you my story. Now we are almost there; free from all of this. You can put it behind you," she began.

"Put it behind us?" Alan called out. "How can we just put it this behind us?" he asked.

The plane leaned to the left, a sudden lurch that caught them all off guard. "I really need to go. Argue it amongst yourselves. What's done is done, whether it was the government or someone else, or even an act of God. We are away from it now." She turned and walked away, a scurry in her step.

"Paul, you have to believe me," Neil began, "You had it all put together. You had already figured out the flu and everything. I just told you who did it. Please," Neil begged.

"I do believe," Paul answered to the shock of the group.

"Really... just like that you change your mind on her?" Leon jumped in. "I mean, I don't know who to believe. Maybe everybody is lying. Hell, I could see our government doing that. They don't care about us, anyway. If anything, it makes perfect sense...Orwellian you could even say."

Paul looked at them all, thinking how to tell them about the distrust that had formed in his mind over Jessica's story. "I never fully trusted her. No flight attendant goes to the pilots that often, not on a flight like this. Every time she goes in, she looked around as if checking nobody is standing behind her. She doesn't act like a stewardess, and well…she's wearing dog tags, small ones, on a bracelet. They might only be symbolic, but when you put it all together…"

"So she lied to us. What the hell is going on? Where are we going?" Tracey asked as she hugged her stomach.

"We are going to Eastern Europe, and I mean *deep* into the East." Neil emphasized the location for them.

"Why?" Paul, Leon, and Monique all asked in unplanned unison.

"Why do you think? We were all exposed to the virus, had close contact to the diseased," Neil began but was cut off by the sound of the remaining passengers turning around to pay attention. News that their proposed fresh start was not quite the thing it had been made out to be had them all riled.

"We were the good group." Robert took his chance to speak. The others were injured or beaten. "We were the ones that got out." For the first time since they had met, Robert sounded young, frightened.

"You think that because you were less damaged than the others you were immune. We all breathed in their blood, we consumed their bodies the moment we killed them. We are more damned than any of them." Neil paused. Out of the corner of his eyes he saw Jessica returning from the cockpit. "Just ask her about the other group, the ones being flown out of a secondary airport, a military base at…" Neil's words stopped a split second before a dark red hole appeared above his left eye. The sound of the gunshot was muffled by the silencer, and it took a few moments for people to realize what had happened. Only when the blood blinded him, and the hole in the back of his head dribbled the first few globs of brain matter, did Neil fall.

A scream rang from around the aircraft, although it was more from surprise than horror. Death had numbed them all.

Fittingly, it was Paul that reacted first, even as the plane's angle of descent continued to steepen. "Where are we really going?" he asked, unafraid of the weapon aimed at his chest.

"Does it matter?" Jessica asked, her voice unrecognizable. The accent she had worked hard to keep hidden burst through, capturing her every word.

"You tell us. Are we heading toward our deaths?" It was Alan who spoke, and he rose out of his seat.

Jessica looked at them all, not just at Paul and those that surrounded him like disciples, but at the entire aircraft. She smiled; a strained expression. "It's too late to change anything now. The plane is approaching the landing zone. The Russian military are waiting. They will escort you to the camp where you will be...processed.

"That's very clever," Paul said, the pieces falling together before his eyes. He looked at his notes. He heard the echoes of everybody's tale of survival reverberating inside his skull, and for the first time, he felt not only hopeless, but sad; sad that he had fought so hard to survive.

"Why save us at all?" Leon asked. His own image had formed just moments after Paul's.

"With every nation in the world watching, zombies walking the streets...it was unforeseen but played into our hands. Everybody is clambering over themselves to help, to prove it wasn't them. We even have a few planes being taken into North Korea. The world is uniting. It's remarkable." Jessica smiled at them. "We could realistically be thinking about world peace, and all for the price of a few bodies and an abandoned island."

Paul stood and stepped into the aisle of the descending plane. His ears popped with that eye watering annoyance that seemed unavoidable. "So we are all to be executed. This is all just a show. Let other nations kill us which gives you something to hang over their heads should things ever turn sour. That's not world peace. That's blackmail. It's a fucking dictatorship in the making. Ruling by fear; retribution is a powerful tool to have in your arsenal." Paul walked down the aisle, taking each step slowly.

"But you know that. Otherwise you wouldn't have cut your wrists. You started this. You wanted Paul to write everything down even though you knew we were going to die. It's too late for you to cleanse your soul so cheaply," Leon spat, his mild manner replaced with a hatred of his own. "We had a better chance out there on the streets," he spat, looking at his daughter who had woken up and stared at them all with wide, terror filled eyes.

"It's too late now. It's too late for all of us. You see, you're right, Paul. I did know...I do know one hell of a lot. The world is going to change. This is just the start. Our day ends with the start of a new world." Beneath them all the plane gave a gentle shudder as the wheel hatches opened, and the landing gears stretched their links in anticipation of the landing. All around them, for those that took the time to look through the windows, snowcapped mountains stretched into a bleak oblivion.

"And you? You just go back tonight, rest up, and deliver another package to some other helpful nation tomorrow? Do you really think they won't see the scars, Jessica? You said it yourself, the world is changing. There is no place for weakness." Paul took another step forward. She held the pistol in her hands. Paul didn't know what he hoped to accomplish, but to simply walk toward his own death like some passive fool was not going to be his way out.

"I know, and Paul," Jessica adjusted her grip on the pistol, her finger wrapping around the trigger, as she adjusted her aim, causing Paul to stop his approach, "you don't have to believe me, but I really am sorry." Tears welled in her reddened eyes. The rest happened in an instant. The gun fired, a fine bloody mist filled the cabin, and Jessica dropped the gun, her face an expression of slack-jawed disbelief. The same expression one wears moments after performing a task they always knew was better left undone. A few seconds later, she fell to the floor…dead.

From the moment Jessica's body hit the floor, an intoxicating cloud of black panic descended over them. It seeped through their pores and sickened their minds. Even Tracy began to babble frantically to herself under her breath. Robert began to hyperventilate. Seeing what was going on, Leon, who prided himself on remaining calm throughout everything he had faced thus far in his life, went over to her. He crouched down in the aisle so he could make eye contact.

Paul heard him start to speak but was more aware of the ground that was approaching so rapidly. They were only a few hundred meters from the ground; there was no time to do anything. Then Paul remembered the gun. It wasn't much, but he was certain that they wouldn't fly into such inhospitable areas without more weapons on board. Moving as fast as the cramped cabin allowed, he sprinted toward Jessica's body where the gun was still clutched in her hand. Bending down to gather it, he felt a shadow fall behind him.

"It's too late," said Robert, the young boy whose tale of sexual depravity was told without a trace of the bragging tones one would normally expect from a fraternity boy.

"No, but I won't go without a fight. There has to be weapons on board this thing. They have to be in the cockpit, it's the only place. Bending down, Paul pulled the gun out of Jessica's hand. He rose and saw the airport stretch out before the plane, the grey tarmac of the runway filling more and more of the window. He could see the military vehicles standing by; their arrival long since expected.

"I'm with you. Let's go." Robert nudged Paul in the small of his back as a sign of his intent.

Paul couldn't say if it was accidental or if Robert had seen the freezing wave of panic begin to settle over his body, but in any case, Paul was thankful to have him there, even if they only had one weapon between them.

Storming into the cockpit, Paul began to bark his orders, hoping the surprise would catch them off guard. Only…there was nobody there. The pilot and co-pilot were gone.

"What the fuck…" Robert asked.

"Drones…we've been sitting in a fucking drone all this time." Paul's voice was empty, the words as hollow to the ears as they were to his tongue the moment he uttered them. The pistol fell from his hand, and the entire plane gave a violent lurch as the wheels touched down. Everybody was caught off balance, the speed and angle of descent far from ideal. Paul fell to the floor, Robert fell on top of him, and the last thing Paul remembered hearing were the screams of the passengers as their fate was sealed.

# CHAPTER 25 – LANDING PARTY

The first thing Paul heard as he found his way through the fog that had settled over his brain was the strange hissing sound as the door he was lying next to released its lock and opened. The light outside was bright, and a harsh wind was blowing. The howls through the open door only served to further heighten the screams of the other passengers.

Scrambling to his feet, Paul made a dash for the gun which lay further inside the plane. His fingers brushed the metal when a shadow fell over him, and a heavily accented voice spoke up.

"I would not do that if I were you." The Russian voice was deep and gravelly; the accent only making it less hospitable.

Paul got to his feet and turned to look at the man that addressed him. His legs wanted to buckle, but he forced himself to stand tall. The man was dressed in military clothes, his jacket adorned with pins and medals, which while shiny and impressive to look at, probably meant much more to someone from Russian heritage.

"What is going on here?" he demanded, looking at the bodies on the floor. Blood still dripped from the ceiling of the plane from where Jessica had taken her own life. A deep red drop fell and landed on the tip of the man's boot which, contrary to the popular image, had not been shined to a mirror-like finish.

"You will answer me." The Russian fought hard against the desire to attack. His defenses and mistrust for the English seemed to be greater than the media would have people believe.

For a while it was as if the plane were empty. That only he and Paul stood there. The Russian soldier's gaze never faltered. He didn't even blink.

"She…there was a fight. The stewardess…whoever she was, shot and killed that man there before taking her own life," Paul explained, feeling his own steely resolve begin to weaken. Three more soldiers stood in the open doorway of the plane armed with heavy duty automatic weapons. From the way they held them, they were not averse to the notion of following Jessica's lead and wiping out the plane. They were going to die no matter what, so did it really make any difference where?

"That is most unfortunate. But there is no time. Come. You must now all come with me. We will take you to the holding camp where you will live until your government finalizes the evacuations, and your lives can begin again." The man turned and left the plane without another word.

The three remaining soldiers entered. Two stood by the door, while a third rounded up the passengers, helping them from their seats and through the aisles.

Outside, two large busses waited on the tarmac, surrounded by military vehicles. Every soldier that Paul saw was armed, and each wore a facial expression that said anything but welcome home. The air was hostile and the niceties forced. Paul realized that knowing the truth changed their viewpoint on things but didn't think it mattered much. The Russians, however helpful they wanted to make themselves look, were far from pleased at being used as a mass grave provider.

The air was colder than any had expected, and by the time they had made it to the waiting busses, the winter air held them all in its thrall. Unsurprisingly, there was no heating on the vehicles—or suspension— they would later come to realize. Nobody spoke as they pulled away. The bodies of both Jessica and Neil were removed from the aircraft and thrown rather unceremoniously into the baggage compartment of the final bus.

The scenery around them changed the moment they pulled out of the airport which was tiny and made Paul wonder how on earth the aircraft managed to land on such a small runway. By the time he looked back, as if he needed to reaffirm his sizing suspicions, the airport was gone, and they were surrounded by trees.

The road that they followed was unpaved for the most part and was certainly not on any map Paul could conceive.

"Where are we?" he heard a middle-aged man whisper to the younger man that sat beside him. It was a common question; one that bounced around the bus like an echo. The vehicle felt like an old school bus. Iron framed, worn out seats, the padding long since gone. The driver sat behind a semi-partition which obscured him from view and from any projectiles that may be thrown his way during whatever journey he was making.

At the front of the bus, standing beside the driver, were two armed guards. They stood motionless, their bodies immobile even as the bus bounced down the pothole-strewn road. The stared at the group, but nobody dared approach them or even call out to them. Paul looked around, trying to find something to occupy his mind. He had left his notepad on the plane. Or rather, he had put it to one side when he went to retrieve Jessica's gun. He didn't know why it bothered him so much. They were being taken to their execution after all. As his eyes roamed the bus, they came to settle on the graffiti that littered the wooden paneled back of the seat before him. It was, he had no doubt, the standard fare: declarations of love and numbers offering the same for a decent price. The Russian text made no sense to his eyes, and he wondered how anybody could read it. He had mastered several languages during his years but never one so complicated at first sight.

It was then that his eyes fell upon something scribbled in the top corner of the seat and hidden beneath a loose flap of cloth. It was not much, only a name and a date, but he doubted many people in Russia would have the name of Charles, nor would they have been riding in the bus only three days earlier. *There are others,* he thought to himself. Paul was unable to remove the smile from his face, and the nudge he got from Leon who had taken the seat beside him made him feel far more at ease.

"I've got your notebook," Leon whispered after a while, timing his words so that they were covered by the din of the heavily revved engine.

"Thank you," Paul managed in response before the glare from the guards silenced him.

After driving for what felt like days but was in actual fact not much more than an hour or two, they came to a stop. Before them was a tall wall, its top wrapped with barbed wire. Spaced every hundred meters or so was a small pillar, equally decorated with the wire, but topped with a security camera.

The guards muttered something into their radios and then left the bus. Even with them gone, the silence remained.

After a few seconds, the guards from the other bus arrived, and the sound of their chatter filled the air. While none could understand their words, the tone of the conversation was unmistakable: apprehension, confusion, and even an undertone of fear.

"Something's gone wrong," Leon whispered to the bus as a whole. The soldier's voices escalated to the point of confrontation and only stopped when one of them appeared on Paul's bus. His face was pale, his eyes wide, and as he surveyed them all, there was a distinct tremble in his hands. His eyes fell on a young girl; she couldn't have been more than eighteen.

"You... come," he managed in strained English.

The girl, who refused to make eye contact with the man, didn't move. The soldier reached out, grabbed her by her long dirty blonde hair, and hauled her from the bus, his own Russian growls almost as loud as her cries. A protest went up inside the bus but fell silent the moment the soldier pulled a pistol from his hip and waved it at them all. He shouted a warning in Russian and then disappeared, pushing the still shrieking girl before him.

"I don't like this." Paul took the chance to whisper to the bus.

The girl continued to scream and fight until the earsplitting wail of a heavy gate being opened on hinges no longer fit for the task drowned her out.

Looking through the front window, Paul saw the complex they had been brought to appear from behind the heavily fortified entry. Even the gate had been covered with brick to create the illusion of no entry. The inside was overgrown. Tall weeds and grass loomed large. A single path ran straight as an arrow through the complex. On either side of the path were single story wooden shacks. The construction appeared as stable as the European economy. The thing Paul didn't see was signs of life.

"Go, go," one of the soldiers ordered, jabbing the whimpering blond girl in the small of the back, forcing her over the threshold, and into the compound. "Walk....Walk, you walk," he ordered.

Small shuffling steps took the girl deeper and deeper beyond the walls. After a few moments, the soldiers began to relax. Their chatter started once more. They turned and ordered the busses to empty. It only took three shouts and a wave of their rifles for their orders to be understood and obeyed.

It took less than five minutes for them to empty the busses and stand in a shambolic line up.

"Where's the girl?" Paul asked while the soldiers were busy taking a headcount and recording something on a series of clipboards. They all had their backs to the compound, and even though Paul's question was more a voicing of a thought that dawned on him than anything more direct, each guard heard him. Their heads snapped to attention, and they spun around on full alert.

The scream came a few moments later, and the first zombie stumbled into view not long after. Panicked, the Russian soldiers all fired their weapons into the creature. Clearly, they had all been briefed on what they were doing and what had happened to bring the United Kingdom into such a condition. Yet Paul also noticed that none seemed to know how to stop the zombie. Blood filled the air as the body collected the bullets fired into it and fell to the ground.

The soldiers started shouting amongst themselves, their captives forgotten. The figure on the ground stood back up and started toward them once more. Its shirtless body was a mess of bubbling meat. The upper torso seemed to move at a slightly different tempo than the legs, twisting from side to side as it moved. The bullets had all but cut the creature in half. Only the spine remained intact. The creature gave a growl, but a final explosion forced a bullet between its eyes, and it fell on the path once more.

Paul stood with the gun in his hands, having grabbed it from the belt of the soldier nearest to him.

Spinning, the Russian military contingent aimed their weapons at Paul. They shouted at him in Russian, their own voices and actions driven not by fear of rebellion, but by fear of being whatever lurked in the camp.

"You need to shoot them in the head. In the head!" Paul spoke slowly, pointing into his own forehead. The Russians didn't seem to pay him any attention, but when the next group of zombies arrived, they seemed to show a modicum of restraint. Their aim was terrible, but the bullets were at least directed toward the head. One fired off the lower jaw of a woman who looked as though her final moments of life had been spent on her back. Her underwear was still wrapped around her ankles, and one sagging breast hung from her bra.

"Everybody on the bus," Leon shouted. The Russians turned to look at him and shouted their response, firing into the ground near Paul and their group. "We need to move. Those things will kill us all," Leon shouted at the Russians. Even as he did so, he saw a group of at least forty zombies appear from behind the huts within the compound. "There are too many of them." He tried, but the Russians refused to listen, and as if to show their defiance, they swiftly put a number of bullets into Leon's chest. Blood frothed from his lips as he collapsed to the ground. He reached out both hands, taking his daughter's hand in one and Paul's in the other.

Everybody screamed, apart from Leon's daughter. She stood in silence; her face pale. Her eyes rolled into her head, and she collapsed to the ground.

Paul moved to catch her, but the rifles, which were not trained on him, for he still held the pistol in one hand, stopped him. The zombie crowd had increased, and they descended upon the Russians who never saw them coming. Paul would later wonder if they knew all along and merely refused to look their deaths in the eye.

The first wave of zombies numbered fifty, and they overpowered the Russian soldiers, descending on them in a snarling fury which ensured that not enough was left over for them to come back from the dead. While the zombies, consumed by their hunger, oblivious to the presence of the others, continued to gorge themselves on the military grade meat, Paul rallied his own troops. Scooping Leon's unconscious daughter into his arms, he led them into the compound.

"We can't go in there," a voice called.

"It is our only chance," Paul said. There is a cabin right here. We head there and barricade the doors," he called.

"He's right. We need to be able to regroup," Monique called out. She appeared beside Paul and looked down at the young girl in his arms. "Poor thing," she whispered.

"Why not the bus? I'm going to wait on the bus," a strong sounding male voice called from the back. "We can drive away," he added, hoping to convince a few of the others to go with him.

The first of the zombies had finished their allocated body part, and raised their head looking for more, their hunger never sated. Their eyes fell upon the man standing by the bus, the others having fled away from the undead crowd, moving along a horizontal plane. It came for the man who fled onto the bus along with the five people who had decided that his advice had been the best. They closed the doors, and immediately the man began to turn the key, which still sat in the ignition.

"Run," Paul called out to the others. The Russian soldiers had been stripped of all their juicy parts, and with the aroma of blood and adrenaline flavoring their palate, they lurched after the others.

Paul ran into the compound. He knew that Monique, Tracey, Alan, and Robert were behind him, moving close on his heels. As for the rest, he neither knew nor cared at that moment in time. He had no obligation to anybody other than Leon's daughter, Keisha, whom he still held in his arms.

As Paul entered the compound, the cold air wrapped around him. There was something stale... something... dead about the place. For the first time since they arrived—a full fifteen minutes ago—Paul thought about the bigger picture; about history. His mind was filled with thoughts about the people that must have been sent to such a camp. The deaths that occurred by nature's own hand or under the guidance of evil minds made him shudder.

Paul and his small group reached the first shack relatively quickly, and with a lowered shoulder and head full of speed, Paul charged the door. It was unlocked and opened inward. He ploughed into the property, crashing to the floor. Behind him, Monique ran in, helping Keisha who had started to come round, and had been placed back on her own two feet by Paul. Scrambling to his feet, Paul ran back through the doorway. He was not prepared for what he saw.

Zombies. A field full of zombies. They had appeared out of nowhere or so it felt. They descended upon the fleeing bodies; drawn to them like moths to a flame. Screams filled the air as the first of them fell. The sound of tearing flesh echoed through Paul like a cold November wind. He saw Tim having his throat ripped out by an older woman who dragged his body to the ground and proceeded to disembowel the man, sucking his intestines into her ravenous mouth like strands of bloated spaghetti. While many of the passengers died, an equal number reached the small shack. It soon became clear that none of the others would make it. Paul, ignoring the chill that ran down his spine, simply stepped back inside and closed the door just as a pleading figure reached the bottom of the steps. They were missing an arm, and had a zombie inches behind them, swinging said appendage like a medieval mace. They never made it up the steps.

There was a small window within the shack, and through it Paul and Monique watched the devastation unfold. The bus roared to life was thrown into reverse and then promptly drove into the bus parked a few meters behind it. It took less than thirty seconds for the zombies that had killed the Russian soldiers to get inside and even less time for the windows to become coated with blood.

"What are we going to do?" Monique asked. Everybody was sitting either on the floor or on the rusty bed frames. In the far corner stood two old wooden cupboards. There was only one door still attached and that only held on by one hinge.

"I'm not in charge here, Monique," Paul answered, his head buried in his hands. "This was supposed to be our ticket out of this. Now look. Look at what our government has done. It's fucking…fucking ended the motherfucking world." Paul threw his head back against the wall of the shack, enjoying the jolting sensation that ran through his neck.

"Easy, Sugar." Monique put a hand on Paul's shoulder. "None of us know what is going on here." She gave him a gentle squeeze.

"We can't seem to catch a break, can we?" Paul let out a frustrated laugh, which became a giggle, and soon after a full-belly chuckle. When he had himself back under control, tears streamed from his eyes, and his side ached. "Oh God, what the fuck are we going to do?" he repeated the question posed to him only moments before, as the walls of the hut began to tremble, and the undead crowd continued to gather.

"We can't stay here." Robert stood up in Paul's moment of lost control. "Those things will break down the walls in no time. It's a miracle that this is still standing at all." He looked around him as he spoke as if suddenly feeling the pressure of the crowd's expectation.

"Then what do you propose we do, Einstein?" asked Paul.

"We're stuck in motherfucking, Russia, surrounded by zombies in an old concentration camp!" a middle-aged and angry sounding man called out above the din of undead fingers scratching at the wood, stripping away flesh and grain in equal measures.

"I don't know… I mean, we could…" Robert stuttered.

"We could go through the roof." Paul stood up and moved beside Robert. "If we get up onto the top of the building, we could move from cabin to cabin. They aren't that far apart. We spread out. Three groups: one with me, one with Monique, and another with Robert here." Paul clapped him on the back as he spoke. "We keep moving, backward or forward. It doesn't matter. We just need to thin out the herd," Paul mused as he spoke, his mind racing through the scenarios and possibilities, hoping that he came up with something before anybody followed up with questions.

Monique took her turn to speak, much to Paul's relief. "We aren't the first group of people here. They have brought others before now. Whatever happened to them, the Russians would have a fortified command center, security, weapons, and food."

"Yes, exactly. If we can get to their stronghold, then we will be in a much better position than we are now. I know we are tired. I know that this is a shitty place to be, and I am nobody's leader, but it is the best chance we have." Paul rounded off the conversation, aware that each small speech he made pushed him more and more into the role of leader.

The door to the cabin shook. The frame splintered. An undead arm, raw and blistered from the cold, shot through the opening. Pus oozed from the fresh wounds and dripped onto the floor like melted cheese.

"We don't have a choice. Quick, you three, move those beds," Paul ordered, raising his voice to be heard above the panic that had spread through the group. "Robert, give me a hand with these cupboards here. We need to move them under the skylight." Paul pointed above their heads to a small, grimy skylight.

Robert didn't need to be told twice and had already started shifting the deceptively heavy units before Paul had reached him.

Heaving, the two men hauled the cupboards to beneath the small skylight.

"You go first," Paul spoke to Robert. "Check that the coast is clear, and then I'll make sure the others come through." Nimbly, with the nonchalance that only youth can provide, Robert opened the skylight and pulled himself through the small opening. As he disappeared, another crash fell against the door, and an entire plank broke free. A zombie head appeared through the gap, teeth snarling and snapping. The face was still covered with dried blood. The hole in the creature's throat turned its growls into whistled exhalations. The beds were slid into their position just in time, with the head colliding with the base of the frame. The tremor in the ground around the hut increased, as, too, did the hungry wail that drifted on the air like the heavy stench of a local landfill.

"Everybody move, now! Those beds will not hold them at bay for long. Come on, quickly now," Paul called, helping the first people onto the cupboards. Robert leaned through the skylight and helped lift people through and onto the roof which cracked and groaned under the increasing weight.

The bed wobbled as the zombie crowd continued to push against the door, while the walls also began to groan and give.

"Hurry now, come on, Sugar." Monique moved through the shack, helping to herd the crowd into the center of the room. Seven people had made it through the skylight when Paul climbed on top of the cupboard and stopped the flow.

"Robert, Robert, there are too many people up there. You need to take your group and move to another building," Paul called through the skylight. He could feel the shack beginning to give. "Monique, you go up next, take your group, and head in the opposite direction." Everything formed naturally in Paul's mind. He simply saw the situation, their options, and the best way to get around them all.

Once Robert and his group had left, each of them surviving the leap to the next shack, Monique went into the open air, swiftly followed by eight of the remaining survivors. One of the beds fell. The front door opened further allowing a second zombie the chance to try and gain access. The first still had his head stuck through the space left by the broken panel, trying to burst through the gap. It got caught in the base of the second bed. A hole in the springs saved the lives of the remaining occupants of the shack.

"I won't fit through that window," Tracey spoke up as Keisha disappeared onto the roof.

Tracey, Alan, and Paul were the only ones left standing in the shack; the second bed was on the verge of falling. The caught zombie thrashed around like a gator caught in a noose.

"It's larger than it looks," Paul added, horrified that he had not thought of Tracey and her belly before.

"Yeah, come on, Tracey, we need to try," Alan insisted. "Paul, you get up on the roof, and help pull her through." Alan spoke as if he were talking about manhandling a piece of furniture rather than saving his wife's life.

"No, I go up last, this was all my idea. You go, help her through. I'll push if needed," Paul insisted as another crash saw the bed topple. The zombie, rather than being freed, trapped itself further beneath the frame and somehow managed to block the door for a few moments longer.

"I can't. My back is shot man. You need to do it," Alan insisted as the barricade finally began to give.

Paul looked from Alan to Tracey. He saw the pleading look in their eyes.

"You need to protect my baby," Alan spoke with tone that made Paul want to weep, and so with a heavy heart, he pulled himself through the skylight. The air was cold, and the layer of sweat that coated his flesh only made the temperature seem that much colder.

There was no time for Paul to stop and feel the temperatures, for Tracey appeared through the skylight the instant that he stood on his feet. Their ascent had not gone unnoticed, however, and the zombies were rattling the shack, causing the entire structure to creak and groan. The plan was working, to a degree. Robert and Monique had both moved their group in different directions. Over half a dozen shacks had people standing on them, and gradually the crowd around his own shack began to disperse as the scent of the fleeing meat wafted through the air and enticed the undead to follow.

"Tracey, give me your hands," Paul cried. Tracey, a slender thing by all accounts, had already had some difficulty in getting her engorged bosom through the skylight, and found herself wedged into the gap moments later. The swollen stomach that housed her unborn child was too large. She held her breath and tried to make herself as thin as possible, and sucking in a stomach that was no longer really responsive to such demands made no difference.

"I can't, Paul! Help me, I'm stuck...help!" she screamed, thrashing about.

"Calm down, calm down, Tracey, and listen to me. Give me your hands. I'm going to gently pull on your arms." Paul crouched down and spoke softly, as an almighty crash beneath them confirmed that the bed blockade had finally been overcome.

Tracey's panic increased further when Alan's screams tore through the roof below Paul's feet. There were sounds of a struggle; a heavy struggle. Adrenaline took over, and Paul heaved on Tracey's arms. She cried out in pain as the wooden frame of the skylight dug into her tender flesh. Her baby kicked and struggled within its water home, displeased with the activity going on around it.

Paul lost himself to the struggle. All around him death filled the air. The exhausted survivors who had run out of energy before the plane even left England were moving slower and slower. Several had misguided their jumps and had fallen to the ground. Their screams echoed in the background of Paul's consciousness. He would only notice the true impact of the loss once he ,too, had made it to safety. In his hands, Tracey's grip slipped, both of their palms greased with sweat. A small trickle of blood stained Tracey's shirt. Paul noticed it, and inside his head he paused for a few moments. He started up soon after, however—what else was there to do? With another great pull, he felt movement. Tracey gave a scream, but slipped higher through the window. The progress fuelled Paul's efforts, and with a concerted effort, he tugged with every remaining ounce of strength he could muster. Tracey came free with a scream that caught the attention of every zombie in the complex. The shower of blood and entrails that came with her also added to the appeal.

Paul landed on his back, Tracey on top of him. The first thing he felt was the warm wetness that spread between them, and while Tracey shook and shuddered, she never made a sound. The coppery aroma of blood filled their air, and when Paul sat up, he saw the reason. Zombies had killed Alan, and it had been the undead attached to the other end of the pregnant tug of war. Their hands and teeth had torn Tracey apart, and in pulling her free, Paul had neatly severed her body. The sounds of ravenous chomping that came from within the shack told Paul all he needed to know.

"Paul, jump, quickly! That place is going to collapse!" Monique screamed as she quickly bounded over the buildings in his direction.

Shock gripped him tightly, threatening to shut his body down altogether. Paul looked over the roof. On all sides, undead hands scrambled at the edge of the shack, reaching for whatever morsel they could find. The shack wobbled and creaked. Paul looked down at Tracey. She was dead, he knew it, yet he could not turn and walk away. He saw her, what remained of her swollen stomach, and then…just before he vomited, Paul saw her baby. It lay on the roof of the shack, encapsulated inside a bloods-smeared sac. Its large eyes were open and seemed to stare at him. *You failed. You killed me!* it screamed at him. *You killed me like you killed your own children. You're a monster!*

Paul jumped backward, his legs buckled beneath him, and he came close to falling from the edge of the shack. The blood was spreading, thick and black even in the cold light of a cloudless day. Then, as he hovered over the abyss of his own existence, Paul saw Monique. She was three buildings away, waving at him frantically. Paul realized then that he had become deaf to the world around him. The noise came back: the grunting and snarling of the undead, the pleas from Monique…something about the shack falling.

As if prompted, the building gave a great tremor, and the sound of cracking wood ripped through the air. Running, Paul leapt from the shack to the roof of the neighboring building. It was in a not much better state of repair, and the undead were soon upon it also, but Paul had no plans to stop. He had jumped three more buildings and caught up with Monique who had turned to leave the moment she saw Paul was moving, when he heard it. The shack they had been sheltering in and then upon was gone. Eaten by a cloud of dust. Hidden by an army of the undead.

*I'm sorry* Paul thought to himself. He felt no better for it. He had no time to further indulge his growing self-loathing, as there was already a crowd gathered around his new position. Leaping, he made his way across the rooftops toward Monique.

The camp was enormous, larger than he had ever dreamed. In the rear was a large, concrete structure which looked as cold in its appearance as the winter weather that slowly worked its way into their bones. The shacks were arranged in three rows, were three rows wide, and at least twenty-five rows deep. He could see the first of the group, those that escaped with Robert, making their way along the far side of the camp. They had separated into two smaller groups; one took the central lane and another took the far side. Both kept relatively good pace with one another. Robert could be easily identified. He would not leave the shack they were upon until the last of the group, in either lane, had moved past him. Ahead, Paul saw Monique, and ahead of her the people she had led to safety.

A cry went up in the group ahead. Someone hadn't made the jump. They had fallen to the ground. Their cries called to the zombies, summoning them like a dinner bell.

"Keep moving," Paul and Monique cried in unison. They knew that stopping to help was just a waste of valuable time.

After what felt like an age, the last of the group reached the officers' area. They knew what it was, for besides the shacks it was the only building on the site. Well, besides the tall circular building that stood in the far corner of the site, and nobody needed to ask twice what its purpose was. The large pit and tractor that stood on the other side of the fence showed where the Russians had planned on hiding the bodies. Paul wondered for a second just how the UK thought they would get away with such a crazy plan.

"How do we get inside?" Monique asked as they stood on the roof of the final shack. The group, whose numbers had dropped to twelve following a few more stumbled jumps, and one man who freely leapt after his wife when he had been unable to save her, pondered her question.

"There is a broken window on the first floor," Robert pointed out. They stood spread across the three shacks with Paul, Robert, and Monique alone on the central building.

"It's a big jump," Paul said as he studied the window. "What do you think, Monique?"

The zombies had kept pace with them, and the crowd around their shack was gathering.

"What other options do we have?" The three looked at one another, and none of them uttered another word. They were covered in sweat, dirt, and blood. None had slept in days, and all knew that making the jump would further reduce their numbers.

Paul looked to his left. He saw—against all odds—the small frail old woman who had first sat beside him on the plane. She stared at him, her old face kind yet weathered. He wanted her to say something, to call to him, and tell him it was okay. That she understood. Yet all he saw in her eyes was hope. In that one fleeting glance she had begged Paul to save her; to let her live on.

"They won't all make it," he said finally, his voice broken.

"Nope," Monique agreed, "but we could save most of them. These shacks won't last forever, Sugar. We need to make a decision," she pushed, even though they all knew what the answer would be.

"What if there are Russian soldiers in there?" Robert asked. The question came at them like a firm punch to the gut.

"I guess we will cross that bridge when we come to it. These things have kind of unified the playing field a little, don't you think?" Paul pointed to the gathered crowd; a sea of unresponsive faces, their features twisted into something horrific beyond adequate description. "Unless…" he paused, staring at the other two.

"Paul, come on, Sugar, they need you." Monique looked at him with wide, worried eyes.

"Robert, you're the youngest, quick on your feet. You jump first. If the coast is clear, we will send the others across," Paul announced, his voice quivering as he spoke. He knew he had to become every bit the executioner to balance out his part as savior.

Robert made the leap through the open window with relative ease. His arms strong even in their weary state, and he hauled himself up and through the gash in what appeared to be an otherwise locked tight exterior. The moment he disappeared, Paul felt his heart freeze. *What if it is crawling with zombies, locked up to keep them in? What if the Russians are there? I killed Robert; I killed another kid.* Paul wobbled on his feet, his legs disappearing from under him. He caught himself before he fell and blamed the unsteady shack they stood upon.

A few moments later, a period of time that felt like hours to Paul, Robert appeared in the window and announced that the room was empty.

It was a start.

# CHAPTER 26 – BASE OF OPERATIONS

It didn't take long for the first person to fall, and while two more jumped across before the zombies had finished their first fistful of fresh human innards, there was an extra weight added to the air. As if even gravity had turned against them.

"I won't make that jump," the old woman told Paul. It was just the two of them left. He had purposefully hung back until the end.

"Maybe you can. See, Robert there will catch you," Paul lied.

"Young man, I may look good for my age, but I was not born yesterday." The old woman, still held a strange and repugnant odor which Paul had first noticed when she sat beside him on the plane, complaining that he was in her allotted seat.

Beneath them the shack began to tremble as the growing weight of the undead increased on all sides. A cold wind whipped through the compound generating a howling cackle of a laugh as it danced between the other wooden buildings, frolicking like a nymph, much to the chagrin of those that stood by, unable to enjoy the freedom.

"Come on, I'm not jumping until we have you in that building." Paul was not sure why he wanted to help this woman above the rest. Their entire interaction had happened at the start of their flight, and lasted maybe thirty seconds at most. Yet there was something in him that refused to give up. Maybe because of her age. She had been through so much in her life, that to have her die at the hands of the undead, on the frozen ground of a Russian concentration camp just felt wrong. She should die in a warm bed surrounded by fat grandchildren.

"Then I shall make it easy for you." She gave another smile, one that highlighted the creases in her flesh, the dried blood flakes that sat between them, and the dignity that she insisted on holding onto as she entered her final moments. Without saying another word she walked backward and fell from the rear of the shack and into the crowd. She never cried out as the zombies ripped her apart at the joints. Paul saw her blood spurt into the air, a thick red; a healthy red.

"Paul, come on, jump," Monique called. Paul turned and saw both her and Robert in the window of the building. He paused, looked around, and saw how the world had changed. In the matter of a few weeks the world had become twisted into a wilderness that would see only the strong survive. *I killed my babies. I saw my wife change. I killed...people. I killed them because I needed to survive. I am strong. We are strong, and we will survive this.* Paul found his strength. Then he wiped the tears from his eyes and whispered a goodbye to the weight that he had been carrying since the first day of the outbreak. Releasing his wife and children to enjoy their forever together, he stood taller and felt stronger that he ever had. He leaped through the window, lifting himself through and into the arms of the two people he now considered his closest friends.

The room they found themselves in was a simple, military grade sleeping quarters. One bunk bed, complete with itchy blanket and khaki colorings, along with a table, two chairs, and a bottle of vodka completed the look. Clothes were folded and neatly secured within the two chests that stood on the floor at the foot of the bed; one against the frame, the other against the wall. There was no sign of a TV or even a radio. A small collection of books stood on the floor behind the chests, and what looked to be a Russian porn magazine poked from beneath the pillow on the bottom bunk.

"Cozy." Monique nodded to herself as she looked around the room. The rest of the group stood in silence. They numbered nine in total. Yet while the zombies could be heard scratching at the walls, each would admit to having never felt safer in all of their lives.

"What do we do now?" a young voice, that of Keisha, Leon's daughter spoke up. It was the first time she had really spoken out since her father's death. It was clear within seconds that she had the same spirit as her father.

"We stick together. We make our way through this place. We have shelter. Our next concerns are arming ourselves for protection and food. Whichever we find first, we take first. If we find anybody else in here…well, that we will deal with as we come to it." Paul took charge, stepping into the role willingly now.

As a group, they walked along the upper corridor of the building. It was laid out in a brutally stark and simple fashion. One corridor. The walls bare and unpainted. The floor was concrete, although there were signs that something had been laid upon it in the past. Every room was the same in terms of size, layout, and contents. There were seven rooms in all on the first floor, and with one floor above them along with the rear of the building, Paul guessed that there would have been up to forty people residing in the complex at any one time.

There were other rooms in the side wings of the building, but they were locked. The rear of the building was much the same as where they entered. Bedrooms, as far as they could tell, but the dust and cobwebs that covered the windows made it clear that this half of the building was no longer in use.

"I guess they only moved in recently," Robert spoke as he swatted at a thick cobweb that dangled before his face.

"Yeah, well, it gives me the creeps," Monique answered. She looked around like a girl in a museum, surrounded by wonder, yet aware of the history that each item told.

"We should keep moving. I want to make sure there are no zombies around before we let our guard down," Paul spoke. His eagerness to leave the cold shadows was well hidden, yet easy to see if one knew what they were looking for.

The first floor was quickly cleared, the window they had used to enter the building was the only visible entry, and by moving the bunk beds in the room—an afterthought that Robert had raised—they managed to create enough of a barricade to ensure that nobody would be able to fit through; at least, not without a struggle.

There were two flights of stairs in the building, and it was quickly decided that if no zombies were found on the first floor, the second would be equally empty, and so the decision was made to head to the ground floor.

Paul's stomach ached. It felt as if it had been tied into a knot as he dismounted the final step. The air on the ground floor was cold. Their breath fogged before their eyes. A low wattage bulb hung naked and alone in the center of the ground floor. The wooden floor told a tale of grand elegance back in the days when the death factory was in full swing. Paul could almost feel the nostalgia: the high-powered military officials' milling around, drinking vodka, and telling stories of how their latest batch of victims had all turned blue in the face, choking on their own swollen tongues during the more recent gassings. Oh, the folly!

"Whoever reopened this place didn't do much in the way of decorating," Paul commented as they walked further into the large hallway. The impressions left by the previous fixtures and fittings could still be seen. Discoloration from where great paintings, statues, and mirrors hung told of lonely times at the end of the wars. A forgotten warrior consigned to serve the Russian regime for eternity.

"Quiet down, everybody. Keep quiet," Paul whispered his command, as a nervous murmur went through the group at the very same moment that a noise echoed through the darkness. "Quiet," he barked once more, doing his best to keep his voice as low as possible, to avoid starling the other occupants of the building.

"What is it, Sugar?" Monique asked, whispering in Paul's ear.

"We're not alone," he answered, and the short sentence was enough to make Monique turn rigid with fear. Paul felt her body stiffen against his, but he had no time to concern himself with her condition. Before they knew it, they were bathed in light, and screaming Russian voices deafened them. Paul collapsed to his knees, hoping that the others would do the same. He had seen enough bloodshed for one day.

"Do you have the bite? Do you have the bite?" A strong, yet scared sounding voice demanded from within the light that blinded them all.

Paul, who had his arms raised into the air, looked in the direction that he thought the voice came from and began to speak. Doing so with a raised voice to ensure he was heard above the screams of his people and the nervous chatter of the Russian soldiers. He knew the other group was Russian because of the heavy accent on the words they spoke.

"No, we have no bites. We are clean." Paul had no idea what he was saying, but he hoped it worked.

"Let us see. All of you, on your feet," demanded the same voice, calmer now it would seem, as a result of Paul's answer.

One by one the group was patted down by a pair of rough and incredibly large hands. Only once the group had all been given the all-clear did the blinding light disappear, though it did nothing more than throw them into a second blind state for a few moments.

"My name is Captain Yuri Shuyvarin. I was sent here to command this station. I take it you are the flight we were expecting." There was something chilling in his words, an undertone that put Paul on edge. He and Yuri had moved off to one side, away from the others after a long discussion to see who the leader of each group was. Both sides were scared.

"Yes, we were attacked at the gate. They killed all of your officers. I'm sorry." Paul added the last sentence as an afterthought. It was the truth, although the level of relief he felt at the demise was almost at an equal level.

The pair walked further away from the group, and after a while Yuri turned and shouted to his small group of men. Paul had no idea what they had said, but it sounded important, and then they turned to lead the others away. Paul made no attempt to stop them. Monique and Keisha looked over their shoulders at him, but with a gentle nod of his head, Paul comforted them from across the room, and they too went off into the darkness.

"You are safe here now. We did not want to run the executions anyway, but the government, they are scared. They wanted to show we had nothing to do with the…"

"Zombies," Paul added.

"Yes, the zombies. It is not normal to be saying this." The Captain had taken on a much more relaxed manner following the departure of his men. "I am leader, you are leader. We must stay strong for the others.

Come, now. We go here. We sit, and talk like men." With a sweeping gesture of his arm, Yuri pointed to a door that opened onto an area Paul would never have assumed existed in such a place: a library.

The room was small, but the walls were lined with a series of bookcases which were in turn filled with all manner of books. A thick carpet lay underfoot. Music played softly in the background, and two deep burgundy leather sofa's stood facing one another in the center of the room, positioned before a large antique desk. The room was high ceilinged, comprised of the ground and first floor. It was a strange room, and given the location and the condition of the rest of the camp, it was even more surreal.

"Please, take a seat. Would you like to drink with me?"

Paul turned his head and saw a large liquor cabinet had been set into the bookcase, hidden behind a panel of fake books, and only noticeable once you knew they were there. "Yes, please," Paul answered in a haze, unsure what to make of everything. For a few moments, he forgot where he was; forgot that the undead had ripped apart his country, that he had killed his family in order to survive, and now stood surrounded by a new batch of the undead in the deepest, darkest corner of the Russian wilderness.

"This is my special place. I come here to…" He paused, after handing a glass with what Paul had already assumed to be Vodka. Yuri's eyes were burning red with tears. "I come here to forget about what I have done; to leave this world behind. We got our orders, and we must see them through. I…it was…I apologize to you for what I have done and for what I should be doing now. There will be no more death here, besides our own I fear." Yuri sank into the leather sofa, shrouded in a cloud of confused self-loathing.

"Orders are orders. You couldn't say no. I understand. Yuri, there is something you need to know. This whole thing is staged. The UK, my country, released this…plague, if you will, upon themselves. They want you all to help hide the bodies, so they can use it as a guilt trip to gain power later on." Paul was surprised at how relieved he felt to pass the message on.

"How do you know this?" Yuri's interest had been caught, and he sat forward in the chair, draining his glass in one shot.

Paul looked at him, adjusted his own seating position, and likewise drank is vodka down. "One of the people on my flight, he worked at the place it happened. He knew nothing about it, but he saw it all happen. Then… well, one of the others killed him. She was with the military, and he blew the secret." Paul hoped that the man would understand. His grasp of English seemed excellent, and his fears were unfounded.

"Is she still here with you?" There was anger rising in his voice.

"No, she died on the plane, too. We are all victims here. But tell me, how did this happen here? The zombies?" Paul was eager to know, as he doubted the Russians invited the previous arrivals into their personal quarters.

"That is unfortunate. One of our soldiers, Andrei…he committed, how you say, the suicide. He could not live with what we did. We laid his body to rest, waiting for the time to come to bury him. He stood up and attacked us. My men and I survived, but as you can see, the damage was already done." Yuri lowered his head, and without speaking, refilled both glasses.

Paul took his, but decided against the overwhelming urge to knock the fiery liquid back in one shot again. He had hardly eaten in days, and already felt his head beginning to spin. Yuri, however, showed no such restraint. His glass was empty a few seconds after he sat down. A silence fell, and Paul looked around the room. It was just as impressive at the second viewing as it was when he walked through the door.

Paul spoke after a period of silence that he felt was acceptable. "I guess that stops Britain's master plan."

"How you mean?" Yuri cocked his head to one side.

"Well, your soldier, Andre."

"Andrei."

"Sorry, Andrei. He was not bitten, so that means the virus they created has changed. It affects everybody. Their plan cannot work because they have infected the whole world. Or will have before long." Paul sat back; a mixture of emotions running through him at the thought.

"Then we are all damned." Yuri stared at Paul with cold eyes that were filled with a raging torrent of anger and fear that would culminate in a total shutdown of the human condition.

"No, Yuri, that is where you are wrong. We are survivors," Paul emphasized the fact. He refused to look at himself, or any of them, as being victims. They were alive. They could still make their own decisions.

"My friend, you have a positive outlook on things, but I do not see how this will help us. We are stuck here." Yuri had lost all tones of superiority, and the use of the word friend made Paul relax even further.

"Well, we can clear the camp, lock it down, plant seeds maybe, wildlife, animals, there must be some we could hunt in the woods. You must have food on site, too. Canned goods, right? This was a military base." Paul felt his stomach rumble.

"You can talk well…"

"Paul."

"Paul. But you have not yet convinced me. However, I do not think you will stop just yet. Am I right?" Yuri gave a laugh, jumped from the sofa, and slapped Paul on the back hard enough for him to lunge forward and almost fall. "Come, we go eat. You were right on that. We have many supplies. So for tonight, we will feast." Yuri lead the way out of the library and back into the cold and concrete general populace area.

They could hear the relaxing sound of forming friendships long before they reached the mess hall. The bare walls of the compound's headquarters echoed, and for a moment, the sounds of life overpowered the bass-line drone of the undead. As they walked past a window that offered a broader view of the compound than the others, Paul allowed himself a moment to pause and look out. The zombies had lost interest in his group. Out of sight, out of mind, was the truest of all statements when referring to the undead. They milled around the compound; British evacuees and Russian soldiers, both victims to a network of political lies.

"It's like peering through the looking glass," Paul remarked when he felt Yuri move beside him.

"I don't understand this phrase," the Russian spoke softly. The wonder of their situation, the hidden wonder in the factual creation of a myth, was not lost on him.

"Like Lewis Carroll's, *Alice in Wonderland.* What I mean is they are the same as us. Two groups, thrown together without understanding why. Only we still have ourselves, our self-control, while they...they are empty."

"Like reflections. It looks the same, but is but a shell," Yuri spoke proudly, pleased that he had understood the metaphor. Paul smiled at the man's enthusiasm and didn't have the heart to correct him. *Close enough,* he thought.

In the mess hall the groups sat, intermingled, with two clear groups having been formed, although there was no clear hard or fast rule governing the split.

"Come, now we eat." Yuri walked into the kitchen and sat down. Paul followed suit. While the chatter continued, a delightfully foreign aroma wafted out of the kitchen area, and a short time later, two large pots of a type of Russian stew were brought to the table. Everybody ate with gusto. The company, even in the face of the long-term odds, had reinvigorated people. The removed threat of immediate execution had lightened the mood in both camps somewhat also.

Night fell, and as people were shown to their rooms, Paul somehow found himself returning to the library with Yuri. He feared a second vodka session, but his concern was unfounded. It was wine. A fine

Merlot which only added to his confusion at the state of the Russian military.

"We will be required to clear this compound. We will work together. No military, no civilians. No Russia, no Britain. We are one. You and I their leaders. So, friend, comrade, shall we work together?" Yuri got straight to business as he took a sip from his wine glass.

"I think that is a wonderful idea. We should work in teams. Your men are soldiers. They should take the lead along with the strongest of us. Each man and woman will need to be armed. We seal off the compound first…"

"You mean, lock them inside…with us."

"Yes, that way they cannot escape, and more cannot come." Paul gave a gentle nod as he spoke, and watched the understanding cross Yuri's face almost before he spoke.

"You are a clever man. We then dispose of these creatures. We have enough weapons; bullets." Yuri was proud of his compound in spite of its former purpose.

"No guns, the sounds only attract more. Knives, bats. Weapons have to be manual, hand-to-hand work. Only shots to the brain actually stop them." Yuri nodded as Paul spoke, listening with intent. The zombies were new to him, and the knowledge Paul shared was the most valuable anybody could ever give another person.

"Thank you, my friend. You have shared with me great details. You could have sent us out alone to our deaths. You are a great English man. But now, let us talk. I have heard of your writing stories. You write down the tales of people, no?" Yuri smiled as he spoke, as if he were in the presence of a truly great name.

"Well, I am not Chaucer, but yes, I wrote down what had happened to people. That is how we learned the truth," he added, taking pride in his own work and amateur detective skills.

"You continue to impress me. Will you still write your stories of the new days that lie ahead of us all?" There was eagerness to the voice that made Paul smile, for he knew what was coming.

"I haven't given it any thought. I mean, I guess there will be many tales to tell." Paul smiled.

"Yes, indeed, many tales of the undead, of heroes like yourself, and maybe even…a strong Russian champion, a second hero to the tales." Yuri spoke with a sudden dry seriousness, and when Paul smiled at him, the pair both broke into a deep laughter.

Paul rose from the sofa, his comfort zone found, and refilled both glasses of wine. He handed one to Yuri and then paced the room, staring at the books that lined the shelves.

"This room was left over from the war time. It was locked away. A secret room until we moved in under orders from the Kremlin. It is quite special here, no?" Yuri talked from the sofa, allowing Paul the freedom to wander where he wished.

"Yes, it is a room I could only dream of." He spoke, walking along the shelves. He came to the desk and stared at the pen and paper that lay there. The upper sheet was yellowed with age, and the pen a fountain point, the pot of ink still in its holder. He reached out and touched the pen, feeling the weight of it in his hand.

The paper, too, was of a high quality and had a generous feel to it.

"The rumor is that Stalin himself sat at this desk. That this room was his, or used by him, and only the highest of dignitaries." Yuri smiled again, enjoying the look of wonder that spread on Paul's face. "Sit, feel it. The world has changed, but history will always remain. We must never lose our history, for good or bad. It has made us who we are today and allows us to determine who we will become tomorrow."

Paul sat. The heavy leather chair squeaked as he found a comfortable position. He reached for the ink and removed the cap. With the pen filled, he wrote across the top of the page.

*We have seen the world of men fall, the dead have risen, but we are survivors, and these words are....*

He paused, before leaving two blank lines and writing in large letters, three lines thick:

*The Diaries of the Damned*

He looked up from the page and saw Yuri watching him intently. He took a deep breath and topped up the pen.

"So Yuri....Tell me your story."

**TO BE CONTINUED...?**

### Who is Alex Laybourne?

Born and raised in the coastal English town Lowestoft, it should come as no surprise (to those that have the misfortune of knowing this place) that I became a horror writer.

From an early age I was sent to schools which were at least 30 minutes' drive away and so spent most of my free time alone, as the friends I did have lived too far away for me to be able to hang out with them in the weekends or holidays.

I have been a writer as long as I can remember and have always had a vivid imagination. To this very day I find it all too easy to just drift away into my own mind and explore the world I create; where the conditions always seem to be just perfect for the cultivation of ideas, plots, scenes, characters and lines of dialogue

I am married and have four wonderful children; James, Logan, Ashleigh and Damon. My biggest dream for them is that they grow up, and spend their lives doing what makes them happy, whatever that is.

For people who buy my work, I hope that they enjoy what they read and that I can create something that takes them away from reality for a short time. For me, the greatest compliment I can receive is not based on rankings but by knowing that people enjoy what I produce, that they buy my work with pleasure and never once feel as though their money would have been better spent elsewhere.

Feel free to stop by my website www.alexlaybourne.com or find me on Facebook or on Twitter

# CHECK OUT OTHER GREAT ZOMBIE NOVELS

## Z BURBIA
by Jake Bible

Whispering Pines is a classic, quiet, private American subdivision on the edge of Asheville, NC, set in the pristine Blue Ridge Mountains. Which is good since the zombie apocalypse has come to Western North Carolina and really put suburban living to the test!

Surrounded by a sea of the undead, the residents of Whispering Pines have adapted their bucolic life of block parties to scavenging parties, common area groundskeeping to immediate area warfare, neighborhood beautification to neighborhood fortification.

But, even in the best of times, suburban living has its ups and downs what with nosy neighbors, a strict Home Owners' Association, and a property management company that believes the words "strict interpretation" are holy words when applied to the HOA covenants. Now with the zombie apocalypse upon them even those innocuous, daily irritations quickly become dramatic struggles for personal identity, family security, and straight up survival.

## ZOMBIE RULES
by David Achord

Zach Gunderson's life sucked and then the zombie apocalypse began.

Rick, an aging Vietnam veteran, alcoholic, and prepper, convinces Zach that the apocalypse is on the horizon. The two of them take refuge at a remote farm. As the zombie plague rages, they face a terrifying fight for survival.

They soon learn however that the walking dead are not the only monsters.

# CHECK OUT OTHER GREAT ZOMBIE NOVELS

## 900 MILES
### by S. Johnathan Davis

John is a killer, but that wasn't his day job before the Apocalypse.

In a harrowing 900 mile race against time to get to his wife just as the dead begin to rise, John, a business man trapped in New York, soon learns that the zombies are the least of his worries, as he sees first-hand the horror of what man is capable of with no rules, no consequences and death at every turn.

Teaming up with an ex-army pilot named Kyle, they escape New York only to stumble across a man who says that he has the key to a rumored underground stronghold called Avalon..... Will they find safety? Will they make it to Johns wife before it's too late?

Get ready to follow John and Kyle in this fast paced thriller that mixes zombie horror with gladiator style arena action!

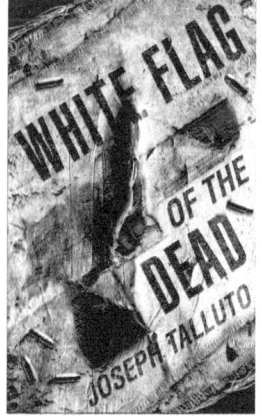

## WHITE FLAG OF THE DEAD
### by Joseph Talluto

Millions died when the Enillo Virus swept the earth. Millions more were lost when the victims of the plague refused to stay dead, instead rising to slaughter and feed on those left alive. For survivors like John Talon and his son Jake, they are faced with a choice: Do they submit to the dead, raising the white flag of surrender? Or do they find the will to fight, to try and hang on to the last shreds or humanity?

www.ingramcontent.com/pod-product-compliance
Lightning Source LLC
Chambersburg PA
CBHW020105180626
46812CB00006B/2473